ONCE UPON A TIME

Also Edited by Michael Ford:
Happily Ever After: Erotic Fairy Tales for Men

rk A RICHARD KASAK BOOK

ONCE UPON A TIME:

EROTIC FAIRY TALES FOR WOMEN

EDITED BY MICHAEL FORD

Once Upon a Time: Erotic Fairy Tales for Women
Copyright © 1996 Michael Ford
All stories copyright © by their respective authors

First Richard Kasak Book Edition 1996

First Printing November 1996

ISBN 1-56333-449-6

Manufactured in the United States of America
Published by Masquerade Books, Inc.
801 Second Avenue
New York, N.Y. 10017

INTRODUCTION

Fairy tales—the very word conjures up fantastic visions of dragons and princesses, goblins and demons. Perhaps more than anything else, fairy tales represent the wide-eyed innocence of childhood, a time when our minds were open to any and all possibilities, and the idea of a princess sleeping for a hundred years was accepted as easily as that some mysterious force called electricity made the lamps glow. After all, magic is magic, whether it can be explained by scientists or not. It's not until we get older that statistics and numbers become the tools of belief, rather than enchanted slippers and pixie dust.

As a child, I used to sit at night and listen to my grandmother tell tales from her homeland, many of which had been told to her by *her* grandmother, handed down by a long line of wise and beautiful women who understood that science just couldn't explain everything. Sometimes the stories were filled with laughter and joy, as she spoke of the midnight folk who came out after the world of humans had been swept up in the arms of night to dance and make mischief. On these occasions I would fall asleep to dream of enchanted mirrors, talking birds, and long hallways that led to somewhere far more interesting that my boring, ordinary bedroom.

Other nights, particularly in the bitter cold of winter, the stories were darker ones, filled with witches and doomed maidens who invariably plucked the rose belonging to the troll king or who turned to stone after peering into forbidden rooms. I loved these stories the best. I liked the struggles the heroines endured, often for the sake of love. As a budding queer, I suppose I gave some passing thought to the princes they were usually searching for; but deep down, I always imagined myself as the one doing the searching. The harder the puzzles assigned, the more I longed to be the one to solve them. Secretly, I half-hoped that the flowers I gathered in the meadow behind the house *did* belong to some vengeful creature, who would demand that I give myself as payment for my transgression.

Often, I would dress up and act out my favorite tales, blind to gender stereotypes or what my "expected" role was. I was just as likely to be tearing through the house playing sly Puss as I was to go chasing the dog around the garden in a vain attempt at getting him to play the Beast to my Beauty. I left milk for the elves and cookie crumbs for the brownies, and on nights with a full moon, fell asleep in my window seat as I tried to catch a glimpse of the fair folk riding the moonbeams. I saw no reason why all of these things shouldn't exist and, like the children in E. Nesbit's *The Enchanted Castle*, I looked for magic behind every corner.

As I grew older, the fairy world grew a little dimmer as childhood dreams were replaced by different desires. Yet it never disappeared completely from view, and time after time I found myself playing out in real life some of the great story lines from the old tales. A lover whose fair hair and rosy skin were so different from my darkness was my Rose Red. Giving up something dear to me in order to please another reminded me of poor Rapunzel, her shorn hair a reminder of a failed love. And as for the Big Bad Wolf, well, some of the things in Grandma's darkened forest are better left untouched after all. Time and again, I found myself reminded of this tale or that, saw in everyday life scraps from the stories I remembered so well.

Talking with my friends, particularly women, I discovered that many of us had been affected by the stories told to us in childhood. Many women I know wanted to be the princess, waiting in a bed of thorns for the awakening kiss of their hearts' desires. Others longed to pull on a pair of seven-league boots and roam the country, killing giants to win the hand of the most beautiful woman in the kingdom. Our reactions and memories were as varied as we were. Some fondly remembered reading the stories and wanting badly to jump into them. Others had harsher experiences, feeling betrayed by the women in the stories and wishing they had been more aggressive, more assertive. Some felt trapped by the messages they found within the tales; others found redemption in the same words. The barest mention of fairy tales would often begin long discussions that lasted late into the night.

I decided to invite women whose writing I admire to go on quests of their own, to venture back into their childhoods and reenter the fairy tales they had visited as young women. I asked them to go searching for what it was that they loved, feared, desired, or scorned in their favorite tales, to bring back the hearts of their chosen stories and refashion them into something new. I asked them to make the stories their own. And because so many of the best fairy tales deal with desire and the attainment of love, and because many women fashion their own ideas about desiring and being desired from these early tales, I requested that the writers explore what spoke to them as sexual beings.

To my delight, nearly everyone I asked to participate in this project accepted enthusiastically. Most knew almost instantly which stories they would return to. Others reread books of fairy tales and came upon forgotten favorites. You will find here many traditional tales, but also many obscure ones, and even a reworking of a classic nursery rhyme. To my surprise, there were very few requests from writers wanting the same stories. The one story that garnered the most requests was "The Twelve Dancing Princesses"; two very different versions appear here.

The result of this foray into the realm of enchantment is an eclectic mix of voices, styles, and approaches. Some of the writers have remained true to the original stories but delved into the erotic possibilities only hinted at in the traditional versions. Others have used familiar characters and recast them in entirely new settings. Still others have created their own fairy tales using bits and pieces from ancient sources. The stories are, by turns, funny, sad, and arousing, depending upon the author's reaction to them.

Just as the styles differ, so does the nature of the erotic content in each story. Some only hint at possibilities, suggesting what might have been; others peer brazenly behind the velvet bedroom draperies and beneath the satin gowns of our favorite heroines to show us what lies hidden there. But whether they feature full-on fucking or simply intimations of happily ever after, each story explores sensuality and desire in a unique way. Each one is an examination of the effect a particular story had on one woman's vision of herself, her sexuality, and the possibilities open to her.

I have chosen to end the collection with Robin Podolsky's post-modern look at "The Twelve Dancing Princesses." While less an erotic story than it is a social commentary on the messages behind our favorite tales, her new story boldly turns the old one upside down. By recasting the characters in a new light, and by demanding answers from a tale that never provided any, she questions the age-old traditions that run rampant in fairy tales and emerges with something uniquely her own. This, after all, was the point of this project.

—Michael Ford
New York
Winter 1995

The Snow Queen's Robber Girl

DOROTHY ALLISON

I wrote about the Snow Queen because I think the world is colder than fairy tales and nowhere near as easy to revise. And also because I believe in magical thinking and the power of good flirting. I like my fairy tales hard-edged.

When she first came to stay with us, she barely talked. Nothing much more than grunts and nods and gestures. "Leave me alone!" she'd snarl, and pull that ragged old jacket up close around her ears. Or, "Don't touch my stuff!" when I went out of my way to tuck her gear back in her duffel.

"Be careful of her," my ma told me. "She's not used to our ways. Seems she was raised off with them gypsy bastards in the north caves. She'd have learned hard manners up there. No manners at all, looks like."

And that was true enough. She used nothing of ours, neither plate nor bowl. She tore her meat off the spit with her knife and ate it squatting by the fire. Drank only what she could scoop with her cupped fist. And though she gobbled Ma's flat-bread, she never touched the greens I'd gathered or the scraggly corn Nadine so prized.

"Pig food," she cursed. "Good for dogs, maybe. Not me." Then took another share when no one complained of her first.

"Raised a thief," my brother told me. "Keep your eyes on her. Don't let her go messing through our things."

I didn't pay him much mind. Don't think he liked her. Well, I know he didn't. But I also know that he wouldn't cross her.

"Scary bitch," he called her, and kept out of her way.

Ma thought that was fine—useful, anyway.

"Your brother needs to learn some manners with women. Not all girls grow up like you, soft-spoken and careful. He's as like to run across her kind as not, once he leaves us. Time he learned."

That was how I felt about it, but who's to say I wasn't just thinking mean. I was tired of my brother's whining, taking the best share of everything and always wanting the place closest to the fire. I thought the gypsy could have done more, taught him her own ways; how to take care with girls and keep out of my way for a change. But she didn't take much interest in us, not my brother or me, though I was the one picked up after her and defended her when old Cot complained that she had no right cutting her meat right off the roast.

"Her ways are not our ways," I told him, wishing a few of her ways were ours. She was a girl like me or Nadine, but she never backed down from the men.

Nadine liked her same as me—which was odd enough. Nadine is like all the touched—very, very careful of strangers. When people come, she hides out in the back of our place. Sits in the corner with a blanket pulled up over her head and watches to see what's what. Comes out only when she's sure there's no threat. She saw no threat in the gypsy, didn't even back away when we brought her back from the wall that day. Nadine's quick to see threat—shy as a mealy rat and twice as quick. Has jumped back from people Ma said were fine and we've learned to take warning from that. Nadine jumps, you know there's cause. Might not be something you'd see at first look, but will be something you see soon enough. Some man with a fast temper, some woman with a sharp tongue, some someone who will rob us or put us all at risk for no reason you'd guess when you first had them sit by the fire.

We live on the edge out here, outside the city, watching what comes and goes, who's been put over the wall, and who's taking a turn on the high seat of the temple. We're not citizens—not anybody at all, the way the temple sees it. They don't even want us to use the water runs off the walls though we do nobody harm with our buckets and carryalls. After all, what is the harm in us sorting through the refuse they toss over that wall? No reason to curse us or set those red dogs on us when the moon is full. That we find use in what they throw away should be nothing to them. Though the things they throw away! My sweet ass.

Like her.

We found her in the midden at the north wall, Ma and me. The north wall's our favorite place. We find stuff there all the time. It's why we go there, looking for stuff the city don't want, stuff we can use, and finding more than the temple-blessed would ever believe. Bodies now and then, the chaff tossed off the temple's threshing table. Citizens are cremated by priests who can speak their names and rites. What comes over the wall is garbage not worth the cost of stoking up the fire. That means people who are not full citizens—the poor, beggars, outsiders, and criminals, most showing the marks of sword or wire rope. But we also find half-finished babies some temple-blessed wife got approval to abort, and now and then the bodies strangled, too well-fed and healthy looking to come over the wall. Ma said it's just what you would expect, citizens tossing others over. Temple-blessed go as easily as beggars, and no one takes the trouble to look after the dead once they hit the rocks.

Only that one wasn't dead. She'd landed lucky on some load of sour pulp with her duffel still tied to her hip and a foreigner's badge still pinned to her shoulder. It was the badge caught Ma's eye, a bright, bright flame against her dark hair, a sign she hadn't paid to stay more than two days inside the city walls and sure sign she was no citizen-to-be. Poor and outlander most likely, and murdered maybe for what had been in her duffel. Ma called me over and had me prod her hard. I had to look close to see she was human. Looked like nothing alive, and her skin was so dark, she almost blended in with the rubbish.

But she was alive. When I pushed her leg, she tried to grab my hand. Her nail scratched my wrist, and I heard the breath hiss between her teeth. The whites of her eyes caught the shielded beam from Ma's little torch. She cursed me then, called me a devil's pup and tried to push herself up. Ma put out her light and pulled me away. We sat still, listening to her thrash about and curse some more. Sometimes, if we wait a bit, people who've been thrown over will die quick enough, and we can strip them as soon as they're cold. It's vile, I know. Sometimes I say my own little prayer as I pull their stuff off, kind of thank them for giving us what they have. Though the temple-blessed say those who die without rites have no power to come back or curse, I figure a little prayer can't hurt. Besides, sometimes the dead provide the best pickings, and I say we should thank somebody. It's not as if we mean harm in what we do. We're just taking care of ourselves, our own. Little enough comes over the wall.

Every time we put the light on her, she kicked some more and cursed a little. Finally we worked away from her and came back only when we were pretty much done. Ma put the light on her one more time, and she lifted her head and looked at us—big eyes shining, and her mouth set in a flat line.

"Ma?" I said, and Ma put her hand on my mouth. The girl just looked at Ma, so it didn't seem she was much of a threat. Ma grunted and put out her hand. She said later it was just to see if the girl would try to attack her, though it seemed to me the palm was open and inviting when the girl reached up and took hold. After that we just had to move slow enough so she could keep up with us. Turned out she had a bit of old blood on her neck from the blow that had sent her over the wall, but no real wound other than that. Whoever had attacked her had meant to be rid of her, not slaughter her and snatch what she had. And once we gave her some water, she straightened up and looked pretty strong. Anyway, no one insisted we run her off once she made it back to our camp.

Except brother. He swore she was cursed and would get us all dead. But Nadine took a place right beside her and that shut him up pretty fast. Things get settled quick around her, and with few words mostly. Which suited her right enough. Like I said, she barely spoke.

Her name was Raven, and she'd fallen in love with a citizen. Well, maybe not a temple-blessed citizen, but a citizen sure enough. Some pale blond thing with soft fingers and milk teeth still pearly in her mouth. Gerda, she was called, the loved maiden our robber girl had tried to protect. Gerda, which proves something, I say. It's a name chill on the tongue, though the robber girl swore she was warm clear through, the kind of female they put up on the walls all draped with flowers when the farmers come up to the city for the ceremonies in the spring.

"She was mine," said our girl. "I claimed her. If anyone was to kill her, it would be me. I bit her ear and tasted her blood, put her in my bed and fed her one of my prize pigeons. She was mine, though why I wanted her I cannot say. She wasn't much."

"A citizen," I said, but our robber girl just spat.

"A slave, my slave. I had a copper collar put on her neck, and she slept only when I had my hand on her throat. She ate only what I put in her mouth and drank from my cup or not at all."

I bit my lip. Nadine giggled from behind my shoulder, as if she knew what I was thinking, knew I wanted to drink from that hand and sleep with that copper collar pulled up to my chin. But the robber girl just chewed on a scrap of meat and stared into the fire, as if Gerda's face burned in the coals.

Not mine. Not me. Our robber girl was still dreaming of her tender citizen, not seeing what was looking her right in the face. Me with Ma's blessing and years of training to be a thief myself, and Nadine with her eyes shining brighter than Gerda's blond hair, the two of us in love with the robber maiden, wanting to be to her what Gerda had been.

"Did you kill her?" I asked. "Did you cut out her heart for not loving you as she should?"

"I sent her north to the Snow Queen," the robber maiden told us. Nadine shuddered at my side. "She'd freed my pets—my wood pigeons and my rats. I took her boots and her robe, put her in my old rags, and sent her north to die in the ice, on the blue lake where frost rules forever. Or come back to me when she would. *If* she would. It's not true that I sent her on my reindeer. That animal ran off before she came, and no, I did not wait for her return. I left on my own, with just my blade, to tour the world and see what was what. If she ever came back, I never will know."

"Ahhhhh!" Nadine leaned over my shoulder and wrapped her arms around my waist. Her sigh was deep and sad, as if she had seen poor Gerda going off into the great dark woods with only the robber girl's rags. Or maybe that she knew our girl was telling us what she wanted us to believe, what she wanted to believe herself.

Poor Gerda. Ha!

I ground my teeth and kept my head down. Hope that bitch took her time dying in the north. Hope the icy wind peeled her skin and split her heart, buried her in the winter waste. Curse her for not valuing what I would kill to have—the love of the robber maiden and her dark eyes shining hot in the night.

Oh, there's no answering the curse of loving what does not love you. Citizens or maidens or robber girls with big black eyes and hair like death's dark shirt on a white winter plain. I took my knife and went off to the midden, hunting through the refuse for something to comfort me for all I did not have. Nadine followed me, head down, crooning a little song into the hollow of her own throat. Near the wall we found another body, some thin-boned creature shrouded in a bloody cape, moaning quietly against a rock.

"Another one," I told Nadine. She put her fingers in her mouth and waited.

I leaned over the body. It made a gentle hissing noise. I used a stick to push aside the hood and saw a lank blond curl fall loose. I did not look to see if it were male or female.

I cut its throat and took what it had.

Sleeping Beauty
FRANCESCA LIA BLOCK

I chose to adapt "Sleeping Beauty" because I am fascinated by the idea of erotic and spiritual love (no matter what the orientation) awakening us from the sleep of childhood, or the sleep of adult pain.

She felt like the girl in the fairy tale. Maybe there had been some kind of curse. Inevitable that she would prick her arm (not her finger) with the silver needle. Did the girl feel this ecstasy of pure honeyed light in her veins, like being infused with the soul she had lost? This Beauty thought not. But for her, that was all there was.

The flood was like an ogre's tears. Mud and trees and even small children were caught in it. Beauty's 1965 Thunderbird was swept away down the canyon, landing crashed at the bottom full of water and leaves.

Fires like dragon's breath consumed the poppies and lupine, the jacaranda trees that once flowered purple in sudden overnight bursts of exuberance as if startled at their own capacity for gorgeousness.

When the earth quaked, the walls of Beauty's house cracked; all the glasses and teacups in her cabinet flew out, covering the floor in a sharp carpet that cut her feet as she ran outside. Chimneys and windows were screaming and wailing. Beauty was amazed at how, with the power all out, she could see the stars above her, clearly, for the first time since she was a child on a camping trip in the desert. They were like the glass fragments on her floor. The air smelled of leaking gas. Her feet were bleeding into the damp lawn.

This is my city, Beauty thought. Cursed, as I am cursed. Sleeping, as I sleep. Tear-flooded and fever-scorched, quaking and bloodied with nightmares.

She went out in the city with its lights like a radioactive phosphorescence, wandered through galleries where the high-priced art on the walls was the same as the graffiti scrawled outside by taggers who were arrested or killed for it, went to parties in hotel rooms where white-skinned junkie singers in lingerie had stayed on the night their rock-star husbands had shot themselves in the head, listened to music in the nightclubs where stunning boyish actors had OD'd on the pavement. When the sun began to come up, Beauty went back to her canyon house where vines had begun to grow through the cracks in the walls. The air smelled acrid and stale—eucalyptus and cigarettes. Her television was always on.

Pop came by in his dark glasses and long blond dreadlocks. He gave her what she needed in a needle in exchange for the photos he took of her. And sometimes she slept with him.

"Sleeping Beauty," he said. "I like you this way."

She was wearing her kimono with the embroidered red roses, her hair in her face. Hipbones haunting through silk and flesh.

"You have opium eyes."

Opium eyes. She closed her heavy lids over them, wanting to sleep.

He photographed her as witch, priestess, fairy queen, garden. He photographed her at the ruins of the castle and on the peeling, mournful carousel and in the fountain.

"It's like you're from nowhere," Pop said. "I like that. It's like you live inside my head. I made you just the way I wanted you to be."

Where am I from? she wondered. Maybe Pop was right. She was only in his head. But there had been something before.

She had been adopted by a man and a woman who wanted beauty. The woman thought of champagne, roses, rosé champagne, perfume, and jewels, but she couldn't have a child. The child they found was darker than they had hoped for but even more lavishly numinous. They had men take pictures of her right from the beginning. There were things that happened at those sessions. Beauty tried to think only of the leopard couches and velvet pillows, the feather boas and fox fur pelts, the flock of doves and the poodle with its forelock twisted into a unicorn horn, the hot lights that were, she hoped, bright enough to sear out the image of what was happening to her. Though she tried, she could not remember the face of the other girl who had been there once.

Was the curse that she was born too beautiful? Had it caused her real parents to abandon her, fearful of the length of lash, the plush of lip in such a young face? Was it the reason the men with cameras had sucked away her soul bit by bit, year after year, because any form that lovely must remain soulless so as not to stun them impotent? Was it what made Old-Woman-Heroine's face split into a jealous leer as she beckoned Beauty up to the attic and stabbed her with the needle that first time?

Because she no longer had a car, she let Pop drive her around. He picked her up one night and took her to a small white villa in the hills. It belonged to an actress named Miss Charm. Pop led Beauty upstairs past the sleek smoky people drinking punch out of an aquarium and into a room that was painted to look like a shell. He told her to take off the antique gold sequined dress and arranged her limbs on a big white bed, tied and slapped her arm, tucked the needle into her vein. Then came the three men. They unzipped their pants and climbed onto her while Pop hovered around them, snapping shots. Beauty did not cry out. She lay still. She let the opium be her soul. It was better than having a soul. It did not cry out; it did not writhe with pain.

"Fuck you, you fucks!" a woman's voice screamed like the soul Beauty no longer had.

The woman had shorn black hair and pale skin. She was wearing a faux leopard coat and cartoony-looking platform shoes.

"Fuckin' get out of my fuckin' house."

"Oh, chill, Charm."

"Leave now," she said.

"Want to join the party?" one of the men said. "I think she wants to join the party."

Beauty felt her empty insides trying to jump out of her as if to prove there was no soul there, nothing anyone had to be afraid of, nothing left for them to want to have. She felt her emptiness bitter and burning coming up from her throat. The men moved away, covering their mouths.

The pale woman helped Beauty to the bathroom and wiped her face with a warm wet towel. Beauty looked at her reflection in the mirror. She had shadows beneath her eyes as if her makeup had been put on upside down. But in spite of that nothing had changed. She still bore the curse.

"You're going to be okay," the woman was saying in a hard voice like: *You have to be.*

Beauty stared at her.

"I know," the woman said.

She ran a bath for Beauty and lit the candles that were arranged around the tub like torches along the ramparts of a castle. She filled the water with oils that smelled like the bark, leaves, and blossoms of trees from a sacred grove. The mirrors blurred with steam like a mystic fog so that Beauty could not see her own image. She was thankful.

While Beauty bathed, the woman stripped off the sheets from

the white bed and boiled them clean. She opened all the windows that looked out over the courtyard full of banana trees, Chinese magnolia, palms, birds of paradise, and hibiscus flowers. She lit incense in sconces all around the room and played a tape of Tibetan monks chanting.

Beauty got out of the bath and dried herself off with the clean white towel the woman had left for her. She put on the heavy clean white robe that must have been stolen from some fancy hotel and walked barefoot into the bedroom.

"Are you hungry?" the woman asked.

Beauty shook her head.

"Do you want to sleep here tonight?"

Beauty nodded. Sleep sleep sleep. That was what she wanted.

She woke the next night. The woman was sitting at her bedside with a silver tray. She had made a meal of jasmine rice, coconut milk, fresh mint, and chiles. There were tall glasses of mineral water with slices of lime like green moons rising above clear pools. There was a glass bowl full of gardenias.

"Can you eat now?" There was an expression on the woman's face that seemed vaguely familiar. Beauty thought of how her adopted mother's face had looked when she would not get out of bed after something had happened with the first photographer. No, it was not that. Maybe she was remembering another woman, before that one. A woman with eyes that were always wet as this woman's were now.

"You remind me of my mother," Beauty said. "My real mother. I thought I had forgotten her."

"How do I remind you of her?"

"Because of your eyes. Because they are wet. Her eyes were always wet."

"What happened? Why was she crying?"

"I used to think she gave me up because I was cursed."

"Cursed?" the woman said.

Beauty pulled the blankets closer over her heavy breasts, breasts that had always seemed too much for the rest of her slender body.

"Blessed," said the woman. "She was crying because you are blessed and because she had to give you up." She was wearing cutoff jeans, the seam split all the way up the side of the leg so that her thighs shone smooth and white as candles. She wore a man's white T-shirt with no bra. Beauty could see her nipples achingly erect beneath the fabric. Her face was scrubbed clean of makeup. Her cheekbones were almost equine. She had a few freckles over the bridge of her nose. "Eat something now," she said.

Strangely, Beauty found that she was hungry. She ate the sweet and spicy, creamy, minty rice and drank the fizzing, lime-stung mineral water. She breathed the gardenias. She watched the woman's eyes. They were like the eyes of old-time movie stars, always lambent, making the celluloid look slicked with water, lit with candles.

"You can stay here as long as you need to," the woman said.

"But I'm going to need—" Beauty began.

"If you need it I'll get it for you. Until you decide you want to stop. I stopped."

Beauty nodded. Her hair fell forward over her face.

"If you need me, I'll be sleeping in the next room."

"But this is your bed," said Beauty.

"It's yours for now."

She stroked Beauty's hand. There was a tattoo of thorny roses on her forearm, over the biggest vein.

Beauty slept for days and days. Sometimes she woke kicking her legs and feet until the comforter slid from the bed. Then she would feel someone covering her with satin and down again, touching her clammy forehead with dry, soft, gardenia-scented fingertips. Sometimes she woke shivering, sweating, quaking, or parched. Always the hands would be there to warm or cool or still her, to hold a shimmering glass of water to her cracking lips.

Sometimes Beauty dreamed she was in a garden gathering flowers that bit at her hands with venomous mouths. She dreamed she was running from creatures who bared needles instead of teeth. One of them caught her and pierced her neck. She was falling falling down a spiral staircase into darkness. She was lying in a coffin that was a castle, suffocating under roses.

One night Beauty heard, through the mother-of-pearl painted walls, the soft, muffled, animal sounds of a woman crying. She got out of bed like a somnambulist. The night was warm and soft on her bare skin. It clothed her like the robe the princess had dreamed of spinning when she found the old woman in the attic—a fabric of gold filigree openwork through which her gem-hard nipples and rough-lace pubic hair pressed out. How many years the princess had dreamed of spinning such a garment. But there were never any spinning wheels to be found in the whole kingdom. And then, finally, when her chance had come to ornament her beauty in the way she wished—erotic, gleaming, prepared for her imagined forbidden lover with the small, high breasts and the wet depth between her legs—she had pricked herself and fallen into the death sleep.

Perhaps it was what she deserved for wanting to make herself more beautiful. And for wanting what she could not have.

Beauty went out the bedroom door and into the hall. Except for the sound of weeping, the house was dark and silent.

In the room where the woman lay, it was darker still. Beauty found her way to the bed by sound and touch. Her hands caught onto something warm and curved and fragile-feeling. It was the woman's hipbone jutting out from beneath the blankets.

"Why are you crying?" Beauty asked. Her hand slid down over the hipbone, across the woman's taut abdomen working with sobs.

The woman reached for a silk tassel and pulled the embroidered piano-shawl curtains back. Moonlight flooded into the room. She handed Beauty a small, battered, black-and-white photograph.

"Do you remember?" the woman asked.

Beauty stared at the two naked young girls, one dark, one light, curled together on a leopard-skin sofa. Their hands and feet were shackled together. It was herself and the woman. That was why the eyes had looked familiar.

"Charm," Beauty said. "Miss Charm."

"I shouldn't have asked you to stay," said Charm. "I shouldn't have made you remember."

"I'll go then," Beauty said. "If you want."

"I don't want you to go," Charm whispered. "I've been waiting for you so long." Her voice reminded Beauty of a piece of broken jewelry.

"I thought they had taken my soul," said Beauty.

"I thought they took mine, too. But they can't. No one can. It's just been asleep."

Charm ran her hands over Beauty's heavy, satiny breasts and down between her legs. Charm's fingers spread Beauty's lips with her first and middle finger, exposing the rosy, engorged whorls that hid there. Beauty dug her fingers into Charm's kitten hair and pulled Charm's head down.

When Charm kissed her, Beauty felt as if all the fierce blossoms were shuddering open. The castle was opening. She felt as if the other woman were breathing into her body something long lost and almost forgotten. It was, she knew, the only drug either of them would need now.

The Butch's New Clothes
ISOBEL BIRD

When I was nine, my parents divorced, and I took a very long train ride from my parents' house in New Orleans to my grandmother's home in Vermont so that I could be out of the way while the details of the separation were worked out. During that seemingly endless trip, I amused, and probably consoled, myself by disappearing into the many different fairy-tale collections my ever-wise grandmother had mailed to me before the journey.

One of my favorite stories was "The Emperor's New Clothes." I was drawn to it, I suspect now, because I liked the fact that only the child in the story knew what was going on and could see things as they really were. I felt much the same way as I watched my parents shredding what was left of their relationship in a bitter battle over summer homes, me, and a great deal of money.

When I set about writing a story for this collection, "The Emperor's New Clothes" came immediately to mind. I wanted to write about what happens when one person in a relationship suddenly sees another person for what she truly is. I also wanted to write about sex roles as the clothing or, more precisely, the costumes that we use to dress up our sexual personas, and what happens when those costumes are stripped away.

Special thanks to Lily August for the inspiration, and for the peach pie.

Sara glanced quickly at the photograph lying on the table in front of her, just long enough for her mind to comprehend what was happening in the shot. Her eyes cut back to the pile of scrambled eggs on her plate. A streak of ketchup slashed across the pale yellow softness. Suddenly the smell of the fried potatoes made her feel sick.

"See," said Jen, "I told you she was fucking around." There was triumph in her voice. It was wrapped carefully in the consoling tones of the smugly confident, but Sara felt the sting nonetheless. Jen loved to be right, and this time she had hit the jackpot. She pushed the photo toward Sara and leaned back in the booth, forcing Sara to pick it up.

According to Sara, the photo had been taken at a recent sex party of the sort that seemed suddenly to be the rage for a certain segment of the lesbian world. It clearly showed a very stern, very butch woman fucking another woman, a delicate redhead, from behind. The photographer had captured the scene at a moment when the butch was entering her femme, her body moving forward as she shoved her cock deep inside. The butch's mouth was set in a satisfied smile, and her hand was caught in mid-swing as she brought it down onto the pale moon of her girl's ass.

The butch was—or had been until the moment the photo had hit the table—Alex, Sara's girlfriend of nine months. The redhead's face, covered by her flying hair, was obscured.

"Pretty," said Sara. "Who is she?"

"I don't know," Jen answered. "She came with Alex. They looked like they'd spent a lot of time together, though. All I know about her is her name—Alice. I thought maybe you'd know."

"No," said Sara. "But it looks like there are a lot of things I didn't know."

Jen pulled on her cigarette, blowing the smoke out in a hazy cloud that settled over the table like smog. For once, Sara was too preoccupied to tell her to blow it somewhere else. "What are you going to do?" Jen asked.

Sara looked at the photo for a minute. Her mind raced with various ideas, none of which were either realistic or legal. She looked at Alex's face, and remembered how she'd told Sara she was going out to play pool with the guys.

"I think I have an idea." She looked up and smiled at Jen over the cold breakfast.

"I have your dick," she said simply. "And if you want it back, you're going to play by my rules."

There was dead silence on the other end of the line. Sara could tell by the faint rustling sounds that Alex was searching the box next to her bed and finding it empty. She could hear muttering as Alex barked a string of obscenities. Then she was back, her voice trembling with rage. "You fucking bitch. Who the fuck do you think you are?"

"I think you've got that wrong, sweetheart," Sara said evenly. "Who the fuck do you think *you* are? *You're* the one who took the randy husband bit a little too far."

It was two days after the morning on which Jen had presented Sara with the evidence of Alex's unfaithfulness. Sara had gone to Alex's apartment the night before, where she had managed to act as though nothing at all were unusual. She and Alex had made dinner, watched a movie, and even had passable sex, during which Sara had clawed Alex's skin perhaps a little too enthusiastically. In the morning, when Alex left for work, Sara had slipped her wandering daddy's dildo and harness into her purse and left.

Now she sat comfortably in her favorite armchair, holding Alex's dick in her hand and feeling quite good about the whole thing. She threw her legs over the arm of the chair, nestled the cock beneath her chin, and listened to Alex rant. "You'd better bring that right back this goddamned minute," she was saying, her butch patter flowing like a stream after too much rain. Sara let her go on until she paused for breath, then cut in.

"Look." She took a sip of tea. "This is very simple. You want your precious manhood back, you do what I say. Otherwise I turn it into a scratching post for Simon." Hearing his name spoken, Simon looked up from where he was curled into a tight ball on the sofa. He blinked his blue eyes, yawned so that his tongue curled out in a graceful dip, and then went back to sleep.

Alex began to scream again. *Jesus Christ*, thought Sara, *all this fuss over a silly dick*. "You'd make a great straight guy," she said into the phone, then giggled as Alex erupted in another fit of rage. The sounds of The Indigo Girls floated through the room, and she hummed along until she was bored with listening to Alex. "Be here tomorrow at nine," she said. "And there's just one little thing I want you to do first...."

The next night, precisely at nine, the doorbell rang. *At least she's prompt*, thought Sara, straightening her dress as she walked to the door and opened it. Alex stood there, not looking at Sara. She was wearing her usual outfit: black jeans, white T-shirt, black leather jacket, and boots. Her short dark hair was slicked back. She brushed past Sara and stormed into the living room.

"Did you do what I told you?" Sara asked, shutting the door.

"Yeah. Now where's my fucking piece?" Alex was trembling with anger as she stood in the living room.

"Not so fast." Sara settled onto the couch. "This is still my game, remember? Your dick is someplace safe. If you're a good little girl, you'll get it back."

"What the hell do you want from me?" Alex demanded.

Sara smiled, pushing her long hair out of her eyes. "Nothing much," she said, "Just a chance to show you the other side. Now, why don't you strip for me and show me what you bought today."

Alex turned her back to Sara and started to unbuckle her belt. "Not so fast," Sara said. "Turn around. I want to look at you."

Alex turned. Her face was red with rage, but she didn't say a word as she undid the buttons on her jeans and let them fall to the floor. As she pushed them down her legs, a pair of pink panties was revealed. She stood, arms across her chest, staring defiantly at Sara, who looked her up and down for a minute or two before standing up and walking over to where Alex stood.

"Very nice." She ran her hand over Alex's satin-clad ass and gave it a little pat. "These look much better than those boring old boxers you usually wear. Very feminine. I assume you have the receipt?"

"It's in my wallet," Alex said, her teeth clenched. Sara reached down and fished the battered wallet from the back pocket of Alex's jeans. She opened it and pulled out a folded slip, which she read. "Victoria's Secret," she said. "Good girl."

Alex bristled at the name. "I'm not your girl," she said.

Sara paused in front of her. She ran a finger along the waistband of the delicate panties. "But tonight you are," she said. "That is, if you want your cock back."

"That wasn't part of this fucking deal," Alex shouted. "All I agreed to was wearing these fucking panties. Nothing else."

"Deals change," Sara shot back, her voice harsh. "You want out, then get the fuck out. But I get to keep your dick. The choice is yours."

She watched Alex's face as her mind weighed the options before her. Sara had been on the receiving end of Alex's similar ultimatums many times. She knew which choice Alex would make.

"All right," Alex said.

"Good," said Sara. "Now, if I remember correctly, I told you to buy a bra that matched those panties. May I see it?"

Alex looked down at her feet. "I didn't get it," she said.

"Excuse me?"

"I said I didn't get it."

Sara drew in her breath. "That's too bad. I really like my girls to be all dolled up. But not to worry. I have some things you can wear. Follow me."

She walked into her bedroom, with Alex shuffling behind her, pants still around her ankles. "Take your clothes off—everything except the panties."

Alex removed her boots and slipped off her pants. Then she pulled her T-shirt over her head. She stood, hands on hips, looking at Sara as if daring her to do anything else. Her large, muscular body was what had attracted Sara to her in the first place. Now, as she gazed at her ex standing before her wearing the daintiest of women's panties, she felt a thrill of power run through her. She went to her chest and brought out a bag she had prepared earlier in the day.

"Since tonight we're just two girls getting together," she said as she emptied the contents of the bag onto the bed, "I thought we'd do some girl things." She held up a lacy pink bra. "Let's start with dress-up."

She walked over to Alex, the bra swinging from her fingers. Alex looked at the garment in disgust, but lifted her arms when told to, and Sara slipped it on. She snapped the clasp closed, adjusted the straps, and inspected Alex's chest. "My, my, my," she said, cupping Alex's breasts in her hands. "Seems those Wonderbras *do* perform miracles. You look like you just stepped out of a lingerie catalog."

"This shit is fucked up!" Alex growled.

Sara smiled. "But sweetie, you always told me you loved how a girl looked all wrapped up in silk and satin. Just like a Christmas present, I believe you said."

Sara ran her hand through Alex's military-short hair. "Oh, this won't do at all," she said. "Just a minute."

She returned to the bed and snatched a long red wig from the bag. It resembled very closely the hair of the girl in the photo that had been the cause of the evening's activities. Sara had been quite pleased with herself when she found it. Now, as she walked toward Alex with it, she thoroughly enjoyed the disgust she saw in the butch's eyes.

"I'm not wearing that thing!" Alex cursed.

Sara pretended to be shocked. "But why not? You always said you liked your femmes to have long hair, right? Besides, if I recall correctly, you have a real thing for redheads."

Alex sneered. "Just give it to me!" She grabbed it out of Sara's hands. "Let's get this little game over with so I can go do something a little more my style, if you know what I mean."

Like fuck Alice is what you mean, Sara thought. She watched as Alex smashed the wig onto her head. It sat crookedly, the bangs falling unevenly into her face. Sara tried not to laugh as she straightened the wig and arranged the dark red curls over Alex's broad shoulders. "Mmmmmmmmmm," she purred. "Beautiful. You're a right little looker, girlie."

"I look like that bitch who dances on MTV," said Alex.

"Oh, not quite yet, you don't." Sara went to her dresser and returned with her cosmetics bag. "But you will in a few minutes."

In a matter of fifteen minutes, she had painted Alex's face up in a perfect parody of high-femme glamour. Alex's lips gleamed in fire engine-red gloss. Her eyes were rainbowed with the brightest blue, and her cheeks fairly glowed with pink blusher. Sara even managed to affix a pair of the longest lashes she could find at the drugstore.

"And now for the finishing touch," she said, pulling out a box of Lee Press-On Nails in brightest red. She took Alex's hands and quickly attached the impossibly long plastic nails to the carefully clipped fingernails.

Throughout the ordeal, Sara could feel Alex's anger and rage trembling through her body. She had spent her whole life running from this very image, although she was drawn to it sexually like a magnet to steel. Sara knew that this was more torturous to her than any of her SM tricks had ever been to Sara, and she was loving it, because she knew that whatever happened, Alex would never break. She wondered, too, if the rush she was feeling was anything like the rush Alex had when one of her blows landed home.

When she was finished, she looked Alex up and down. She was by no means a pretty femme: there was just no hiding the butch daddy beneath the girlie costume. "Go lie down on the bed," she said simply.

Alex stomped over to the bed, her muscular thighs and heavy step incongruous with her getup, making it all the more amusing for Sara to watch her. Alex lay down, and Sara went to the bedside table. She pulled open the drawer and removed the familiar wrist cuffs that Alex had used on her so many times before.

"Uh-uh." Alex shook her head. "None of that."

"No play, no dick," Sara said quietly.

After a brief stare down, Alex presented her wrists, which Sara wrapped tightly in the leather cuffs, securing them to the head-board. "Now wait here," she whispered in Alex's ear. "Daddy will be back in a minute." Alex bristled at the "daddy" reference, but kept her mouth shut.

Sara went into the bathroom and shut the door. After what she knew was a long enough time for Alex to have gotten good and angry again, she came back out, bringing with her a razor, towel, and shaving cream. She laid these on the table next to Alex and left silently, allowing Alex time to take in the razor and think about what was going to happen next. As she ran water into a bowl, she heard Alex muttering.

She returned to the bedroom, carrying the bowl. She set it on the nightstand and dipped the razor in it. As she uncapped the shaving cream and squirted some into her hand, she looked at

Alex. "A good femme should always be smooth for her daddy," she said. She rubbed the cream into Alex's armpits and removed the hair deftly, rinsing the skin clean. She then moved down and repeated the procedure on Alex's legs, slowly scraping away the fine black hairs until her skin was silky and her muscles stood out in sharp relief.

When she pulled down the pink panties and moved toward Alex's cunt, the butch squeezed her powerful legs shut. "No goddamned way!"

Sara twisted the razor in her fingers. "It's either this," she said, "or I do a bikini wax. Your choice."

Alex allowed her legs to be parted, and Sara began the delicate job of defoliating her pussylips, drawing the razor down first one side and then the other. She even forced Alex to lift her legs and spread them so that Sara could shave the area around her asshole. When it was done, Alex's skin gleamed white and bare against the sheets. Sara gathered up the shaving paraphernalia and returned it to the bathroom.

When she came back, she fetched a pair of high heels from the closet and put them on Alex's feet. They were a little small, but the effect was what she wanted, and certainly Alex's comfort was immaterial. She stood at the end of the bed and looked down at the captive butch, all dolled up in femme drag and looking for all the world like a two-dollar whore.

She got the camera. When Alex saw it, she started to thrash around, screaming. "Get that fucking thing out of here!" she bellowed. "You fucking stupid bitch, I'm going to break your goddamned neck!" Her body flailed against the mattress as she tried to break free from her restraints.

Sara knew from experience that Alex could never break the cuffs' grip. As Alex bucked and twisted, she snapped picture after picture, the Polaroids fluttering to the carpet like leaves. As she did, she teased Alex. "That's it, baby, give me more. Give me more.

Make love to the camera, baby doll." When she finished the pack, she gathered them up and looked them over. There were some great shots. Her favorite was one of Alex with legs spread and panties around her calves, her mouth pursed in what looked like a kiss as she arched her back and clenched her red-nailed hands. The face was unmistakably hers, but the body was all wrong.

"I really like this one," Sara showed the photo to Alex, who was huffing and puffing as she tried to regain her breath.

Alex looked away from the proffered photo. "Fuck you!" she said.

Sara went to her desk and picked up a small manila envelope. As Alex watched, she placed the photo inside and sealed it. She then wrote something on the envelope. She did the same with a handful of the other photos, then brought the envelopes over to show Alex. On each one she had written the name and address of one of Alex's butch buddies. On the one that contained her favorite photo, she had written Alice's name and address. It had taken a little detective work to get them, but the look on Alex's face told her it had been worth it.

"If you are not a perfectly behaved little girl," she said. "Every one of these goes into the mailbox outside my building. Do you understand?"

At first Alex refused to answer. The veins in her neck throbbed as she looked at the envelopes and then at Sara.

"Do you understand? Yes or no."

"Yes," Alex hissed finally.

Sara smiled. "Good," she said. "Then we can get on with it." She placed the stack of envelopes on her dresser, where Alex couldn't help but see them, and went back into the bathroom. "Daddy will be right back," she called over her shoulder to Alex.

When she came back into the room, she was wearing nothing but Alex's dick. When Alex saw it, her eyes turned hard. "You cunt!" she screamed. "You fucking cunt! How dare you wear my cock—"

"Shut the fuck up, bitch," Sara screamed back. She stormed

over to the bed and smacked Alex hard across the mouth, smearing the lipstick unevenly across her cheek. "Who the fuck do you think you are, talking to your daddy that way."

"Give me my dick," Alex said evenly. Her hands had balled into fists, and one of the nails had broken off.

"Oh, I'm going to give it to you, all right." Sara brought the tip of the cock close to Alex's cheek. "I'm going to give it to you real good. Daddy's little girl is going to get just what she deserves."

Sara pulled Alex's panties back up around her waist. "Keep yourself covered," she said in disgust. "Little fucking tramp."

She climbed onto the bed and straddled Alex's waist, pinning her down. She could feel the rise and fall of Alex's breathing beneath her, the beating of her heart as it pulsed against her thighs. She stroked the dick between her legs.

"Yeah, you're a pretty one." She ran her hand over Alex's chest. "Daddy likes you." She pinched one of Alex's nipples hard through the bra. Alex jumped beneath her. "Oh, did you like that?" Sara cooed. "Maybe I should just take this off, then."

Leaning over, she pulled a knife from her bedside-table drawer. She held it, glinting in the air for a moment, before using it to cut the bra away from Alex's body. She then ran the sharp point under the mounds of flesh and up around the nipples. As she did, Alex's breathing became more shallow, and her nipples swelled. Sara was surprised.

"What's this?" She flicked one of the hardened points with her nail. "Is someone turning into a bottom before my very eyes?" She dropped the knife and pinched Alex's tits, pulling on them viciously as she talked to her. "Filthy fucking whore," she said. "Want Daddy to play with your tits, is that it? I bet you play with them yourself when no one's around, don't you?"

Unable to help herself, Alex was moaning, the sounds of pleasure coming out as muffled barks. Her eyes were closed, and her reddened lips were parted. Sara's cunt jumped as she realized that

Alex was in her control. She stopped playing with her tits, and Alex let out a sigh of both relief and frustration.

"That's enough for now," Sara said. "But just so you don't forget what it felt like, you're going to wear these for a while." She reached once more into the drawer and removed two spring-operated clamps. With two quick snaps, she affixed them to Alex's nipples, causing her to scream out in a mix of pleasure and pain. Sara hoped it was more of the latter.

Leaning forward, she smacked Alex's face with her dick until Alex looked up at her. "Suck it!" she ordered.

When Alex didn't respond, Sara forced the head of the cock between her lips. Surprised, Alex didn't have time to lock her jaw before the thick shaft was pushing into her throat. She gagged as she attempted to take it in.

"Like how it feels?" Sara teased, pumping her hips a little so that the cock slid in and out of Alex's mouth. The lipstick smeared along the pink sides as the shaft glided in and out. Alex was helpless as she was fed more and more of the prick.

"You're a natural cocksucker," Sara taunted. "Now do a good job, and maybe I'll let you have this back."

Alex's mouth worked up and down the length of Sara's dick. At first, Sara simply fucked her mouth. Then she pulled out, forcing Alex to lean forward and take the head between her lips. "Tease it," she ordered. "Use that blowjob mouth of yours on Daddy's big cock."

Alex strained against her cuffs, leaning forward to take all of Sara into her mouth. Sara held herself just out of reach, until Alex's tongue was fully extended in a vain attempt at reaching the dickhead. Then she grabbed her by the hair and slammed the cock forcefully into her again, choking her. She loved the feeling of being in control, of watching Alex take her cock into her throat.

"You keep that up, and Daddy just might come down that pretty little throat," she said.

She pulled out, leaving Alex gasping for breath. "That's enough," Sara said. "Actually, it's more than you deserve."

Moving down the bed, she pushed Alex's legs apart and yanked her panties down. "What's this?" she said, fingering the material. "Feels like someone got a little bit wet. Couldn't be you liked sucking Daddy's dick, could it? Greedy little bitch."

She ripped the panties off and held them to her face. "Smells like a little girl," she said. "A very horny little girl who can't control her own pussy."

Balling the panties up, she shoved the wet crotch into Alex's mouth. "Suck on that while Daddy inspects your pussy," she said.

Forcing Alex's legs wider with her knees, she ran her fingers over the smooth lines of her labia. Alex had never allowed Sara to touch her cunt, and now Sara made up for it by taking her time. She tickled the skin, then pulled the lips open and ran just the tips of her fingers along the sensitive edges. She looked up at Alex and saw that her head was thrust back against the headboard.

Sara slid a finger into Alex's cunt and felt the walls contract tightly around it. "And all this time I thought you were a real man," she said, slamming another finger in alongside the first. A roar escaped the gag in Alex's mouth.

Sara pulled the panties out. "What was that?" she asked. "Did you ask me to use another finger?"

Alex didn't answer, so Sara began to fuck her, sliding her fingers in and out until they were glistening with juice and she could feel Alex's body begin to shake. Then she stopped.

"Do you want me to fuck you?" she asked.

Alex didn't answer.

Sara slid her fingers in and out again, keeping Alex on the brink.

"Do you want me to fuck you?" she repeated.

Alex nodded almost imperceptibly.

"I can't hear you." Sara pinched Alex's clit.

"Yes," she whispered.

Sara thrust a third finger inside Alex's swollen cunt. "What?"

"Yes," Alex screamed. "Yes, Daddy, I want you to fuck me."

Sara pulled her hand out and slammed her cock into Alex's pussy, driving it home in one swift stroke. Alex rose off the bed, a howl ripped from her throat as Sara's dick impaled her. Sara knew nothing had ever been inside Alex before, and she imagined the pain must be terrible. This only increased her excitement.

Pulling back, she hammered Alex's cunt with vicious force, pumping away at her in swift thrusts. Grabbing Alex's legs, she hoisted them over her shoulders and toward her head in a classic porn film position. She liked the view this gave her of Alex's cunt and of her cock slipping in and out of it.

"Nice fucking pussy," she said. "Makes Daddy's cock feel good."

Alex was moaning, her head thrown back as Sara fucked her for the first time. Her high-heeled feet dangled over Sara's shoulders, and each time Sara pounded into her, the clamps on her nipples pulled, causing her to cry out.

"What a sweet cunt," Sara said. She felt her body begin to tense as she neared her own climax. "You like being fucked by your own dick? You like taking it up your cunt? Take this!"

Alex answered her by coming in a long, shuddering orgasm. Her whole body tensed, and Sara felt the walls of her pussy clawing at the cock inside her. It pushed Sara over the edge, and she allowed herself to be swept up in the tail of Alex's come. "Fuck!" she shouted, plunging one last time into Alex's hole.

When it was over, she looked down at Alex. The wig had slipped off and fallen to one side. Her eyes were closed, and her lipstick ran in smears down her chin. Sara reached over and undid the nipple clamps, making Alex cry out as the blood rushed in. Sara pulled her cock out of Alex and unfastened the harness. She dropped the dick on the floor. Hearing it fall, Alex opened her eyes.

"Now get dressed and get out!" Sara unclasped the cuffs at Alex's wrists.

Alex scrambled off the bed. She quickly pulled on her jeans and her T-shirt. Without a word, she picked up the dick and started for the front door.

"Not so fast," Sara said.

Alex turned. Her face looked like a watercolor painting left out in the rain. The strong butch facade had been cracked. Sara walked over to her, a crisp twenty-dollar bill in her fingers. Folding it up, she tucked it into the waistband of Alex's pants. "Thanks," she said. "Let's do it again sometime. Oh, and tell Alice I said hello."

Without a word, Alex opened the door and left. Sara went back into the bedroom and began to clean up. As she threw the torn panties and bra into the wastebasket, she noticed the stack of envelopes still sitting on the dresser. She picked them up and began to laugh and laugh.

Go Tell Aunt Tabby
WICKIE STAMPS

I wrote "Go Tell Aunt Tabby" so that I would not have to be alone on this earth. So that, when it is 3:00 A.M. and the Furies sweep into my mind, I can pull out the story, read it, and remember that there was a time when I was held, when I was loved. I wrote "Go Tell Aunt Tabby" to keep myself company.

Most people come into this world in between their Mama's legs. Not me. I was born on my Mama's soft, warm breast. The time of my arrival was sunrise. I know this because the first thing I saw when I opened my eyes was the sun casting its long shadows across my Mama's back. I also know that a window was open because a cool breeze off the St. Francis River was blowing over me and I could hear the waves lapping gently against the pilings down by the water's edge. I also know Mama was swinging back in her big old rocking chair. Her legs were pushed out straight, her thighs hard, and her arms were wrapped firmly around me. The exact moment of my arrival was several stanzas into "Go Tell Aunt

Tabby," my Mama's favorite song. It's a crazy old tune about an old gray goose that Aunt Tabby murdered because she wanted a down comforter.

Because Mama was humming "Go Tell Aunt Tabby" when I was born, I knew she had been singing for a while. Mama always started humming after singing a few stanzas. And I'd bet money I was attached to Mama's breast at the crest of my right ear. Because that would explain why that part of my ear is just slightly crumpled. It just didn't want to pull away from Mama's breast.

I also know that my ear was pressed hard against Mama's slowly rising bosom because I was trying hard to catch the tune that was moving so low and slow within her. The creaking of the rocker, the sun casting its rays across those long, wide, polished boards were what I remember surrounding me. Just me and Mama, wrapped together, away from anyone but ourselves.

Because I had the taste of tears in my mouth, I also know that, when I was born, I was right in the middle of a cry. I was in the same place then as I am now: smack-dab in between my tears and a woman's sweet consolation.

I can guarantee you it wasn't my idea to venture forth into the world. Or, maybe it was. After all, I was a restless child. But I can assure you that whatever the cause of my removal from my Mama's breast, when my bare feet touched those cold, wide-planked wooden floors, I was pouting. I always am.

My first adventure was into my own front yard. There I met my four older siblings: Katrina, Rags, Tom, and MF. They were the meanest children on God's good earth. I never lasted long among this evil brood. Soon I'd run screaming back to Mama. After all, I was a delicate and cowardly child. Mama was never hard to find. I'd just follow the smell of her Tabu perfume that always swam around her or I'd listen for the jangling of her silver bracelets. Usually I'd find her in the bathroom. She'd be in there putting on her lipstick or straightening out her girdle.

"What's wrong, sugar?" she'd ask in that sweet singsong voice of hers. She'd cup my face in her left hand, tilt my head back and, with her right hand, push my matted hair away from my tear-streaked face. As she'd console me she'd be picking the twigs out of my hair and banging the dust out of the seat of my jeans. Mama was always cleaning something or somebody. Sometimes she'd spit on her fingers and scrub my dirt-streaked face. For I was also a very grubby child. Throughout her scrubbing and her inspection, Mama would be humming that crazy old tune.

Quite honestly, I'd milk these times with my Mama for every-thing I could. I'd hold on to my whining, tears, and pouting for as long as I could. But no matter how hard I'd try, Mama could always sweet-talk me out of my misery. Invariably, I would blush, break out into a sheepish grin, and bury my face in the folds of her perfumed silk slip.

By my teens, things started changing between me and my Mama. Maybe it was because she stopped singing "Go Tell Aunt Tabby." Maybe it was her drinking. Or mine. But to tell you the truth I think I just decided it was a sin to love a woman so.

It was around this time that I saw Mama in the tub. It was about 5:30 A.M. I remember the quiet and semidarkness that accompanied that hour. I got up and wandered out of my bedroom toward the bathroom. I started to step in. When I saw Mama's profile, my foot stopped in mid-stride. Mama didn't see me. She was sitting in a shallow tub of water, washing herself with a washrag. The bath-room was low lit. Steam was rising from where Mama sat. She was humming that crazy old song of hers.

Even in the tub she was moving, busily rubbing her skin with her washcloth. But now she was moving just a little slower, sort of peaceful, maybe thinking thoughts she had only when she wasn't with me. I remember the splash of the water in the quiet morning air. Her humming.

I just stood in that doorway watching Mama tending to herself.

I knew I shouldn't be standing there in that doorway. So, I turned and walked back into my bedroom.

Soon after this, Mama started drinking again and I left home for good. She died over twenty-three years ago while I was hitchhiking across country in pursuit of some consolation. I never made it to the funeral. My sister MF buried Mama with those silver bracelets.

Me? I'd take my broken heart and bury it in a world of trouble. It would be a long time before I'd come back around again. But no matter how deep my misery, the sound of a barmaid's jangling bracelets or the whiff of her heavy perfume would always turn my head. And, in between my boozing and my battles, I'd often nurse my hangovers in diners where the older waitresses always called you "sugar." Just for a moment these women and their ways could wash away my misery. Just like my Mama had.

I'd go on to fall in love with big-busted, wide-hipped women. And sometimes when I'd be walking out of their bedrooms still hitching up my jeans, I'd walk past the doorway of their bathrooms and pause. For just a moment I'd rest my elbow on the bathroom doorway, take a deep drag off of my cigarette, and steal a glimpse of these women brushing their hair, putting on their lipsticks, or sliding their stockings over their thighs. I don't know if, in fact, they'd be humming, but in my memories they certainly were.

In between lovers, I'd eventually return to visit Mama's grave. Even at her graveside, there was that silence I remember that settled around us after she finished humming her old song, filled only the with creak of her rocking chair. Touched only by the breeze of the St. Francis. I, usually empty-handed as I was during her life, would just stand there at that grave. Sometimes I'd stoop down and, with tears running down my face, dust off her tombstone, always wishing there was a tree to block the heat and shade from Mama as she had shaded me. MF had made sure the tombstone was pink granite, Mama's favorite color. And MF had fought with Tom, who said he didn't have any money for Mama's tombstone, that he needed all he had to pay for the house he was buying. Me, I had no money to contribute. Too deep in drugs. And myself. Tears flowing, shame resting nearby. I, now alone, would wrap my arms around my knees and rock myself as Mama had, still angry that she had been in my life and had shown me there is a place of silence, coolness, an eye in the hurricane called my life. As I squatted there, I'd find myself humming that tune, humming for me and Mama. No breezes now, no hope lay before us or between us. I, angrier still, that she had left me long before she died, her song, her solace, stolen by the world around us.

I live three thousand miles from where my Mama is buried. On my desk is her picture. Young, like a girl. I, old now, with a younger lover, find myself in times of woe, when fear swims near, wrapping my arms around my lover, rocking her slowly, asking "What's wrong, sugar?" The tone of my voice an exact mirror of my Mama. Tears stream down my face as I rock her, knowing that I learned my solace and consolation in another melancholy place.

It's taken me a long time before I'd let myself rest my head high up on a woman's breast. And longer still until I'd let another woman stroke my hair. For, as you may have gathered, it is a melancholy place for me up there on a woman's warm, soft breast.

Puss in Boots: Or, Clever Mistress Cat
CAROL QUEEN

Besides the fact that I've always loved kitties (and pussies...) and boots, "Puss in Boots (Or, Clever Master Cat)" seems tailor-made for a queer to subvert. Puss is an underdog—or perhaps I should say undercat— hero who subverts the dominant culture through his quick-wittedness, and who makes himself indispensable from a quality-of-life point of view. Who among us can doubt that a culture without sly, subversive, queer artists would be worse than a day without sunshine? Dashing Puss, in the fairy tale, substitutes feline fluidity for macho heroism. Thus he was easy to gender-bend into Darling Puss, clever femme/female kitten of the underclass who lives, as so many in her position do, by her wits. It was a pleasure to put a queer sex-worker's spin on this tale, and I dedicate it to all of us kitties who live by our wits and look fabulous in tall boots. Meow!

There was once an old patriarch, one who had been a king of industry, who on his deathbed determined how his riches would be divided among his children. No sooner had the old man thus decided his children's futures than he died. To the eldest son he left factories and holding companies. To his second son he left his stock portfolios. To his youngest child, a daughter, because he was a patriarch, he left nothing but the house in which she lived—which he stipulated she might never sell—and the family's young serving maid, Kitty.

Nell, the daughter, was secretly glad at that, for the maiden Kitty was fair and clever and had always favored her. But she was furious at her father for leaving her brothers all the family's riches. No doubt he expected that she would soon marry, but there was slim chance of that. She herself was not so inclined. Still, she worried that Kitty would not want to stay on serving her, a woman who suddenly had hardly any money.

But "I would have stayed with you anyway," declared Kitty, when she heard the will read. She had long ago taken a fancy to the rich man's daughter. She was clever and knew, as the daughter did not, that they might, in fact, find happiness together, now that their lots were more equal. Still, she knew she must do something to provide for them. The patriarch's daughter knew nothing of earning a living, nor of being poor.

So Kitty lived with Nell in her great house, though no money came to them and they lived without luxuries. Now that they were alone together—for Nell's brothers were off managing their companies and portfolios—they began to amuse themselves by exploring what they had, which is to say, each other. Kitty, who was not sheltered from the ways of the world as Nell had been, taught her friend much about the worldly amusements. As love grew between them, Kitty became more sure than ever that she must provide for the two of them.

One day when their store of food had grown low and they had sold many of the great house's pretty furnishings to get some extra money, Kitty told Nell that they must go out to a particular shop. "You must buy me a pair of good boots, my darling," she said to her lover, "because I need them to seek our fortune." Nell did as Kitty told her to do, for she depended greatly upon Kitty's wit and resourcefulness and feared the day they would be hungry. So out they went through the broad boulevards and narrow alleys of the town, until they came to the shop where Kitty would choose her boots.

"But my dearest Puss," cried Nell, for that is what she called Kitty in private, "what kind of shop is this?" For the place was full of lewdly painted women and improbably dressed men. "Hush, darling," Kitty quieted her, "they are all only seeking their fortunes."

Kitty chose a pair of very tall boots, with glossy black heels and pointed toes. Nell paid for them, after which they had very little money left.

The next day Kitty clothed herself in a tight black dress which showed her loveliness to very good advantage. Nell had never seen Kitty wearing such a garment, and Kitty was late in leaving the house owing to Nell's strong reaction. After Kitty had put on the dress a second time, she drew on her new high boots, took up a little whip she had found among the patriarch's effects, kissed her lover on the mouth, and promised to return before evening.

"But where are you going, dressed so provocatively, darling Puss?" cried Nell.

But Kitty said only, "Hush, my love, I go out to seek our fortune."

Kitty went out through the broad boulevards and narrow alleys of the town, until she came to a house she had heard of wherein several women lived and sought their fortunes, on a daily basis, from wealthy men who craved strong amusement. The women knew Kitty well, for here in this house, many years ago, the old patriarch had found Kitty's mother and brought her to his home to serve him privately there. The women now drew Kitty in with exclamations and open arms; and when she told them she had come to seek her fortune, they arranged to get a client for her that very day. Afterward she gave the women some of the money she had earned, to thank them for getting her employment, and they agreed she had done very well and was welcome to come again the next day. Then she visited the shop again where she had got her boots, and there she purchased a black corset and some lace-and-silken underclothes. And Kitty went home to Nell that evening with money in her pocket.

The next morning Kitty set out again, this time with her corset cinched tightly under her dress, which made her look more comely than ever. "Puss! Please be careful seeking your fortune!" Nell cried, but she no longer asked where her Puss might go. They had dined very well the night before, and Nell knew that Kitty was very, very clever.

When Kitty reached the house, she declared to the women that her name would be Mistress Cat, and that she would return every day if they would have her. "Oh, yes!" they said, "for we are delighted to have you working here with us, and the name Mistress Cat suits you very well. We already have told all our clients about you. You have three appointments booked so far today."

So it came to pass that Mistress Cat, as Kitty came to be called by all who knew her except her lover Nell, who still called her Puss and nothing else, met great success in seeking her fortune. For she was young and fair and devilishly clever, so that rich men with a taste for strong amusement loved her and visited her, bringing money and gifts. In return, she would demand imperiously that they strip naked before her, and she would mercilessly ply the whip she had taken from the deceased patriarch, that in fact had belonged to her mother before her. She would send them into paroxysms of pain and pleasure using her whip and her wit and her biting tongue, and they praised her as comely, clever, and cruel.

One day Nell could stand her curiosity no more. "Dearest Puss," she pleaded, "please tell me whence you have all this money! Can I not help you earn it, to lessen the work you have to do, which so often takes you away from my side?"

Now Kitty knew that Nell had grown up rich, and so was unaccustomed to doing any sort of labor; she knew also that because her lover was as fair as she, and tall, and could be exceedingly haughty, that she, too, might earn a fortune very successfully, if she could be taught a taste for the work. And in fact, Kitty reasoned, if they were to work together, they might even earn enough to invest well, which would keep them until they were old.

So she told Nell to wait for her a moment, and she would reveal everything to her. She bade her lover kneel before the fire with closed eyes until she came to fetch her. "Then, my pretty one," she murmured, "your Puss will tell you every secret, and teach you how you may earn your fortune, too."

Kitty ran up to their room and put on her tall boots, which she wore every day to the house where she worked; she laced up her tight corset, let down her fair long hair, and painted her lips crimson. Then she took up her mother's whip and went down to her lover, who waited for her with closed eyes before the fire.

Nell heard Kitty come up before her; then she felt the sharp toe of her lover's boot on her shoulder, and Kitty's foot pushed her down until her lips were almost brushing the floor. "Kiss my booted foot," she heard Kitty say. "The boots you bought for me with the last of our money, the boots in which I have earned our fortune." And Nell did so, wondering at the voice Kitty used, so different from her usual sweet voice, so magnificent. She kissed the pointed toes of the tall black boots, and found that the act of kissing them made her want to kiss them all the more passionately.

"Rise up now and open your eyes and look at me," said Kitty. "I am Mistress Cat, and I am strong and clever, and I love you enough to provide for you. Now what will you do for me?"

Nell saw her Puss dressed in her finery—Mistress Cat, as grand a figure as she had ever seen. Her eyes grew wide with awe, and for a moment she was silent because she could find no words to say. Then she whispered, "What...would you have me do, my

Mistress?" Then, trembling a little, she waited for her Puss to reply.

"I would have you serve me, my Mistress, my love, as I have served you all these many years," said the bold Mistress Cat. Then in her heart Nell was glad, for she loved her Puss dearly, and it seemed wrong to her that they should be together only because her father the patriarch had left Kitty to her in his will.

"Then how shall I serve you, my Lady?" cried Nell. "Only tell me, and I will hasten to obey you."

At this Kitty rejoiced, for she knew by Nell's answer that her plan was sound. So she asked that Nell's hands to be extended before her, and bound her wrists with a strap of soft leather. "My love, walk into the kitchen and pour me some wine, and bring it back here to me, taking care to spill none of it." Nell looked at her bound hands with great consternation. Then she glanced up at her Mistress Cat and said with a small smile, "My Lady, this will I endeavor to do."

As she sat before the fire, Kitty heard sounds coming from the kitchen that told her Nell was managing to pour the wine, even with her hands bound as they were. Presently Nell rounded the corner, her hands still bound before her, and walked slowly toward Kitty. She clenched a small tray in her teeth, upon which rested a stemmed wineglass, perfectly full of good red wine. When Nell arrived at Kitty's feet, she knelt ever so carefully before her, lest she spill a drop of the wine as her Mistress had warned her she must not do. Smiling, Kitty took the glass from the tray. She raised it to her still-kneeling love, then took the tray out of Nell's mouth so that she might reach down and kiss her.

"That was smartly done, my love," Kitty said. "Now stay kneeling there whilst I drink my wine, for you are very pretty to look at." Bound as she was, Nell sat immobile with her eyes cast down, waiting for Kitty to finish her wine.

"Now, my darling, I would like you to draw a bath for me," Kitty said at length, and Nell managed to get to her feet and went to do as she was asked. Kitty followed her, that she might enjoy the sight of her bound love doing her bidding.

Nell was obliged to undress Kitty in a most awkward and tantalizing way, for Kitty did not untie her hands. "With your teeth, then, wench," Kitty said idly, and found that it amused her greatly to have her garments removed, piece by piece, by her lover's teeth. The corset proved especially challenging, but Nell managed to work the knot apart and tug the lacings open. At last Kitty stood there in only her tall boots, and Nell went to kneel before her, but Kitty took pity on her and bade her stand, removing the boots herself. Then, before she stepped into the bath, she untied Nell's wrists. "Wash me, my darling," Kitty said, sinking into the bath, and Nell took up a sponge and did as she was told.

"Now dry me," Kitty continued, stepping at length out of the water. With great concentration, Nell did so, marveling at the way her Puss's nipples rose up at the touch of the towel, loving the steam rising from her pink skin. So overcome was she by Kitty's loveliness that she dropped to her knees again, kissing her pretty feet.

Smiling, Kitty drew her up. "Come now, my impetuous one," she said, "you need not do that here, but come to our bed." Blushing hotly, Nell followed Kitty out, and when her Mistress lay herself on the bed, Nell went back to kissing her pretty feet, up the arches and over the ankle, and up and up until Kitty bade her to "Stay *there*, kiss only there!" So Nell served Kitty with as much devotion as Kitty had ever shown to her.

The next day Kitty showed Nell how to wield a whip and how to speak imperiously, and told her what to say to the men who would come to make use of her services. She taught her how to bind and to torment, to use a man's manhood to bring him low and cause him to weep and grovel. Nell took to these lessons well, just as Kitty had suspected she would, and the following day Nell went with Kitty to the big house.

"Here is a new Mistress," said Kitty. "As you see, she is tall and comely, with a haughty air and a taste for seeing men crawl before her. She shall be called Mistress Sapphire, for her eyes are blue as jewels."

"Welcome!" cried the other mistresses. So they introduced Mistress Sapphire to each gentleman who visited that day. By the late afternoon, she felt quite wealthy, as three men had paid her handsomely to kneel before her and accept her wrath. Mistress Cat, too, had been visited by several men.

"Come, my darling Nell," said Kitty as they left the house. "We must go to buy you some boots of your own." So they went through the streets to the little shop, and Nell used her own money—the first money she ever had earned—to buy a pair of tight black boots that laced up her shapely calves, showing them to very good advantage. Then they walked out into the streets arm in arm, laughing together, and went to sup at a good place; and Nell bought their meals, too, with the money she had earned herself.

Now their days were very happy, for except when they parted to see their own clients, they rarely left each other's sides; and Kitty no longer had any secrets from her love, telling her even how it was that her mother had come to live with the patriarch, Nell's father, in his fine big house. So it was no surprise to them when a gentleman appeared at the house where they worked, boasting of his riches and requesting the services of the finest Mistress on the premises. It was Nell's eldest brother; but he did not recognize his sister at all, nor Kitty, so changed were they from the quiet sister and saucy serving girl he had known in his youth.

Nell quickly whispered to Kitty that she did not want her brother's money, but that Kitty should go with him. She added that her eldest brother was deathly afraid of mice. "Perhaps," she laughed, "that is information you can use."

So Mistress Cat stepped forward and motioned to Nell's boastful brother to follow her, which he did, for she was exceedingly comely and walked with great pride. When they came to her private room, she bade him strip naked before her, that she might see what sort of man he was; and, she bound him to a table and belittled him severely, so that his manhood stood straight up; and seeing this, she bound that, too. Then she told him he was not man enough to look at her, and tied a blindfold over his eyes; after which she tickled him with her long, sharp nails and dangled a bit of string over him, and told him she had loosed a mouse on him, and that it was running about on him whither it wished. Though he pleaded with her most piteously, she did not relent from making this mouse, as she said it was, run about, and when it reached his manhood and began to crawl upon it he gave a great cry and emitted most violently, out of terror.

Then Mistress Cat became even wealthier and better known, for thereafter Nell's wealthy brother gave her anything she asked, and many men visited the house and petitioned for her services, having heard tales of her from him.

It came to pass that the house grew so successful that it was too small for all their business. The women who lived there declared that it was time to search for a bigger location, but large houses were scarce to find. So Kitty and Nell offered up their big house, the house Nell had been left by her father, the patriarch.

And in the end, their wealth grew so great that they were able to purchase their own stock portfolio—a better one than Nell's brother had been left by their father—and they earned enough money to keep themselves richly, and their house full of women as well. And although they no longer needed to work, they often did just the same, for they were both amused by the way men crawled and mewled before them. And at home Nell continued to serve her Puss, her clever Mistress Cat, just as she had on that first night. In this way they lived many happy years together and, for all I know, they are living there still.

The Nightingale
CECILIA TAN

This has always been a mysterious tale to me. In the original fairy tale, the nightingale is taken from the woods to please the emperor; and then, when a mechanical replacement for her is brought from Japan, she falls from favor and is sent back to the woods. Despite this shoddy treatment, she returns at the end to chase the demons of death away from the emperor. It seemed to me the elements that needed full illumination were her relationship to the kitchen maid who brings her to the emperor in the first place, and her feelings that brought her back to save him in the end. There are issues of loyalty here: to king and country, to something larger than oneself, subservience and submission. There are also the tales from the romantic poets who believed that the nightingale's song could only be so beautiful, so sad and full of pain, because the nightingale pierced its breast with a thorn. Searching for a context to explore both the issues of loyalty and masochism, I found the nightingale became a performance artist and the emperor an underworld Mafia figure. (The quotes through-out are taken from Fairy Tales by Hans Christian Andersen, *a facsimile of the 1884 edition.)*

"It is my pleasure that she shall appear here this evening," said the emperor.

The knife girl writhes on a stage scuffed with boot marks and stained with wine, blood, water, and sweat. The knife is alive as it twirls in her hands, electric as it flashes under the lights, cruel as it opens her skin and the wound cries blood. A golden ululation issues from her throat as the blood flows, and she sings, entranced, transforming her pain into ecstasy, her self-destruction into sacrament.

She is jarred by the empty sound of Michael's cough echoing off the walls of the club. He is standing between Carl and Karen—Karen, whom the knife girl had almost forgotten was there.

"I've seen enough," he says to Carl, and rubs his eyes against the flickering of the lights. Knife girl sees him pull his coat and fine silk scarf tighter around him, even though the club seems warm to her. "She's hired. Set it up." Michael, whose name she remembers because he is the owner and she knows it is important to remember it, turns away from the stage and disappears through a black door behind the bar.

Carl comes to the edge of the stage, the silver piercings around his face flashing in the lights, and says, "Well, Night, that's it. See you in a week."

And then Karen steps forward. "Night? You okay?"

The knife girl presses a hand to the cut in her arm, and the bleeding stops. Now Karen will take her home, and Night will use the edge of the blade to slice Karen's clothing from her, the cold edge of it to harden her nipples, the pinpoint of it to flick her clit, and the smooth pommel to fuck her until she cries. The knife girl knows this with a certainty that makes her close her eyes and press her lips together in something like a smile.

At last they met with a poor little girl in the kitchen who said, "Oh, yes, I know the nightingale quite well."

They had been lovers perhaps a month when Karen had explained it all to her, the club, her bartending job, Michael's underworld ties, and Carl's idea to turn business around. Business had been bad—so bad that Karen could lose her job, Michael could lose the club. "They want a performance artist. Michael's heard about that show you did at Artspace and wants to see you. I told him I could…introduce you." Night had kissed Karen on the lips and told her of course she would go.

> *The nightingale sang so sweetly the tears came into the emperor's eyes.*

The knife girl stands in the darkness of the DJ booth beside the stage and breathes deep. In a few moments, she will step beyond the veil of darkness and into the glare and flash of the lights. Karen told her Michael even spent some extra money to install better lighting and a fog machine. Announcements of her performance have been made in the right publications, to the right people. Night takes deep breaths and waits for the moment to arrive.

The lights dim, and she takes her place in the smoke in darkness. Faint music rises and then the lights, and then she unfolds herself before the crowd. She lets the rhythm of the music curve her spine and the faces at the edge of the stage become small whitish blurs as she spins the knife in the air.

The knife. It is warm in her hands as she begins to sing to it, and a little sweat shines on her skin as she dances. The marks on the stage are obscured by the smoke. The knife girl feels that she is the moon, rising above the storm. The knife flashes like lightning, and she lets her tongue taste the sharp tang of the metal. She feels the eyes of everyone in the room on the knife as she presses it to her skin.

Not yet, she thinks. More foreplay before the penetration. But her voice is getting shaky as she cuts the gauzy material from her breasts. The song changes, becomes more breathy and desperate. Night plunges the hilt of the dagger toward her crotch and hears someone nearby gasp. The knife swoops and slices open her leggings. She sinks slowly to her knees.

She hugs the blade to her cheek like a lover's hand, singing, pleading, singing, until she lets her hand fall and the knife scratches a red line along her jaw. The pain opens her eyes and makes her breath deep, her song loud. With one hand covering her bare crotch, she draws swirls with the knife tip across her breastbone. In a few places, the tip parts the skin, and blood begins to run down her belly toward her crotch. She crisscrosses the lines of old scars until the blood flows as easily as her song. Her pubic hair is sticky with her own blood and she brings her hand up to smear the blood across her eyes. The mask of war, the mark of death.

At that moment, she looks up. With her bloodstained eyes, she sees Michael in the DJ booth, looking back at her with his eyes full of hunger and sadness.

> *"I have seen tears in an emperor's eyes," she said. "That is my richest reward."*

He looks at her the same way when she goes to collect her pay at the end of the night. He counts out the bills and holds them in his hand for a long moment, his eyes focused past her on something only he can see.

"Michael?" She does not lean against his desk, nor look away into the dim stacks of papers that crowd his office.

His gaze snaps back to her with a little shake of his overgrown hair. His small beard and mustache are neatly trimmed, she notices. He holds the money in his hand, as if he knows when he gives it to her she will leave. "Is your name really Night?"

Her eyes, dark and placid, do not waver. "Do you want me to try the piercing thing next week?"

"I…sure, whatever." His fingers touch hers as he hands her the money.

Now, the whole city rang with praises of the bird.

The knife girl's tongue dances on the edge of her lover's clit. Karen is squirming, but her bonds hold her pelvis still while the knife girl uses the tender tip to torture her. The knife girl has lost track of time, lost in the sensation of Karen and the rhythm of her tongue moving.

"Ahh! I can't take it anymore!" Karen pulls hard on her bonds trying to shut her legs, but to no avail.

Night looks up. Something else, then. She sucks Karen's swollen clit into her mouth. Her jaw begins to tremble as she snags the flesh between her front teeth and begins to close them. Her fingers slide into Karen's cunt. As she bites down, Karen screams, and Night feels the spasms around her fingers as Karen comes.

While Karen lies limp, Night loosens the bonds and tucks coils of rope like white cobras into her bag. She leans over to kiss Karen on the cheek.

Karen stops her with a hand on her shoulder. "Don't ever do that to me again."

Night's eyes close in a long blink. "Do what?"

"I didn't like it."

The knife girl considers whether or not her remark should cut. "Your body did," she says.

Karen's hand connects with Night's cheek, a sudden but not forceful slap. Night holds her wrists then and drags her full weight on top of Karen. "Tell me what you didn't like."

Karen twists her head to the side. "I'm not like you. I don't like pain."

Night releases her suddenly and stands up. "You're not supposed to like pain. If you did, it wouldn't hurt so much."

Karen sighs and sits up in the bed. The only light comes from the street lamp below the window, making Night's face look blue, her lips dark. "I'm sorry I hit you," she says, watching Night for a sign of forgiveness. "I…you know you stir up a lot of crazy feelings…." Night is so still, she could be a statue of herself. "And you've been getting so…at the club, your show is so extreme sometimes, it scares me. I mean, I know that's what gets the big crowds—the publicity and everything. It's great how we're doing, but I just get a little freaked out, okay?"

Night listens to Karen go on in this vein for some time before she changes the subject. "So what was attendance last night?"

"You mean Michael didn't tell you? It was our biggest night ever."

A big crowd, a rapt crowd, people who would not be the same today as they were yesterday. Except Karen, who is easy to distract from her apologies because she does not really mean them; and Michael, who always watches her with the same expression. The knife girl chews her lip and wonders what she will dream about tonight.

She was put into a golden cage and was allowed to fly out every day….

She sits in a darkened corner of the club while insistent rhythms thrum the wall around her. Carl turns a watchful eye her way as he passes through the club, a walkie-talkie by his ear. He is the one who explained it to her: that her presence draws people on the nights she is not performing, that the scenesters and curiosity seekers alike would come to catch a glimpse of her, hoping to meet her and spin their own myths about her. This corner, up beside one of the bars, is not easily accessible from the dance floor. Michael often sits here while he surveys the crowd. Night has made her appearance here several nights this week and is not surprised when Michael takes a seat next to her.

When he turns to her with bloodshot eyes and puts his hand on hers, and then buries his face in his arms, though, she wonders. And when she takes him back to his office and he knocks the papers from his desk in a rage and then beats his fist upon it, she wonders. And when he regains his composure and apologizes and suggests that she should leave him alone, and when she takes his chin in her hand and rakes his throat with her nails, and makes him hurt, and when he falls to his knees, his eyes closed, his breath shallow, then she wonders. She makes him come with one hand on his penis and one hand around his throat. The knife girl knows better than to say anything about it.

The knife girl lets Karen make her come. She curls up into a ball until Karen coaxes her open, soft hands and probing fingers seeking out her pleasure spots and manipulating them. Night's throat opens with soft cries as Karen's fingers saw at her slippery clit. Karen pumps her fingers in and out of Night's soft cunt, rubs her thumb over Night's clit, fast, slow, hard, soft, and still Night does not come. Her cries become longer and her breathing deeper, but she does not come. Karen, tired, takes Night's nipple in her mouth, sucking hard and letting her teeth graze across the hard flesh. Night decides to let her think that is what she needs, and she lets loose a wail. Karen does not notice that as Night comes, Night's fingernails are digging into her own buttocks.

When they are both relaxed, Karen brushes Night's hair from her face and says, "You are so beautiful when you come."

"Thank you," Night says.

"Why don't you do it more often?"

"Because I don't need to," Night answers.

"But I like to make you come."

"No," Night says, and though she does not intend it, her voice is cold.

The knife girl arrives early to the club, before the doors open and the adoring public arrives. She sheds her coat and carries it to the back room, led by voices. Carl and Karen are talking in Michael's office.

"There's seriously something wrong with him." Karen.

"No kidding." Michael.

Night pauses outside the door to listen.

"I mean, I think he needs to go to a hospital or to a therapist or something. Doesn't he have insurance?"

Carl laughs. "Yeah, the mob. Look, he can't go to the nuthouse. They'd never trust him again."

"He doesn't have to be committed. I think he just needs medication or something. Prozac. I don't know."

"I've worked for him four years. He gets like this sometimes. It'll pass. Just keep it quiet, or everything could fall apart around us—you hear me? Something happens to him, and this place goes with him."

Night goes silently back to the main room and stands under the white house lights, thinking that they look like the lights on a train as it bears down on a crossing. That night, after her performance, she tends to Michael again. He is in his office alone, his head on his desk, an empty bottle of rum at his feet. With her knife pricking the soft, lethal spot behind his ear, she tells him she knows what he needs. With her mark carved into his skin, where it joins self-inflicted scars, some old, some new, she knows she is right.

One day the emperor received from Japan a present of a golden bird.

And so it goes for the knife girl, as her performances continue, on the stage, with Karen, with Michael, and it seems to her all will remain that way, until the day she sees the courier leaving Michael's office. A dark-haired man with Asian eyes and an impeccable suit. He inclines his head toward her, as if acknowledging her as worthy of notice, and then disappears.

Inside the office she finds Michael with a dreamy look upon his face and a needle—not her kind of needle—upon his blotter. That night he does not come to watch her performance, and when she visits him later, he responds dully and thanks her for coming as if she'd fixed a broken sink for him or some other necessary but small task. She leaves him to find Karen swamped with customers at the bar. Carl ushers her to her secluded corner table, and she waits there for the night to end.

The next night, she tries again, but Michael sends her away. "Look," he tells her, "we've got to have a little variety to keep the crowds coming down here. Why don't you take a few weeks off? It'll create a great buzz. I've got some other acts who can fill in." The knife girl knows when she is being cut loose.

The emperor and the court now fell in love with the new golden bird and the nightingale was allowed to fly out the window…and then a real grief came upon the land.

The knife girl is not surprised when Karen comes home early one night a month or so later, angry and fuming. "He was so fucked up tonight! Everything's going to shit at the club," she tells her. "These Japanese business types are hanging around, throwing their money around, but business is down, and Michael doesn't even seem to want to do anything about it!" Karen looks around the small apartment they have been sharing and exhales. "He's fired two other bartenders this week because we couldn't afford to pay them." Her voice edges on hysterical. "It's like he doesn't care anymore."

"He doesn't," Night whispers, but Karen hears her.

"What do you mean, he doesn't? That club is all he has." Her fear makes her bitter. "And that's all we've got. Or did you forget that I'm the one with a job?"

Night has not forgotten. "I wish I could see him."

"Excuse me?" Karen takes a step closer to Night, out of the kitchenette and into the dining/living area. "How can you miss that bastard after he fired you like he did?"

Night knows she should remain silent, but she does not want her lover to think that Karen owes her nothing. "I thought maybe I could help him."

"Help him?" Karen's jealous streak interprets her meaning and cannot help confirming it. "You were sleeping with him?"

"Not exactly," says Night, sounding small.

"Not exactly? Not *exactly?*" Karen's face fights between stricken and angry. "Night! You...after what you did..." She can't speak; she only sputters.

Night waits silently for a moment, then says, "Do you think I should try to help him now?"

Karen recoils from her, eyes narrowing. "What do you mean?"

Night wishes she could explain these things, these things she can only express with tears and cut flesh and songs. "Nothing," she says. "I'm sorry."

"You cheated on me, slept with our boss behind my back, and all you can say is 'I'm sorry'?"

Night says one more thing. "Perhaps I should leave now."

"Did you love him?"

Night does not answer. Karen is irrational; no answer will satisfy her. Besides, the knife girl does not think there is only one kind of love. Karen has never thought to ask if Night loves her. She is too afraid of the answer.

Cold and pale lay the emperor in his royal bed.

The knife girl does not expect thanks. She does what she does for her own feelings, not others. It is her feeling of loyalty that propels her down the dark hallway to Michael's office. Loyalty to him, the man that built the temple for her sacrament; loyalty to Karen, who needs Michael more than she will admit; loyalty to an ideal, a way of life and living that the knife girl must prove to herself. She must prove it to Michael. She shivers with the thought of the confrontation to come—it will be a hard argument to win, and he will probably just send her away again. But she has to try.

She opens the door to find him slumped over his desk, as if he fell asleep after working late. But he is not asleep. She knows it as she lays a hand on his shoulder. He is near death.

Night pulls him from his chair, knocking papers, books, the phone from his desk as she drags him onto it. His chest barely moves—he barely breathes—as she climbs astride him. "Come on, Michael!" she whispers, urgent breath through her teeth as she shakes him. "Come back to me!"

She slaps him across the face and watches the redness of her handprint appear. It is the only reaction she gets. She slaps him across the other cheek, hoping some deadened nerve endings will fire. This is about pain, she thinks. If you can't feel pain, you can't care. People cry at my shows because they can feel the pain I am going through.

The knife, never far from her, cuts his tie from his neck and opens his shirt. She runs her fingers over old scars. I understand you, she thinks. I know why you cut yourself. Because it is better to feel pain than to feel nothing at all, the emptiness. Remember?

She finds the drawer is full of syringes, the needles in a separate package from the plungers. She discards the plungers and opens the needle pack. She fans them in her fingers, chisel points outward. Remember?

She begins with his nipples, heavy with nerve endings and so responsive in the past when she used to pinch them and make him worship with her. The metal slides through his flesh, the left, then the right, and she slaps him across the face again, a guttural growl coming from her throat. I know you felt that!

She feels electric, as if she has started a motor somewhere, connecting her to him. Her nails rake his body as she chooses another place to pierce him, and sinks the needle into his upper arm. She puts another and another through, in neat lines like stitches up his arm. Come on, Michael, feel it! Pain is life, life is pain, so live!

Night cuts open his pants and squeezes his genitals, strokes him, scratches him, until she thinks he takes a deeper breath. One hand pinches a bleeding nipple while the other yanks on his ball sack. There are more needles to go through there, and his perineum, like a ladder climbing between his legs. She drags the point of a needle along the underside of his penis and stops with the tip poised against the cleft of the head.

If you die, the ship sinks with you, Night thinks. I do this for you, and for me, and for Karen. As she drives the needle through, Michael gasps and clutches at her, like a drowning man rescued from icy seas.

The knife girl lets the blade trail down her lover's back, as her lover arches into the knife's caress. The lights pulse red, then blue, but Night sees only one thing: the ecstasy in Karen's body as she shudders. Night runs her teeth over her neck and shoulders. There are gasps from the audience as Night tears Karen's bra away. One hand goes to Karen's crotch while the other holds the knife between Karen's bare breasts; and as Night's teeth sink in, Karen comes.

Svya's Girl
KATYA ANDREEVNA

The traditional Russian story I have rewritten is called "Svyatogor's Bride." The original is about Svyatogor's inability to escape his fate—he is to marry the maiden from the dung heap. By the time he does marry her, she has been transformed by a stroke of his sword. I picked this story and chose to write from the maiden's point of view because I am interested in her transformation. I have experienced many periods in my life in which my sexuality was shut down. The maiden's awakening through cutting is what drew me to this story.

Long ago in the Land by the Sea, Maiden lived in a modest dwelling. Although known for her great beauty and vigor, a strange lethargy had overtaken her. She had ceased combing her thick, dark locks. Her clothing had become dirty and ragged, her body weak from inactivity. Most days she sat in her chamber and gazed from the window.

One evening, a sparrow landed on her sill. It hopped and chirped excitedly at her.

"Do be quiet," she said.

But the bird kept up its chatter.

"Am I to accompany you?" she asked the bird. Finally, following the bird's lead, she strolled from her abode. Slowly she moved through the streets, her joints creaking from disuse, her wild hair swarming her head like a cyclone. Passersby stared at her disheveled state and drew away.

After what seemed like days, Maiden entered a place of great merriment, a tavern she had frequented before the onset of her malaise. As in the past, she waved to the barmaid and passed into the dimly lighted back room.

As always, the room swirled with energy. By the door, two women were binding a third to a chair. Moans and sighs rose from the crowd gathered around the large table in the middle of the chamber.

"A typical night at The Cave," she thought, and sank to the floor in a corner. She blinked her eyes, adjusting to the feeble light. She watched as a powerful woman with silver hair pinned a young woman to the floor. The silver-haired one drew a thick rod from under her garments and with it entered the young woman, who gasped and wrapped her legs around the body above her.

Slumped against the wall, Maiden yawned. "Perhaps I should have bathed," she thought, settling deeper into her torpor. By midnight the passions in the room had reached a boiling point. Women cried out and shook in waves of pleasure. Couples, threesomes, and the group at the table wrestled satisfaction from their bodies in their own way—slaps rang in the air, while the slippery murmurs of lapping tongues created a soothing susurration.

As the ecstasy in the room reached a crescendo, Svya entered. Her appearance was met with intense pleasure. Svya, a renowned traveler, was a favorite in the community. Tall, strong, and commanding, she wore a pair of carefully tailored men's breeches, a hat with a plume, and a richly brocaded vest. A long, jeweled sword hung from the finely tooled belt at her waist.

"Svya, join us," the woman tied to the chair called.

"Svya, where have you been?" another woman asked.

"Out seeking my fortune," Svya replied, striding into the center of the room. Maiden glanced at Svya with a cold eye. She had heard tell of this glorious Svya and, in the past, she had most desired to meet her.

Svya approached. "Who do we have here?" she asked, leaning down.

Maiden tried to smile. Her wooden cheeks felt as though they would crack from the effort.

Svya snorted with laughter and spun on her heel. She grabbed a passing blonde and, pressing her against the wall, sucked greedily at her breast. Barely breathing, Maiden watched. As her eyes followed Svya, her hands drifted numbly down the flesh of her own cool thighs. But the heavy chill pressed against her, anesthetizing every pore.

Svya made the rounds of the room, massaging breasts, sucking toes, doling out quick spankings. And Maiden watched.

As dawn approached, exhausted women slumped out of the room. Still Maiden lay in her corner, her eyes open, although her body slept. Once again, Svya drew near. She smiled down at Maiden.

"Have you not moved all night?" Svya asked.

Maiden struggled to sit up.

Svya unsheathed her gleaming sword.

Maiden remained perfectly still, but somewhere deep inside, her soul twitched.

Svya drew the flat of the sword up the length of Maiden's leg. She thrust her legs open, and Maiden offered no resistance. Crouching between Maiden's legs, Svya parted her fur lips with the hilt of her sword. She pressed the smooth, cool handle to Maiden's clit and then pushed inside her.

Maiden lay still.

"Can you feel this?" Svya asked.

Maiden moved her head slowly from side to side. With a sucking noise, Svya withdrew her sword from Maiden's womanhood. She grabbed the still-pungent hilt and pressed the sharp point of the blade to Maiden's breastbone.

"Well, can you feel this?" she asked.

The cold steel of the carefully crafted sword—colder than Maiden's cold skin—sliced through her thin blouse. As Maiden inhaled, the slight motion caused the blade to break her skin. A part of Maiden wanted to shove her chest forward onto the steel spike, but her body remained immobile. Maiden took a deep breath and drove the point into the scanty flesh of her sternum.

As Svya drew the tip of the blade down Maiden's chest, the steel flashed cold, then hot. Maiden's breath filled her lungs in short bursts. She tried to speak, but merely gasped as the stinging sword caressed her.

When Svya reached the central point between Maiden's smooth breasts, she withdrew the blade and watched Maiden for a moment. Then sheathing her sword, she cast a handful of gold pieces in Maiden's direction and strode from the chamber.

Maiden looked at the trickle of blood that ran from the wound on her chest.

"Yes," she said, as if Svya still stood before her. "Yes, I can feel that." She breathed deeply and her pulse throbbed in her chest, in her wrists, at her temples. A great weight fell away from her body as if she had been cut free from a girdle of thick bark. Like the live green wood below, she tingled with newness. She touched the mark Svya had left on her. Suddenly, like the rising sap, she was flooded with desire.

"Where is Svya?" Maiden demanded.

"I guess she left," one of the few remaining women answered and headed for the door.

Maiden grabbed the woman. Fondling her breasts, Maiden

pushed her against the wall. Maiden sucked greedily at the stranger's neck, rubbed against her legs.

"Svya," she thought. "Svya."

Maiden took the money that Svya had thrown. Days and nights she searched for Svya to no avail. She began to travel, searching out craftswomen far and wide. They made for her many a mysterious device dedicated to female pleasure and pain. She tested them all herself, but every new toy merely increased her desire for what she had not felt, the hilt of Svya's sword.

When Maiden came to the Great City, she opened a shop to sell her precious goods, and the fame of her great beauty and strange implements spread throughout the land.

One day Svya came to Maiden's shop. Svya gazed long at the Maiden's wares. Maiden gazed at Svya, her well-muscled legs encased in white breeches, her strong arms, her shining sword.

"Kind Mistress, please, explain the use of this implement," Svya asked.

While Maiden explained, choosing her words with care, her heart beat steadily between her legs. She eyed Svya's sword.

"I would be happy to demonstrate the implement," Maiden pronounced finally. Svya smiled and followed Maiden into a private chamber.

"I'll need to warm up a bit," Maiden said. She grabbed Svya's arm and steered her to a chair. Maiden slid the sword at Svya's waist around so that it fell between her new customer's legs. Raising her skirts, Maiden climbed into Svya's lap and lowered herself into the hilt of the much-desired sword. The sword was both cold and hot, as it had been when it awakened Maiden from her sexless trance. Maiden moved slowly. The weapon was larger than Maiden had remembered. She rocked from side to side as she engulfed the sword, allowing it to caress every inner fold.

Svya stroked Maiden's hair and unbuttoned her blouse. "You are a bold one," Svya whispered into Maiden's ear. "This pleases me."

"I have awaited this a long while," Maiden said, driving the sword deeper inside herself. Maiden rocked on Svya's stiff stem. Her movements became rapid and abrupt. Maiden began to pant. The hot-and-cold sensation of the sword's steel flooded her whole being. Her body shook in quick spasms, and a deep groan crawled from her throat. Maiden drooped against Svya's shoulder for a moment, inhaling deeply. Raising her head, she laughed a full, round, satisfied laugh.

Svya sucked on Maiden's earlobe. "What is this scar at your breast?" Svya asked, running her thick fingers along the thin slice of white.

Maiden's laughter rang out. She squeezed Svya in her arms and Svya squeezed back. They kissed long and deeply.

After some delay, Maiden replied, "Once I was a prisoner, but a beautiful knight set me free."

Svya stroked Maiden's flushed cheek, and Maiden felt herself swimming in the blue pools of Svya's eyes.

"I will tell you the whole story someday," Maiden said, removing her blouse and unbuttoning Svya's vest. "Now I will demonstrate the implement."

Hungry Wolf and the Three Capable Femmes
CRISTINA SALAT

There once was a party where female participants were asked to dress either butch or femme in the extreme and then explain why they identified more with one label than with the other. Almost all came as butch because, these women said, femmes are "frivolous," "vacuous," and "still oppressed."

I beg to differ.

The word femme *is linked intrinsically to the words* female *and* feminine. *There is power in that. Feminine should not mean frivolous; it should connote one type of woman in all her soft, colorful splendor.*

I consider myself a capable femme. What's more—rather than being attracted to my mirror opposite, the "butch," who is often glorious, it's true—I tend to swoon over other capable femmes. And so this story began....

Wolf was not pretty; she was dashing. She had short brown hair, long brown limbs and a smile that could charm femmes into bed...or so it had always been.

Wolf had been a butch-about-town, overindulging her libido,

for many years. But now she was almost forty. Tasty one-nighters were no longer good enough. She wanted breakfast together the next morning and every morning after. She wanted to play house—no, not play it!—live it. (Recent therapy had taught her the difference.) Wolf was hungry for the real thing. It was time to settle down.

Of course, settling down entailed finding just the right femme to settle down with. Color was unimportant, but other details were not. Wolf wanted someone pretty but not straight, someone shy but not too shy (especially in bed!), and most importantly, someone who appreciated Wolf's glorious butchiness and said so often.

Now Wolf had her eye on one particular femme named Straw who lived down the lane. Straw had quite a nice thatched tropical dwelling with skylights to play (live!) under. She also had long, wheat-colored hair, pink, pink skin and breasts that swayed gloriously under her clothing. Oh, how Wolf loved the idea of sucking on big, beautiful breasts. And this time she would stick around to suck on them again and again and again. (Wolf's therapist had been right; abstaining was the best thing she had done for herself in years. It had made her hungry to commit.) So Wolf went a-courtin'. She brought flowers and a book of feminist fairy tales that she and Straw could read together in bed after spending the night.

Straw, it turned out, had a delicate appetite and only picked at the steak Wolf brought. As Wolf devoured her own, she imagined reaching out to pinch the dark nipple circles of Straw's breasts, evident even beneath her clothing. Wolf hoped, when the breasts were unclothed, she would find large, wrinkly nipples, and this thought caused her to smile with feral charm and raise her eyes to meet Straw's. Unfortunately, Straw was looking elsewhere at that moment and their gazes did not meet. *Later*, Wolf thought patiently.

But after dinner Straw gave Wolf a friendly good-night cheek kiss and led her to the door.

What a wasted evening, Wolf reflected on the way back to her cave. *She didn't laugh at my jokes. Anyway, her nose is too big, she is too*

round and too pink, and I can not have a girlfriend who doesn't appreci-
ate fine steak. Besides all that, she is too materialistic for me. I do not need
someone who owns a fancy thatched hut. I need someone who needs me.

The next weekend, Wolf called a woman named Stick. Stick had silky mocha skin, loved a good pork chop, and was not rich. She lived in a log cabin which, simple as it was, felt more like home than Wolf's dark, empty cave. Stick was a bit too skinny for Wolf's taste (big breasts did not swing like pendulums under her clothing), but they'd had a fine time on previous dates. So Wolf turned on the charm.

They went for a night walk in the woods, talking of dreams and walking close to each other to avoid sharp bushes. Wolf kept a chivalrous eye out for snakes, dangerous crevices in the path, and low-hanging poisonous plants; putting herself between anything harmful and her date. Their arms brushed, sending shock waves of longing up Wolf's spine. Finally she took Stick's hand. It was so warm, she could not help picturing this sensual creature nude, long and slim, rolling onto her back and opening herself to whatever Wolf might try. How many fingers would Stick take willingly? Would she have a small, secret nub that unfurled when exposed, and caused Stick to moan and squirm when kissed? Wolf's own hand began to sweat.

In the moonlight, Stick's black Brillo strands of hair shone electric like an ebony halo. Wolf smiled at Stick and Stick smiled back. She had the most beautiful smile. It said: You are *very* interesting to me. What had Wolf been thinking last weekend? Gone were the days that she would sleep with just anybody. Stick was so much warmer than Straw, and Wolf deserved someone warm and caring to love.

Wolf squeezed Stick's hand, thinking, *This is it.* But when they returned to the cabin and Wolf said, "How about a nightcap?" Stick shook her head and smiled.

"Not tonight. But thanks for a nice evening."

Wolf leaned against the doorjamb in her most provocative pose. "The night doesn't have to end just yet," she said, reaching for Stick's shoulders. "How about a massage? You seem a little tense."

Stick's smile faded. She shrugged Wolf's hands away. "If I'm tense, it's because you're making me uncomfortable. Good night." She closed the door, shutting Wolf outside.

I've lost my touch! Wolf thought, suddenly paralyzed with fear. All those years of mimicking Sidney Poitier and James Dean, all those femmes that had swooned, and now that she really wanted to love someone, NEEDED to love someone....

Wolf went home to her cave. The someone she needed was not Stick—that's all there was to it. Stick was too skinny and quiet. She was probably a turtle in bed, and Wolf preferred wildcats. The right wildcat was out there. Wolf would find her.

The following weekend, Wolf called on Clay. Clay worked at the local butcher by day and for animal rights by night. She lived in an abandoned adobe yurt at the edge of the county. In other words, she was interesting. Much more interesting than Stick, or Straw, and much cuter, too. Perhaps she was a bit young, but she had thick corkscrew curls and was neither too skinny nor too plump. What did age matter? Wolf asked Clay for drinks. Maybe that had been the missing ingredient with her previous dates. Many of Wolf's earlier forays into bedrooms were led up to with alcohol. So what if Wolf no longer drank? Her date could.

Clay sipped one tequila sunrise, then another. Then Wolf took her dancing at the local club. Instantly Wolf spotted Stick sitting near the pool table, skinny and alone, with dangly earrings and lips painted rose red. Wolf grabbed Clay's young hand and led her to the dance floor. Let Stick pretend to watch pool, while secretly watching her dream butch swoop a dream femme across the floor!

But the dream femme did not want to be swooped.

"I don't dance country-western," Clay said, pulling her hands away. "I like to do my own thing." And she proceeded to sway and dip in a truly embarrassing fashion. Wolf was mortified. It was all she could do to shift from one foot to the other until the song ended.

"I need a drink," Wolf said the second the music changed.

"Oh, I love this song!" Clay waved. "I'll keep dancing."

Wolf left the dance floor, striding fiercely between couples. At the bar, she ordered a tall, stiff Coke. The bartender—a cute, aging fox with dimples—winked and put two cherries into Wolf's glass. Wolf hardly noticed. She was busy watching Clay on the dance floor by herself. What was the world coming to? Young femmes dancing alone, and not to please their butch.

Clay was not alone for long. A woman in a T-shirt dress danced up to her and said something. Clay nodded and they began dancing together. The new woman had long wheat-colored hair and heavy breasts that swayed provocatively under her dress. It couldn't be…of all people…

It was. Straw and Clay danced a hippy-dippy dance, not touching, but aware of each other. And then Wolf witnessed something truly incredible. Beautiful big-nosed Straw leaned over, swirled up a fistful of Clay's thick, wild hair and pulled her forward with smooth golden charm for a kiss!

It was not a friendly kiss. It was a wow-you're-hot-when-can-I-see-you-again? kiss. Wolf could almost feel their tongues getting acquainted. Impossible! Femmes wanting—not a glorious butch, but each other? It wasn't right. It wasn't safe.

As if they heard Wolf's thoughts, Straw and Clay moved apart and stopped dancing to talk. Then Clay left Straw on the dance floor and headed for the bar.

"Wolf," Clay said.

"Oh, there you are!" Wolf exclaimed.

"I know we're here as friends," Clay said too brightly.

But you want to be more, so much more, Wolf prayed.

"But I feel a little awkward. I just met somebody...."

I am going to kill myself, Wolf thought. She could not muster even a pretend smile. Wolf nodded in Straw's direction. "That femme?"

Clay beamed. "Isn't she gorgeous? I haven't met anyone interesting in ages!"

Shoot me now, Wolf thought.

"Let's get together next week, okay?" Clay danced off with a wiggle of her short young fingers.

Wolf was floored. Had the world gone crazy during the time she was out of circulation, acquiring health? How could two femmes possibly connect? Who would protect them? Neither one could pass as a man; they could never walk down the street holding each other without everyone knowing. And they'd certainly be sorry once it came to sex. What would they do, race each other to bed to be the bottom? Wolf flexed her own long, perfectly buffed and moisturized fingers. *I am being small*, she realized, feeling a slow bitterness parch her mouth. Where once her strength was alluring and necessary, perhaps now women found her ugly and unimportant. Times had changed. It seemed that femmes now wanted each other for love. Wolf's brand of beauty was obsolete.

The next weekend, Wolf stayed home grieving the past when finding a mate had been as simple as going to a bar and spotting her complementary type. But a revolution had occurred—one, in fact, she had prayed for. The old days were gone. Even if she would never know love, she did appreciate no longer being shot at or clubbed for being herself.

Unless...she could change with the times....

She could grow out her hair, and perhaps shave her legs and buy a spring frock to show them off. Wolf looked in the mirror, tried to imagine this new self and thought, *screw love*. She was a jeans-and-leather wolf of almost forty. Some things did not change. Anyway, who needed love? To hear her friends talk, 98 percent of the time, love led to heartbreak. Did Wolf need to experience heartbreak? No, she did not.

But she was still lonely. And horny. So the next Saturday night, she decided to cruise the local sex pavilion and at least find herself some good nookie. Maybe with a femme, maybe with another butch—her therapist had always said Wolf should stretch her horizons and grow. It was time to stop living in the past. From now on, Wolf would live only in the present tense.

The sex pavilion is lit with dark red lights. Music thumps from tall speakers. Wolf unzips her leather jacket, allowing her solid stomach and black sports bra to show. She runs long fingers through short hair and tries to act like the last time she felt irresistible.

No one pays much attention. All eyes are focused on a pillar at the far end of the room. Wolf saunters over to where she can see. A swarthy young femme is winding a long scarf around the pillar, tying a curvy blonde to the post. It can't be.... It is. Wolf watches Clay knot the scarf around Straw's waist with a mischievous grin. Wolf scowls, thinking, *This community is the size of a pinhead.*

Clay unbuttons Straw's flowered sundress. *I will move to another county*, Wolf decides as Clay lifts one of Straw's milky breasts and sucks in as much as fits in her mouth. *Spoiled brats*, Wolf thinks as Clay shifts her hands downward to ease Straw's panties over swelling hips, succulent thighs, sweet hairless calves and delicate ankles.

The two femmes that Wolf dated are oblivious to the eyes that watch them. They do not look rich or immature. They look blissful. Clay nuzzles her face along the length of Straw's ample thighs, nudging her nose close to the wheat-colored bristle between Straw's legs. Her tongue darts out once, quickly, between the bristle. Wolf can almost taste the dampness that is surely pooling there. *I am starving*, Wolf thinks, watching miserably.

"Quite a show."

Startled, Wolf turns to face…Stick. Tall, skinny Stick with her rose-red lips has caught Wolf staring.

"Disgusting, isn't it?" Wolf mutters, embarrassed by her hunger.

"Oh, I don't know. I'd much rather see a happy couple going at it than a bunch of strangers. Nice leather jacket." Stick fingers Wolf's arm. "Want to dance?"

"Dance?" Wolf asks.

"The music's terrific here," Stick says. "So much better than at the club."

So they dance. Stick swoops to Wolf's lead. Her baggy pants and dangly earrings flow. Stick is quite a good swooper, on the beat and energetic. Eyes turn to watch them. They swoop the night away until they are too hot and sweaty to swoop anymore. On the way to the soda bar, they pass naked Straw, still belted to the pillar, belly to belly with naked Clay, who is pumping slowly while they kiss. Wolf notices that young femme Clay is not shaved. Her dainty leg fur about rivals Wolf's own. Isn't that funny? A femme with fur.

As Wolf and Stick pass by, Wolf restrains herself from reaching out to touch Clay's perfect buns framed in their leather harness. She wonders what type of lovestick Clay is gliding into Straw. The thought of it makes Wolf wet. She yawns so her interest won't be obvious and orders two Cokes.

"I'm having a fabulous time," Stick says. "I'm glad my friends talked me into coming. I'm glad I bumped into you!"

"You are?" Wolf asks.

"Of course."

Wolf raises one practiced eyebrow. "That's odd. The last time we went out, I had the distinct impression you gave me the brush-off."

"Because I didn't sleep with you?"

"Well…yes."

Stick smiles sweetly. "I prefer someone to get to know me first."

"The times they are a changin'," Wolf sighs.

Stick laughs. "Isn't it great?" She is extremely pretty when she laughs. She reaches into her Coke, pinching the cherry and holding it out to Wolf. Wolf stares at Stick's lively mocha eyes and then at her skinny fingers, suddenly knowing just what they might be capable of.

Imagine, glorious Wolf entertaining the idea of being done by a femme, rather than doing. But she is tired of fasting and is open to suggestion. Suddenly nothing seems more delicious than whatever glorious scene Stick might have in mind.

The maraschino cherry touches Wolf's mouth. She takes the red flesh between sharp teeth, a small growly purr escaping her lips. Music throbs from nearby speakers, echoing through Wolf's body, beginning a pulse, down low. Anticipation flows thick through brittle obsidian fur to dampen the crotch of Wolf's jeans.

Stick grins and leans closer. Her ebony halo brushes by, electrifying Wolf's cheek.

"So, gorgeous," Stick whispers, moist mouth against Wolf's ear. "Let's go to your place for breakfast."

The Little Macho Girl
KATE BORNSTEIN

I'm going through a very dark period of my life right now, and I love how dark these fairy tales really are—especially Hans Christian Andersen's. His stories were, I think, my introduction to SM. As a child, I would go to sleep fantasizing myself the little mermaid walking upright, each step sending sharp blades deep into the soles of my feet. Or I'd be the girl who trod on a loaf, bound in hell, fully immobilized for nearly all of eternity. But the ultimate for me was always the little match girl. I mean, she dies, right? I think I've always been crushed out on Death.

In retelling the story, I tried to stay close to Andersen's style: He never apologizes for his cruelty, makes no excuses for the pain he inflicts, or the injustice of the worlds he creates. And there's so much love and spiritual awareness in the suffering of it all, no? It's what I keep looking for in my own SM play—the jewel in the crown, that beauty and glory.

It was terribly cold and nearly dark on the last evening of the old year, and the snow was falling fast. In the bitter cold and encroaching gloom, the wind whipped through the clothing of any poor souls stranded out this evening, to freeze them in their very tracks.

She clicks the remote once.

"Fuck The Weather Channel," she says to herself. "Goddamn depressing, that's what *I* say."

The *American Bandstand* guy has replaced the images of the storm on her forty-eight-inch screen. Dick somebody, right? What the fuck is he laughing about?

Safe and warm that night inside her office on the thirty-fifth floor, she draws her bare feet up beneath her in the large leather chair behind her executive-sized desk. Her shoes were ruined or gone: both pairs she'd brought to work that morning. A young man had lifted her not-yet-out-of-the-bag Reeboks on the subway. He'd been part of a gang of performance artists, who'd laughed as they'd danced off with her running shoes, saying they could use them as cradles for the twin births in their nativity program. She had to wear the fucking Guccis to the office—ruined those suckers in the slush, damn it. *And* she'd had to carry those goddamn sample cases the whole way, as though she were no more than a common salesperson. She shudders and draws her feet farther up beneath herself. Leave it to the Chinese Army to want to do business on New Year's fucking Eve. Well, she wasn't going to lose this account—no way. Sheffield and Buck had bids in, but her own company's blades were going to be *the* official knives of the Chinese Red Army, and it didn't matter to her whether she had to miss New Year's Eve to cinch the deal.

But the phone does not ring.

The fax machine is silent.

Damn it!

Click. The large-screen television in her office offers up the evening's news: family shots, parties.

Click. Couples going out for dinner and drinks. Fuck 'em all.

Click. A diamond is forever.

Click. The television winks out.

She glares balefully at the phone. General Ping is over an hour late. Bastard had *better* call—she isn't about to go through this day without closing that deal. If she doesn't sell this lot of blades, the CEO is going to hang her ass out to dry. She snorts once. *That* asshole is most certainly at the company party right now, smiling that ice-cold smile of his, the one he'd taught her when she'd first joined the company, the smile she scares herself with in the mirror nowadays. She's vice-president in charge of overseas marketing, and she can play hardball with the toughest of the guys. But tonight is going to make or break all of that.

She shudders involuntarily and hugs herself—a gesture she hasn't done for years. Her fingers trace the toned muscles of her forearms. No sign of the scars anymore—Doc did a good job. Ha! She'd paid him enough!

Click. More parties, more people laughing, dancing, singing, laughing, kissing…laughing.

Click. Silence.

She doesn't dare leave the office without this deal. Her eyes drift to the sample cases, and before she can stop herself, she opens each one. Revealing row upon row of gleaming, razor-sharp cold-forged steel blades.

One more glance at her arms, scar-free now for…what was it? Four years, ever since she joined the company. Four years since she'd become as hard as she had, as cold as any of the assholes working here. No…colder. Four long years since she'd made herself bleed. She looks longingly down at the blades.

"Yeah…yeah…what the fuck," she says softly to herself. It'll take the edge off waiting for General Whatsis-Ping to call. She barks a short laugh.

"Or put the edge on," she whispers.

Slowly she draws a long, curved blade from the sample case—she cannot stop the small animal cry that escapes her lips. Holding the blade between the thumb and forefinger of her left hand, she scrapes it lightly across the fine down on the back of her forearm. Oh, yes: as sharp as she might hope. Hell, she used to do this with her father's razor blades!

She takes a deep breath and, eager and sure, cuts the warrior mark into her upper right arm.

Ohhhhh, yes.

The warmth of the pain spreads swiftly through the rest of her body.

Yes, yes, yes. It really is a wonderful cut: blood dancing out behind the blade and trickling down her biceps. But more truly wondrous, it now seems to her that she is kneeling beside a small burning brazier with polished brass feet and intricate brass ornamentation. She can see the irons heating up to white-hot. With a small whimper, she lifts her thighs to present herself for the brand when, lo! The blood from her mark stops flowing, the brazier and irons vanish, and she has only the red-stained blade pressed between her fingers to remind her of this vision.

Breathing heavily, she shakes her head. Omigod! she thinks. I can't go back into that space. No no no—I've got too much going for myself in this job, can't give it up for *that*. Yet, even as she thinks *no*, she takes a second blade from the case and slashes more deeply across the first mark on her arm. She cries out in joy and pain. The blood pours willingly down her arm. And where one or two drops fly from her blade onto the wall, it becomes transparent as a veil, and she can see into the room beyond: a dungeon! Beneath bright lights, a young slave lies on a table, eyes closed, a ceremonial dagger piercing the upper thigh.

Who's that laughing with such pure delight? The creature on the table? Or herself?

What is still *more* wonderful, the slave jumps down from the table, and hobbles across the floor, knife in thigh and all, right up her. But the bleeding in her arm ceases, and once again she is left alone in her darkened office.

"Gotta stop this shit," she says aloud, but she has already grabbed the third blade and, crooning softly to herself, she cuts a deep circle into the top of the vertical slash on her arm. Blood seeps from her wounds, suffusing her with a warmth she hasn't felt in years. A moan escapes her lips as she lifts her eyes to the next vision: herself, pierced with hundreds and hundreds of needles, each sparkling and dancing in the light of the now blazing brazier. Taller and taller she grows, this pierced apparition, until the needles themselves seem to her like stars in the sky.

Stars indeed. The bleeding has stopped, and she's looking out through the office window into the New Year's Eve night. A star falls, leaving behind it a bright streak of fire. "Someone is dying," she thinks to herself, for the woman who first collared her, the only person who had ever loved her, and who was now dead, had told her that when a star falls, a soul was leaving the physical plane.

She drags a fourth blade through her arm. Blinking, dizzy, she lifts her head to see…her first owner, the woman who had first put a collar round her throat and called her "mine."

"Ma'am," she calls out to this vision, her voice hoarse with tears uncried for four long years, "Please take me with you. I know you'll disappear when my arm stops bleeding. You'll vanish like the branding irons, the slave with knife in thigh, and the girl who was pierced like the night sky itself."

She quickly takes blade after blade from the case and cuts here and there, everywhere—all over her body, for she wishes so deeply to keep her lover with her. Her blood flows with a heat that is more intense than the summer sun itself, and her lover, who has never appeared so large or so beautiful, takes the still-bleeding one into her arms and makes a final cut: deep across her throat.

"You knew I always wanted to do that—didn't you, love?"

She can no longer speak to answer, only shake with ecstasy. And they both fly upward in brightness and joy far above the earth, where there is neither coldness of heart nor hunger of soul, for they are together and they are in love.

In the dawn of morning, there lies the young woman, with pale cheeks and smiling mouth, curled up in her overlarge leather chair. She had bled to death on the last evening of the year; the New Year's sun has risen and shines down through the window upon a slashed and bloodless corpse. The woman still sits, in the stiffness of death, holding the blades in her hand, many of which are yet stained with her dark blood.

"It's because the China deal fell through," said some.

"She couldn't take the pressure," said others.

And in the very highest offices, they agreed, "It's a man's job after all."

No one ever imagined what beautiful things she had seen, nor into what glory she had entered with her lover, on New Year's Day.

The Girl Who Loved the Wind
CHRISTA FAUST

This simple and little-known story had a great deal of influence on my budding sexuality. I always had a passion for storms and often ran naked through the rain when I was a little girl. (Still do sometimes, whenever I can get away with it.) On the night I received the invitation to this anthology, the Santa Ana winds were blowing so fiercely that trees were being knocked down and stop signs scattered. How could I refuse her, my first love?

Once, a very long time ago, before you were even born, my love, there lived an old Sultana. She had lived a hard life, this Sultana; seen war and death, love and loss and all the sufferings of this great wide world. There was only one thing left that still brought her joy, and that was her daughter Danina.

Danina was a brilliant and beautiful girl. Her hair was the color of warm brandy, shot through with glistening twists of amber and gold flowing all the way to the ground behind her. Every day the servants would bind it up with ribbons and pearls and gilded butterflies and agree that truly no princess had ever looked finer.

But Danina's beauty was troubling to the Sultana, who loved her daughter more that life itself. She knew of the dangers that lurked out there in the big bad world, ready with teeth and claws to devour beautiful young girls; for hadn't she once been such a girl herself? So, to protect the beautiful and innocent Danina, the Sultana built the Sanctuary to keep her daughter safe.

The Sanctuary had one hundred rooms filled with every wondrous thing that might capture a young girl's attention and imagination. It had every toy, every luxury. No expense was spared. There were the finest musical instruments and more books than a girl could read in seven lifetimes. There were smiling servants to wait on Danina hand and foot and tutors to teach her the magic of numbers and language. But of all the diversions in her hidden world, Danina's favorite was the walled garden.

In this garden was every sweet fruit, every exquisite flower. And, at the far end, beside an adolescent weeping willow whose thin green arms were just beginning to bend beneath their own weight, was a little stone bench. If Danina sat there in the dusky purple twilight, she sometimes caught the tantalizing scent of the sea.

On the morning of her sixteenth birthday, Danina woke with a strange melancholy twined about her. She sleepwalked through the birthday celebration that the smiling servants had arranged for her, feeling nothing but a nagging restlessness, a indefinable longing in her heart. When her mother came to wish her a happy birthday, Danina was careful to put on a smile to please her.

After it was over, Danina went out into her garden and sat on the little stone bench. As she watched the sun slipping down in the west, glistening on the shards of broken glass that topped the garden wall, she heard a new voice, a low, breathy voice that sang softly in the treetops.

"Who are you?" she called out.

"Who am I?" the voice answered. "I call myself the Wind. I

carry birds and autumn leaves on my back. I hold thunderstorms in the cup of my hands. I am not always kind."

Danina shook her head. "Ridiculous. Everyone here is always kind."

"I am not," the Wind answered.

With that, the Wind came down and pressed a cold kiss to Danina's lips, bringing her the flavor of the sea, of faraway places. Her soft lips parted beneath an invisible tongue while strong arms held her immobile, frozen as if caught in the center of a whirlwind. Salt stung Danina's skin as chilly fingers teased her hot young flesh and plucked the golden combs from her hair, playing in the long, silken tumble, then whipping away as quickly as they had come. Alone and awash in curious heat, Danina shuddered and pulled her cloak tighter around her.

The next day, as a servant combed the tangles from Danina's hair, she told the old woman what the Wind had said.

"Silly girl," the servant said, smiling wider. "Every one here is always kind. You must have been dreaming."

But throughout the day, Danina could not forget the Wind, her stinging caresses, her salty kisses. Again, as the sun sank below the edge of the wall, Danina stood with her arms outstretched, waiting.

It was not long before she heard the Wind's song in the trees.

"Who am I?" she sang. "I call myself the Wind. I can turn a child's pinwheel or tear the roof from a house. I can guide a ship to distant lands or dash it to pieces on jagged rocks. I am not always kind."

Trembling with newborn sensations, Danina gave herself to the Wind, to her strong fingers. She lay back on the green grass and let the Wind tear her dress, pull loose her hair. The Wind's icy teeth bit into Danina's warm skin, pulling at her budding nipples and teasing the newly awakened flesh between her legs. She felt wild, alive as never before. The Wind's kisses brought her the flavors of a thousand places, the rich mélange of coffee and spices from the market and the dust of bones and ashes from the cemetery. The warm promise of tomorrow's bread and the hopeless stink of a beggar left to die alone. Tears flowed from Danina's eyes and the Wind lapped them up with her long tongue.

"Danina," another voice was calling, a bland, ordinary voice. "Danina, where are you?"

Then servants were pulling Danina with hot hands and covering her with her cloak.

"You mustn't go outside in such terrible weather," they scolded— kindly, of course, still smiling. "You'll catch your death!"

But Danina was full of her new love. She could think of nothing else. When her mother came to visit, Danina told the Sultana of her new friend.

The Sultana was horrified. She demanded that the evil woman who had ravaged her daughter be found and put to death at once. She forbid Danina even to speak of it. She locked Danina in her room and ordered that the garden be watched night and day by armed guards.

But that day at sundown, Danina stood at her window, heart pounding furiously in her chest. She had never in her life deliberately disobeyed her mother. She never had reason to, for weren't her mother's rules laid out for her own good? Yet she could not forget the Wind's wise mouth, her demanding touch.

As she stood with her fingers on the window catch, Danina's body tormented her as never before. The secret place between her legs felt huge and swollen, smoldering as if ready to burst into flame. She felt she would die without the Wind's icy tongue to quench that fire. So when the Wind whispered to her through the cool glass, Danina threw open her window and invited her lover inside.

The Wind played and danced in the gauzy curtains surrounding Danina's golden bed, tossing the silken sheets and laughing. She took Danina in her strong arms and laid her down on the rumpled bed, singing songs of distant lands, of love and pain and redemption. She pressed rainwater kisses to Danina's closed eyelids and hungry mouth, slapping at her hot flesh with open palms and whipping her hair across her face.

Lifting the girl completely off the floor, the Wind spun her like a storm-tossed rose petal, caressing that liquid slit between Danina's parted thighs. Then, just when Danina felt herself surrendering to the lush sensation, a stinging pain sliced across her upthrust ass. She struggled weakly, but the bed was so far below and she was afraid of falling, of the Wind leaving her forever. Again that cold lash bit into her warming ass and she bit into her tongue to keep from crying out. She thought of the Wind's low song, *I am not always kind*, and as the pain sizzled again across her virgin flesh, she felt a terrified elation. The Wind held her tight; the pain was as unavoidable as sunrise. Danina felt utterly powerless in the face of such intense sensation. There was nothing to do but give in to it completely, to let it wash over her and fill her. The caress between her legs quickened, the lashes falling with inescapable rhythm until the two blurred into one exquisite torment, until she thrust her hips shamelessly to meet them. That icy touch was so cold that it burned, and the burning was excruciating, delicious, building toward some unimaginable crescendo.

And then it was upon her like a summer storm, lightning through the depths of her belly and thunder in her veins, filling her young body with sensations the likes of which she had never even imagined. Tossing back her head, she cried out, finally, unable to stop herself.

The servants heard Danina's cries and, mistaking them for distress, came bursting in with armed guards close behind.

The Wind laid Danina down gently and pressed a final kiss to her lips before ripping the tattered silk scarf from around her neck.

"It smells like your hair, and your sweet skin," the Wind called as she spun away with the colorful scarf trailing behind her. "I will always remember you, Danina."

When the Sultana saw the dark welts crossing Danina's ass and thighs, she was furious. She ordered that all the windows in the Sanctuary be boarded up, that all the cracks be sealed. No expense was spared.

Danina was heartbroken. She walked up and down dark, stuffy hallways, sat alone in still, empty rooms, dreaming only of the Wind, who was not always kind. As the welts on her skin faded, she was filled with a sense of aching loss. There was an emptiness inside her that grew deeper with each passing day. She would not play any of her beautiful instruments. She would not read any of her lovely books. She would not eat. She would not speak.

Finally her mother came to her in despair. "I cannot bear to see you so melancholy," the Sultana said. "What can I do to make you happy, my daughter?"

Danina closed her eyes. "If I could go to the seashore, I would be happy."

The Sultana organized a party of servants and armed guards at once and had a covered chair brought to Danina's room. When Danina was inside, the Sultana closed the heavy curtains and surrounded the chair with guards as servants lifted it high on their shoulders. Thus protected, Danina traveled to the seashore.

On the beach, the Sultana opened the curtains to let Danina see the ocean. As soon as they were parted, the Wind swept them aside and gathered the overjoyed Danina up in her strong arms, carrying her off into the twilight sky.

"Who are you?" the Sultana screamed, shaking angry fists in the air.

"Who am I?" the Wind sang. "I call myself the Wind. I am not always kind."

With that, the Wind dropped Danina's silk scarf at the Sultana's feet. The Sultana gathered up the soft fabric and pressed it to her cheek. It still held a lingering scent of her daughter in its delicate weave, but it was not the bland sugary scent of a child. It was the warm, smoky scent of a new woman. The Sultana hung her head, tears falling across the pale sand, because she finally understood.

Hans and Greta
LINDA SMUKLER

"Hansel and Gretel" was one of the most prominent fairy tales in my child-hood—a story constantly read and told and acted out by the neighborhood kids. I've written about the story once before (in "Tales of a Lost Boyhood" from my book Normal Sex*), but as I sat with it while thinking about a piece for this collection, I became more aware of the vast transforma-tions embedded in the story: girl into boy into girl, young into old into young, evil into good into evil, love into cruelty into love, home into wilderness into home, nourishment into starvation into nourishment. And, of course, the intimate connection between once-suffered abuse and future sexual pleasure.*

I.

Mom's outside weeding vegetables. Or tending chickens or milk-ing the cow. While she's out, I wear my brother Greta's clothes. When we can, we switch. He wears my clothes. I wear his. My name is Hans. I'm a girl. But you can't tell from the outside. You can't tell that Greta is a boy, either. His hair is long and he would play with it in front of the mirror all day long if he had a choice. Combing it to the side. Piling it on top of his head. All his pride is in that hair. Me, I couldn't care less. Chopped it off when I was seven. Mom was furious. She's not my real mom, but someone Dad married because my real Mom died when Greta was born. Maybe that's why Greta's the way he is. Me, I don't remember my real mom at all, but I think she had yellow hair. I'm twelve now. Five years later, and I still don't think my stepmom's used to my hair. She'd have to tie up my hands for a year to get this head of hair to grow. I actually don't put it past her to do that. But I guess she has other things to worry about. Greta and I play like we are our real mother and father all the time. He's Mom. I'm Dad. We can do this out at the tree which is our make-believe house. Greta always wears my dress-up dresses and wraps his thin arms around me. He's a very good mother. A very good wife. Gentle kisses. They make me crazy sometimes and I push him down into the mud and have to lie on top of him. I can feel everything under those thin dresses. I tell him I love him like this: "Greta, Greta I love you, dearest." I am the best husband in the world to the most beloved wife, and Greta's little cock is my cock and even though he's only ten it gets hard. So mine does, too. See, I know these things. He sometimes lets me touch him. But we can't get caught by our stepmom. No, we can't get caught. One time she found us on top of each other and she grabbed me off and pulled Greta up and tore our clothes off and made us stand outside naked with our arms straight up above our heads. "You will be pure," she said. It was so cold. And we had to stand for four hours. Greta cried and shook. His arms fell down once, and Mom rushed out yelling: "Look. This is what you are!" She pointed down to his little cock shriveled up from the cold. Greta sniffed hard and tried to pull in the snot running down his nose. Mom pulled his arms back up and told him to stand still. Me, I stared straight ahead. She wasn't going to make me cry. I kept whispering to Greta that it would all be okay. We made it through somehow until Dad was due home and she let us come back into the house. She told us that she would do it all again if we told and we knew she would. That's why we can't get caught. But we haven't stopped playing. We just hide ourselves better.

II.

One Year Later. Life's pretty hard these days. Dad's a woodcutter. Did I say that before? He can't sell wood anymore. It's a "depression," he says. We don't even have seeds for the garden. No chickens. No cow. Nothing. Greta sleeps with his hand in mine and will sleep only when I'm here. He's so thin. Even thinner than I am. His hipbones hurt me when he curls up next to me. But I don't complain. I can hear a lot through our bedroom walls at night. Our parents always fight. Always. That keeps me up, too. I don't think Greta hears any of it. Two nights ago I heard Mom say: "No. You sleep there on the floor. I can't have you near me tonight." My father said something back, but I could not quite hear what. Mom's voice was clearer. "We've been without food for three nights. Three nights and three days!" she yelled. "We'll just take them into the woods and leave them." First I didn't hear anything from my father. Then I think he said, "No." At first, I didn't know what they were talking about.

Now it's been two more nights. We did have a bread crust to eat yesterday, but that's all. I can't sleep again. I'm too hungry. Greta's asleep, but he's restless. Moaning in his sleep. And I can hear my parents on the other side of the wall. Mom says the same thing she said before: *We'll take them into the woods and leave them*. Dad says, "No" again. He sounds firm. "I can't do that." "You have no guts," Mom says. "Maybe you should go into the woods and get lost yourself. It's me or them." There's silence for a minute. I hear the sheets rustling. "Look at that," Mom says. Look at what, I wonder.

"I know how much you want it," she says. "Want me. You've wanted me for days. For weeks. Haven't you?" I hear my father get up and sit down on their creaky old bed. Mom's voice again: "That's right. Look at how you look. Can't control that, can you?" There's silence again for a minute, then she says: "Oh, no. Not until you say you will leave them."

"I won't," Dad says. Then I hear a strange noise. I realize it's him. Groaning. Like a lot of air let out of his lungs. "You like that, yes?" Mom asks. Dad groans again and Mom continues: "You will do it. You will do what I say."

"Yes," Dad says breathlessly. He gasps. I can't hear any more words. Just noises. Shouts. What are they doing? I start banging my fist on the wall. They can't hear me. Dad's howling now. She's hurting him. But he yells, "Don't stop!" My foot kicks at the blanket. I can't help starting to cry. I never cry. I know we are lost. Our father will do nothing for us. There's nothing to do but save Greta and myself.

I am going to save us. After a few hours, I get up out of bed and go outside. I sneak out so quietly, I'm more quiet than a deer. There's a path of white stones around our house. I fill my pockets with stones. When I am done, I sneak back into the house and upstairs. I lie down next to Greta without taking off my clothes. He hasn't woken. I'm finally able to sleep.

Early the next morning, Mom pushes into our room all cheerful. She tells us to get up and that we are all going into the forest to cut wood. No breakfast, of course. We just march off. Greta is sleepy, so he doesn't notice how I reach into my pocket and drop a stone on the ground every few steps. Dad won't look at me. He has a tight smile on his face and says things like: "Isn't this part of the woods beautiful? We've never been this far before—we should come here more often." Mom says nothing. She just walks briskly off to one side of us, like she's doing her morning exercises. Greta asks why we have to go so far when there is plenty of wood closer. Dad says we are looking for a "new special kind of wood that will be easier to sell." I just keep dropping my little stones. No one notices.

We walk deep into the woods. I have no idea where we are. Finally Dad stops and nods to Mom. I try to catch his eye, but he turns away. We all start to cut wood. Not special wood. Just wood. Greta doesn't question it. I don't know why. Maybe he knows something strange is happening. We cut wood all day and when it starts to get late, Dad stops and makes a fire. Mom turns to us and says: "No sense all of us walking to the house, since we just have to come back in the morning. You two stay. Your father and I will go and do chores and see you right here tomorrow." I reply, "We can't stay. It's too far, and Greta will be scared." I don't often use my brother as an excuse for anything, but it's the only thing I can think of saying. Mom gets very stern and says, "He's getting older now. It will be good for him to stay out one night. Might make him more of a man. And good for both of you to learn a little self-reliance." Greta starts to cry, but I clamp my hand over his mouth. "Yes, Mom," I say, not wanting to argue and thinking about my little stones. "We will see you in the morning."

Dad turns and does not look back. He just marches off through the woods as fast as possible. Mom tries to be nice, but I just look away and ignore her. Finally they are gone. I sit down in the dirt. Greta starts to cry again. "Don't worry, dear brother," I say to him. "We will sleep near this warm fire, and in the morning, everything will be fine. I promise." I pull him to me, his body warm and damp from work. I am proud of how smart I've been, how sure. "Dear boy, don't worry." I say again. My brother stops crying and falls asleep to whispers of confidence and comfort. He is safe in my arms.

I wake Greta in the middle of the night when the moon is high and full, and the warmth of the fire has burned down. The little white stones reflect the light of the moon; it is easy to follow them in the dark. Both of us feel rested from our sleep, and by the time the light comes up in the morning, we find ourselves on familiar ground. We are at our front door by breakfast time. Mom and Dad are actually eating—a simple breakfast, but breakfast nonetheless. Our father shouts with joy when he sees us. Mom cries out, "We were just getting ready to leave to find you! Why didn't you stay?" But there are no signs of preparations. "Oh, well," she continues, "here you are. Maybe we won't go back into the woods today. There's so much work to do around the house." Dad offers us some of his meager breakfast bread. I give a bite of mine to Greta. Even though there is nothing edible growing, Mom puts us to work weeding the garden. Perhaps in hope for better times.

Two nights later, I hear my parents arguing on the other side of the wall. Mom wants to take us into the woods again. Dad says no, that it didn't work the last time. But Mom insists she knows why and that it will work this time. He still says no, but within an hour, through the same shouts and howls and groans, I hear him agree to anything she wants. I'm not as surprised this time. I just slam my fist down on the bedcovers. I realize that I've almost woken Greta. But he just turns over and stretches. When I'm sure that he's back in a deep sleep, I slip downstairs. But when I try to open the door to the outside, I find it locked. Mom must have figured out my plan. I look all over for something in the house to make a trail in the woods, but all I can find is some old stale bread crumbs. Not very many, either. I scrape the bottom of the drawer, gathering what I can, and climb back upstairs to bed.

It's not even light yet when Mom comes into the room to tell us that we're going into the forest to cut wood again. Greta does not seem to mind—after all, everything worked out fine before. We walk even deeper into the forest this time, and I drop bits of bread crumbs all along the way. Again, our parents tell us to stay the night and that they will come back in the morning.

After they leave, I hold Greta in my arms near the fire. It is colder tonight. As I run my hands down my brother's chest, I realize how similar our bodies are. My hair is short, my brother's long. One of my hands cradles his ass in his ragged pants. He pulls my other hand between his legs. He wants me to stroke him and I do, erasing all our fears of the night.

I wake my brother when the moon is high and the fire has gone out. I start to look for the trail of bread crumbs, but I can't find a single one. The owls, the squirrels, the rabbits, the foxes, must have eaten them right off the ground. We try to walk in the direction of home, but soon we are completely lost. We walk until three mornings have passed since we left our father's house. No food. No water. An endless forest. Greta can barely put one foot in front of the other. He cries every few minutes. Then he starts to laugh and to talk like a crazy person, seeing things that are not there.

I must be going crazy, too. I see a huge snow-white bird, bigger than a grown man, sitting on a branch. It's a huge snow-white bird that talks. It says: "Follow me. I know where you can get food." Real or not, I don't care. We do follow, taking only about ten steps before we find ourselves in a clearing. I see a house built of pastries and bread, the sun streaming down on a roof tiled with wafers and cakes, windows paned with crystal sugar. I stop, not trusting my eyes. But Greta keeps walking, his arms outstretched, his mouth open. He reaches the house and touches a wall made of chocolate. A piece crumbles off into his hand.

"Wait!" I warn him. But he pays no attention. He puts the chocolate into his mouth and closes his eyes. "Hans," he calls to me. "You must come." He reaches again for the wall as my hunger pushes away my caution. I reach for the wall, too, take a piece of chocolate and put it into my mouth. It tastes like chocolate, but it also tastes like a tender piece of meat—lamb perhaps or chicken— some potatoes on the side, and gravy. We eat more chocolate, and wafers and sweet butters from the windowsill, the clearest sugars and honeys from a windowpane. I am filled with a sense of well-being. Greta just smiles. He doesn't stop smiling. We are no longer worried about finding our way out of the forest, about getting home. We want to eat, to sleep. We are happy.

III.

The wind seems to come up a little and I think I hear a voice—more a whisper, really. Do I really hear anything? It seems to say: "Nibble, nibble, like a mouse. Who is nibbling at my house?" I listen harder. "Do you hear that, Greta?" I ask. Greta thinks it's just the wind. Then I hear it again. Suddenly I see an ancient woman walk out the front door of the house. She leans on a crutch. Greta steps back. Again, I don't trust my eyes. As the woman gets closer, her wrinkled skin turns smooth and firm. The crutch falls aside. She stands tall. Her ragged clothes turn whole and are covered in jewels. Her clouded eyes become piercing and clear. She reaches out her hand to us. I cannot move. My heart feels stunned. I realize that my mouth is open. I've never seen anything like her. Anyone so beautiful. She takes my hand and I feel a charge travel from her arm and hand into my hand up my arm into my heart, down through my chest, into my belly and below.

I don't understand how I walk from outside to inside, but suddenly we are inside the house. I can't take my eyes off this woman as she sits us down at a table covered with a white cloth, laid out with milk and apples and nuts and pancakes. Greta is chattering about something. Giggling, actually, but he seems very far away, and I don't really care what he is talking about. I can't eat anything else, even though I know I should still be hungry. The beautiful woman says nothing. She just stares at me. I stare back. I want to lower my eyes, but I can't. I'm terrified and incredulous at the same time. I try to shift off the chair, but I feel bound. I cannot move my arms, my neck, my head, my calves, my feet. For some reason, only my thighs and my rear end can move. I don't understand this. I slide back and forth, trying to break the hold the woman's eyes have on me. My dungarees pull tightly against my crotch. She smiles at me and I blush in shame. I see myself as this woman must see me—wiggling ridiculously back and forth on a chair. Just like Greta dancing in front of a mirror in a dress. Did the woman think that I was purposely trying to…? Trying to what? I am horrified—I feel more like a young girl than I ever have in my life. Suddenly the woman stands up and walks directly over to me. Her long skirts are in my face. I breathe in as hard as I can and feel faint from the deliciousness of her smell. She steps back and takes my hand. Greta's, too. She walks us upstairs to a bedroom which holds two little white beds. She motions to me to wait while she picks Greta up and lays him on one of the beds. He falls asleep immediately. The woman turns to me. I say, "I am not a child; you don't have to pick me up." She picks me up anyway and lays me on the other bed. She pulls the covers over me and brushes her lips against my cheek. Her hand travels down my body through the covers. "Your name is Hans," she says. Or I think she says. Her lips do not move. She stands up. As if on a string, my body rises up to follow her, but she gently pushes me back down into the mattress. "Sleep now." And I do, immediately falling into a sleep full of longing and rest.

The next morning, the beautiful woman wakes me gently. She does not wake Greta, who sleeps soundly. "Come," the woman beckons as she pulls me out of bed. She leads me downstairs and outside to a tiny stable. I do not remember seeing the building the night before. There are two small rooms inside.

"You will call me Agnes," the woman says. "And this is where you will bathe." The woman holds my hand tightly and does not let go. The bathing room is tiny. A metal tub filled with water stands in the center of the floor, taking up almost all of the space.

"Undress," Agnes demands in a suddenly cold voice, completely different from the warmth and kindness of the night before. My clothes are filthy, but I do not want to take them off. "Undress!" Agnes demands again. I don't move. She seems to get taller, heavier. Her body expands to fill the tiny room from side to side. Suddenly she reaches across to me and grabs the waistband of my pants. With one wrenching pull, the rags fall to the ground. In another, even faster motion, she rips open my shirt. Her scream deafens me.

"A girl!" Agnes howls. I try to run past her out the door. But the door slams shut. The two of us are locked in the tiny room. Agnes' thighs and arms trap me between the wall and the basin. Her huge hands pick up my skinny body and throw me into the water. The frozen water. "A girl, a girl!" she screams as she roughly washes me all over, scraping away at my calves, my thighs, my private parts. "A girl, a girl!" she shouts as she pushes into me deep and hard to show me exactly what I am. I am so cold. I try to fight her but she is a monster, ten times bigger than I am. Finally I am overwhelmed by darkness. The pain and the cold disappear.

I must have fainted, because when I wake up, I am lying on a dirt floor. I can't see anything in the pitch black, but I am naked. When I touch the dampness on my skin and put my fingers in my mouth, I realize that I am bleeding. I cannot find my clothes in the dark. I am freezing from the damp and the cold bath and there is nothing to cover myself with. I crawl around the floor. I must be in the other tiny room. I cannot get out. I call for Greta. Scream. He cannot hear me.

I hold myself curled in a corner of the room when Agnes opens the door. The light is so intense after the darkness that I cannot see anything but a shadow.

"Here, my dear 'boy,'" Agnes says, her voice melodious again. Warm. "Look at you. You look cold. Let's put some fat on those bones." I try to pull away as she gets closer, but she picks me up with those huge hands. I still cannot see her clearly. I kick at her form, but she grasps both of my legs with one hand, sits down, and holds me in her lap. My legs stick straight out. I do not understand why I cannot move them. Agnes holds my arms, too, so that I can't move any part of my body. I am held like a board across Agnes's lap. I want to ask where Greta is, but I can't seem to talk. "There, my dear boy," she says. "You *are* cold." She bends over me and blows warm air across my body. Her breath fills me with heat. I am desperate for her breath, which blows harder and stronger, a stream right into the center of my body. This is warmth. This is life, a current suddenly focused between my legs. I cannot move, can do nothing to stop her. I do not want to stop her. She blows on me until my whole body shudders, is flooded with light and heat. Agnes strokes me, caresses me until I am convinced that nothing bad can happen. She feeds me delicacies—meat and pastries—which she says Greta helped her cook. She tells me that Greta is a wonderful helpful child, that she likes her immensely. I realize that Agnes still thinks that Greta is a girl. Agnes makes me believe that Greta is well and happy. I want to know more, but I still can't talk, can't ask any questions at all, before I fall into a deep contented sleep.

I wake again after many hours. Alone. Naked. Curled back into the corner of the dark room with the dirt floor. I am freezing, wet. It's as if I've had a cold bath again. No matter how tightly I hold myself, I cannot get warm. I've never felt so cold. I think I hear something crawling. A rat. More than one. The cold does not let me sleep. I pray to faint. Hours go by. I scream, cry. Nothing—no one—can hear me.

Suddenly the door opens and Agnes pushes into the room. "Where is Greta?" I scream. My voice has come back. "What have you done with Greta?" Agnes will not answer. She ties a rag around my mouth so I can no longer scream. She pulls my limbs away from my body and stands me up against the frozen stone wall of the room. I try to hold myself—to protect myself from her, from the cold—but Agnes ties my hands and feet to bolts in the wall. I can do nothing. I do not expect what Agnes does next. She begins to sing. A low soft hum at first, then a full song. I can't believe what I hear. The melody enters me, travels through me, warms me, clothes me. She begins to rub warm oil along my legs with her hands, no longer rough, but silken. My body, so cold, begins to warm. Even the wall at my back fills with heat. I do not understand anything except that my body is getting warm again. I no longer worry about Greta, or where I am. I have lost my will. I feel myself writhing against the stone until my body shudders again. Agnes feeds me the most delicious morsels imaginable, right there on the wall. She tells me stories of Greta, how 'she' walks the dog, bakes bread, studies sums, plays in the stream. Do I dream these stories? I do not know. I fall asleep.

The same thing happens over and over. Day in and day out. Week after week. The cold baths, the frozen dirt floor, the icy walls. Then the warmth of Agnes's hands, her probing, the scalding heat at the center of my body. Nothing else is real. Agnes.

IV.

She says she cannot tell whether or not I'm getting fat.Lately, she bites into my neck every day, stopping herself before she breaks the skin. Then she steps back and stares at me. Today something is different. She comes into the stable earlier than normal, and I am, as usual, terrifyingly cold. She begins to warm me, but then stops. She tells me to hold out my thumb. Some clarity comes into my frozen brain. It's dark enough, so instead I hold up an old chicken bone that has fallen into the dirt. Agnes feels the bone and yells, "You are still too skinny!" She gets up and storms out of the tiny room. This is not what I wanted to happen. She cannot leave me like this. I need her to come back. I rock back and forth for a long time, holding myself, calling her name.

Suddenly the door opens and I look up into the light where I expect Agnes to fill the doorway. But I see nothing but empty space. Slowly my eyes travel down to a smaller form, a tiny shadow in the doorway, which rushes toward me. Someone familiar, a small, thin body. "Warm me, warm me, warm me…," I mumble. The tiny body rubs against me and says, "Hans, it's me—Greta. It's Greta." I don't understand. This body feels so small, so light. "Get me Agnes," I demand. "Bring me Agnes."

"Agnes is dead," the body says. "We are free. We are free!" The body keeps repeating that. I start to cry and weep. "No! Where is she?" I scream. I call to her. "Agnes is dead, I pushed her in the oven," says the small voice. I get up and run around the room. I tear at my skin. "Only she can warm me. Where is she?" Greta stands away from me until I exhaust myself. Finally I lie down in the dirt. Greta puts his arms around me gently and does his best to comfort me. I finally begin to understand that Greta was a prisoner, too. That there was no dog, no play, no sums. That Agnes meant to kill us. That Greta has pushed Agnes into the oven meant to cook both of us for dinner that very night.

We walk out of the tiny prison that has been my home for the last weeks. I feel the sun and it warms me, but it does not push away the grief in my heart. I do not understand why I cry when I look back over my shoulder at the candy house. I insist that we go back and gather Agnes's ashes out of the stove. I scatter her ashes over the garden, the house, the pile of bones from the meals that were meant to make me fat. As the last of the ashes billow away, a flock of white birds rise up through the clouds and begin to sing. Their song is the same song Agnes sang to me in the stable.

V.

Before we leave, we find a great treasure in and around Agnes's houses. We carry as much of the treasure as we can on our shoulders. The white birds lead us through the forest to a lake. A large duck carries us across graciously, one at a time. The same white birds lead us to our father's house. He is overjoyed to see us, certain that we had perished in the forest. Our stepmother is gone. Our father, haunted by guilt, could no longer live with her.

In the future, I become my father's son. He lets me wear the clothes I've always wanted to wear. I have many lovers, but am never quite satisfied. In my lovemaking, my limbs often get very cold, and I am always haunted by my memories of Agnes.

And Greta, dear Greta, becomes the most beautiful and desired damsel in the land.

Rapunzel
SHAR REDNOUR

"Rapunzel, Rapunzel let down your long hair."

When on a date with someone new, I say right at the beginning, "I don't give head to dildos, and DO NOT, under any circumstances at all, pull my hair." I am, and always have been, extremely tenderheaded and thus, as a child, was caught between horror and confusion to hear that Rapunzel allowed her hair to be pulled so that the witch and prince could climb up the tower. I would look at the illustrations of her and search for a pain in her face. I knew that I would have punched anyone who touched my hair right in the teeth and sent them tumbling to the thorns below. Rapunzel and I are opposites; that has always intrigued me.

It's really no wonder that she becomes a masochist in my version of the tale because frankly, I've known it about her for years.

The man, the woman, the witch. Rapunzel.

It was the herb that they had wanted, the herb rampion, rapunzel, to save the wife. It could heal her. She was too young to die. The man was willing to sell his soul; but the witch wanted what she could not have, what the woman could give her. The witch said, "I will give you life for life. I will give the herb rapunzel. You will pay me with the first life you create. You bleed as you birth her. I will take her when she bleeds." And so it was.

Rapunzel had always watched her, the witch, Madame Lenora. She lived behind Rapunzel. Crooked apple trees and a stony hedge that led to a tower marked the boundary between them. The fence was crumbling, completely gone in some places, so the stones really just made a nice perch from where Rapunzel could watch. But she had watched Madame Lenora before she was old enough to sit upon the fence. From her wooden kitchen seat in her mother's window, from the porch steps, from the ground, crawling until she could see between the stones and the trees to the old woman working in her garden. The man and his wife sometimes stiffened at the sight of Madame Lenora, but they said no unkind words about her; and if they noticed Rapunzel's fascination, they never worried aloud over it.

Rapunzel would see her in her garden working quietly, steadily, with the many herbs and plants. On occasion, she cooked in a large caldron at night. Once a month, she accepted visitors, with whom she traded potions for trinkets, milk, woolen socks, or metals.

Madame Lenora had silky black hair that she kept pulled loosely off her pale, hard face. She did have creases on the hardness, lines between her brows and slanting out from her eyes. Her lips were blood red, but not moist with paint. And her eyes were the color of coal. Every day she wore a black skirt that fitted closely down her hips and swayed out slightly past her knees. Although always pressed and immaculate, it was not hemmed. The bottom hung jagged in tatters that dipped longer in the back, dragging past her ankles. Her black leather boots had pointed toes and were tailored to her feet and ankles. They had no buttons or laces, but simply split down the middle from just over the arch of her foot to the top of her ankle. Rapunzel could see glimpses of Madame Lenora's calves between the swing of the tatters and the split of the leather.

Rapunzel would climb up on the fence and watch Madame Lenora's crooked fingers do their work. To most people, her hands seemed a horror—the knuckles bulged and bones bent. Her long fingers looked like fat knots on a twisted tree. Rapunzel was fascinated that Madame Lenora could move them so fast. They plucked blossoms or leaves and could till the earth around a growing plant.

Rapunzel studied the witch to see what hint of a thought would be reflected in that stern, motionless face as she worked those fingers. She never smiled with her mouth or eyes. Her lips never pursed in anger. Rapunzel studied until her eyes spotted one of the few shows of emotion to scratch that perfect ivory mask—a tiny pulse throbbed in her temple if she was concerned.

Madame Lenora would take a herb to her long thin teeth. If she was pleased, the right side of her mouth would curl up and her eyes would twinkle a little. That also fascinated Rapunzel because her mother, when pleased with a good garden or well-cooked meal, smiled, but her smile was simple. Madame Lenora captivated Rapunzel before she could put these feelings into words because Rapunzel watched before Rapunzel had words.

Catching a moment of expression from Madame Lenora made Rapunzel's heart stop. She felt ecstatic; yet, instead of joy showing itself in dance, it caught in her throat. She would run home and muse fiercely under her bedclothes about what she could do again to catch the witch's notice.

It was that driving urge to please and capture the witch's notice that sparked Rapunzel to sing. One day Rapunzel lay on her belly on the stones, eating berries when Madame Lenora broke her silence and said to her, "Your hair often reminds me of streams of honey, but in this light, it's as if you caught the sun." That was it. She bent down and began to garden again. Rapunzel nearly fell off the wall; berries fell from her gaping mouth. Then she began giggling without control and tumbled to the ground. She danced around her own yard until she opened her mouth and began singing a happy song, a song that spooned around the trees while Rapunzel dipped and lifted her tongue trying to make flowers with her notes. She sang as she fell to her knees and crawled back to the garden, sliding between two crumbled stones. She sang and plucked at the grass beneath her.

Madame Lenora stood upright and turned to Rapunzel. For a brief moment, her hard face melted. Even had they not been alone, no one but Rapunzel could have noticed. The witch walked slowly to Rapunzel and stretched out her gnarled fingers to cup Rapunzel's chin. Rapunzel stopped singing and wanted to retreat, fearing that she had upset the old woman, but she also felt a burning that urged her to press herself into the witch's hand.

Madame Lenora said, "Sing, Rapunzel. Sing for me now."

Rapunzel turned her soft lips to the inside of the witch's hand, kissed it, then replied, "Yes, Madame." And so she sang.

As it turned out, of course, Rapunzel was promised to Madame Lenora to become hers, like her garden or like her caldron. But before Rapunzel was even aware of her promised soul, her bond was with the witch.

Well into her young womanhood, Rapunzel bled. Confused and embarrassed, she told no one. That night in a dream she saw Madame Lenora hovering in midair outside her window. Lightning flashed around the witch, and her black hair snaked around her head. She heard Madame Lenora whisper in her ear, "You're mine now, Rapunzel. Wake and come to me." Rapunzel walked out of her parents' cottage door, never to return.

Over the next few years, she learned how Madame Lenora wanted her home kept and what her personal needs were. She was carefully trained in how to keep the herbs and the other elements for the witch's potions and in how to assist the witch on trading day.

Rapunzel grew into a woman. Her skin was tanned from the sun, her muscles, fed from her labors, toned her curved flesh, her hazel eyes were like autumn, and as for her honey-golden hair, well, her hair grew. It had always been long, but since moving to the witch's house it had grown yards. Madame Lenora seemed very pleased with this, so Rapunzel, in turn, was also pleased. She sang and brushed her hair for an hour every evening after completing her chores and turning down the witch's bed.

It was during this time that the dreams began to become dark and fierce. Rapunzel would wake with her heart pounding and a strange, foreboding ache burning between her thighs. She could never completely see what was happening in the dream—just sense blackness and fire all around, hear her own screams, and see flashes of blood-red swirls in the blackness. Her eyes would come to her Madame's shoes; there she would focus all her attention and find comfort in her dream. She would try to force her eyes to see her Madame's place in all this turmoil, but could see only spots of stars or cracks of fire. She would wake worried in the morning, but as her gaze fell upon Madame Lenora, Rapunzel would be overwhelmed by the urge to please those black eyes, and the dream would flee from her mind. As for her thighs, that was a different matter. The aching continued until one day she found the spot that could tip off her pleasure. From then on, she released her urgent tension while thinking of sitting at her Madame's feet or imagining those gnarled fingers working up a potion.

One evening at the end of a trading day, a large, buxom woman came to the witch's garden. She wore a black woolen cape with purple velvet curling around its edges and carried a small woven valise in her gloved hands. The cape parted at her neck to drape around her high, bountiful chest. The woman paid no mind to the trading, but stood staring at Rapunzel as she ran potions in and out of the cottage.

Madame Lenora said good-bye to her last trader, then turned to Rapunzel. "You have grown into a young woman and are no longer a girl. We shall mark this passage," she said. Her black eyes seemed to drill into Rapunzel. "We will talk of it later." She wrapped her hand around Rapunzel's neck. "At this time I want you to go into the cottage and undress for Dame Winster, a fine tailor. You will be clothed appropriately for your passage."

"I need no finery, Madame, I only—" Rapunzel's voice hovered, stopped by the turn of the witch's black eyes to her. "I, oh, I am sorry, Madame. Yes, thank you so much. I shall comply with Dame Winster. I long only to fulfill your wishes." She swallowed hard and followed the Dame inside.

Dame Winster instructed Rapunzel to undress completely. The Dame's eyes revealed her pleasure at studying Rapunzel in her nakedness. Feeling the desire in those eyes set a match to Rapunzel's cunt, and at the same time made her heart tremble as the dark dreams had. The Dame took a measuring tape to her legs, then ran it tightly between her cuntlips and in between her asscheeks. She wrote numbers down for Rapunzel's waist and hips, then ran the tape between Rapunzel's hard nipples. "I'm glad Madame Lenora has someone to...care for. This is all I need." She laughed, then left.

Rapunzel had been dreaming, grinding her pussy into the mattress. Madame Lenora watched Rapunzel's ass rise and fall through her thin shift as she moaned in her sleep.

"Rapunzel, awaken." Madame Lenora towered over her. From the darkness in the window it was apparent that the sun barely kissed the horizon. "In one and a half rotations of the earth, your passage will begin. Our preparation begins today. Arise."

Rapunzel stood with her covers hugging her. Madame Lenora reached out with one hand and ripped them to the ground. Rapunzel stood naked in horror and shock. She straightened her shoulders and stuck out her chin, "Madame. I wish to keep my body warm."

The witch pressed her fingernail into Rapunzel's shoulder.

Rapunzel's lip tensed, but she willed herself frozen. Maybe she was becoming a woman, she thought, because normally she would never feel the need to defy Madame Lenora. She loved the witch with all her heart and knew the Madame always knew best. But this time her chin would not budge, and she found herself captured in her motionless body.

"You," the witch said, trailing her fingernail down Rapunzel's flesh and leaving a red trail that rose into welts before her eyes, "my beautiful Rapunzel, you will be very, very"—her nail sliced across Rapunzel's small, full breast to the center of her chest—"warm tomorrow night." Rapunzel felt the witch's nail go deeper, and she inhaled sharply. "Today you will throw all your clothes into the woodpile. You will wear nothing at all until I tell you." Rapunzel felt her cunt swelling up, and she couldn't remember why her chin was stuck up so defiantly. She wanted to fall to the ground and lick Madame's boots until she felt the witch's contentment. She also wanted to throw herself against the witch's hand until she bled. Instead, her head fell back and her breathing quickened.

"You want to grow up so badly." The witch continued her journey downward; blood streamed from beneath her rigid nail and trailed around Rapunzel's navel and into her golden triangle of hair until it pooled at her magic button and dripped to the floor. The warmth against her spot made Rapunzel gasp. She thought she was going to swoon. "You are already my possession, Rapunzel, but soon you will be all mine."

Madame Lenora pulled her finger away and Rapunzel stumbled forward, "Of course, Madame, let me pleasure you." *Oh, her horrid mouth!* "I mean I...I am so blessed. My gratitude reaches around the world a thousand times over, and still it is not enough." Rapunzel slowly raised her hazel eyes to meet the witch's gaze. Her nipples hardened into leaden pellets.

The corner of Madame Lenora's mouth curled. "Today you will find stairs leading up to the top of the tower."

"No, Madame, there are no stairs."

"Rapunzel!" The witch slapped her hard across the face. "Do not question me again." Rapunzel fell to her knees and tears welled up in her eyes, not from pain, but from confusion and humiliation. Part of her wanted to beg forgiveness for upsetting the witch, yet part of her was simply aghast. She knew how to please Madame Lenora, which was not easy, and that was precisely why Rapunzel took such pride in it. She labored hard at her skills to please Madame Lenora—a witch who sent fear into every other creature. Rapunzel felt as if she were being ripped into three beings: one groveling in horror at her misbehavior even if she didn't understand what she'd done wrong, one wanting to defend herself, and one begging to throw her cunt at the witch's boot.

"Take my caldron, my chest, the baskets of supplies, and all the firewood to the top of the tower." Rapunzel's eyes widened—she could not possibly carry the large caldron. The witch put a finger to Rapunzel's mouth. "You will hurt, but you will have the strength."

Rapunzel went out into the growing light of day to see that a marble staircase curved around the tower as if it had always been there. She did all of her chores naked, and her cuntlips swelled so that she thought she would burst with every step. She strapped the caldron onto her back with leather sashes. The witch watched as Rapunzel kept her legs bent and parted wide. The cold iron pressed into the crack of her ass.

Rapunzel labored all day and into the night. The final piece to go up the marble stairs on Rapunzel's back was a large X-shaped cross. She anchored it four feet from the caldron. She fell asleep curled in her old clothes, now in a woodpile on top of the tower.

Again she was awakened by the witch—by the voice that pierced her soul. The witch stood against a blue-violet sky. Her hair was loose around her shoulders, and a small fire burned under the caldron.

"Braid your hair in one braid until you reach the last four feet.

Then divide your hair into eighteen braids and weave these into each braid." She gestured to a large basket filled with strips of hide, iron loops, birch strips, animal claws, sharks' teeth, dried thorny roses, and jagged pieces of crystal, rubies, and amethyst.

"Weave your hair with love, Rapunzel, and sing for me." Then she was gone again.

Rapunzel sat by the fire as the sun rose to the top of the sky and as it descended. She rocked back and forth, singing. Her fingers were as nimble as the witch's, and seemed almost as strong. Her pores opened and a feverish heat pulsated from her moist skin. She forgot everything except the witch's words: "Weave your hair with love and sing for me." She thought of the witch touching her braided hair, looking down at it without disappointment. She felt her love of her own body surge through her, and sat on the thick braid as it went down her back and then curved under her ass and pussy. She wove the small braids in front of her, laying them side by side so that they fanned out across her lap. Her voice echoed throughout the garden as she sang. Her fingertips bled and her joints ached. Calluses wore on her palms. She fell into a weary but fulfilling sleep.

At sunset the witch appeared with her hair once again pulled back. Rapunzel rubbed the fog from her eyes, sat up, and smiled into the witch's face. Madame Lenora smacked her hard across the face. Rapunzel's nostrils flared, but her nipples hardened and blood throbbed to her cunt.

"Get up, Rapunzel." Rapunzel's feet were laced into calf-high boots with pointed toes. Her waist was cinched by blackened hide and encircled with silver links that also ran up the center of her chest to a loop around her neck. Two chains stretched out from it like a cross to biting clamps fastened on her nipples.

Words flooded Rapunzel's throat, "Mistress, I think I am afraid. Not of you, but of the darkness, of my dreams."

"Do you love me, Rapunzel?"

Rapunzel began weeping. "Let me pleasure you," she murmured, as if only to herself. She hung her head.

Madame Lenora hit her hard across the face again, knocking Rapunzel back. Rapunzel tasted blood on her lip. "You are mine, Rapunzel. You will be mine."

"I am yours at this hour as always, Mistress. I do not understand." Rapunzel's voice rose.

"You will understand, Rapunzel. Now stand and follow me."

Rapunzel followed the witch as she began to circle the caldron. The fire rose with her circles, growing stronger, making the liquid contents boil into mountainous popping bubbles. The witch threw handfuls of ingredients into the caldron and chanted words that Rapunzel did not understand. Rapunzel followed, stumbling in her wrapped and stilted feet, dragging her heavy hair behind her. The moon appeared low and orange in the sky. Gusts of wind raged from every direction, sending sparks shooting from the tower. The cross grew large and black in Rapunzel's eyes—it gained life and seemed to prod at her each time they passed it.

On the last circuit around the cross, Madame Lenora, as if a flash of lightning, was no longer leading Rapunzel, but holding her shoulder from behind. "Place yourself here."

"Oh, Madame, I—" Her voice trailed off as she realized the Madame's intentions.

The witch placed Rapunzel's braid in front of her, in between her breasts, then had Rapunzel straddle the fat golden hair-rope. She lashed Rapunzel's wrists and feet to the cross. Rapunzel faced the fire and could see into the bubbling caldron from her perch. The clamps on her nipples bit at her as the chains pressed into the cross. Her tanned skin instantly began to glow from the heat. Madame Lenora ran her hand down the inside of Rapunzel's thigh. Then the other. The pale silken curls that covered Rapunzel's swollen cuntlips were damp from sweat and desire.

"You long for my touch, Rapunzel?"

"Yes, Madame."

Madame Lenora ran one finger down Rapunzel's spine, leaving Rapunzel's young, tight skin rippling. The witch reached between Rapunzel's legs and cupped her pussy. Rapunzel's whole body began to quiver and her breath was reduced to short gasps—she hadn't known how much she ached for her Mistress until this very moment. A torrent of desire and need burst through her body. The knowledge of her need seized her mind and soul like the slaps across her face. She began to grind her pussy against her Mistress's hand. The witch parted Rapunzel's lips and pressed a bulging knuckle against Rapunzel's button. Rapunzel rubbed and twisted against the callused knot.

"You desire me inside of you?"

"Yes." Tears seeped from Rapunzel's eyes.

The witch withdrew her hand. She stretched her arms out behind Rapunzel's, then pressed her nails into Rapunzel's flesh at her wrists and in one swift motion ripped bloody lines down Rapunzel's arms. Rapunzel threw back her head and screamed.

"You are mine, Rapunzel!" The witch's voice rose over the fury of the wind and fire.

"Yes, my Madame."

"You will be *all* mine."

Rapunzel cried in frustration, "I am yours…. I am yours."

The witch screamed, "Sing, Rapunzel, sing to save your soul."

With her head still back, neck and shoulders taut, Rapunzel's voice rang out high and shrill as it sliced up from her soul at the base of her cunt, through her belly, through her throat, finally to shake through her teeth. It rose into the air and then curved—hovering like a lasso around them. Her voice was the only thing keeping her alive, reaching up to the sky and her Mistress.

The witch reached down between Rapunzel's thighs and grabbed the base of the thick braid, following it hand over hand to where the braids began to divide. Then she turned to face Rapunzel's back. When she pulled on her whip, the fat part of the braid pressed into Rapunzel's pussy. The witch stretched a length of the whip high over her head.

"Rampion!" she yelled into the storm, then swung the woven whip down into Rapunzel's back over and over. Rapunzel's song jolted and snaked like the whip itself. Her eyes burned from streaming salty tears and the singeing smoke of the fire. Her arms pulled against the ropes with every slam of the whip, but her song did not stop.

The sharks' teeth, crystals, and rose thorns ripped into Rapunzel's back. The witch set a rhythm to her stroke that mounted steadily. Each slam of the hair bore welts into Rapunzel, pricked cuts into her, planted knots under her flesh, and sliced lines into her. Blood began to run from her wounds until it poured over the blackened hide and down her ass. The hair whip absorbed Rapunzel's blood and wiped it from her back, only to spring forth more. The leaded whip matted and grew even heavier. Rapunzel's hips gyrated into a blur, burning her cunt against the thick braid that matted, too, with drippings from her pussy. Fire wrapped around the cauldron and danced right up to Rapunzel's eyes. Madame Lenora's blows rose furiously, and Rapunzel's voice began to climb again until it ensnared the sky and purpled the moon.

A magnificent crashing of stones gained on the roar of the wind and fire. "Give yourself to me now, my Rampion, now," Madame Lenora commanded firmly into Rapunzel's ear, as if she were close behind her.

In that moment, the outermost cells of Rapunzel's body began a quiver that grew into waves that crashed at her core and twisted up through her cunt, belly, heart, and throat. Her body undulated fiercely, and only the bruising ropes cradled her.

"You are mine, Rampion, mine." The witch's voice seemed like a mist around Rapunzel's face, so close, almost in her, that she could breathe it. Time ended for Rapunzel. She floated above herself in a perfect clarity that wasn't captured as simply thoughts, but was felt to be so real and filling throughout all of her being.

The witch released the whip, then brought her hands and voice to the sky with an utterance of closure.

Rapunzel awoke days later, nestled in a bed of straw against the ledge of the tower roof. Dried blood and come cracked on her skin as she stretched, and the matted whip of her hair scratched against her. Her body was stiff. Her head and back ached, but nothing like they should have.

The cross and large caldron were lying harmless against the far ledge. In their place was a small fire with a kettle of boiling water hanging over it. To the side there was a large pot filled with water, a bowl of fruit, and a metal bathing tub. Rapunzel opened a chest to find a cup, bowl, and ladle; jars of salve, potions, and tonics; and a bottle of oil with rose petals in it. There were no longer any stairs.

Rapunzel slowly made a bath for herself. She did not undo her hair, but instead dipped it yard by yard into the water until it was clean—adornments and all. She soothed her skin with ointments and quenched her thirst with a juicy apple.

She went to the ledge of the tower and looked down at the garden. Madame Lenora was working her fingers around the plants. Rapunzel began to sing lightly, and the witch looked up at her. A smile curled from the corner of her lips.

The witch gardened during the day, and Rapunzel sang for her. Many nights Rapunzel slept alone, but many others Madame Lenora came and took pleasure from her. The Madame would say, "Rapunzel, Rapunzel, let down your long hair," which Rapunzel would do gratefully. Madame Lenora would then climb the hair to the top of the tower. Rapunzel's cunt (and heart, for that matter) was always swollen. She would beg to lick the Madame's boots clean or to pleasure her in any way. On occasion, Madame Lenora would even let Rapunzel grind her cunt on the witch's boots until she came, then she would lick all the pussyjuice from the boots as well. On the nights with full moons, Rapunzel's singing could be heard for miles and miles. The witch and Rapunzel were very happy, and they continued on this way for quite a while.

Saint George and the Dragon
PAT CALIFIA

I am fascinated by the connection between monsters and dykes. Women who refuse to be conquered or governed by men are frequently seen as being inhuman. Revolt against the patriarchy is such a seditious act, and we are even relegated to the pages of mythology, as in tales about Amazons, who of course never really existed. Any powerful creature that mystifies or destroys male control, like the sphinx or the Gorgon Medusa, is seen frequently as female. Today, dykes who do not conform to the lesbian mainstream's sexual mores are also seen as monsters. Leather dykes, sex workers, and transgendered women are defamed and demonized by women who are afraid we have gone too far. The twin threats of being treated as a dangerous, evil creature, or being erased as a fable that never really existed, are powerful forms of social control. If we are going to be free, women have to find the courage to become monstrous. In this fairy tale, a young woman who is an outcast despite her powerful status as a duke's daughter is forced to encounter the dragon. What happens to her does not follow the scenario of "virgin sacrifice" that her frightened fellows had planned.

The iron-bound wheels of the ox-drawn cart did not cushion any shocks as they ran over rocks and ruts. Bound in a standing position, George was unable to brace herself, so she bounced along with each jar and jounce, wincing a little at the bite of iron about her wrists. The higher they went up the mountain, the fewer people accompanied them. First ladies and lords had peeled off, the ladies holding clove-spiked oranges or candied rosebuds to their noses, the gentlemen holding the ladies' elbows. Her father and her sisters had not even attempted the climb. They had waited at the castle gates until the wagon was out of sight, then gone within and ordered that the drawbridge be taken up. As if a slab of wood, no matter how thick, could protect them from a creature that spewed fire. As if stone walls, no matter how high, could keep out something that, for all its size, flew higher than any hawk or eagle.

The peasants had been more hardy, and since it was to placate them that George had been forced to make this journey, they might have felt obliged to persist and witness her sacrifice. But by the time she got to the top of the mountain, George thought, only her father's guards and the priest would be her companions. The rough ride should have been enough to make her miss the carriage that her sisters commandeered for their rare forays into the outside world. *But nothing,* she thought bitterly, *nothing will make me miss any part of that false and horrible world, the grand court inside the castle that rules this scorched land.*

For the land was covered with cinders and ashes on either side of this road, which wound like a scar up the tallest mountain in the kingdom, as if it had been drawn with the claw of some monster even greater than the dragon, for which everyone was keeping a surreptitious lookout over anxious shoulders. As if, George thought sarcastically, by seeing it they could avoid it, as if it could not outfly a running man or horse and pluck it heavenward in its ravenous jaws, brushing aside any resistance as if it were meaningless, like the flirtatious raps her sisters gave overbold suitors with the tips of their fans.

She felt sorry for the boy who was leading the oxen, though. She could not see his face under his large floppy brown hat. But his slim shoulders and short stature told her he could not be fully grown. This task the soldiers would not do, as it was beneath their dignity to be seen guiding beasts of burden. Perhaps this was understandable. Most of them would have been farmers, if they had not discovered some talent for brutality that encouraged them to think that wielding a spear or sword in her father's army was a better sort of life than following a plow or cursing droughts, floods, and plagues of insects. She could see the peasant boy ahead of the wagon, plodding on, doggedly putting one foot before the other though he must have been terrified. Perhaps he was too dull-witted to be afraid. Or perhaps he was even more afraid to look backward, to see her naked body stretched taut between the two shafts of the prison cart.

At that thought, George smirked, and for a few moments did not mind the rip and burn of iron at her wrists, the jolts that sent pain thudding up her spine.

The dragon had been in residence for some weeks now. At first its presence was only a rumor. The first peasant who came running to the palace to announce that the mountain was belching smoke and flame had been flogged for seditious rumors and turned loose to warn other serfs to hold their tongues. Father Paulus had gone to investigate. The possibility of <u>proving</u> Satan's existence on earth was a powerful incentive indeed if it had succeeded in getting him to stray from his chapel and his portion of the plank in the great dining hall. Think what sermons he could preach with fire and brimstone coming off the mountain in a magnificent backdrop behind him!

Father Paulus could not be whipped for treason. And so George's father, the Duke, had asked for volunteers to slay the scaly scourge of his domain. There had been only one, a pale young knight who was the least-favored suitor for his youngest daughter Mimsy's hand in marriage. The Duke had no son, and so this blonde, blue-eyed child was his heir. Percival had no demesne of his own, whereas all the other knights who sighed with love, mooned about as if they had fevers, and stole one another's poetry, could offer the Duke an alliance with some other great house. Percival no doubt hoped that if he distinguished himself in this hopeless cause, his case would be advanced. George believed he was the only one of the group who might genuinely care for Mimsy. She might have liked him for that, incomprehensible as she found his choice of romantic objects, if he had not once cornered her after a drunken banquet and crudely demanded her favors.

"Don't you want to see what it's like, then, before they pack you off to the convent?" he said, trying to be nice about it, hurting her hands, which he had restrained.

"And if I am with child, Sir Knight, what convent will have me, then?" she asked. His shrug said it was no concern of his, this trifling bit of women's business. So she kneed him sharply in the groin, and he called her a name that knights usually spoke only in all-male company, and in reference to women who were for sale. George did not care. It got her loose, and she was glad to run to her own quarters and bar the door. Father Paulus had attempted to have her father remove that bar, saying it was unseemly for a woman to be able to seclude herself from the rest of the household. But it was just one of many changes the fussy little priest wished to make in the castle, and the Duke had never seen fit actually to tell a particular man to go and do it, so it never got done.

Because the kingdom was handed from eldest son to youngest, and then from youngest daughter to eldest, as the eldest daughter of five (her sisters were Pansy, Tansy, Fancy, and Mimsy), George was last in line for the succession and last in everyone's thoughts. It gave her a certain freedom, this indifference. No one cared if she taught herself Greek as well as the priest's Latin, or spent her day bent over a book rather than a loom or an embroidery hoop. Her father had tried to make her take over management of the kitchen, but she was hopeless there, and (tired of cold soup and raw joints) he did not complain when she delegated everything to an older servant who knew how to cook and manage the supplies. No one seemed to notice if she took a horse and rode into the village, ostensibly to do good works. Even Father Paulus could not accuse her of being unwomanly for distributing loaves and dried fish among the less fortunate. George didn't like visiting the villagers much, even though they called her a saint. She was appalled by the dirt, the grinding ignorance, and the cruelty with which they treated one another. But it bought her a few afternoons in which she could roam the countryside, alone and untroubled.

Had she wanted to "see what it was like"? No, George thought, she had not. It did seem unfair to her that happiness must always consist of escaping from the presence and influence of other human beings. Surely somewhere, women found companionship without the condescension or coercion that colored her interactions with her father, the priest, her sisters, and everyone else at court. But where? Not in this realm—that was certain. And whatever it was she wanted, or could have wanted, from another human being, it was not Percival's indifference and thinly veiled violence.

Locked in her tiny room, George picked up her hand mirror and tried to see what could have drawn such unwelcome attention. Was there perhaps a glint in her eye, some hint of wantonness she was not aware of, that had secretly signaled Percival to pursue her? She could not find it. She saw what she had always seen: a girl with a forehead that was perhaps too broad, a jaw that was too solid and strong, clear gray eyes without a hint of coquetry, eyebrows that were too thick for beauty, a proud nose, a mane of chestnut hair that she kept unfashionably short because it was so curly that brushing it out was a painful ordeal.

It was her father's face, and George suspected it had been that resemblance which had made her mother (while she lived) so distant from her eldest daughter. It could not have pleased her sire, either, to see features which would have better graced a son, worn every day by a useless female.

When Percival went out to fight the dragon, he wore his tournament armor. George saw him off with her sisters and the rest of the court, though she had forgotten to bring a silk scarf to wave. She thought it was silly of him to wear those chased and engraved plates with their decorative curls and spikes of metal. This was no pass with lances in a meadow, with bleachers full of ladies saying "ooh" and "ah." This was deadly combat, a combat he was not very likely to win. Then it occurred to her that perhaps Percival did not expect to win, and he simply wanted to be remembered at his most dashing. Still, she remembered the way her wrists had felt, trapped by his mean fingers, being pushed down toward his groin, and she did not feel sorry to think that he might soon be dead. On the whole, she felt rather sorrier for his horse. Dragons were said to be fond of horsemeat.

The court waited a week, and Percival did not return. Then it became clear that something else must be done. The dragon had taken to raiding cattle from some of the more distant pastures. The peasants were afraid to follow their flocks up to the grazing lands. Her sisters and their ladies-in-waiting were afraid to promenade along the battlements. The priest's sermons about repentance and evil were making even the Duke, who had a strong stomach for talk of eternal damnation, a little bored and uneasy. George wondered what he would do. She knew that the Duke planned to ride upon his neighbors to the east as soon as a convenient excuse could be found. He did not want to risk any more of his fighting men in an attack upon a creature that could destroy all of them. It would be demoralizing; recruitment would falter.

When Baby Mimsy came to George's chamber one night, bearing a two-handled cup full of hot liquid, she knew that no good could come of it. Mimsy never visited George, barely spoke to her, hardly acknowledged her tall and overly intellectual sibling as one of her own clan. Mimsy was everything George was not: short, delicate, blonde, cleverly painted, elegantly coiffed, graceful of carriage, soft of voice. She also beat her serving girl with a spiked strap, or had—until George sneaked into her chambers and threw it in the fireplace.

The consequences of that piece of philanthropy had not been what George had anticipated. The serving girl, afraid of losing her place and being sent back to the village, had tattled. Two days later, a merchant had visited them; along with cloth and spices, he had books to sell. George had been a spendthrift and bought two of them, a slim collection of ballads by the leading poet of Aragon, and a thick volume of fantastic tales of some Italian trader's travels to Cathay. The Duke had confiscated George's new books and given them to Mimsy, who had cast them into the fire. "What did you expect when you destroy other people's property?" she had said smugly.

"Too much reading causes a brain fever among females and fosters disobedience," Father Paulus had added, staring piously at the ceiling. George was then sentenced to attend daily readings of the Epistles of the Apostles by the priest, in lieu of private time to study. This was supposed to cool her brain and foster obedience. Mimsy had a new strap made that was even nastier, and things went on as before, except that everyone thought George even more a hopeless gawk and a figure of fun.

So it was not surprising that George greeted Mimsy with suspicion and refused to accept her invitation to drink from the steaming cup. "What is it?" she asked, sniffing the mist that rose from the dark liquid.

"Father Paulus says it will help you to sleep, and will make things easier for you on the morrow," Mimsy gushed.

George raised a bushy eyebrow and stifled an impulse to shake her sister until her teeth rattled. "What happens to me on the morrow, pray tell?" she prompted.

Then Mimsy had the grace to look ashamed. She scuffed her toe on the flagstones and examined the guilty dance of her slipper. "I am to be married, George," she said finally. "Father will announce my betrothal tomorrow. And it would not do to have a pall cast upon the wedding. Are you not happy for me, George?"

Her sister refused to answer her, and continued to stare at her, waiting for the rest of the story. Resentfully, Mimsy got the rest of it out at last.

"Everyone knows that the only way to get rid of a dragon is to offer it a virgin sacrifice," she said airily, as if this were an announcement that the rushes in the banquet hall had been changed. "Then it will fly away for a year and a day. Well, you can't expect us to find a virgin among the peasants, can you? They're all born rutting. You've always been fond of the common people, George. Can't you see how much they will love you for taking care of them in this grave matter? And what did you have to look forward to, anyway? I should think you would be grateful. Isn't this better than going to a boring old convent?"

"It is not," George said firmly. She hated the thought of living behind cloister walls, being compelled to fast and pray, and was grateful that the Duke's ambitions made him reluctant to send her off with the appropriate escort. But she refused to absolve Mimsy of blame. "You have given me a death sentence, little sister. Shame on you for allowing our father to place this burden upon you. If he wanted me to do this dreadful thing, he should have come to me himself."

"No one is *asking* you to do anything, George," Mimsy replied, nettled. "We are, in case you forgot, all subjects of our father, his to dispose of as he will. He can marry me to whomever he chooses and send you off in the morning to placate the dragon. It is our duty to accept him as our sovereign and sire and be grateful for his constant love and care, as we are grateful for God's beneficence."

"Somehow I do not feel loved just at the moment," George said.

Mimsy shrugged and offered the cup again. "It's getting cold," she said. She had not really expected George to be reasonable.

"Of the two of us, you are the one who will have the hardest time falling asleep tonight. Drink it yourself," George snarled and slammed her door.

She had sounded brave enough until that, but once Mimsy's light, mincing steps went away, George paced her chamber like a caged bear before the baiting. Then she remembered the poison. Heloise, the midwife, had given George a good stock of herbal remedies, in case someone at the castle needed doctoring. Father Paulus would not let Heloise minister to members of the court. He would have called her a witch, if the Duke had been the sort who could take time off from plotting to steal his neighbors' lands to burn. He was a careful man who would have begrudged the price of the wood. George knew Heloise from her scouting trips into the countryside. In small doses, the steeped essence of certain berries was a powerful aid for women whose birth pangs had stopped before the child had emerged. Taken in larger doses, it killed.

George took out the simple and looked at it. Then she put it away. The same part of her that refused to let Father Paulus's epistles bludgeon her into submission refused to die now.

But that did not mean she would cooperate. She refused to go down to the throne room in the morning. Her father had to send armed guards to fetch her. And they were nonplussed at what they saw. George had hacked off all her hair. "Why keep it when the dragon's breath will singe it off soon enough?" she said bitterly. But it was the rest of her appearance that made the men mill about and look to their sergeant for direction. She was wearing not one stitch of clothing. "I wish to take nothing from this house with me, where I am going," she said, certain that her remark would be heard and repeated by the scandalized courtiers who lurked behind the warriors. She had chafed all her life under the strictures and pettiness of other people. Now they had singled her out as a sacrifice because none of them liked her particularly or could find a use for her. Surely she was entitled to drop any pretense of caring what they thought. She felt more dignified going to her death sky-clad than she would have felt tricked out in the yards and yards of fabric that made her feel, when she was trying to walk somewhere in a hurry, as if she were a ship foundering beneath too much canvas. The air was pleasant, and she wanted to feel it caress her body for as long as she might until her flesh was caressed by flames.

The sergeant unhooked a cloak from his shoulders and draped it over her. "Please, my lady, wear this for my sake," he begged her. "If your father should think I dragged you out to be shamed in front of the common people—"

"It is not the common people who are shaming me," George said tartly, but she suffered the cloak to remain upon her shoulders until they got outside and chained her to the wagon. Father Paulus had the temerity to bless her and ask the multitude to join in a prayer that almighty God would lift this scourge from the land, wicked though they all were and deserving of divine chastisement. George waited until his eyes had closed in admiration of his own eloquence, then shifted her shoulders and allowed the cloak to drift to the wagon bed. Father Paulus thought the gasp that came from the crowd was a tribute to his oratory and kept his eyes closed tightly. The look on his face when he turned to see her revealed in Eve's garment was priceless.

And its memory was enough to comfort George now and make her laugh, even here, bound willy-nilly for a death that would surely be more painful than anything she had ever known, including the leg she broke when her father's grooms insisted on trying to teach her to ride sidesaddle. After that, she had been certain she would be banished from the stables, but it turned out that her father could not bear to have anyone who was infirm near his person. Eventually the grooms, the master of the hounds, the falconers, and the villeins who assisted them had come to depend on George's presence because of her ability to doctor animals that their Duke valued above the life of a servitor or fosterling. She turned a blind eye to their gambling and poaching, and they said nothing about the men's hose, doublet, and jerkin she stashed in the stable for her rural jaunts, or the plain but well-oiled saddle that she used to perch astride her favorite gelding.

At the sound of Princess George's pealing laughter, one of the men-at-arms looked back at her, and shook his head. He said something under his breath to the man who marched up at him about courage. Or was it craziness? George could not quite hear. As if it was easy to tell the difference.

They were near the summit now. The road had petered out in a sort of natural plateau. The soldiers stopped marching, and turned around in unison. Under the barked orders of their sergeant, they marched around the prison wagon in two rows, dividing around it like a river surging past a large rock. The man who had made the muffled comment to his friend about craziness or courage gave George a discreet salute. Well, it was nice to have someone look on her naked body with approval before she died. Father Paulus passed her by without so much as a glance. He did not even bother to trace the sign of the cross in her direction. He had finally given up on her salvation. That was almost worth this wretched ride.

The soldiers did not wait upon the boy who was unharnessing the oxen, apparently not thinking it worth their while to extend their protection to him. The sound of tramping feet and clanging mail shirts, scabbards and shields, rattling arrows and spears, had faded completely before he succeeded in deciphering the tangle of leather and metal rings that drew the wagon after the brace of oxen.

But still he lingered, until George was impatient. What did he have in mind, a little rape before he returned to his father's furrows? Well, if he was able to do her an injury in the precarious position she was in, George thought, more power to him. But the face that she saw, when finally the ox driver turned in her direction, was not the face of a boy.

"Heloise!" George gasped.

"Yes, it's me." She climbed into the wagon.

"Oh, I'm so glad to see you!" George cried. "Quick, let me go. Do you have horses hidden in the woods? We'll be miles away before anyone thinks to look for us. Come, Heloise, why do you delay?"

The wise woman shook her head slowly, and took off her hat. For the first time, George saw strands of gray wound through her dark hair. "I can't loose you," Heloise said regretfully. "Those cuffs are closed with a bolt hammered home. No key would do you any good. And even if I had a key, I would not spare you from your destiny."

George thought she had given up all hope before dawn. The sight of her friend and teacher had brought it back, and it was cruel to lose the thread of her own life twice in one day. So even Heloise feared the Duke's retribution. "Oh, that's bitter news," she said dully.

Heloise stood close to her and touched her shoulder lightly. Her hand trailed down George's bare arm and back, then moved up again to outline her throat and caress her cheek. "Don't despair," Heloise said. "Other people have never been able to tell you what to do or cloud your clear vision of their folly, dear heart. Don't let them blind you now. The world is a much larger place than even you or I suspect, sweetheart, and miracles happen every day."

"That sounds like something Father Paulus would say," George sneered.

Heloise laughed. "The marvels I anticipate have little to do with Father Paulus and his hidebound notions of holiness. They are pagan glories, like this wonderful thing I am going to show you now."

As they conversed, keeping their heads together and their voices down (the habit of fear of being overheard was hard to break),

Heloise had continued to run her hands up and down George's body, making her shiver in a way that the brisk morning breeze had not. Now Heloise took George's head in both her hands and kissed her on the lips. Terror and recognition bloomed together in George's breast: "I must not do this," and "I must have this" twined together, stealing her breath. It was too unjust to be made to leave the world when she had just discovered this amazing thing—not just the pleasure the kiss had given her, but the great cloud of warmth and love and sensuality that surrounded her.

"Oh!" George cried. What else was it possible to take, to give, in this new realm of feeling?

Heloise nodded, and said nothing at all. She looked as if she had heard George's unspoken question, but she did not answer it.

"Please!" George tried to climb down from the wagon. "Take me with you! There must be a way. Save me, Heloise, save me!"

"I envy you," Heloise said. "Even if I could save you, I would not. You have been chosen, George, but not for me."

It took every ounce of George's royal composure to keep her from kicking and screaming. She was determined to keep her dignity, even in the face of this new betrayal. She knew only by the chill air upon her face that her tears were falling. She would not weep openly, like a bawling cow.

When her tears ran out, George knew she was alone. No other member of her species dared remain upon this cursed mountain. She also knew that she was not going to wait, bound like a chicken for the hatchet. Her mean-spirited sisters and small-minded Father Paulus and the Duke himself imagined they finally had her trapped, subservient to their will, helpless to evade the inevitable. Well, they were wrong again. She would prove it. The iron was implacable, but her flesh was not. The fetters were on the large side, anyway. Taking a deep breath, she resolutely drew her hands down as far as they would go inside the unforgiving metal that constrained them. Then farther. Farther. She leaned her whole weight against her poor injured hands and pulled, pulled as if she were trying to yank down the sky. She dared not stop. She dared not free one hand and then the other. She could not be this brave again. There was pain, but more dreadful than the pain was the noise she felt as much as heard inside her own hands, as if her finger bones and wrists were being ground into meal.

"Guess I never will learn to play the twice-damned harp," she said, or perhaps she only thought it very hard, because her hands had folded in half and were sliding on the lubricant of her own blood. Free, free, free! The hot agony that lived at the end of her arms was a small price to pay. For a moment she thought she would lose consciousness, but the breeze picked up, and birds suddenly flew up from nearby trees, and she came back to herself with a twitch. "Nor ever mend tapestries again," she told the rowdy cascade of blackwings, and that time she knew she spoke aloud. Her tongue, at least, was not broken.

In order to get out of the wagon, she had to kneel, then throw her lower body awkwardly over the side. She tried to hold herself up with her elbows until her feet could find the ground; but the wagon was too tall, and she fell. She woke up in its shadow. The day had progressed without her. It was heading into afternoon now, and she was hungry and thirsty. She hurt more than any creature she had ever tended. Of that she was sure.

George crawled from beneath the wagon, sat, and then stood. What now? She realized that she had a choice. She could do what she had earlier urged Heloise to do, and flee. There were thick woods on the other side of this mountain, and outlaw bands roved there. But would outlaws use her any more kindly than Percival had thought to do? Even if she managed to bring down green vines and wrap herself up in them? What would outlaws do with a woman who would rather read a book than rock a cradle?

Perhaps she could wind through the forests and into a neighboring kingdom. But would they not ransom her straight back to her father? If they even believed her claim to be of royal blood! She hardly looked the part of a princess in need of a knight-errant.

No, George realized, she was done with all that. She was done with the world of war-hungry men and the women who flattered them and slept with them and cleaned up after them. She was done with it all. And, in fact, she had never belonged there in the first place. They had been clear enough about that, even when she was not. It seemed to George that she had always been treated as if she were a monster. Her kindest and noblest impulses made her repulsive to the people who ought to have loved her, and her strength and intelligence simply deepened their contempt. So let the monster go to its own kind.

She went up the hill then, breaking through the underbrush because there was no longer a trail. She did not watch where she placed her feet. What did she care for sharp stones now? She was the walking dead, an inhuman thing, abandoned and cast out. She had triumphed over pain and her body's frailty. Perhaps she was invincible. She would see. She would go up the mountain and see this thing that had terrified everyone for miles around. It would be worth it, to see something that could frighten her father, even if she could only look at it for a moment before it snuffed her out.

After trudging for a hundred paces, light-headed and full of this sort of reverie, she came to the dark mouth of a cave. It was like the entrance to Hades, and a sulfurous smell came from it, like the thick smoke that billowed from the forge. There was a little clearing in front of the cave, scorched clean. *Suckling pig*, George thought incongruously. Then she saw that she was not the first to have come this way, for on the ground lay the body of Sir Percival. From the smell of him, he had been roasted in his tournament finery, and George had to admit (when her stomach growled) that he smelled far more delicious now than he ever had spreading his elbows at feasts or rattling his weapons in the lists.

Not three feet from him lay the dragon. She (for it was somehow undeniably female) was beautiful. And dead. A lance had pierced her chest and splintered on the rock face behind her. She was only the size of a foal. Was this the omnipotent demon that made Father Paulus rage at and bully his congregation? George felt the tearing sensation in her chest that she always felt when an animal was mortally wounded. "No!" she shrieked. "This must not be! No, no!" She ran to the still, twisted thing, which lay on a bed of her own crumpled wings, and fell to her knees at the dead dragon's side, barely noticing the shooting pains in her hands as she forgot they were useless to break her fall. She scooped the head, the neck, up across her forearms and cradled it to her bosom. Now she did not care who heard her weep. This was her miracle, and it had died before she could come to its rescue.

The dragon's silver scales were iridescent, like the light that refracted through a prism, or the sparkling of opals. She seemed clothed in a strange, rich garment of jewels. Despite their metallic appearance, the scales felt warm and supple beneath George's hands. They had a slippery, silky texture. George barely noticed that she knelt upon a puddle of rubies, a small heap of gems whose color was so fine they would have bought the Duke an army large enough to overturn the king himself—dragon's blood, wasted on this fallow land. She was too busy gazing into the dragon's golden eyes, which still seemed to contain some vestige of shrewd awareness. The slit pupil was black, like the eye of a snake; but for some reason, George was not afraid to think of that eye, living, turned upon her. She would like to see what this creature would have thought of her, encountering her without weapons or any intention to do harm.

It was a solemn occasion. George spoke as if to one living, not knowing how much she resembled her father addressing his troops before a skirmish. "The battle was bravely fought, my little one, and you did not fight in vain. Your foe is vanquished. He paid dearly for the hurt he gave you. Valiant one, brave one, you were a hero, and

I am your witness. Fly home, little warrior. Fly home where pain will never trouble you again." Somehow, George made her stupid, floppy hands close the bright eyes. She held them until she knew the respectful semblance of sleep would remain. And all the time she wept, her tears flowing from the same bottomless well of grief that she had found within herself when her mother died, and had thought sealed, never to flow again.

At first George thought the day was slipping into evening more rapidly than she expected. It grew dark, and the breeze quickened until it seemed a wind blew that would herald a rainstorm. But this was not a cold, wet wind; it was a hot wind that heralded drought and famine. Still the wind grew and grew until George could hardly hear herself weeping. But she did not stop petting and cradling the creature's head and mourning her cruel death.

Then the earth shook, and George had to turn to see what new adventure this strange day presented.

It was the dragon. She was beautiful. She was enormous. And alive! As George watched open-mouthed, she spread her wings the way a peacock will spread his fan. Their magnificence was blinding. The adult dragon's muzzle was glittery black, and George could see small fires playing about her horned mouth. George realized she held this being's child, that it had died defending their cave. Percival could never have put so much as a scratch on this furious mother, armored in rainbow light and guarded by jets of scalding flame. He was nothing but a child-killer. There was no more honor in his quest than there would be in drowning kittens. *So much for chivalry*, George thought, *I should be frightened*. But what was the use of running? Mutely, she indicated the broken body of the dragon's daughter, and edged back a little on her knees.

The dragon's gaze took in the scene. Her whole bearing was full of despair and grief. When her golden eyes rested on George, she thought she would die from panic and something else, something like the feeling she had had when Heloise first kissed her and showed her all the things a mouth could say without actually speaking. She pointed wordlessly toward the knight, and the dragon examined him, too. All the spikes along her spine became erect like a porcupine's quills and rattled. Then she stood on her back legs, raised her huge gothic head to the sky, and screamed. George knew they would hear that scream as far away as the castle. It was a terrible noise, full of so much anguish that she felt rocks should break and trees topple as it passed them by.

Without thinking, George got to her feet and went to the desolate mother. As she approached, she noticed a pair of shapely breasts high upon the dragon's chest, covered with scales, as was her entire body. Though they would have been out of place on the body of a lizard or a serpent, the two creatures that the dragon most resembled, George thought they were beautiful on Celosia (for somewhere in her mind a voice told her that was the creature's name). *Of course she has breasts*, she thought. *She loved her daughter and cherished and cared for her.*

Closer still, while the dragon shrieked and clawed at the sky, George saw that the nipples were very swollen and the breasts uncomfortably taut. The death of her daughter had made Celosia's milk dry up, or perhaps she had the milk fever that nursing mothers sometimes contracted. George knew there was only one treatment for that, to drain the swollen breast and apply a cooling poultice.

So she walked up to the dragon's belly, put her hands on either side of the left breast, and closed her mouth around the scaly black nipple. Abruptly, Celosia ceased to rebuke the elements, and her wings came down around George, forming a protective tent. She smelled like burning incense or spices, like fresh-cut pine, like steel being beaten into a new shape, like coal and the inside of a mine.

The dragon's milk was bitter. It burned going down, scorching George from the inside out. But she did not think to gag or spit it out. She was a doctor now, ministering to a patient. It left a complex, not unpleasant, tang on her palate, like the resinous wine of Greece. The hunger and thirst that had tormented her was gone. Patiently, she drained the inflamed breast, soothed it with her hands, then turned to the right nipple. What she got from this one was as sweet as the other had been acrid. It cooled the places in her that had been scorched by the other fluid, healed her and seemed to ease the throbbing in her hands. She found that she was touching Celosia's belly, soothing her as Heloise had done when George was bound. Trapped inside the dragon's wings, she felt safe for the first time in her life. She tried awkwardly to embrace her, though she was far too small to cradle or comfort such a giant.

One of the wings drew away, allowing the cool air of the rapidly approaching evening to intrude. George shivered as the dragon took her whole body within its taloned hand and lifted her up for examination.

They were face to face now, gray eyes and gold, the tiny eyes of a puny human woman and the enormous orbs of a mythological creature big enough to topple houses with one flick of its toe. But George did not feel intimidated. She felt blessed, as if she were meeting an equal, or making a friend. When the dragon opened its mouth, there was a tiny part of her that thought, *Oh, dear, this is when I get charred and chomped*, but it was a raspy wet tongue—not flames—that greeted her. Celosia seemed to want to return the favor that George had done her. She bathed the girl with her enormous forked tongue, and George found herself wriggling with delight under this strange massage. When the dragon licked at her thighs, George felt compelled to open them, and found herself riding a tongue that was twice as big around as her forearm. She thought for a moment she had gone mad, because she was shaking and talking nonsense, then she realized that this was the bliss her sisters giggled about finding in their husbands' embraces.

Well—no, it was not, but that was as close as those benighted things could come to imagining this ecstasy. This was something far finer than any clattering, punch-drunk knight had in his gift. Only Heloise might have been able to pull off something just as delicious, George was willing to wager.

Then the dragon repeated the caress, and George quit comparing Celosia to anything or anyone else she had ever met or read about. Oh, to be turned and licked and admired and sampled again, as if she were a morsel too tasty to be lost by consumption, oh, it was amazing! And the most amazing thing about it was that George could swear Celosia knew exactly what she was doing, and was laughing about it.

Then George was set down gently upon her unsteady pins, and Celosia seemed to be waiting for something. George looked up expectantly, hoping to be told what to do. She felt a little nudge between her ears, something like a tickle deep in her brain, and then a voice that was like the roaring of a fire being stoked.

"Ah, there you are," Celosia purred. "Any mortal with the wit to ferret out my name must have the old knack of speaking mind-to-mind with one of my kind. We are well met on this sorrowful day, friend George."

"Well met," George said, a little frightened by this new ability.

"Fear not," Celosia said. "Any more than I should fear to spread my wings and fly. As you will do before the sun will rise. Are you my beloved, come to replace the child of my body?"

"Am I?" George wondered.

"You are what you will to be," Celosia thundered. "What is your will, dragon maiden?"

"To be with you forever," George's heart cried before her mind could censor it. "To go where you go, to see marvelous things, to be strong and powerful and wise. And to know…to know the pleasure that you do, the bond of love and the care and sport that true lovers share honorably with one another."

"Then come to me. If you are my beloved, you have only to

love me," Celosia said huskily, and the power of her thoughts made George's throat feel warm and full.

So she explored the body of her beloved, with eyes and hands and tongue. Celosia reclined for her, folding up her wings and batting her eyes flirtatiously. As she grew more excited, she lashed her tail, but she was careful not to strike her small companion. Finally, George dared to put her hands upon Celosia's finely shaped and sizzling-hot funnel. By now the dragon was roaring and writhing, and it seemed to George (though she knew little of such things) that the time for subtlety had passed. It did not occur to her to wonder why she was able to push her hands, which had been mangled so badly, up to the elbow in the boiling welcome that awaited them. Nor did she particularly notice the pale lines that were crossing her skin, faint triangles that were a little raised up, that shimmered even in the fading light of this dying day. She pumped with much more enthusiasm than she had ever shown for churning butter or rinsing clothes, and Celosia cried out with joy. George felt herself weeping again. To be able to create such happiness in the wake of tragedy was a blessing she had not imagined. George wondered if she had ever been sure before that she had really delighted another.

The ripples of Celosia's pleasure had thrown George a little distance away from the dragon. She was still drunk with her triumph. George had never thought of pleasure as something she could bestow on others. Sex was supposed to be something you waited for, something that was done to you, the way hawks got hooded or heifers were branded. She had never felt so powerful, so alive. She was so exultant that she was not frightened when the first spike pierced the skin behind her spine, and a row of them rippled quickly up her back, growing in rapid succession like the wicked thorns on a giant's rose. The last thing she said as a human being was, "Celosia, I love you," and then her face elongated into a reptilian muzzle, her arms and legs thrust her far, far, from the ground as they grew thick and long as the masts of a great ship, and her body became a scaly, twisty thing of agile wonder.

She was blue, George knew, examining her own armor. She was a rich sapphire color, like the liqueur distilled from wildflowers. Newborn, she shivered in the night air, suddenly frightened, afraid of this new form, this new life. But Celosia crossed the space between them in two huge easy steps and took George's nostrils between her jaws.

"Receive the breath of life," Celosia said, and spewed a boiling stream of elemental energy into George's maw, and from thence into her very bowels. The furnace in her belly caught, and George was comforted, no longer uneasy or unsure. Celosia laughed with delight.

"A fine companion I have found for myself on this mating flight, though I never thought the price of love would be my precious daughter."

George understood that it was time to give the little dragon's abandoned body an appropriate farewell. Celosia was gathering wood for the funeral pyre, snapping off ancient trees as if they had been daisies and arranging them about the little one's body. George helped her, gradually getting used to the power and grace of this new form. Being large and powerful did not mean being clumsy, she was grateful to discover.

When the wood was laid, the two of them stood back and ignited it together. Green as the wood was, it caught like straw. George knew the rest of the forest would probably follow into the inferno they had triggered.

"You will be hungry soon," Celosia said. "New-made changelings always are. We must feed you and then begin our journey home." She showed George where home was with a series of mental images imbued with love and contentment. Home was far beneath the earth, in its hollow center, where a second sun blazed and dragons circled it in lazy games of flight and passion. And George also knew the appropriate food for her kind: gold.

Dragons did not eat cows, horses, or men. They consumed treasure, which was their right as children of the great earth mother. And it was for this that men hated and hunted them. Once they braved the chilly realms of Upper Earth to seek out rare veins of precious metal and shared their spoils with the two-legged tribes who shared a blood bond with them. It was dragon kin who had learned the secrets of forging molten metal and shared them with other mortals. Now dragons came only rarely, to make a name for themselves, or to see if it was really true that all human beings were dragons'-bane, greedy oath breakers who no longer sang to welcome the beat of metallic wings. Celosia had been trying to make a name for herself by having a great adventure. She had lingered in Upper Earth only because her child had been born early, and the fledgling was not ready to undertake the strenuous burrowing homeward.

"I know where all the gold in this kingdom is kept," George said, eyeing Celosia with love and devotion. The ironbound chests full of her father's wealth were kept behind a door that was guarded day and night. He might as well have entrusted it to the wind's protection.

"Then let's away," her lover said, and sent a warning cry into the night.

Lighting their own way, they returned to the castle that had never been George's home, to the people who had never been her family, to take back everything that had been stolen from her.

The Piper

JENIFER LEVIN

This story has the affective resonance of myth. The Piper is the Trickster, a seemingly mottled, laughable clown who (like the seemingly effeminate god Bacchus) reveals him/herself in the divine androgyne's full, potentially dangerous power persona only after absorbing unbearable misinterpretation and insult—when it is too late for uncomprehending humanity to save its sorry ass! The Pipe is the phallus of the god/goddess. As such, it has sacred connotations. I believe that femme gay men and butch lesbians serve the (widely unacknowledged) function of the mythological Trickster archetype in America's national psyche. For all these reasons and more, I was drawn to this tale.

Spring was full of chilled rain that year, smog-heavy; the mushrooms were in bloom. I'd walked charred forests and marshland filled with bones. Then slogged along a muddy road with so many others and their sad carts and possessions, all of us heading for Hamelin. Artisans, mendicants. Quack doctors, barbers, penitents. Women and their children, hooded infants bosom-shrouded in the rain, fathers' brows beaded with effort of the pushing, the hauling, and the mud. Children clutching rudely carved toys. Children's eyes, children's smiles, fresh powder smell of innocence. I searched them out; I looked away. The long intermingling lines of people moved on, stumbled, slowed, and stopped, miles away from the city gates. So many wanted shelter. The gatekeepers, taking full advantage of war and plague, were busy exacting tolls. Behind them factory spires twisted out of smoke and I saw it then: The rat, a dark angel, red-eyed, teeth spiked and wings spread suspended over the town, over the city, of Hamelin.

I took a job as deejay at The Mountain Club, where queers went at night. Everyone knew about the place.

When I say *everyone* I mean, of course, *us*—not straight people; not Hamelin at large. We queers knew. We danced there and caressed and had too much to drink in the dim corners, on the hot-lit Mountain dance floor every night. We lived day in and out for that era between midnight and 3:00 A.M., when everyone—*our* everyone—was there. To show up alone at that special time was to announce your availability. Bargains were made, liaisons begun. And black-market perfume became a riotous, urgent smell, rising with a mist of cigarette smoke and scotch in the strobe lights' flashing. The Mountain was special; not just anyone could walk through her doors. We wanted dykes hungry for power and surrender inside. And we wanted no straights. Spotting them was my specialty, hovering as I did in my booth above the dance floor. A lot of them did manage to get in, though, because they'd heard about the great dancing, the music, me; or because they had a bet with someone or were bored, or curious, or frustrated. I hated them even more than I hated the politicians and professors, even more than I had once hated rats, or the virulent plague itself. But one—a delicate exquisite young thing with long dark curls and wounded eyes—was the daughter of Hamelin's mayor. The Mayor was law in Hamelin.

We paid him off—through a series of designated emissaries—with a suitcase full of cash each month. A suitcase I delivered to the first in a chain of nameless goons with guns. In return, the Mayor let us alone. I noticed his daughter, of course; everyone did. She was so beautiful—we were all a little bit in love with her. I never dreamed she was in love herself.

Oh, and copious peddling of this or that was acceptable, even desirable.

Did I forget to say that we provided Hamelin's straight residents with a great service, by absorbing much of the city's criminal element after hours? The discreet commercial criminal element, courtesy of the Mayor: those with useful gifts to barter or trade. The war was staggering along, as usual. The plague was at its height. Politics had passed us by. We heard about it now and then—politics, the war—and scoffed in a kind of amazement. It was all old news to us, anyway.

I played music. Women danced to it. One of those girls was the daughter of the Mayor. And I—I watched her as she danced.

Perfume. Sweet, sweet sweat. There's a feeling to damp cloth, to how a femme brushes her silk sleeve across your face, carrying away the wet. Cigarette tips soaked in wine, on a table. The twisted metal cap to some lost poisonous bottle. A bracelet. Smell of hair against a neck. All these sensations drifted through me as I played music and watched women dance, until most nights there was nothing else inside me at all except sensation and an endless subliminal series of elusive memory—no real thought, no grief. When I'd first arrived in Hamelin, just one more ruined refugee, things had been different: I'd stood at rigid, exhausting attention all night looking over the crowd, contemplating my injured life. But as time went on and the plague failed to touch me, this tension was soon swept away by the continual breeze of sensation, nightly blasts of color and texture and smells, until I was just exactly what I was, the Piper— no more, no less—standing there momentarily scrutinizing, or sitting back to watch everything pass by, and that was just fine.

The less-timid femmes always approached me. Not because I was beautiful—I wasn't, not at all. But to some I seemed attractive in a strange, brooding way, and rumor said I did it right in bed. Go figure. I understand little about how to judge or rate love when it's purely physical; the truth is that I partook of it so rarely. Out of choice. It's hard to touch or feel through a plastic bag. Eventually, my long stretches of chosen celibacy were accepted by the brothers as a sort of personality quirk, like a funny way of tying your shoes, of stabbing out a cigarette. And eventually I, too, was accepted as one of the less-dispensable fixtures at the Mountain, along with the bouncers, the bartenders, and the regulars.

It was easy to forget the plague in there; easy to think that this little basement space was the world: a world of women dancing and drinking and kissing under white-hot flashing lights. Because when you worked at The Mountain, what you saw of life was pretty much contained within its walls—a cavernous converted cellar and first floor in an otherwise-condemned neighborhood over on the West Side. I got there by evening, worked until closing time, then stayed for free drinks. Maybe before six there would be breakfast—coffee, dripping eggs on thin toast and that foul after-hours taste on the tongue. Or maybe I'd skip food, take my pills, and begin the trip home.

I walked crosstown often, especially in summer. That early there weren't many hearses. Just me; just the rats. I'd feel sometimes as if the streets were my own private property; I'd jump off curbs, tread the white dividing lines on broken cement, while to the east smog sifted over the river, orange fires glowed in the burning parts of town, red sky dimmed to yellow then yellow-gray, the sun rose. Home was some hellhole of a squat I'd claimed with force and ingenuity, my own private, sacred space: roach-infested, clogged pipes, multiple locks on doors and windows, steel bars and rusted metal alloy shutters entrenched in walls and sills against the continuous assaults of the homeless, the desperately addicted and ill, those who slept behind garbage cans nightly and tried to break in each lawless day. Home was dishes crusted in the sink, mail unopened, phone calls unanswered or desperately awaited, Black Talon bullets filling extra clips for the semi I carried everywhere. But most of all home was just a bed: a soft unmade bed to fall into. I'd keep steel bars and shutters closed, sleep the sunlight away. And when an alarm clock rattled me awake it was evening again, time for The Mountain.

I'd get out my pipe. I'd strap it on. I'd throw on a shoulder holster, too, and the semi, some extra clips. Boots. Shirt. Suit and tie. The gun, the clothes, they were just for sheer survival. But the thing that gave me a calling, a name—was both a necessity and an extravagance. It was tool and fetish; it was bold, bold delight; it meant that I aimed to please; that I didn't just play music—I ran the fuck, I led the dance.

"That for me, hon'?" bolder girls would ask, squeezing my trousers' crotch like a plea.

I loved those nights.

It was on such a night—during a break when I'd left a tape on and slow music drifted from it, signaling a lull—that the daughter of Hamelin's mayor, that exquisite curiosity seeker, brushed up against me as I made way through the crowd. Her eyes rounded with surprise. Looking into them for a second, I fell in love. I don't know why. Then collected myself and winked, took her hand, led her through the gaggle of sweet-smelling, sweat-smelling bodies. She seemed willing. Her hand beat a pulse into mine, gentle, rhythmic. But just shy of the dance floor, that hand began to shudder like the rest of her and she pulled back. My guts churned. No, she mouthed into my ear, leaving a lipstick trace, No, please, not yet. I let her go. Then stepped just out of reach until she followed me along.

I pulled her to me. The tape segued into a slow, slow dance.

Her arms went around my neck. For a while we moved together quietly; I could tell that she liked it.

Then I did something I hadn't intended: Midway into the slow, slow dance, I reached down and pulled the back of her blouse until it fell out of the silk and leather that trapped it, cupped both my hands against the smooth wet flesh underneath. I felt my hands moving with perfect grace somehow, etching deliberate circles on the naked small of her back. And I could feel my own thighs shaking into silk and cotton. Voltage went up my spine, buzzed around the back of my neck, I moved my lips and tongue on her ear, her dark curls covering my face until we stopped dancing and swayed against each other. Something sweet buzzed, swooned, burned a blank over everything. I felt my head drop back as if it had some pillow to rest on instead of just air, and the sweet thing spread, hot, colorless, then shot up and out the top of me. When the music changed, we stood there pressed together, breathing.

Sorry, I said—and I was—but I didn't know why, or even if I'd said it out loud. I pushed her away gently, then headed for the door, bumping lots of elbows and breasts to get there. Moved outside and a gust of smoke blew with me. I could smell it on my hair, hands, the odor of ash on sweating cloth that stuck to my chest, a hint of death. There was another smell, too—something indefinable. I'd caught a whiff of it when her stray dark curls had brushed my neck: her perfume, mixed with whisky. A rat scuttled across the tops of my shoes and vanished.

"Hey, you there. That's no way to be."

Smoke and dull lights spilled out the noisy door once more, got muffled when it closed with a thud. She stroked my arm and I let her; but when she pressed against me for a kiss, I turned my own face away. Then held her firmly at arm's length. I'd felt her breasts and hard nipples through the shirt; they reminded me of the left-over quivering at my own core, reminded me of the fact that my own legs were still shaking, and I didn't want her to see.

Breeze blew from somewhere, bringing a scent of garbage. The alley wall held me up. Pull it together, Piper, I told myself. Regain control. Too many hours between now and dawn; you don't want any mistakes. But the girl looked injured.

"Oh, honey, why not?"

"Your daddy wouldn't like it." But that wasn't really it, and we both knew. The night air was cooling my flesh; I could seize a little control now. Instinct said to wait. I watched her lips make words, but no sound came out:

Why not?

In the shadows her face was disbelieving, then humiliated, her voice desolate.

"Please."

"Please, what?"

"Don't go."

"Why? You like me or something?"

"Yes."

I eased my grip, let her wilted body come closer. "Tell me how much. How much do you like me?"

I ran a hand along her neck, up her cheek, to the beginnings of tears on an eyelid. The lips moved again: *please* they said, silently. I traced them with a finger, smudged lipstick and tears away, brought the finger back to my own mouth to suck it. It occurred to me that if she carried plague, we'd both die soon. For a moment, I thought she would fall; she was shivering all over now, not fighting anymore. So I relaxed and let her fall forward against me, took her face between both hands, and turned it up until the mouth opened, just so, lips quivered as I teased them with my tongue, then they seemed to melt away like ice on a flame when I kissed them.

I let her hands stay against the backs of my thighs, let myself be pulled forward gently, rhythmically, then released, again and again. I played a game with her lips, holding them open with my fingers sometimes, sometimes only with my tongue. I was in control now, and it felt good. Suddenly I'd become cold, full of clarity, of a boundless ability to plan and intuit—but I was still walking a narrow line between having all the power and losing it completely, and I knew it. I moved back away from her, plucked her hands off to hold them between my own. The dark eyes met mine fully: pained, wanting, afraid. I wondered what the fear was—an invitation? Rats whimpered in the darkness. I wondered how she'd slipped out of the mansion this time; I wondered if the Mayor usually sent spies after her, and where they were right now.

"What do you think happens now?"

"Now? You—you —"

"I what?"

"Come home with me."

I laughed, softly. "Won't your daddy mind?"

"He's somewhere else. Until Wednesday."

"Busy guy. Somewhere else? Why'd you lie like that? There's nowhere else to go."

I passed a hand over her breasts. They were gorgeously soft under the barrier of cloth, nipples stiffened, aching to burst. Maybe it was a kind of pity that made me stop. That, or the thudding of my heart. I would touch them later, anyway, and when I did she'd be naked; but there was plenty of time between now and then.

Gas was rationed; it mostly went to the hearses and politicians' cars, anyway. So we took a bike rickshaw all the way uptown. Passing through neighborhoods of withered prosperity, where garbage cans burned in the streets. Passing the last church left in Hamelin. The minister was a fundamentalist sort who hated queers. He was always decrying us in the morning papers, accusing us of bringing plague to the city. He and his wife and children huddled together on steps in the rain as we passed. A mass of drenched, miserable, shivering refugees around them. Hoarsely, he shouted.

"Hallelujah!"

Shuttered windows turned blankly on them. The preacher's collar was frayed and gray. He wore dark-rimmed glasses, but one of the lenses had cracked; a thin strip of masking tape ran diagonally across it.

"And why, my friends—why have you come to Hamelin? What forces brought us here together, some of us starving, some of us lame, some of us tired, but all of us full of God's glory, to stand here, together, in this city, this last remaining outpost of civilization? I'll tell you, my friends!" He paused. Raindrops streamed across masking tape.

From the crowd came a shrill "Tell us, brother!"

The preacher breathed in rain. "The forces that weave their ways among us, that bring us all here to stand together, my friends, in humanity's last place; these forces are the power of the Lord! The power of God to ordain and uphold, to avenge and lead the righteous!"

"Amen!"

Our rickshaw clattered on.

The Mayor and his daughter lived in one of Hamelin's last existing villas: a compound surrounded by high gates and barbed wire. She paid the driver well. He coughed into both fists, and I wondered if he had flu or plague, wondered if he would live out the night; and, if not, who would bury him. She opened the gates with a special remote. We walked past gardens, ponds, and trees shrouded with light mist. It was a place of dark beauty, seemingly separate from the whole dirty city that surrounded it—quiet, flowering, an island of rural calm. Then I saw the mayoral mansion: a vast fort of wood and stone standing starkly in the rain.

A door slid open; she led me inside.

It was quite still. Somewhere an ancient clock ticked. The floors were high-gloss walnut, the rug antique Persian. She pulled a cord and sashes flew across glass, obscured the empty sparkle of pool and patio; she pressed something on the wall, and golden light rose dimly from each corner, aimed so that shadows played across the expensive things placed everywhere. I stood at the carpet fringe. Six crystal brandy snifters waited on a bar. "Would you like a drink?"

"No."

She turned once to smile—inviting, a little amused. Ran her hand along an armchair. It came away dustless.

"Have a seat."

I did. "Your parents like collecting things."

"Mommy's gone. The plague. She didn't like it—collecting things, I mean—not especially."

"Your father, then."

She shrugged. "His staffers, really. Daddy—well, he doesn't know the difference. He just pays lots of money to the people who *do*. 'Get nice things,' he tells them. 'Make it look like I come from wealth. Make it look like the plague can't touch us here.' Important people pay him to make sure things outside stay just like they are. Everyone dying all the time. Dead people—they leave chairs and desks and beds, expensive things, and if the rest of their family's dead, too, Daddy's men just go there and they bring stuff back. Or they sell it. They take a percentage. They bring the rest of the money back and they give it to Daddy. And he gives it to—to the important people."

"What about you? You like what they bring back?"

"No. It reminds me of death. I want to get out—"

"To go where?"

"The Mountain," she said. And laughed. Then poured good burgundy into a snifter and sipped some. In the light it looked like ink, swimming around the bottom half-inch of frail crystal goblet.

"My name's Cheri," she said. "I've been watching you for months."

I rose to touch her.

Later, in her room, she opened her arms. For a moment she looked like an expanding shadow against lamplight, dark wings spreading. I stepped nearer. Carpet muffled everything. I knew that maybe I was going somewhere I shouldn't. But that seemed inconsequential now; even getting plague seemed like a tiny thing; I was just where I'd planned on being. Stepping into the soft shadow her arms made was like stepping into a satin cloud, lightly encompassing. Petals, I thought. Gossamer exquisite, closing over a bee. Still, the bee found what it was looking for—buzzing right into the core of the bud. And when it died, it died sucking nectar.

I slid my hands along her forearms until the shirtsleeves bunched. There I was, fingers trapped between flesh and silk. I kissed her lips softly, then each eyelid, on the tip of my tongue tasted salt, perfume, mascara gone bitter, hinting death, like a wine cork left to dry. I could feel her shiver. She was trying to reach me, searching for my belt; I wouldn't let her.

"Cheri, I'm going to kiss you."

"Do it then, just do it."

It was liquid warm, made me think of clear water covering skin completely, reminded me of the first time I'd touched another woman's tongue with my own, and the two-way shock that had gone through me then—shooting straight up into my head, obscuring every thought, then down to my belly and all parts below. But that had been so long ago. Before the war. Before the plague. Now, in this time, I could watch her eyes close while my own stayed open; I could keep my thoughts alive, despite the crazy electricity jumbling every muscle, making my breath sound faster; I could ache deep down, yet—somewhere above it all—calmly observe myself aching, and know that it did not matter.

I traced lines along the back of her neck. Reached down simply to free silk from silk once and for all. Then touched naked torso underneath. She made a sound like a sob.

"Is it time to take your clothes off, Cheri? I think so. I think it's time."

I'd seen many breasts in my life. Hers seemed new, though, a pair of something rare and beautiful: plump in a way I'd never have suspected, pink-tinged brown circling each nipple, puckering gently when I touched them. I let myself get a little lost. I let hands that didn't feel like mine undo all the buttons and zippers. She ran a palm over me, between flaps of shirt. I grabbed her hand, pressed it to my mouth, and licked my own sweat off.

"God," she said, "how does it taste?"

"Well, you'll find out, won't you?"

She slid down until her knees hit the carpet. Like praying, I thought. Only no words sounded. And maybe what she reached for now and took into her mouth had a different power than prayer—sacred or profane, I didn't know—but, in any case, it would not lead to salvation.

When I pulled her up, she let out a louder sound and arched back onto the bed. I tugged at each silk leg. The pants peeled off easily; I didn't stop to fold them. I kissed the flesh they left behind instead, silky skin darker than my own; for a second I saw my wrist against the quivering top of her thigh, different shades of skin. The sight made me want to shut my eyes and lose myself again, but I didn't.

"Honey."

It was a whisper. Cheri twined fingers through my hair, pulled my lips up to brush belly skin, breast skin; I took her nipples in my mouth again, ran my lips in circles along her neck. I could have stretched out fully on top of her then and kissed, long and deep. But I held myself up and apart instead, staring down at her against a background of blue satin bedcover. A gift from her father. Had it once belonged to some victim of the plague? Probably. In the light, her hair blended in: loose dark curls on a dark sheen. She breathed quickly, lightly. Her forehead was damp. When she blinked, the sweat gleamed.

"You're still half-dressed. No fair."

"Maybe I'm shy."

"Ah." She smiled. "We'll see." Then she toyed with zippers and leather, something opened with a clink, and for a second it felt like the rest of me would fall open too, onto satin and flesh, everywhere. We moved together a little. Everything throbbed. Dancing, I thought. Slow dance. I held her hips up against me.

"Save me," she said.

"Your sheets," I asked. "Are they silk?"

They were—dark rose-colored, fresh and smooth, the pillows goose down. I wondered whether her daddy's goons had taken them, too, from the bed of another plague victim; she'd said as much. But did it matter? Did it matter to the dead? Satin cover peeled away, thick dark quilt folded underneath. I held the small of her back and watched curls spread against the rose-tinged shadow. Then eased down on top of her so our hipbones clashed, but I wouldn't go inside her—no, not yet. I twined my fingers through her hair as if it were a good-luck web I'd fallen into, not disaster—but gently; webs are fragile things. Her breath came against my cheek, fast, sweet. She pressed against me, begging, and we kissed. Maybe it was the way her tongue searched under and over mine, trying to suck, then release, that made me match the sounds she was making with my own somehow, whispers, whimpers; that made me move in rhythm like waves on sand while Cheri strained under me, trying to catch and keep me, finally gave up and wrapped her legs around me in one wet desperate motion, nostrils flaring like something wild.

"Inside." She bit her lip raw. "Please, please. Go deep inside."

"Whatever you want, you know you can have it."

"Really?" she said. And sobbed.

I pulled away then, held the perfect instrument there between my own legs, found a perfect dark triangle of Cheri waiting to match it. I slid fingers through the tangled damp hair, a thick, open, impatient wetness that smelled faintly of the sea, and I heard her moan deeply and then slid inside her against pliant wet walls, over the soft nub of something electric. Her hips swayed forward to take me in, slowly at first, then urgently. She stiffened slightly. Something like suffering went across her face.

"Ah—careful—make it last—"

I was teasingly motionless for a while, watching damp glimmer at the edges of her half-closed eyes, listening to her breathe raggedly. Then her whispers sounded raggedly, dreamily. "I'm sick," she said. "I'm dying. I've had plague since last summer."

Something smashed the back of my neck and head; it was heavy and cold. I could hear a thud far off: my own body, half-dressed, falling.

I was standing when I woke—or, rather, being held up by big hands grasping each arm. But my head dangled forward, and through the blur of swollen eyes trying to focus I could see garbage crusting each boot tip. The boots were mine, on my feet; they wobbled against the surface of rare, expensive Persian carpeting, speckled now with tiny drops of blood. Something tickled my face; the blood was coming from me. When my neck snapped alert, the blood ran into both ears. I could feel my collar soaked and loose— someone had taken my tie. Cheri, I thought. Remembered her curious femme fingers—trembling, unknotting. With battered lips, I smiled.

"Listen. Carefully. To what I am about to tell you."

The Mayor sat behind a redwood desk. The bookshelves around him were full of other people's books, dimly lit chestnut, walnut and redwood, a blur of scarlet. His goons supported me on either side, but I sensed them rather than saw; my ears rang full of blood. I could smell their sweat and mine.

"You exist because I allow you to. Because I work it out with the powers that be. Because I have pity." The Mayor's voice echoed like something from the other end of a tube, his whining tenor bent, warped, the vowels elongated. He laughed. "No, not really. You live because you serve a certain purpose. Never forget that. Hamelin's full of rats and plague. Not the rats and plague you see all around you—no—I'm talking about the rats and plague that stream into this town like rain from all the high places, the places of money, the places of war. The rats that water your beer and dilute your medicine and sell it all back to you at black-market prices. The rats that finesse deals, barter lives for cash, make sound investments, make money from suffering and illness, make money from money and death. These rats you never see. The plague *they* spread will grip you silently, tenaciously, and you'll never even feel the terrible illness that has invaded your body and soul—as it invaded the body of my wife, and now my precious daughter—never, until the very end. But understand this, and understand it clearly: Do not underestimate the power of these rats. You live because they haven't yet bothered to kill you. Because they haven't gotten around to noticing you. But *I* notice you. And with a word, a letter from me, a memo, *they* will notice you, too." He sighed. "You see, I am just middle management, really. But I shuffle the papers along."

The two goons I never saw tossed me down stone flights into the street. It was after-hours time—between four and morning. They'd taken my money, my gun. Rats ran over me there in the sewer, and blood dripped out of my ears for a long, long time, until sunrise threatened and a hearse rattled by, and I crawled to a corner pump for water.

It's no fun nursing a broken face. They'd stormed through my squat while I was away and wrecked everything. For many nights I shivered, half-naked, on a torn old mattress. The phone rang sometimes, once, twice, forlorn, then stopped. Whoever wanted me also did not want me or the trouble I'd bring, and I imagined her face hovering over the phone pad, fingers pressing buttons, terrorized into a grotesque ambivalence. Finally, one evening I crawled to the bath, then staggered through the remnants of my possessions toward a splintered mirror, bruised hands fumbling as I eased into a few shredded, mottled clothes. I wrote a letter and addressed it to the Mayor:

> *Understand that your suffering is no ticket of admission. No automatic entry badge to some illusory paradise of respect. When I come around next time, you and the people you work for will pay, and receive nothing in return—except a continuation of emptiness. It is like that, emptiness: a mirror. You can see your foolish greed gazing back.*

When I limped down into the street and slipped it into a mailbox, things seemed changed. There were fewer sounds than usual. The rats had multiplied so drastically that some were starving to death; they scampered around my feet feebly, blindly, their tiny ribs showing, dancing over human corpses stacked high near the trash. And the roads were deserted—not a beggar or bum, not a hearse in sight.

I limped past one group of bodies spread out like a fan—feet toward the gutter, eyes staring open—and I recognized the preacher and his family.

You should have loved us, I prayed, silently. Loved me, even me. That was your salvation; you let it pass you by.

The Mountain was dark, windows boarded up. No notices posted. No lines at any doors. It had ceased to exist so suddenly—as if a light had suddenly been snapped off forever, and now the place was just one more nailed-shut building in a long and dreary row of them on a dying city's street. Even the sign was gone.

I turned to see her watching.

Her shadowed face was puffy; someone had hit it.

"Daddy said he killed you. I came back anyway."

There was something, I thought; something I ought now to say. But I just faced her silently.

She shrugged; it was a steadying motion, to stop herself from shivering. Fever radiated from her.

"There's a big rat in there."

"Yeah?"

"Really, really big. He's sick. He's full of plague. I think that maybe he's dying now."

I reached across the trash-strewn space of street to pull her in and hold her to me, and our bruised cheeks pressed together. Candle, I thought, light, fire. I am going to steal his fire. His future. And keep it safe somewhere as if it is a jewel or dream, somewhere protected, hidden, safe from waste and greed and plague.

"Cheri—"

"Mmmm?"

"Let's go."

It hurt to tear the boards away. Rusted nail points scraped my flesh. Those goons had done their job, but not irrevocably.

While she watched, I pulled the old door open. Something big with a whiplike tail raced past us hissing, spattering germs. She gasped. Fell into my arms. It hurt, but I lifted her up, took her in, sealed the door behind. Inside The Mountain burned a light, from some deep part of the cellar. It dimly illuminated the busted mirrors and jukeboxes, smashed stools, tables, bar. I laid her down gently. Then stretched out next to her on the cold, cold floor, unzipped pants and reached between her legs, and fucked her for hours, fucked her back to life. She came out of the death swoon from cold to hot to fever. When the fever broke with a deep, deep, moan her lips and breasts were warm again, and full, and she opened her mouth and eyes.

Later we stood, dizzy. Now the power between us had shifted: I leaned against her shoulder feeling frail; she supported my tired, tired, weight.

The light came from far below, from a place I'd never been. Was it war? Plague? Death? No, I thought—love! Perhaps that was just illusion—love, I mean. Yet the hope of it seemed sweet.

So we headed toward it, she and I, feeling along the walls for direction when shadows fell too strong, our shod toes inching ahead. We walked knowingly somehow, though this way was strange to us.

Gammer Ermintrude's Revenge:
A Love Letter from Snow White
JOAN M. SCHENKAR

Erotic writing has always made me uncomfortable. I can't read it with-
out giggling, and I don't write it without wincing, preferring—but only
in this matter—the life form to the art form. Fairy tales, on the other
hand, I consider to be as wide as the world and just as serious: They have
provided both dark and light directions for my theater work.

In "Gammer Ermintrude's Revenge: A Love Letter from Snow
White," the collision of these two attitudes helped to produce a satire.
From the story of the inseparable sisters Snow White and Rose Red,
who rescue both a dwarf and a prince and are themselves "rescued"
from their close relationship by royal marriages, and from the story of
the lone Snow White, concealed by dwarves, pursued by a vengeful step-
mother, and possessed by a necrophiliac prince, I have raised, like a
rabbit from folded cloths, the alcoholic and intrepidly lesbian Gammer
Ermintrude—determined, at ninety-one years of age, to avenge herself
on the Brothers Grimm for stealing her best stories by telling them a story
they'll never forget. (The Grimm boys did extract most of their material

from elderly female fabulists—none of whose names I've seen credited on editions of Grimm's Fairy Tales.)

Out of these Grimm tales, too, I have made a Snow White with literary and epistolary aspirations, an inflated and genuinely insincere writing style, and an erotic interest in interior decor that far outstrips her attraction to any possible partner, including her beloved sister and constant bedmate, Rose Red.

I regret that constraints of time and mind did not allow me to provide Rose Red's response to Snow White's love letter, a response which would surely include a serious critique of her beloved sister's use of the parenthesis as a part of erotic speech.

Another time, perhaps.

Olde Gammer Ermintrude is in a foul mood this morning. Not her first foul mood of the week by any means, but certainly her worst one. Drinking morosely from a two-liter stein of Bavarian ale— alcohol content 26 percent—she meditates on the pains and humiliations of living the artist's life in nineteenth-century Germany.

Three pfennigs! Why, in all her ninety-one years, she has never been offered so little recompense for her storytelling services. Three pfennigs! The *nerve* of those two fat folklorist brothers from Frankfurt exploiting her like this! She draws deeply on the ale once again, trying to find a more comfortable position for her generous derrière on the three-legged stool beneath it. Now, just what *was* the silly patronymic of those solemn bourgeois scribblers? Ah yes. Grimm. *Die Brüder Grimm*, as they introduced themselves. The Brothers Grimm. A descriptive surname, Ermintrude is certain. They looked *exactly* like undertakers.

Gammer Ermintrude hates the Grimm brothers. She hates them because they are rich, she hates them because they are prim (they sit and even stand with their black broadcloth knees pressed together), she hates them because they speak High German in her presence as though she can't understand it, and she hates them because she is giving them, *far too cheaply in her estimation*, her fabulous stories for their collection of German fairy tales. She also hates them on general principles, and here she thrills with a little atavistic shudder of malevolence, *simply because they are men*.

The Grimms—Ermintrude can't think of them separately and she feels in her *bones* that they are sleeping together—will return this afternoon for another display of Gammer Ermintrude's fabled abilities as a *raconteuse* of little-known fairy tales. Ermintrude's well-attended recitations are always held here in her filthy little hut—for in the tradition of many spoken-word artists, Gammer Ermintrude uses her humble home as a performance space. (Ermintrude doesn't actually think "performance space," she thinks "recital hall." And the phrase "spoken-word artist" is not in her vocabulary.)

Ermintrude shares the hut and all her other earthly belongings with her close companion of fifty-six years, Olde Goodie Grizela. Grizela, the love of Ermintrude's life and, incidentally, the most flirtatiously attractive woman in the principality half a century ago (what a story *that* seduction was), is also the local *vendeuse* of healing potions and sexual stimulants. Her herbs hang drying everywhere in the filthy little hut, while her retorts and alembics drip steaming possibilities on the earthen floor. Goodie Grizela is out at the moment searching for mandragora and Indian pipe somewhere in the deep, dark, Prussian woods.

Gammer Ermintrude knows that this afternoon will be yet another painful, wasted four hours of her beautifully nuanced narratives being constantly interrupted by those irritating Grimm brothers. They will ask about word origins, they will request foreign pronunciations, and they will no doubt require her to repeat each tale, *word for word*, at least four times as they have done in the past. And all the while they will be taking their terrible, precise, unnerving notes. The thought of their pens scratching in unison at the parchment drives Gammer Ermintrude deeper into her beer.

And now that Ermintrude thinks of it, and this is one more thing to add to the endless list of grievances she is accumulating against the Grimms, those two brothers are *extraordinarily smelly*. She doesn't know if her delicate sensibilities can bear another four enclosed hours with the fat, stinking beasts. She begins to wish, not for the first time, that she were drinking something stronger—something to fortify her against their awful odor. Something more like...schnapps.

Of course, Gammer Ermintrude's *own* personal body *bouquet* could never be mistaken for a bed of edelweiss. And nineteenth-century plumbing being what it is, there is generally a fairly persistent lavatory odor about her filthy little hut. Then, too, Goodie Grizela feeds twenty or thirty stray cats a day here, and the hut has no windows. In this fascist, Saxe-Coburg–crippled country, you are *taxed* for having windows; and all of Gammer Ermintrude's stories and all of Goodie Grizela's herbal potions taken together do not earn them enough money for *taxes*, means that there is something very like a "sick-building syndrome" in the old ladies' wretched domicile—a hundred fifty years *avant la lettre*.

Gammer Ermintrude takes another deep draught of ale and thinks with pleasure of how the Grimm boys stumbled out of the hut yesterday, reeling and puking from the atmosphere. It gives her something to look forward to this afternoon.

All Gammer Ermintrude wanted from this day was to drink more ale, fondle her beloved Goodie Grizela until they both cooed their mutual satisfaction, and then pore, for the thousandth time, over the manuscript fragment of Hildegard von Bingen's *Salve Regina* which, miraculously, has been in the old couple's collection of works by women these thirty years and more.

This hand-scriven medieval treasure was acquired from a grateful client of Goodie Grizela's in exchange for one of her inadvertently successful herbal decoctions. It has pride of place in the old ladies' hovel. Grizela values the manuscript far above the Shroud of Turin or a fair copy of the *Malleus Maleficarum*; Ermintrude likes to look at it every day and think with wonder of the shining beacon of female power that was Hildegard von Bingen.

And now, instead of honoring the work of a sister genius (and, Ermintrude is certain, a fellow pervert), and pleasuring dear Olde Goodie Grizela in new and interesting ways, Gammer Ermintrude has to recite, once again, from her precious store of perfectly crafted fairy tales for these stupid, unfeeling, *inartistic* brothers. And for nothing. For *nothing*. Or, what is even worse, for *next* to nothing: Three miserable pfennigs!

Ermintrude swallows the last of her ale in a positively volcanic mood.

Yesterday, she broods, those unsmiling *auslanders* forced her to tell the stories of "Little Red Cap" and "Rapunzel of the Golden Hair" at least five times. With special emphasis on the subjugative states of the young heroines in which, Ermintrude feels, the Grimm boys took far too much pleasure. Her throat is still sore from the effort, and her feelings are still hurt from the unresponsiveness of her audience.

No applause, Ermintrude remembers with a shudder. Those swinish brothers couldn't stop taking notes long enough even to clap. What do they think I am? A machine? (Ermintrude doesn't actually think "machine," she thinks "spinning jenny.") To spin out stories all day long without encouragement? Ermintrude yearns to remind the Brothers Grimm, preferably in mephitically foul and trituratingly abusive language, that all performers of the spoken word require a *tsunami* of positive response, not to mention a *Himalaya* of hearty reinforcement, from their audience members.

This afternoon the Brothers Grimm are expecting to hear Ermintrude's gloriously unique versions of the old fables of "Snow White and the Seven Dwarves" and "Snow White and Rose Red."

Gammer Ermintrude reflects that it will be confusing to tell those two tales side by side with all their sameness of flowers, fruits, dwarves, and objects made of glass. She wonders whether she shouldn't simply conflate (she thinks "conjoin") the two tales and be done with it. Those inspissated Grimms (Ermintrude doesn't think "inspissated") certainly wouldn't know the difference. And, just for variety, she could tell it in another voice, too, perhaps an epistolary ("letter-writing" thinks Ermintrude) voice. As she contemplates the artistic difficulties before her, Ermintrude waddles over to the crock of beer in the corner of the hut, dips her stein in once again, and brings it to her lips in a long, lovely, life-affirming swallow.

Refreshed and refueled, Ermintrude eructates softly and scratches a pendulous underarm. Urrrrppp. Scratch scratch. Urrrrrrppp. The exercise stimulates her cognitive faculties. An idea, or something like an idea, begins to sprout gills and fins and does a tentative butterfly stoke around the pool of alcohol perfuming her hypothalamus.

Stories, she thinks. Those boring burghers want *stories* for their three pfucking pfennigs? Urrp. Ha *ha*. *I'll* give them stories. Stories they won't soon forget. Urrrrrrrp.

Gammer Ermintrude drinks deeply once again from her tankard, smacking her lips with evident satisfaction. She thinks of her old darling Goodie Grizela's still-plump and still-desirable thighs—just like a nice fat little hen she muses—and she fingers her own withered labia familiarly through the pocket of her kirtle. The response is disappointing; her mind is elsewhere.

I wonder, she calculates, what the chances of extracting another two pfennigs from those cheapskate Grimm boys would be. Poor, she decides with a heavy sigh, very poor. They have the mentalities of bank managers. I suppose I'll have to settle for some form of revenge.

Then Gammer Ermintrude sits back down on her seat with a

wicked, and by now, *utterly* inebriated laugh. The kind of laugh that, a century and a half previous, would have gotten her the stake, the stocks, or the ducking stool. And she begins to rehearse in her head the *really interesting* fairy tale she has decided to tell the Brothers Grimm this afternoon. It is a very different tale from the ones she has promised them and she is very certain it is like no other fairy tale that has ever been heard or spoken or written down before.

And, as she rehearses the story to herself, Olde Gammer Ermintrude feels her foul mood begin to rise like the morning sun. She knows now that her revenge—the only revenge worth having, the revenge of the Spirit of Art upon the Cretins of Commerce—is going to be elaborate, effective, and completely satisfying.

And for the pure pleasure of it, Gammer Ermintrude speaks aloud the first few lines of her new fairy tale, the fairy tale like no other, the fairy tale which the Brothers Grimm will be hearing in a matter of minutes:

"Ever since I can remember, all young women in the kingdom of Bavaria have crept into each other's beds under the dark cover of night. Though they were sisters, Snow White and Rose Red were no exception. From the time of their earliest childhood, Snow White and Rose Red enjoyed each other's bodies with unrestrained passion and unregulated emotion. And when the persecutions of their Wicked Stepmother forced Snow White into hiding with the Seven Dwarves, Snow White and Rose Red continued their love story with secret messages, each in her own distinctive style. I remember very well the only letter from this correspondence I was allowed to see...."

Snow White to Rose Red   *28 June*

Dearest Rose Red,

At last, my darling, I am able to smuggle this little love letter into your waiting, willing, incredibly dexterous hands—kissed, I know, by every courtier who comes near you. Well, let the fawning fools kiss your hands. *I'll* kiss all the rest.

A woodsman with the most beautifully endowed loins I have seen in years (always excepting your own, my love) has just come upon this hideous hovel where I have been restrained so long from your embraces. The woodsman promises to carry my letter to you—if he can *find* you, that is. The cretin lost his way in the surrounding woods (isn't that just *like* a man not to ask directions) and stumbled on my secreted little slum wholly by accident. You'd think someone whose entire profession is *trees* would be able to hack a path thru a small second-growth *forest*, wouldn't you? But *no*. He is as directionless as a kiss without consequences. (All *our* kisses had consequences, didn't they, Rosie? How *much* I miss those consequences!)

Fortunately for our clandestine correspondence, only the somnolent Sleepy is here guarding me today. And he, as usual, is collapsed in a kind of fugue state on the floor. The rest of my midget captors (I *hate* calling them dwarves, the term doesn't do justice to the very real perversions they practice and, besides, "midget" is a *much* nastier word than "dwarf") have already marched into their gold mine doing that ghastly Hi-ho Hi-ho thing they sing every morning. Considering that I was raised (as were you, my love) on the music of Fanny Mendelssohn, Cécile Chaminade, and Hildegard von Bingen, the Hi-Ho Hi-Ho song is a terrible blow to my softer senses. I can only add this affront to the long list of horrors I've endured in my seven-year imprisonment here—

horrors that include confinement in a kitchen, sensory depri-
vation, forced maid service, and (the *worst* for a budding
femme des lettres) constant exposure to truly *awful* grammar.

Seven years my darling! Seven years away from you with
only the occasional curl of hair or smuggled scented note to
heat the blood and stimulate the olfactory sense. (I *did* receive
that little pubic patch you sent by chimney swallow in January.
Thank you a thousand times, dearest—it sustained me
through the winter.) The moment I am freed from this endless
rotation of kitchen duty and dust detail, you and I must and
will bring legal action against the dwarves, our stepmother,
the kingdom, and whomever else is responsible for our painful
separation.

But there I go, behaving just as I did in the old days in that
quaint, but perfectly appointed, cottage bedroom we shared.
So eager to speak with my little sister Rose Red that all my
sentences come tumbling out in droll disorder. How *well* I
remember that cottage bedroom, my darling: The divinely
scented Rigaud candles we lit every night to consecrate our
love, the intricate hand-blocked William Morris wallpaper
gift-wrapping our walls, the 500-thread-per-square-inch
pure Egyptian cotton Porthault sheets (you should *see* what
I'm forced to sleep on here) on our deliciously disarrayed
burnished-brass Charles P. Rogers bed...

Ah! those sheets! And what we did *on* them, *under* them,
in *spite* of them.... Forgive me, my love. Desire for you always
provokes me to digression. And I *do* still lust after our little
luxuries. You've no idea, Rose darling, what horrible crime
I would commit *at this moment* for breakfast on a silver tray!

As I was saying, I was able to gain the woodsman's promise
to deliver this letter to you by inviting a few of his awkward,
yet strangely arresting caresses. There *is* something about
working with wood that encourages the weaker sex to raise

the sapling of talent in the forest of the senses. But the woods-man's small gifts in that department didn't distract me for long—for I had my darling sister Rose Red firmly in the middle of my mind and a letter to get to her! Besides, Rosie, I know in my deepest heart that someone as passionate as you has not been celibate for seven long years. And it's perfectly all right, my love, I forgive you in advance. Absence certainly makes the heart grow colder and the body hotter. I'm sure you've noticed.

Well, my dearest, I know you'll want a full report of my behavior, sexual and otherwise, since the last loving letter. The truth is, I have been leading a prisoner's simple existence in this cloistral cottage. My nights are given over to romance—I try to imagine you in every position ecstasy and fantasy make possible. And my days are devoted to practicality—I do my concentrated best to accept every sexual opportunity that comes my way.

Yes, Rosie, even in this sad concealment I have been able to honor the memory of our perfect love (just how perfect only you and I will ever know) with a few rehearsals for its next delicious expression. In descending order (and in perfect honesty), I have made love with women (in every way my first choice), a few available men (always a distant second selection), and the occasional consenting furbearer (very good for variety, and the woods are full of them). Of course, I am not exactly in a position to discriminate widely—or, actually, to discriminate at *all*—but *you* know how completely country life and pastoral torpor can dull the senses and I *do* try to hold my end up. As it were.

You'll be happy to hear that I *have* refused the poisoned advances of our wicked, *wicked* stepmother whose last attempt to kill me (only yesterday morning, I'm sorry to report) involved a dildo as sharp as a Sabatier and a vibrator running sufficient voltage to electrify an elephant. Is the woman *insane?* Is she even a *woman?* Does she take me for a *fool*, for heavens sake? (These are rhetorical questions, Rosie dear, and you needn't bother to answer them: Your last letter featured *two whole pages* of responses to my rhetorical questions.)

Because I know how your mind *leaps* to the ledge of inference, I hasten to mention that I also refused the advances of six of my seven dwarf captors (they actually prefer sex with each other, anyway, the grotesque little things) and then slapped the one called Doc to the ground the *moment* I discovered his name was *not* an honorific diminutive indicating advanced degrees in literature. Silly me, *I* thought the little fellow was a Doctor of Philosophy. Well you *know* how bookish I've always been, my love, and frankly I was *desperate* to discuss the forty-three lesbian poems of Emily Dickinson with *someone*. *Happily*, I discovered my mistake in time. I mean, can you *imagine?* Sex with a tiny *miner? And* a discussion of Emily Dickinson?

I tell you, Rosie, my life here swings between the loathsome and the lugubrious and, unfortunately, I have no one to blame but myself (well, no one to blame but my extraordinary beauty, to be perfectly accurate). Because of that old canard of my being fairest in the land, I have suffered seven years of protective custody in a ghastly witness-protection program run by small ugly day laborers. You remember how my wicked stepmother's tiresome mirror started this whole beauty-contest business. Of course anyone who listens to a talking mirror deserves what she gets. And, besides, we all know what *her* jealousy is made of (the theories of that Viennese misogynist pervade even *these* woeful woods, my darling). But the jealousy of that wicked woman is not *my* problem. *My* problem is getting out of here alive and still libidinous. Ah,

Rosie! How I long to run my nails over the nacreous surfaces of your silken undergarments. And how often I imagine draping myself in our divinely sheer *broderie anglaise* duvet cover flocked with the *petit point* fleurs-de-lis. I thrill at the anticipated sensations, Rosie, really I do.

I miss you terribly, my red Rose. Every fragrant stamen, petal, leaf, and hip! I think of you constantly and dream of your rubicund embraces, the roseate colors of your "nether lips," the essence of crimson and scarlet that is your own personal body bouquet. Ahhh, even now I deliquesce as I dream of you, Rose Red. My sister. My lover. My multifloral darling.

Our time together seems to me like a fairy tale.

Enchantingly yours,
Snow White

Avi Shmacha and the Golden Yidlock
KAREN X. TULCHINSKY

My fairy tale is based on an old Yiddish folktale from Poland. In the original the main character is Aaron Shmacha, a man. Aaron Shmacha is homely, slow, socially inept, and poor. He is shy, keeps to himself, and though he has his eye on a young woman from his village, he knows he is not worthy of her and figures he will spend the rest of his life alone. One day the prophet Elijah, disguised as a beggar, appears on Aaron's doorstep. Aaron invites him in, offers Elijah his only crust of bread to eat and his bed for the night, while he sleeps on the floor. In the morning the beggar is gone, but he has left a golden yarmulke (a skullcap worn by Jewish men for prayer). Uneducated Aaron doesn't know the real name or purpose of the yarmulke. He calls it a Yidlock, and when he puts it on his head, his whole life changes. Suddenly he is handsome, charming, and wise. He meets the woman of his dreams, they marry, and live in happiness the rest of their days. I interpret the Yidlock to be a miracle, a turning point in life when someone is rewarded for patience and kindness. In other words, sometimes from out of the depths of despair, someone or something comes along that changes a person's life for the better. That even when things aren't going your way, if you have hope, you have everything. As Harvey Milk said, "You gotta have hope."

Avi Shmacha had no luck with women. She had never been truly in love, and no one had ever truly loved her. She had never really dated much, either. She wasn't very good at it. She lacked the confidence. She lacked the skill. And Avi had bad luck. She wasn't bad-looking, she just wasn't very noticeable. She was a loner, timid, the type who would hang around in dark back corners of the bar, drinking beer and girl watching in silent, passive invisibility. In group situations, she was the quiet one at the corner of the table. She laughed at the right times, listened well, and was socially acceptable, but Avi just didn't know what to say most of the time. While others were witty and charming, she was tongue-tied, unsure of herself, and shy. There were times when, for a brief moment, Avi had a girlfriend, but never for long. Just recently she had been dating a woman. It lasted almost two months, but then her lover left her for Avi's good-looking, smooth-talking next-door neighbor. For a long time, Avi felt betrayed, and more recently, depressed.

Every day she dragged herself in to work. She was a production assistant at her local gay paper, *The Rainbow News*. She liked her job well enough. She enjoyed working in a queer place, where she could be fully out all the time, but sometimes it made her sad. All of her co-workers were in happy relationships. She was the only one who showed up to work parties without a date. She was sick of happy couples. Being near their bliss made her feel worse. Lately, on Friday nights she had taken to buying a six-pack of beer and sitting alone in her bachelor apartment all evening, getting drunk and watching the two or three videos she'd pick up on the way home from work. She'd watch anything, but she especially liked old Hollywood musicals, Fred Astaire, Gene Kelly, Debbie Reynolds, *Oklahoma*, *South Pacific*, *My Fair Lady*. She'd sing along with the musical numbers and cry at the tragic parts. Her favorites were the sad scenes where the hero died in the end or the lovers were cruelly separated by evil forces. She'd watch the scenes over and over. Rewinding and replaying the most heart-rending parts. The misery of these fictional characters soothed Avi Shmacha. She was living her life vicariously through the movies. It was kind of pathetic and definitely lonely. Avi was in a rut and did not know how to get out.

The Friday night before Valentine's Day things got even worse. Avi's best friend, A.J., with whom Avi had spent many a lonely Saturday evening commiserating together about their sad single state, called to say she had fallen in love. Somewhere in her heart, Avi was happy for her friend, but the thought of being the last single dyke on earth only compounded her own unhappiness. She went to the video store and rented *West Side Story*. It seemed like the thing to do. She liked Tony's dying in the end. It was more true to life than all those happily-ever-after stories she was raised on. It comforted her to see bad times fall on other people, too. It allowed her to feel like her life wasn't so terribly awful after all. About half way through the movie, she realized it was not working. Bernardo had already forbidden Maria to see Tony. The lovers were heartbroken, but Avi didn't feel one bit better. Frustrated, she fast-forwarded to the really sad part, where Tony dies in Maria's arms. She replayed it five times. It didn't make her smile, as usual. It only made her feel worse—jealous, even. At least Maria could say she had found the great love of her life, even if he died soon after. And Tony? Well, he was dead, wasn't he? At least he was out of his misery. At that thought, Avi knew she was slipping deeper and deeper into desperate despair. Some sense of self-preservation told her she should go out. Anywhere. Just out. She needed milk and was practically out of toilet paper. Even a short trip to the twenty-four-hour grocery store would be better than staying at home. She threw on a pair of black jeans, a T-shirt, and her black leather jacket. On the way out the door she grabbed her plain white motorcycle helmet and her black leather gloves. Outside on the street, she stood beside her bright red Honda scooter, waiting for its small engine to warm up.

The Save-On-Groceries store was brightly lit, with fluorescent lights everywhere. Easy-listening music seeped out of speakers mounted high on the walls. People walked down the aisles, slowly stopping to read labels, compare prices, squeeze fruit, and order deli items. Avi pushed past an obnoxious het couple who were kissing and hugging shamelessly, right in the canned-soup aisle. She headed directly for the snack-food section. Depression was as good a reason as any to stock up on cookies, potato chips, chocolate bars, ice cream, and Pepsi. She was standing in front of the cookies, debating between Oreos and Fudgeos, when she heard the unmistakable sound of a runaway shopping cart, hard rubber wheels against polished linoleum floor, the rattle of wire mesh, apples dropping, a crash as a milk bottle exploded against tile, metal cans clinking furiously against each other. For a moment Avi thought there was an earthquake, but then she realized it wasn't the ground that was shaking—it was the walls. For the next few seconds cans fell off shelves, boxes bounced through the air, fruit and vegetables rolled down the aisles. The sound of wheels grew louder and Avi saw a shopping cart heading right for her. Instinctively she dove out of the way, right into a cardboard Mr. Christie display, featuring three smiling children with chocolate-smeared faces happily munching on the latest in cookie chic, Oreo Triple Stacks.

In the fall, Avi bumped her head against a stainless steel shelf and for a moment lay on the floor, out cold.

Through the hazy throb of a long, hard headache, Avi heard the sweet melody of a soft golden voice, one that reached deep inside her heart and wrapped tender loving arms around her instantly, seductively, profoundly.

"Are you okay?" the voice repeated.

Avi shook her head to clear the stars, and the most beautiful woman she had ever seen came slowly into focus. Radiant soft brown eyes, long black hair, full lips covered in rose lipstick, high cheekbones, a lovely, strong, sensuous face. She was dressed in tight blue denim shorts and a slinky, low-cut hot-pink sweater. Avi could see the strap of a black lace bra underneath, resting seductively on her lovely shoulder. The woman's voice was gentle, soothing, sexy. A sense of peace flowed over Avi Shmacha. A small, delicate hand came down and gripped her shoulder tenderly. Avi's heart flipped over in her chest. Desire surged through her body. She was In Love. This was the woman she had been waiting for all her life. This was her Princess. The Woman Of Her Dreams. Her Other Half. Her Girlfriend. Her Lover. Her One And Only. Her True Love. Her Bride-To-Be. Her Sweetheart. Her Baby. Her Life. Avi knew exactly how Tony felt the first instant he saw Maria.

There's a place for us. Somewhere, a place for us. Hold my hand and I'll take you there. Hold my hand and we're halfway there.

She tried to sit up. The heavenly hand helped her.

"Are you okay?"

Avi smiled bravely and reached back to feel a huge bump growing on the back of her head.

"Can you stand?" The enchanting woman's perfume was enticingly exquisite. Avi inhaled deeply, even swooned a little bit.

"I think so."

"Let me help you. Put your arms around my neck." Avi thought she was going to die of happiness. She did as she was told. The beautiful woman put her arms around Avi's back. "Okay." Avi looked deep into the Princess's eyes. She thought she saw them smile. "On the count of three." Avi felt her True Love's breath on her cheek. "One. Two. Three."

With all her might, Avi stood. Her legs were wobbly, but her Princess held her up. Avi laughed to herself because they had it all wrong. She was the butch. She was supposed to help the Damsel in Distress, not the other way around. But she figured that feminism had changed all that, so she might as well enjoy herself. Anyway, it's not like the Butch Police were there monitoring her every move.

Just in case, however, she glanced over her shoulder to see whether anyone was watching.

"Can you stand by yourself?" The Princess smiled as she spoke.

"I—I'm not sure. I think so."

Slowly, her True Love slipped her hands away from Avi Shmacha's waist. Avi missed them the second they left. She felt as though someone had suddenly rocket-launched her spirit into outer space, far out into the cosmos, and, helpless, she could do nothing but watch as Her One True Love grew smaller and smaller, and she—Avi—was banished once again to the far reaches of the universe, floating aimlessly, unattached to anything or anybody. Avi could barely contain the moan that rose in her throat. Reluctantly, she released her hands from around her Sweetheart's neck. She thought she saw disappointment in her Sweet Pea's eyes, but it could have been something else, too. Shyness, maybe, or perhaps pity.

"You were out cold for a minute. You must have hit your head."

I love you, Avi wanted to say, but in this day and age you just didn't get away with saying those kinds of things to perfect strangers. She didn't even know if Her New Girlfriend was straight or gay. What if she freaked out? What if she screamed? What if she had a boyfriend? For the first time, Avi glanced around. The aisle was littered with fallen boxes, bottles, and cans. People were yelling. A baby was crying. There was the periodic crash of a stray bottle falling to the floor, boxes sliding from shelves, bulk grains pouring from plastic cases. From outside, the wail of a distant siren grew closer.

"What happened?" Avi asked her True Love.

"Look." Avi's One And Only pointed. A huge yellow truck had

crashed through the front window. It now sat halfway in and halfway out of the store, wheels spinning, smoke streaming from its engine, tiny shards of glass scattered all over its windshield, hood, and on the floor. The front bumper was mangled. The side doors of the rig were thrown open and on the ground a thick golden syrupy liquid spread out onto the asphalt parking lot. Broken bits of glass reflected light from street lamps, like diamonds. In fancy old-fashioned script, painted on the side of the truck were the words *Golden's Miracle Honey, 100% Natural.* The driver—a woman—appeared unhurt and stood beside her rig, hands on hips, eyes wide, shaking her head back and forth over and over, as if she was trying to register what had happened. Her truck must have gone out of control, which is exactly how Avi's emotions felt. She looked again at the face of her Lover-To-Be and her heart filled with magic. She knew she was destined to be with this woman as surely as she had ever known anything in her life. Her Betrothed didn't know it yet, but that would come in time, Avi knew. She smiled wide, even though her head hurt. She could never remember being so happy before in her life. She stuck out her hand slowly.

"My name is Avi," she whispered.

Her Beloved smiled, the most wonderful smile. "I am Akami." And she reached out her hand as well. When they touched, Avi held the sweet hand in hers. She felt love all through her body, exploding inside. She was aware of nothing but Akami, her beautiful face, sensuous body, sweet harmonious voice, and of her own heart beating wildly in her chest.

Suddenly the music from the speakers went off. There was a crackle, and then a man's voice.

"Attention, shoppers."

For a moment, Avi thought he was going to announce the weekly specials.

"Please try to stay calm. I repeat. Shoppers, please try to stay calm." At just that second, a woman down the aisle screamed and then fainted. Her husband dropped to his knees and leaned over her, helpless.

"There's been an accident," the voice continued. As if no one had noticed. "If you are hurt, please stay where you are. Medical help is on the way. If you are not hurt, please leave your groceries and walk in an orderly fashion toward the nearest exit."

People all around took that as a cue to load up baskets with food and run out the side doors without paying.

Avi knew nothing but happiness, as she turned again to face her Beloved. Just then, a Giant butch with a crew cut, leather jacket, and Doc Martens stomped over.

"You ready?" she growled. Avi could tell that the large woman was Akami's lover. Her heart sank right through to the basement.

"Loran, this is Avi," Akami said.

Loran nodded curtly. "Come on. Let's get out of here."

Slowly, reluctantly, Akami slipped her hand away. Avi's heart followed. It was wrenched abruptly from her chest, leaving nothing but a large and empty hole. Lovesick, she secretly followed Akami all the way home and hid in the bushes across the street, watching and waiting. Akami and the mean Giant girlfriend lived on the main floor of a house on East Eighth Avenue, not far from Avi's place, in the local dyke ghetto. A white stucco house, with green wood shutters and a flower bed in front. Pink and red roses grew up the sides of a white picket fence. A cobblestone walk curved up to the front door. A chimney poked up from the center of the house. Like out of a fairy tale. From what Avi could see, however, their relationship was more like a horror flick. Avi knew this because after that day, she spied on them all the time. The oaf watched a lot of football and drank a lot of beer. She often went out by herself at night, would throw the front door open, jump into her battered big blue pickup truck, and roar off into the night. She never helped out around the house, and sometimes Avi could hear her yelling at Akami. Avi forced herself not to go charging in, because how could she explain spying on them from across the street? But she swore to herself if she ever suspected the Giant was hitting her Beloved, she'd bust down the front door and punch the living daylights out of the brute.

Meanwhile she spent her days at work pining over her Future Wife, waiting for the day when they would finally be together. And she spent her nights hiding behind a large pink rhododendron bush across the street from Akami's house, where she had a clear view of the living room and part of the kitchen. She had figured out that the bedroom window was along the side of the house but, short of being inside the neighbor's place, there was no way she could see in. Sometimes she wished she could. Other times when she was sure her Sweetheart was having sex with the cloddish Giant butch, Avi was glad she had no way of watching. She knew it would tear her up to see that.

On the nights when the ogre took off in her truck, Avi was tempted to knock on the door and dashingly sweep her precious Princess right off her feet. She had it all figured out. She'd dress up real nice, in a jacket and tie, ring the bell, and wait on the front stoop with a dozen long-stemmed red roses. Akami would answer the door, draped in a black lace nightgown, one strap sliding seductively down her succulent shoulder. Her hair would be a little messy and her face would be soft and sexy. She'd recognize Avi instantly. Wordless, they would gaze into each other's eyes. Slowly, almost imperceptibly, they would move toward each other until their lips met. Avi would take her Beauty in her arms, and they would kiss passionately, furiously, haphazardly crushing the flowers between their aching bodies. Her arms would be around her Lady Love's waist, whose sweet, soft hands would be around her neck. An ageless lust would push up from the depths of her soul, crashing forward like the pounding surf of open ocean. Salty, wet, blue, black, bottomless waves, rolling, crashing, colliding hungrily, breathless, desperate, and free. They would be swept away in a titanic storm, overtaken by their passion, lost in its rhythm. Avi would hold her Sweet Babe in her arms, kiss her deep and long. Akami would call out her name as Avi slowly slid her nightgown down. Her hands would be on her Beloved's breasts, nipples growing hard under her fingers. Akami's legs would wind their way around Avi's, their mutual need pushing and pressing against each other, unaware of everything but their love, their desire, and their bodies which, naturally, fit together perfectly. Everything would go into soft focus, just like in the movies, and Avi would carry her love off into the sunset, where for the rest of their days they would be happy.

Oh, how Avi longed for the courage to approach the Love Of Her Life. She'd fantasize about their meeting over and over, from her spot in the bushes, but she never quite worked up the guts actually to move. She had come close once or twice, but just as she'd stand, smooth down her hair with the palm of her hand and take that first step toward the house, she'd hear the all-too-familiar rumble of the Giant's battered pickup truck and she'd slink back to her hidden perch across the street.

In a very short time, Avi had become a woman obsessed. Every night, she'd gobble down a hasty supper alone and ride over to her Beloved's little house. She'd go three blocks out of her way, sneak through the back alley, and settle in for the evening. She'd bring a chair, binoculars, a camera with a telephoto lens, a thermos of hot tea, and usually some snacks. She'd stay until the lights in the little stucco house went out and her Princess went off to bed. Sometimes she'd stay a little longer. Then, slowly, sadly, she'd gather her things, strap them to the back of her scooter and, dispirited, despondently make her way home to her lonely apartment six blocks away. At first, Avi's friends kept inviting her to dinner, out for a drink, or to their parties. But as the weeks turned into months and Avi continued to reject their invitations, one by one all her friends disappeared, until the only people she saw outside of her

Betrothed and the Giant were the people she worked with. And as time went on and she became quieter and more reclusive, even they spoke to her less and less and less, until they addressed her only when absolutely necessary. Since most of her work was behind a computer screen, that didn't happen very often. Sometimes weeks would go by and Avi had not uttered a single word.

Two years to the day that she had first laid eyes on her Love, a miracle happened. She was at her post across the street in the bushes, watching Akami's house absentmindedly, feeling kind of blue. She was starting to lose hope. Some days she feared her dream would never come true. She knew it was crazy to spend every single night alone, hiding behind two big bushes, waiting and watching. Every day she told herself she would not spy on her Beloved anymore. And every night she broke her promise. She just couldn't stay away.

It had been a quiet evening. Avi's beautiful Lover-To-Be was in the kitchen cooking—muffins, as far as she could tell. Probably for the ogre's lunch. It had been lovely at first, to watch her Princess flow through the kitchen, measuring ingredients, humming softly to herself, wiping her delicate hands on her lacy white apron. But then she had gone to sit at the table, which was out of Avi's view. She knew Akami was still there, but couldn't see her. And the oaf was at her usual spot, watching the football game from the living-room couch, a can of beer in one hand, a bowl of pretzels in her lap.

The rumbling grabbed Avi's attention. It was beneath her feet, under her chair. It felt as if the whole ground was shaking. She leapt up. A terrible roar was hurtling down the street. She could see a large yellow truck barreling down the hill. It sped closer and closer. Avi gasped. The truck was heading right for her Beloved's little house. Avi ran out of the bushes and toward the street. There had to be something she could do. She yelled. Suddenly, the truck swerved to the left. The world went into slow motion as the yellow beast jumped over the curb, across the green lawn, and stopped mere inches from the house. A gargantuan butch leaped from the seat, marched up the cobblestone walk, flung open the front door, and stomped over to where Akami's half-drunk Giant girlfriend trembled in fear and disbelief. The even-larger truck driver grabbed Loran by the scruff of the neck, picked her up, and threw her against the back wall of the living room. Avi watched the whole scene from the middle of the lawn, using her binoculars to get a better view. She couldn't hear, so she moved closer and hovered in the doorway.

"I know it's you been messing with my girlfriend," the huge truck driver bellowed.

"No. No. You're mistaken." Loran groveled.

"No such luck, Casanova. I found this picture in her purse." She held a small square photo an inch from the Giant's nose. "That's you, all right."

"Okay. Listen. Why don't you put me down. Maybe we can make a deal or something."

"A deal? What? Like money? You think you can buy me?"

Loran groveled further. "No. No. Course not. Please. Don't hurt me."

"Hah! You're lucky I didn't run you over."

"Please. Just put me down. Let's talk about this."

Avi watched in awe, as her Beauty entered the living room, a look of righteous indignation written all over her lovely face. "Yes, Loran. What a good idea. Let's talk about this."

The truck driver held Loran tightly by her shirt, pushing her farther up against the wall. She winked at Akami. "Go ahead, honey. Take your best shot."

"What? You mean hit her?"

"Sure—why not?"

Yeah. Why not? Avi thought, hiding not-so-carefully on the front stoop behind the door frame.

Akami thought about it for a moment. "No. I don't think she

deserves it." She moved closer to Loran's face and spoke quietly. "It's over, Loran. I should have expected something like this from you. I trusted you. That's the worst part. I trusted you."

"Please, babe. We can work it out."

"Work what out? You disgust me. Get out of my house."

"Please, baby."

"Get out."

"You heard the lady." The truck driver barked. Without so much as stopping for her coat, the oaf weaseled out of the truck driver's grip, crept past Akami, and scurried out of the house, with her tail most definitely between her legs. She raced past Avi, jumped into her pickup and rattled up the road. The truck driver tipped her yellow baseball cap ever so politely. "Sorry to barge in on you." She nodded and headed for the door. "Oh, and sorry you had to find out about it this way."

Akami just stood where she was and shook her head sadly.

On her way out, the truck driver bumped into Avi who, by then, was standing right in the middle of the doorway.

"Oh. Sorry," the driver said.

"That's okay." Avi grabbed her hand and shook it enthusiastically. "Thank you. Thank you very much."

The driver raised one eyebrow, pulled back her hand, and walked across the lawn to her truck.

Inside, Akami was struck with a strange feeling of déjà vu. When Avi turned to her and their eyes met, a sense of the familiar grew even stronger. She walked toward Avi, until she was standing before her. She studied the handsome face, looked deeply into Avi's Shmacha's sad brown eyes. The recognition was so strong that she knew everything all at once.

"It's you," Akami said softly, her words like music.

"You remember me?"

Akami did remember. "The grocery store. The accident. You fell and hit your head. Oh, my God! Look. It's the same truck."

As the driver pulled the huge yellow rig out into the street, they stood and watched. Neither one was surprised to see the words *Golden's Miracle Honey* painted on the side.

Some ancient, deep-buried body memory rose in both women simultaneously. Wordless, Avi raised one hand. Akami did the same. When they touched, it was like finding a missing piece. Avi's heart swelled, and desire, which began somewhere deep in her belly, spread throughout her body. Akami was so lovely. She was wearing a tight black dress that hugged her hips and exposed her sensuous cleavage. In her white lace apron, she was innocence and sex combined. She had the same rose lipstick on her lush full lips that Avi had seen the first day they had met. Avi had dreamed of kissing those lips a hundred thousand times. She smiled at her Princess, who smiled back. Just like Avi, Akami knew in her heart their meeting was meant to be. There were times over the last two years when she had thought about the handsome butch she'd met in the cookie section of the twenty-four hour grocery store, had wondered when they would meet again, sure that the day would come when they would. Had known it all along. Had felt it in her heart and sometimes very late at night, especially during a full moon, deep inside her belly and down to her cunt, which ached with desire.

"I've been waiting for you," she said as Avi held her hand tightly.

"You have?"

"Of course."

And then the most wonderful thing happened. Akami stepped up on her toes and kissed Avi. It was just how Avi imagined it would be. Magical. Sweet, hot, passionate, fiery feelings, swirling, burning, aching, rising, full, happy, sensuous, love, lust, circling all around and within. Akami threw her arms around Avi's neck. Avi held her Sweetheart tenderly around her slender waist and pulled her close. They were aware of nothing but the taste of each other. Sweet like honey. Pulling, sliding, in and out. Avi's hands held Akami at the small of her back. Her Princess pushed her breasts against her. They couldn't get close enough. Avi kissed her Baby all over, her face, her neck, and down. Hands everywhere all at once. Touching, stroking, grabbing. In the doorway of the little house, passion rose and fell like the tides. Avi held Akami tightly, kissing her everywhere. Akami moaned and buried her face in her Truelove's neck. Avi was so overcome with desire that she forgot who she was. Like the Knight In Shining Armor she was destined to be, she reached down and scooped her Lover up into her arms, carried her inside the house, where she lay her down on the living-room couch and lay on top of her, pulling her tight, trying to get closer, closer, and closer still. Drowning in lust, they clutched at each other, tearing clothes away, one by one. Black jeans, white apron, lacy bra, shirts and socks, all ripped off. They were lost in their breath, their bodies, their need. They were drifting away in a deep, wide expanse of pleasure. Confidently, Avi slipped off her Lover's black panties and slid two, then three fingers inside her wet cunt. She knew just how her Angel liked it. Hard and slow. Slow and Hard. Then faster, faster, more, yes, deeper, harder, yes, yes, yes, baby, oh baby, oh lover, oh god. Oh god. Oh god, yes. Akami clutched Avi Shmacha tightly, breathing heavy and fast as she came, the rise and fall of her passion so beautiful it almost broke Avi's heart. As her breathing calmed, Avi held her with strong arms. And they both knew she would never let go again. Avi was sure the reappearance of *Golden's Miracle Honey* truck was no coincidence. Something magical had happened. She was a changed woman. Where she had once been clumsy, insecure, inept, now she was charming, confident, gallant. Every fantasy she'd ever had was coming true all at once. With her Princess, she really was a Prince Charming. For the rest of the night, she took her sweet Lover with all her passion, all her love, and the desire of ten Don Juans, kissed her mouth, neck, face, and breasts, fucked her hard and fast, slow and soft, all through the long, lovely night, while her Beloved moaned and sighed with pleasure.

And they lived happily ever after.

The next day, over a light breakfast of yogurt and granola, like true lesbians, the new lovers decided to move in together. After all, they were in love. Avi went to the phone and rented a U-Haul for the very next day.

The Story of the Youth Who Went Forth to Learn What Fear Was
HEATHER LEWIS

Initially I felt drawn by the title; but when I read the story, I wasn't convinced I wanted to work with it. I found the ending particularly unsatisfying. It reduced the story to a joke with a disappointing punch line. But still the story stuck with me—became the one I wanted to do, or redo. Refashioning it allowed me to compress all my favorite themes into one simple tale.

A certain father had two daughters. The elder possessed an obedient and compliant nature. She brought joy and promise to her father. And when the people of the village happened upon her running his errands, they said to themselves and each other, "She will marry well," and "Look how she brings happiness to her father."

Not so with the younger. Though guileless and pure of heart, she could not obey without question. She could not keep from questioning, and so could not behave in the manner required by her father. When the people of the village saw her, they whispered and hissed, "That one is trouble. No good will come of her." And as time passed they named her Trouble, laughing and taunting her as she passed.

Because Trouble's heart was tender, these public jeers wounded her. At home it was no better. Her elder sister delighted in ridiculing her, and their father had long since convinced himself of his younger daughter's useless character and missed no opportunity to remind her of this.

Though she had not begun this way, Trouble came to believe what was said of her and determined to find what was the matter. One night the father bade his elder daughter to fetch him tobacco and spirits from a friend beyond the village border. As this trip meant crossing the church graveyard and then taking a path through the forest, the elder daughter replied, "Oh, no, Daddy. I could not venture there. Not in the dead of night. The very thought makes me shudder."

The younger daughter, still eager to please and fearless, volunteered. But, instead of the praise she had hoped for, more ridicule ensued. The elder sister laughed and said, "Yes, you go. You are too stupid to know to be afraid."

And their father joined in, saying, "Yes, go on, then, for we need not concern ourselves with what comes to you."

So the younger daughter ventured out with these words in her heart. As she walked, she began to believe perhaps this was the thing the matter with her.

Two nights passed. On the third, the father and his daughters gathered by the fire to tell stories with some others villagers. The stories were of ghosts and goblins and things under the earth. As they were told, the listeners and teller alike would say, "It makes me shudder to hear such tales."

The younger daughter sat in a corner, away from the others, as she always did when people gathered. Lonely and bewildered, she said to herself, "It does not make me shudder. I know nothing of shuddering. I think that is the trouble with me."

Not long after, her father called to her and said, "You must go out and fend for yourself. I cannot keep throwing my good money after bad."

Still eager to please, the younger sister said, "I will learn to shudder, and then I can earn my keep."

Hearing this, the older sister laughed loudly and cruelly, saying, "What a good-for-nothing dolt you are."

Their father did not laugh, but angered, said, "You shall soon learn what it is to shudder, but it will not earn your keep."

The father came at his younger daughter with his strap, but this did not frighten her. It never had. It only made her sad and pained her a little and bewildered her again that she could not ever seem to please him.

He left off lashing her but, though tired, he was not finished with his anger. "Get out of my sight. You bring nothing but trouble. Take your trouble somewhere else and do not return here. And tell no one you came from here. Never speak of me to others. Tell no one you carry my name, for you bring me only shame."

And he threw a bag of coins to her, and watched her limp away, feeling not heaviness in his heart but only hardness. He had done no wrong, he had used her as any widowed father would use a daughter. His elder daughter he'd used, too, for the things a wife must provide—cooking and cleaning and so forth. She had no complaints. He had asked this younger one only for the other things a man must have, no more. There was nothing the matter with him, only inside her. Of this he was sure.

But Trouble was not sure of anything. And her heart felt heavy as she dragged it away. And she felt her father's hardness, for she could always feel what others felt. As she clutched his bag of coins, she determined one last way to make him proud. She would make her heart as hard as his.

Perhaps she could not feel fear because her heart was too crowded with these other things, these useless things. It felt too much else to have a place for fear. "Yes," she said to herself, "this is what must be done. I will harden my heart and that will teach me to shudder, and these other things inside that cause trouble will go away. I will be like everybody else."

She walked and walked the road all night and when day came a man drew near her on the road. She was still muttering to herself about shuddering, and he had overheard. He said to her, "I know a place where you can learn to shudder."

The girl was overjoyed. "Take me there."

The two together walked farther down the road to a field. Once there, the man pointed to a tree in the center of the field. Seven men hung from its branches, swaying in the breeze. "Go there," the man said. "Spend the night beneath that tree, and you will learn to shudder."

"Is that all?" the girl said.

The man nodded, so she said, "If it be learned so easily, you will have earned this bag of coins. Come back in the morning. If I know what it is to shudder, this bag is yours."

She made her way to the tree and sat beneath it, waiting. And the wind blew stronger as the sun set and her companions above whirled around her. She did not shudder, though. All she felt was cold. She built a fire, but the wind grew stronger still and bit her face and hands. The men above her began to knock and bang, capturing her attention. And though she had promised to keep her heart hard, she could not. She thought, If I am so cold, they must be colder still.

She climbed the tree, and carried each one down to sit by her fire. They did not move, but sat pressed against one another. And they seemed not to notice when their ragged clothes began to catch on fire.

She yelled at them to beware of the fire, but they did not heed her words. She yelled that she would string them up again, but they still paid her no mind. Angry now, she carried them back up, one by one, and hanged them again. When she had finished with the last one, she climbed back down and, tired from her labor, fell asleep.

The man awoke her the next morning, wanting the bag of coins. She said, "But I have not learned yet. At first I could not keep my heart hard, so I carried them down so they could warm themselves. I thought, 'This is my trouble.' But then my heart became hard toward them because they let their clothes burn and paid me no mind and kept me no company. I strung them back up and my heart was truly hard, but still I did not shudder."

The man looked at her. Backing away, he said, "What kind of girl is this?"

The girl got up and began again to walk the road. As she walked, she worried aloud, saying, "If I could but shudder," over and over until she walked in step with her voice.

At midday a wagoner overtook her and called down to her, "What's that strange walking song you sing?"

Caught unaware, the girl said, "It's not a song. I need to learn to shudder."

Taken by her at once, the wagoner said, "Who are you?"

"I do not know."

"Well, where do you come from?"

She repeated, "I do not know."

"Who is your father?" the wagoner asked finally.

"I cannot tell you."

"Well, one so fair should not have to walk alone. Come along with me."

The girl climbed up and off they went. But as they drove along the girl spoke again of her desire to learn to shudder. The wagoner looked upon her with curiosity. And the girl sensed something else within him. She entreated him to speak of what he knew but had not said.

He reined in his horses. Stopped there in the road he gazed at her while still not speaking. She felt him weighing things in his mind before he spoke at last, saying, "I know of a place not far from here where you may learn all you need know of shuddering."

The girl's eyes grew wide and hopeful, so he continued haltingly, telling her, "There is a haunted castle nearby. Venture inside it, and you would surely learn to shudder. But you would not come out again. No one has. That is why the Queen has promised her daughter's hand to anyone who spends three nights there."

The wagoner told more. He told of a treasure stolen from the Queen. It lay within the castle guarded there by demons. Only one who spent three nights there could free the treasure, and for this would lay claim to a portion of it. But the girl heard little of what he said. She cared not for fortune. Nor did she care for the hand of the Queen's daughter. She knew nothing of women's hands; had never felt a woman's hand. Her mother had died as she was born. And what she knew of men had come at the hands of her father. She cared only for her quest to shudder.

"Please," she said, "take me to this Queen."

The wagoner agreed but reluctantly, and they set off again. When they reached the Queen's palace, he pulled his horses to a stop. At once the girl started to jump down, but he took her arm to slow her. She turned to him and he lay one palm gently against her cheek. And as he did this the girl felt a tremble begin somewhere inside her. But it passed so quickly that she could not quite grasp its feeling.

She looked to the wagoner with questioning eyes. He said only, "I do not want one so fair as you to meet her end in such a place, but I know I cannot stop you."

The girl wondered at his kindness, a thing no one else had shown her. She wondered, too, at the heaviness in his heart, a thing she had felt from no one, but had felt only inside herself. And then there it was again, the little tremble and then gone again.

And as she made her way to the Queen's gates, she gazed back to see him looking after her. It gave her pause, but she pressed on.

She quickly struck her bargain with the Queen. The Queen allowed her three things and three things only—and not living things—to take with her into the castle. Without hesitation, she chose a fire, a turning lathe, and a cutting board with a knife. These things were carried with her to the castle.

As the first night approached, the girl made her fire and sat beside it with her other things close at hand. But she grew sad, believing she would not find her quest here. And she thought again of the wagoner and his gentle hand. And wondered about hands not used for hitting. She tried to recapture the trembling she had felt, but she could not. It had been too fleeting, just a murmur.

She poked her fire and waited as it grew darker, and darker still, outside. As this day turned to the next one, she heard a sound. A whimpering came from a corner, a howling saying, "We are so cold."

"Well," said the girl, "come warm yourselves by my fire."

Two great panthers came from the shadows and sat on either side of her. Their eyes grew fierce in the firelight. And their great tongues came out their mouths, licking themselves with blood thirst. And strangely, they said to the girl, "Let's have a game of cards."

The girl agreed but, still thinking as she was of hands, she asked to see their paws. They showed them to her and she saw great claws there. She thought, 'These paws will not be gentle with those long, sharp things.' Aloud she said, "Let me cut your nails so you may better hold the cards. And swiftly she grabbed each by its neck and fixed their paws to the cutting board and cut their claws.

But when she let them up again, she saw this had not made them gentle. The blood lust still shone from their eyes, and she could feel no hearts in them at all. So as they came at her, baring teeth longer and sharper than any claws, she took her knife and slashed their throats.

Done with these two, she went to retake her place by the fire when from every crevice and corner came ferocious animals, swinging white-hot chains and growling fiercely. She took up her blade again and, holding out her arm, began to whirl and whirl, slashing throats and bellies until no more came at her. She now stood in their blood and some of it bubbled in her fire. She looked about her and said, "What a mess!"

She took the nearest beast and cleaned her blade on its fur and then began hauling carcasses out the door, one after another. And as each one hit the outside air, it vanished from her hands. When she had finished her cleaning, she sat again beside her fire and grew sleepy. Seeing a bed in the corner, she took to it. But soon as she had, it began to jump and move about, taking her all around the castle.

And she, who had not known beds except her father's and had otherwise slept on floors, said to herself, "Now I see what all the fun is. Why people talk so fondly of beds and make so many jokes about them. And why they say they've been in them but have not slept, but had a great time nonetheless."

But just as she thought this, the bed came to a halt and then threw itself atop her. She kicked it off, saying, "I've had enough of this fun." And again she took her place by her fire and lay down to sleep there on the floor, as was her custom. But as she drifted into sleep she said to herself, "I still know nothing of shuddering and I do not think I'll learn it here."

The Queen came the next day, for the castle was safe by daylight. When she entered, she saw the girl still sleeping on the floor and naturally thought her dead. The Queen moaned aloud, crying, "What a shame, for I would've liked so fair a girl to have my daughter's hand. I believed in this one."

The Queen's voice woke the girl, and the praise and kindness of her words brought a curious fluttering to the young one's heart. But then it had gone again. Seeing the girl alive, the Queen spoke joyfully, and asked happily how the night had been spent. The girl said only that she had fared well, but had not learned to shudder.

The Queen, whose aims were quite different from the girl's, said, "I'm so pleased that you are well."

The girl remained in the castle. As that day turned to night, she heard a great tumult growing louder and louder from inside the chimney. At last a great busting, breaking sound shattered the air, and half a man lay before her. And then the rumbling began again until his other half popped out. When these two halves were joined, they made a monstrous figure.

Then more noise, and more men came from the chimney in bits and pieces that joined together. And these ghoulish beings pulled skulls and bones from inside the chimney. They set the bones as ninepins and used the skulls as balls and set about to have a game.

The girl stopped them, saying, "If you let me play, I'll make your skulls roll better. The ghouls looked to her and then at each other and, all agreed, they handed her the skulls. She fixed them with her lathe, making them smooth and round. And in gratitude they let her throw the first one. And so she put her fingers into the eye sockets and her thumb where a nose had been. And she threw the skull, knocking down all the bones.

She had some fun with them, but at the first signs of light, they vanished, as did the bones and skulls. And now, alone, she remembered that she had not yet found what she was seeking. A sad and hopeless feeling grew in her, broken only by the Queen's midday visit. Seeing the girl so sad, she asked, "Have you not yet shuddered?"

And the girl felt something again, that small quaver too swift to capture. She felt it because the Queen had remembered her quest and remarked upon it with earnestness. And, too, she seemed grieved that the girl had not obtained it.

So again she was left alone to wonder and try to conjure that flighty, fleeting thing, but she could not. As this day turned to the next, more men appeared, carrying a coffin. Inside it was the girl's dead aunt. And though this relation had treated her no better than the others, her heart welled up and she bent to touch the dead woman's cheek. But it felt cold as ice, yet burned.

The girl next carried her dead aunt to the fire to try and warm her there. She held fast to her, but none of this would do. The girl thought and thought of something else to try and finally a new idea came to her. She said aloud, "When two people go to bed together, it is said to warm them. I'll try this, aunt."

So she took her aunt to bed and sure enough as they lay together the dead woman grew warm and soon began to move a little. The girl felt good in this and cried out, "See, I have warmed you."

But her aunt rose up and shouted, "I will strangle you!"

The girl had had enough of threats like these from family, so she said, "No, you won't," with great force behind her voice. And force was in her body when she seized her aunt and dragged her back to her coffin and shut her in there. And the men who had brought the coffin carried it back out.

Once again the girl sat by her fire. She poked at it without energy and nearly wailed because she had not learned to shudder. A figure appeared, neither man nor woman, neither dead nor live. Grotesquely misshapen, it held all the features of all the family this girl had ever known. And so there was this one's eye and that one's ear, and another's nose, and what of these could not fit on its face were strewn here and there upon its body.

Yet there was just one set of hands—the kind that hit and strangle. And just one set of feet—the kind that kick and squash things underneath. And just one heart—a dry and hard and shriveled thing to be clearly seen through papery skin. And this huge monstrosity bellowed out, "You will learn to shudder from me. You will shudder as you die by my hand."

The girl cried back, "I will *not* learn from you. What I learned from you has been all wrong. I'm stronger now than you."

"Is that so?" the figure said mockingly. "Well, then, you must prove this now."

"I need prove nothing to you, but if perhaps you will learn something from it I will try and show you."

The two went down a passage together. There stood an anvil and an ax. The monstrosity took the ax and knocked the anvil to the floor. With much gloating, it handed the ax to the girl, saying, "Can you do better."

Without a word, the girl took the ax and with one hand brought it down on the anvil, splitting it in halves. But the monster did not concede her victory. Instead the thing turned on her to kill her, but she used the dull end of the ax and began to bludgeon it.

At first she felt heady and roused with hate. It heated her and drove her on. Vengeance coursed through her veins, but soon it lost its fire. She took no more pleasure from delivering these blows. Found no satisfaction in revenge. And so, when the figure fell and lay at her feet, begging for mercy, she relented cautiously.

The monstrous thing then said, "You have won. I will release to you the castle's treasure."

The girl cared not for the treasure. Still she followed the creature for the Queen's sake. But she kept hold of the ax, for though the creature had shrunken and paled and she believed its words, she would no longer let her kindness blind her where it might well be unfounded.

Immense and overflowing, the treasure took three huge chests and still spilled out. The creature told her that one chest was for the poor, one for the Queen, and the third for her. Then it faded away. And as it did, the girl felt some sadness at its passing. She felt alone once more.

The Queen came at midday and rejoiced to find the girl alive and rejoiced, too, upon seeing the treasure. But the girl was not so happy. The Queen said kindly, "Come, now, what is it? You have freed the castle and shall marry my daughter. Are these not good things?"

"Yes, yes, but I have not yet shuddered."

The Queen regarded her fondly. "Perhaps you will still shudder."

And though the girl felt a knowingness in these words, she did not quite believe or understand. Instead she decided to forgo her quest, that it might no longer be hers.

Much merriment ensued. The girl met the Queen's daughter, a much older woman who had waited long for one who could free the castle. But the daughter was kind like her mother, and beautiful, too, and they soon married with great celebration.

On the night of their wedding, the two went to their bedroom. And there they found candles burning and flowers and a fire roaring in a great fireplace. Amidst all this stood their wedding bed, a huge, soft feather bed with pillows of all sizes and shapes. It promised much comfort.

But the girl hung back at the doorway, unsure whether to enter. Her bride asked what the trouble was. Feeling somewhat small and ungrateful, the girl said, "I cannot help it. I still wish to know what it is to shudder."

Her bride gathered her up in her arms and carried her in. And lay her down in the bed and undressed her and then undressed herself. And when they had nestled there together, the girl's bride said, "I can teach you that." These words were spoken with unarguable knowingness.

And then the woman's hands traveled the girl's body with the same knowingness. The girl began the kind of trembling she had felt only partly. She turned soft, trembling, fragile. And the woman's hands touched her in ways and places she had never known. And the woman kissed her, too. No one had ever done that.

And as the woman kissed her, the girl grew fearful in her trembling. And the woman's hand went inside her, feeling warm and gentle there, and this began her truly shuddering. And she shuddered and trembled and cried out before she grew peaceful again. And the woman's arms were strong around her, and she felt drowsy in them, though now and then the woman would trail her fingers gently where her hand had been and set the girl shuddering again.

And as they lay there, the woman asked the girl, "Was my word not true?"

The girl nodded happily and dreamily. And she took the woman's hand and put it against herself, wanting to know more of this shuddering, and know it to be hers.

Goldilocks and the Three Bears
DORSIE HATHAWAY

My mom began reading me fairy tales before I was two. My heart pounded every time Goldilocks went into the bears' house! Half of me couldn't believe she was doing it; the other half was fascinated that she dared. I made my mother read the story over and over. I'm sure it warped me, because I grew up with the perverse belief that I could break the rules and get away with it, just like Goldilocks. (Yes, I put my poor mom through hell in my teens. I'm trying to make it up to her.)

I'm certain now that "Goldilocks" was always a queer story. The bears are living up in a house in the woods just as nice as you please, everything looks the same as everyone else, except that they're bears—visibly different, mysterious, scary, unapproachable. One could only imagine how the bears lived—and that imagination was savage, yet on closer look, inside, they have relationships, furniture, regular meals. Even seeing it up close (taboo), Goldilocks glimpsed the bears' regular family life. She could interact with all the external stuff, but she could never be a part of the bears' life.

Transgression, sheer terror, and escaping with your life—what more could a kinky girl want?

Author's comment: Another version of this retelling had Goldilocks given to Devin as a butch apprentice in training, with weekly head-shaving routine. But the story wouldn't work that way because Goldilocks had compromised the bears' safety and security in the first place. She had to remain an outsider.

Once upon a time, there was a young dyke living in the City. Her name was Goldilocks. She was irrefutably Blonde. Goldilocks had a bad attitude. She hated her life. She hated her name. She especially hated her hair. It was a constant source of vexation. It seemed to grow faster every time she cut it. Seriously faster. It was a curly golden curse. No one could take her seriously with hair like that.

Her college sweetheart, C.C., moved out in February after a real wingding of an argument. It started with conflict over who would have the car that weekend, and escalated into a laundry list of sins of omission and commission accumulated during the past year. Included: The accusation that Goldilocks was a perpetual fuck-up in the area of laundry. More specifically, that she had thrown C.C.'s delicate lingerie into the extra-heavy-duty wash cycle with the denims…and then into the extra-heavy-duty dryer. On hot. Goldilocks thought she might be guilty as charged, but she really didn't understand what C.C. would have preferred she do with the spooge-covered lacy things after a hard night's workout.

She didn't know what to say to begin to make things right, and according to C.C. she couldn't do anything right, and hadn't for some time. There were more accusations. Most of them true, but that was beside the point. She didn't like being blindsided. Goldilocks was seriously pissed. She sulked for a while and decided that it wasn't going to get her anywhere. She left to go get drunk, and came back the next morning to find her things out on the street. C.C. kept the apartment, the heavy-metal collection, and the kitten: Goldilocks didn't even protest. She moved into a studio in the Mission and thought about cutting designs in her forearms.

She considered therapy, but didn't have insurance, and the waiting list for sliding-scale therapy in the city was very long, unless she was suicidal, in which case they could see her in three months. Goldilocks went to work most days, and spent her spare time reading porn from the apartment building's lending library. She stomped a lot on the way to work.

Since the breakup, she wasn't making any headway on her student loans. Five years of college meant big debt. The mail came at three o'clock every afternoon, and at least twice a month it contained something threatening from the government. Every night, she tried not to think about the loans, working for Big Apple Pizza on the four-to-midnight shift. A friend once suggested that she wait and open the mail when she got home, but she knew she wouldn't sleep if she read threatening mail before bedtime. So Goldy did her thinking about the money she didn't have while she had eight hours to work with her hands, taking out her frustrations on the dough. She felt like a circus freak on display, tossing dough circles in the window. People stood outside just four feet away, watching her like a trained seal with a ball. Sometimes they applauded. She wished they'd leave tips instead.

Goldilocks wished she had studied engineering or computer science, instead of Sixteenth-Century European Literature. She suspected that the Big Apple Pizza manager, Jerry, had hired her for her looks: every other member of the "front office" staff wore a white toque, while she had a see-through hairnet. She would have preferred a toque. Every time she asked, the answer was, "They're on back order." The assistant manager, a cute dyke from Brooklyn, jokingly referred to Goldilocks as "The Great Blondini." Yeah. On display all day long in the front window, and she couldn't get a date to save her life.

Goldilocks fantasized about a radically different life, one in which she didn't have to make any decisions. Her favorite books contained tales of dominance, submission, or long service. Those were the ones that left her hot and edgy. While reading *The Market-place*, she jerked off every night. The stable scenes made her hot.... *I'd muck out the stable, wear a bridle and bit, or sleep in horse shit if it would make my owner happy.* They'd probably even make her learn to do laundry right. It could be A Good Thing.

One sunny day in April, when her restlessness had reached critical mass, Goldilocks decided to blow off work and go for a hike. She couldn't afford to take the night off, but it was that or start throwing pizza at the customers. She'd been thinking about razor blades and carving up her arm. Time off might be a good kick in the ass: nice hike, some fresh air, trees, lizards, exhaustion. *Bliss. As long as I don't run into any bears.*

Bright and early, Goldilocks packed everything she thought she'd need for her hike: Serengetis, her pocketknife, bottled water, a sack lunch. The metro bus map that passed for art in her apartment was rife with possibility, especially at the edges, where the roads vanished into the wilderness that was The County. She picked a random stop by closing her eyes and pointing. Around 11:00 A.M., Goldilocks stepped off the bus near Mariposa Road and went for a walk in the woods.

Goldilocks walked slowly at first, amazed at the number of homes lining both sides of the mountainous road. They started thinning out after the first half mile. Her hair was already getting damp. She gathered the mass of it in her hand, and tied it back with a bandanna. She reached for her water and then remembered. *Still on the bus. No big deal,* she could get water from someone's hose. All the houses she'd seen so far had security gates and dogs. She moved on, climbing into the hills, breathing a little harder. *Exercise is A Good Thing,* she told herself, panting. Houses were spaced farther apart here. She passed a mini-manse with a pair of Mercedeses in the driveway and a pair of llamas in the adjoining field. *Some weird yuppie dream. Gotta be Silicon Valley refugees.*

After that house, it seemed that Goldy crossed some invisible line into the past. Now, all the houses were different, older. Some clearly reflected hippie roots: There were *three* geodesic domes, and a few houses built from assortments of scrap building materials. Goldilocks was really thirsty now. *Must be about two.* Her head ached, and her legs needed a break. She was hungry, but didn't think she should eat until she had something to drink. Frankly, peanut butter and jelly without a drink was intimidating. Goldilocks kept hiking.

She hadn't seen a house now for nearly a mile. The road here was gravel and dirt, narrow, with deep ruts on either side where cascading spring rains had cut channels of their own design. It hadn't rained in a month, though. She was thirsty. She thought about turning back, but coming around a bend to the left, she arrived at the end of Mariposa Road and discovered an interesting house. It was a soaring A-frame, with a second-story balcony and a black front door. Closer inspection showed that the door was covered in leather. *Excellent!*

Goldilocks stepped up to the front porch and knocked, and discovered that leather was a very good sound-deadener. There was a pull-cord next to the door, and she pulled it. Inside the house, she heard a muted bell. She waited. One minute. Two minutes. No answer. She had to pee. Shifting her weight from one foot to the other, she called a hello up to the second story. Still, no one answered.

Goldilocks walked around outside of the house, peering in all the windows. Three chairs in the living room, and three at the kitchen counter, and no people. Really thirsty now, and she had to pee, and there was no one at home. She bit her lower lip. She knew that people peed in the woods, but she'd read so many fairy tales about little girls lost in the woods and eaten up that she'd as soon burst than risk meeting a bear (even though she was twenty-one and weighed 170 and was standing there in broad daylight).

Bees hummed around the sweet peas climbing the lattice around the back porch. *Bears. Hm.* Now she really needed to pee.

Goldilocks jiggled the back-door handle a bit, turned it, found resistance, and then turned it harder. It was locked. She was very thirsty. The bees were loud. She was annoyed and swatted at them. To the front door again. Again Goldilocks pulled the bell and waited for an answer. One minute. Two minutes. She hadn't tried the front-door latch before. She pressed the latch and pushed. To her great surprise, the door was unlocked. She was sure that no one would really mind if she just used the facilities, so Goldilocks opened the door farther and let herself in.

Goldilocks barely noticed that it was a very tidy house. She zipped through the living room to the kitchen, rummaged around until she found a glass, and helped herself to water from the free-standing cooler. She didn't notice the dusty yellow bootprints she left in the entryway and living room. She didn't notice the water she dripped on the kitchen floor, even when she walked across it on her hurried search for the bathroom.

It was upstairs, just to the left of the landing. She peed for two minutes, thinking that it was probably a good thing to have forgotten her bottled water, and headed back to the kitchen. There she drank more water, and started on her PBJ. The kitchen was clean and utilitarian, and there were several shelves of amber jars simply labeled HONEY. While eating her sandwich, Goldilocks looked in the refrigerator. Lots of glass jars without labels—probably weird natural foods. Nothing interesting there. She opened all the cabinets just to see what was inside, inadvertently leaving peanut butter on two of the door handles.

The living rooms had three different chairs. There was a large black leather-clad recliner, a medium-sized overstuffed rocking chair, and some lightweight modern balance chair that looked uncomfortable. She tried sitting in each of them for a minute. The balance chair nearly threw her on the floor. She couldn't figure out how to sit on it. The big black recliner was too tall to sit in comfortably. She dropped some crumbs on the rocker and tried to dust them off. She finished her sandwich and then went upstairs to pee again. Goldilocks left a faint trail of muddy bootprints across the living-room floor on her way.

She felt dirty. And sweaty. And tired. Eyeing the shower, she wondered where the owners of the house were, and how soon they might be back. She could take a shower pretty quickly.... Probably not A Good Idea. She settled for wetting a towel and running it all over her head and arms. It had a funky, earthy smell, something she couldn't quite place. Not an offensive smell, just...rich. While drying off, she realized how tired her legs really were. She hadn't slept well last night and had been hiking for a couple of hours. It couldn't hurt to just *look* at the rest of the house before leaving. Tossing the towel over the top of the shower door, Goldilocks stepped into the hallway and entered the first of three bedrooms.

Frigging Better Homes! She whistled. This must be the master bedroom: hushed, imposing, with polished wooden floors, dark woods, and a Persian rug. There was a sunken tub in one corner, a massive four-poster bed with a heavy quilt, and a nightstand. On the far wall was a gun rack, with two well-polished rifles locked in. Everything in the room gleamed, as if the owner didn't really live in it, but just kept it that way for special occasions. *Maybe they were on vacation.* Next to the gun rack, floor-to-ceiling windows opened onto the balcony she'd glimpsed earlier.

Crossing over the rug to the bed, Goldilocks left the unmistakable imprint of her boots, along with more dirt. The bed was firm. She tried bouncing on it, but it was too hard. That same smell from the towel was strong here. There was a large trunk with an ornate brass padlock at the foot of the bed. Fingering the lock, Goldilocks wondered what was inside. *Probably sex toys.* No sign of a key.

She opened the nightstand drawer, but all it held was a silver comb and a stash of honey sticks. *No one would notice if I had just one.* Biting the top off with her teeth, Goldilocks sucked down the sticky amber, jamming the empty wrapper in her back pocket. She didn't notice when it fell onto the carpet as she left the room.

Around the corner, the next room had a more lived-in look. A femme room, for sure. Wood floors again, a high, queen-sized four-poster bed, two nightstands, an antique dresser with a large mirror, and a freestanding full-length mirror. The bed had flow-ered sheets and a matching quilt, and five feather pillows. The heavy scent she had noticed earlier was strong in here, too. Goldilocks tried to sit on the edge of the bed, but it was so high that she had to turn around and climb up. She didn't think to look for a bed step. She didn't notice the smudges of yellow earth her boots left on the dust ruffle. *Way cushy.* She sat in the exact center of the bed and fell back against the stack of pillows, making a great *whoosh*. Lying flat on the bed, she saw several eyebolts in the ceiling. *Some-one's been having fun.* Then she noticed the canes on the wall. *Uh-huh. Big fun!*

Goldilocks clambered off the bed and checked out the balcony, leaving a damp spot on the pillow and goose down scattered on the floor. She opened the door, and stood out on the narrow deck overlooking the garden at the back of the house. She was surprised to see white boxes on stands in the backyard. At first she thought they were for bunnies, and then remembered she'd seen the same thing on that *Nova* special about killer bees. *Bee ranchers! That explained all the jars of honey in the kitchen.*

The last bedroom was more like an oversized closet; cozy, yet livable. *Hope they got a cut on the rent.* Its saving grace was the small skylight set up near the peak of the roof. The room must belong to a young person—Chicago Bears and Chicago Cubs posters on the walls, a mini-stereo, and a single bed. Goldilocks sat on the bed, testing. She lay down on it. *Just right. Warm here.* Goldilocks yawned. She stretched out on the bed and closed her eyes for a minute. She thought about the people who lived in the house, and wondered how kinky they really were, and if they'd ever thought about owning someone like her....

Ten to seven. Riley, Max, and Devin were returning from their city jobs. Devin collected the day's mail from the box near the road, and they headed up Mariposa in the 4x4. Dinner tonight would be fabulous. Watsonville artichokes, a crunchy baguette, and fresh salmon steaks for the grill. Max's tomatoes would make a great side dish.

Max growled, opening the door. "Devin!! You forgot to lock the door again!"

"I'm terribly sorry, Mistress." Devin bowed hir head.

Riley, a half-step behind Max with the groceries, stopped suddenly. "Stop—someone's been in the house." Yellow footprints were clearly visible on the living-room floor, and other things looked disturbed. The house had been spotless when they left that morning: Housekeeping was a required part of Devin's contract. Max backed up. Riley unholstered hir service weapon, growling, "I'll check it out." Max went back to the truck and sat down to wait. Devin stood nearby. Both were far more anxious than they appeared.

Riley expected to find the electronics missing but, at first glance, everything seemed to be in place. In the kitchen, a glass on the counter and muddy footprints. It was eighty fucking degrees already and no rain since February; where did *mud* come from? Riley's boot skidded on a puddle of water next to the cooler. *Boot. Water. Whoever had been in the house must have come on foot. Goddamn!* Devin's computer, shut down, kept silent watch on the workbench in the common room. *Whoever it was—probably kids—must have been looking for jewelry, money, anything small enough to carry away.*

The burglar should be long gone, but the muddy bootprints led to the stairs and there were none leading out the front door. Deeply pissed now, Riley went creeping up the stairs, trying to be impossibly quiet, pulse roaring in hir ears. Someone had been in the bathroom, it was obvious…and there was a damp towel hanging over the shower door! *Someone had decided to make themselves right at home. Goddamn.*

Mud on the floor and bootprints going in and out: Riley followed them cautiously to hir own bedroom door, standing wide open. Both prized rifles were still locked in the gun rack. That was a relief. Small relief. There was dirt on the floor, and the bed looked messy, but there was no one there.

Max's room was worse…mud on the dust ruffle. Riley grimaced. *There would be hell to pay for this!* Max craved safety and security, and this was a violation she wouldn't soon forget. Riley crossed the room cautiously; the balcony doors were open. Nobody.

Coming down the hall, Riley's heartbeat slowed, whu-thump, whu-thump…. Squaring hir shoulders, exhaling slowly, sie came around the door to Devin's room. There on the bed, faintly snoring, was the burglar! The form on the bed mumbled, moved, and rolled over. Dyke! A very blonde dyke. This somehow made Riley more furious. Sie put the gun to the offender's head, cocked it slowly, and growled, "What the *fuck* are you doing in *our* house?"

Goldilocks had been dreaming. She remembered bees, and honey, and being in the high pines and eucalyptus, but kept smelling bears. She was wandering, lost, and she had to pee again and she was nervous. In the deeper woods, close by now, noise, and heavy breathing, and there it was…a low growling. Startling awake, Goldilocks came face-to-face with an armed and very angry bear. Her eyes widened. She put her arm out to get off the bed and was tossed onto the floor, facedown. A boot pressed heavily between her shoulder blades. Goldilocks tried to say something, but no sound came out. Her arms were pulled up roughly behind her, and she found herself handcuffed, staring at a very shiny black boot. *"Get up!"* the bear-person growled. Goldilocks pulled herself back and stood with difficulty, trying not to pee her pants.

Max and Devin wondered what was taking so long. It had been ten minutes, at least. Motion at the front of the house now, a curly-haired blonde kid, handcuffed, Riley behind her, grim-faced, holster unsnapped. Sie marched the kid around the back of the house.

Shaking violently, Goldilocks tried to figure out what had just happened. *I'm still dreaming. I'm having a nightmare. Bears don't live in houses, and they don't wear SFPD uniforms. Any minute now I will wake up.* She was sitting in the dirt behind the back porch, hand-cuffed to a laundry pole.She felt like she might throw up. Goldilocks would have asked for help, but she didn't expect any, and believed the bear-person might kill her. Her face felt funny. Her throat was tight, and her head hurt. She thought she might cry, and then she was angry because she hated to cry, and then she started to cry anyway. And then she couldn't stop. She tried to be quiet about it.

Still smoldering, Riley helped a shaky Max out of the truck.

"What is going on?" she asked.

"This snot-nosed *kid* broke into our house, that's what happened. I can't tell yet what's missing." Devin followed behind. Normally, sie would have been expected to open the door for Max and Riley, but this was not a normal situation, and Riley looked dangerous. Devin kept a respectful five paces behind, carrying the groceries.

Inside the front door, dirt tracked across the oak floor. All the chairs had dirt on them, and the cushions were squashed. A line of ants marched to and from a large bit of *something* next to Max's favorite chair. In the kitchen, yellow mud streaked the floor. Max started to go in, but Riley intervened. "Floor's wet." Devin took note of the mess and whistled softly. Sie'd left the house spotless that morning. At least the computer was safe. Her dissertation had not been backed up in a few days.

Yellow bootprints led all the way upstairs, where they took stock of their rooms. Riley shadowed Max protectively. Nothing was missing, but the house was a mess.

Max tightened visibly as they surveyed her room. The last time someone had broken into her house, she'd lost something irreplaceable. She turned away and went downstairs. Riley held her hand, dusted off Max's favorite chair, went to the kitchen to get her a cup of tea. Devin began dispatching the ants. Max sat back and rocked, and inhaled and exhaled, and tried to gather her thoughts.

In the backyard, Goldilocks felt her shoulders begin to cramp. She tried to slide her arms up and down the laundry pole, but couldn't move them more than an inch. She crossed and uncrossed her legs, but felt icky no matter what. Her arms itched. Her face was hot. She couldn't even wipe the snot off her face. Inside, she could hear boots on floors, low voices, water running. A bee buzzed near her left shoulder, then lit on the side of her neck and started walking around on her. She could feel the tiny feet and wings brushing her face. She wanted to scream. *I'm not dreaming, and this sucks.*

"So what's the plan?" Max said quietly after Riley brought her tea. Riley paced. "I know what I want to do. Drag her ass down to the sheriff's office and bring charges. Breaking and entering. Of all the goddamned nerve!"

Max waited a minute, watching Riley pace. Then, quietly; "What do you think she was doing here? There's nothing missing. So she's not a thief. Maybe we should ask her." Max got up from her chair to stand behind Devin, who was watching the kid from the back door.

Riley was still on a rant. "I see kids like this all the time. They're all spoiled rotten by the system; they're all carrying, dealing, stealing, robbing, or fencing, or some combination! You know I have no patience with kids like this."

Max suppressed a grin. *Yes, because you were one.* "Devin. Tell me what you think."

Devin turned to face Max. "I'm sorry, Mistress, Master. I left the door unlocked. I let you down. This is all my fault." Silence. *I deserve this, and more.* "I don't know why she is here. Perhaps I can talk to her."

Max nodded. "Talk, then. Five minutes." Devin nodded and stepped outside.

Goldilocks faced away from the house. She was afraid to look up. Nearly sunset. The day's heat was already waning, and a steady southerly breeze had begun. Her face was sticky. Goldilocks was chilled and feeling more miserable by the minute. Under other circumstances, handcuffs were promising, but this seemed to promise only pain, imprisonment, or death.

"Well? What *were* you doing in the house?" The voice came from behind, low, quiet, startling. Goldy turned to look at the person...compact, not stocky, not skinny, just...well constructed. There was a little mustache, and longish hair, and there was thick black hair curling over the back of the hands. Goldilocks tried to think of an answer. "I was thirsty." *Oh fuck.* "I...was out hiking and I needed to stop. No one was home. I knocked." The slender bear didn't change expression. Goldy again: "I'm sorry."

Max slipped out the front door and went around to the garden for tomatoes. Back inside, she watched Devin and the kid from the kitchen. Riley was furiously chopping ingredients for dinner. The garlic would go in first, but dinner would be late. Devin slipped wordlessly in the back door, closing it behind, waited to speak until spoken to.

"Well?" Riley growled.

"Sir. She says she was out hiking, sir, and stopped to use the facilities." Devin kept a poker face. Eyebrows raised, Max considered this scenario. Riley was chopping veggies hard enough to leave fresh gouges in the cutting board. "Why the fuck should I believe a story like that?" Devin didn't respond. Max, quietly then:

"What if it's true?" She went to the window and looked again at the kid. She appeared to be shivering.

Devin had discovered Goldilocks' backpack in hir room. Riley went through everything. Several bus schedules, a pass with a picture and name: Goldy. A hairnet? Crumpled sack lunch. Sunscreen. No valuables. No drugs. *Shit.* "Let's have dinner and then figure this out." Their hearts had all stopped pounding; maybe dinner would be okay.

Devin took an old sleeping bag outside. "Here." Sie unzipped the bag and tossed it across Goldy, who looked uncomprehending. "You're going to *keep* me here?"

"For the moment," Devin replied and vanished again. Goldy shivered under the sleeping bag and wondered what would happen. She was sure she'd be killed or eaten by bears. She wished she had stayed out of their house. She was hungry again, and cold, and felt sick inside.

Inside, Devin served dinner and waited for a decision. Washing the dishes afterward, while Max and Riley conferred, Devin vowed to make door locking a reflex. Her mission in life. Any atonement would be preferable to this waiting, knowing how displeased they were. *Patience.* Max: "Let's go." She headed out the back door. Riley followed. Devin stayed five steps behind.

By now Goldilocks was a cold and humble mess. She hunched into the sleeping bag and tried to look small when the bear-people came out. The big one with the gun looked menacing. She was very hairy; Goldy couldn't figure out exactly what she was dealing with. She settled for staring at her boots and decided it really didn't matter. The femme one was furry, too, with longer hair, and intimidating in a different way. *A top.* She spoke first. "What's the story, kid? I hope you don't make a habit of inviting yourself into people's homes."

Goldy's answer tumbled out in a flood. "I'm really, really, very sorry. I was out hiking and forgot my water bottle and I needed to stop and there was nobody home and so I let myself in…I had no right to…and I'm sorry, ma'am." Goldilocks stared really hard at the boots, hoping she sounded properly apologetic.

The big one lost it. "Do have any idea how close I came to killing you? We should throw your butt in jail. Who the fuck do you think you are, going into people's houses and helping yourself to the kitchen and the bathroom and the beds? Do you know what a mess you made?"

Goldy stared harder at their boots. "I'm really sorry. Please tell me what I can do to make this up to you. Just tell me what to do; I can follow orders." She still didn't dare look up. Her shoulders hurt. She tried to move a little and winced. The handcuffs were cutting into her wrists. In a small voice, she volunteered, "Maybe…I could be of service?"

Max narrowed hir eyes, looked hard at the kid. "Not in our house. You showed no respect for us." She turned and disappeared. The scary one produced a set of keys, unlocked the handcuffs. "Get your ass out of here. We never want to see you again." Goldilocks was pulled to her feet by a surprisingly warm hand. The hairy one shoved her backpack into her grasp, and Goldilocks found herself facing the road. Goldilocks turned back to look at the house just once, and thought she saw the slender bear watching her, but could never be sure. It would be a long way home.

EPILOGUE

Following her misadventure in the woods, Goldilocks cut her hair short, moved to a different apartment, and started working out at the Y. Some things she could change. Worked overtime, even though she wasn't sleeping well. Got the toque. She thought about the bears a lot. She wished things had turned out differently between them. Goldilocks taught herself to do laundry.

Late in the summer, during a hot spell, Goldilocks was at work, tossing pizza dough as usual. She looked up for a moment, and thought she saw the slender bear. Her heart caught in her throat. The person was just turning away. They didn't make eye contact, but Goldilocks caught a look at a brand and tattoo on the left shoulder. It looked like a key superimposed on a bear paw. There was a lot of color; it must be fresh. Goldilocks could never be certain if that's who and what she saw. By the time she'd gotten to the street, sie was gone. She had been scared for a minute, seeing the slender bear, then furious. Raging. Couldn't make herself understood, but she was scaring the customers. The boss sent her home. That night, the dream started. It was always the same.

She was warm and sleepy. The sun shone, and she was naked on a strange little bed in the middle of the woods, under a canopy of fir trees. She was way turned on, and touched herself, but wasn't getting off. Her fingers were sticky with honey. Then there were bees. She told them to go away, tried swatting at them, but they started swarming on her. She was so afraid that she couldn't move. She knew she should try to move, hide, run away. But she couldn't get up. There was a house about one hundred yards away. She wanted to get up and go in the house. She couldn't move. Then she knew that if she went to the house, the doors would be locked. There was a heavy scent on the wind, something earthy. She knew what that meant. There were bears in the woods...and she couldn't move. She closed her eyes tightly, hoping she'd wake up, hoping the bees would go away. Close by now, snuffling noises, bootsteps crunching, growls becoming a roar. Cold steel on her neck. Jolting awake, muscles tight, skin crawling, always wet. Goldilocks felt scared, and small, and inexpressibly sad.

The Shoes That Were Danced to Pieces
RED JORDAN AROBATEAU

I chose to do this story after my wife picked the title from a book of German fairy tales she got at the library. The idea of twelve daughters appealed to me, and I was happy with the story after reading its first line.

Once upon a time, there was a Queen who had twelve daughters, each one more beautiful than the other, and several kinkier than the rest. They all slept together in one chamber in a huge circular water bed, and every night when they were in it, the Queen locked the door and bolted it. But in the morning, when s/he unlocked the door, s/he saw that their shoes were worn out with dancing, and no one could find out how that had come to pass. Then the Queen caused it to be proclaimed that whosoever could discover where they danced at night should choose one of them for his wife and be ruler after the Queen's death; but that whosoever came forward and had not discovered it within three days and nights would forfeit his life.

It was not long before a Rich Person's son presented himself and offered to undertake the enterprise. He was well received, and in the evening was led into a room adjoining the princesses' sleeping chamber. His bed was placed there, and he was to observe where they went and danced; and in order that they might do nothing secretly or go away to some other place, the door of their room was left open. But the eyelids of the prince grew heavy as lead and he fell asleep, and when he awoke in the morning, all twelve had been to the dance, for their shoes were standing there with holes in the soles. On the second and third night there was no difference, and then his head was struck off without mercy.

Many others came after this and undertook the enterprise, but all forfeited their lives. Now it came to pass that a poor lesbian soldier, who had been wounded on the battlefields of war, and of love, and could serve no longer, found herself on the road to the town where the Queen lived. There she met an old transvestite, who asked her, "Where ya' goin', honey?"

"I hardly know myself," she answered, and added in jest, "I had half a mind to discover where the princesses danced their shoes into holes and thus become King. But this is only a fantasy, because surely they are straight, and the Queen is, too. Ain't they? And I would be beheaded for just the thought."

"Not so," the old transvestite replied with a lisp. "For I know the Queen Mother, the ruler of that land. I know her well. As a matter of fact, I knew her *when*. And methinks all is not what you might believe regarding the Queen and her twelve fair young jazzy daughters. Yes, as a matter of fact, that is not so difficult to believe." Then the old transvestite told the soldier a secret. "You must not drink the wine which will be brought to you at night, and you must pretend afterward to be sound asleep." With that she reached into her wardrobe of finery with gnarled, diamond-studded fingers, fiddled with her cherished possessions and, somewhat reluctantly, produced a little cloak all studded with rhinestones. As she handed it to the soldier, she said, "If you wear this, you will be invisible, and then you can steal after the twelve princesses."

When the soldier had received this good advice, she fell to the task in earnest. Taking heart, she went to the Queen and announced herself as a suitor. Much to her utter amazement, she was as well received as the others (who had all been men), and royal garments were put upon her. She was conducted that evening at bedtime into the antechamber, and as she was about to go to bed the eldest daughter came and brought to her a cup of wine. But the lesbian soldier, being a recovered alcoholic and clean and sober for some years, faked drinking the wine. By tying a sponge under her chin, she let the wine run down into it, without touching a single drop. Then she lay down, and when she had lain a while, she began to snore, as if in the deepest sleep. The twelve princesses heard the noise and began to giggle. As the snoring grew louder, they began to laugh, and the eldest said, "She, too, might as well have saved her life. What a waste. She was kind of cute."

"Yes, she was rather cute in that studly butch soldier costume," replied another.

"I'm not so sure she is studly—what of that tacky, femmey little cloak she has brought along in the brown paper bag?" said another. "With rhinestones? Who *is* she trying to fool?"

"She deserves to die for spying on us!" cried the eldest.

"And quickly," another agreed venomously.

With that, they got up, opened wardrobes, and began to dress. A few began to press their hair. Others sprayed the air with perfume. They brought out pretty dresses, stiletto heels, fishnet stockings, leather bodices, lacy pink-and-white corsets, black see-through teddies, strings of pearls and diamonds, and began to dress themselves. The eldest aided the youngest, of whom she was actually quite fond. They helped each other as they primped before the mirrors.

Some of the princesses were white as snow, with fair blonde hair and pale blue eyes; others were of the finest ebony, with rounded features and soft doe eyes of liquid brown. They were an interracial bunch, for the Queen had seen fit to adopt these daughters from hither and thither all over his/her Queendom when they were but babes, abandoned as casualties of wars and famines by their natural mothers. The Queen had raised them with tenderness, educated them with the finest tutors, and saw to it that they were fine young girls, strong and healthy. But as Queens are liable to be, she was somewhat nervous and worried, and she busily dreamt up horrors which might befall her daughters. Thus she imprisoned them at night to keep them from the troubles of young women, declaring: "These are my girls! Nobody had better mess with them, or off with his head. And *I mean business*. Keep your hands off my girls!"

The princesses knew their father/mother loved them dearly, but also knew that s/he was a bit out of touch with the times. They were growing young women who needed to be pleased. All had desires of the heart and of the flesh, and it was with these passions that they burned at night. So it was by selling off pieces of their fine jewelry that they had been able to bribe some of the servants to help them construct an elaborate escape passage under their bedchamber so as not to distress their beloved father/mother the Queen, nor to jeopardize their royal positions (they lived high on the hog in the castle), but to enable themselves to party hearty and indulge their steamy desires of the flesh at night.

They preened in the mirrors and sang. They popped their fingers and sprang about and rejoiced at the prospect of the dance, as young women are inclined to do. Only the youngest said, "I know not how it is that you are so happy. I feel strange, as though some misfortune—some twist of fate—is certainly about to befall us."

"You are a goose who is always frightened," one said scornfully.

"She's clueless," said the eldest. "Have you forgotten how many Kings' sons have already come here in vain? Don't we have our little scheme perfected? Daddy/Moms ought to know we hate male suitors. It's what s/he gets for trying to raise us to be normal—ugh! And as for that soldier, I hardly had any need to give her a sleeping draught, the booby would not have awakened anyway, she's so exhausted from walking all those miles."

When they were all primped and curled and decked out in their finery and ready, they looked carefully at the lesbian soldier. But she had closed her eyes and did not move or stir, so they felt themselves safe enough. The eldest then went to her side of the bed and tapped it, whereupon with a great sloshing of water it immediately sank into the earth, and one after another they descended through the opening, the eldest going first. The soldier, who had watched everything, tarried no longer. Putting on her little rhinestone-studded cloak, she followed after the youngest daughter into the opening. Halfway down the steps, she trod just a little on her dress. The youngest princess was terrified and cried out, "What the hell is this? Who is pulling at my dress?"

"Don't be silly!" said the eldest.

"You *wish* someone was pulling your dress," replied another.

"Simple wench," exclaimed the eldest, chastising her sister. "You have caught it on a nail. Don't be such a worrywart! You're just as bad as our father/mother the Queen."

Then they went all the way down the stairs, and when they were at the bottom, they were standing in a wonderful, pretty, queer nightclub. It was magnificent. All of the lights were of silver and shone and glistened like stars on the ceiling. The soldier thought, *No one will believe this! I've never seen such a fab place. Girls with girls and boys with boys. I must carry a token away with me.* She grabbed a napkin imprinted with the name of the nightclub off one of the tables, but it was partially under a drinking glass, and the glass fell off the table and broke on the floor with a loud retort.

The youngest cried out again, "Something is wrong! Did you hear the glass breaking?"

But the eldest reproached her sisters. "One of you has fired off her gun for joy because we have gotten rid of our prince so quickly.

Which of you tramps is it? Put it away. We don't need firearms in here—this is not a dive. This is a *nice* place."

After that, they came into the second level of the nightclub—a dance floor. Around the outer circle of the floor there were platforms, booths, and bar stools of gold. Moving through the room, they went outside to another dance floor on a patio adjoining a dock, complete with a salad bar and chefs in tall white hats carving huge hams and roast beefs. There was also a line of full-length mirrors, in which the finery of the twelve was reflected with the light of bright diamonds.

The lesbian soldier started grabbing at matchbooks, bar napkins, menus—anything—as evidence of where she'd been and what she'd seen. This made a racket, and again the youngest started in terror. But the eldest still maintained that the noise was caused by one of them firing off one of the little guns which they all carried for protection as a salute of their superiority in outwitting yet another hapless prince.

The twelve princesses went across the dance floor of the open patio to the dock, on the harbor of a great lake. There waited twelve little boats, and in every boat sat a handsome butch dyke prince, refined and rich. Very rich. The princes were waiting for the twelve, and each took one of them with her into her boat. The soldier seated herself behind the youngest princess.

Her rich butch prince said, "I wonder why my boat is so much heavier today. Has my pretty young princess been at the royal table stuffing herself and gaining weight? My darling, why have you grown so fat? I shall have to row with all of my strength if I am to get across the lake."

"What should cause you to say such a thing as that?" snapped the youngest. "I'm not any heavier than the last time. It's *you* who are more tired. It's the warm weather. It's making you more tired. I feel very warm, too. In fact, I'm *hot!*"

On the opposite side of the lake stood a splendid, brightly lit castle with an orgy room in the basement, from whence resounded the joyous music of the moans of many orgasming women. Delicious aromas of kettles of food filled the air. Inside, the tables were set with gallons of drink, and entertaining the crowd was the famous belly dancer, Delphinia. Every pleasure the princesses could desire was awaiting them, and behind the castle doors were all the makings of a raucous, sexual, sensual, and erotic party.

The butch princes rowed there. Each took her princess by her maidenly hand in a charming butch manner and led her to a little cubicle and laid her down on a sumptuous bed—individual bed of her own, not one gigantic bed with some sister elbowing her in the side or snoring perfumed breath in her face. There in the scented and warm spray of air they began to make love in ways which pleased them.

Ah, thought the youngest, *the lights on the ceiling are so like a starry galaxy, so pleasant to look at*. As she lay on her back, her garments being parted and her milky thighs spreading, she felt her lover enter her, and soon she was being fucked. As the soldier observed, a voyeur studying them all while shrouded in the invisibility of the rhinestone cloak, the twelve indulged in a range of passions, from the tender vanilla caresses of the youngest, barely sixteen, to a perversity of experience of the eldest, who was thirty-two.

At the second cubicle, the butch of the second couple knelt upon command before her dominant royal princess, sucking the pink nipple upon each of her milk-white breasts. As the dom princess condescended to spread her royal legs, the handsome slave prince slid down between them and began to probe through the pubic hair and lips of her pussy with fingertips. She licked and sucked greedily, stopping only to raise her head, mouth dripping with savory cuntjuice, and gaze up from time to time from between the princess's spread thighs to her face, which was watching sternly, and ask, "Is it satisfactory, my Mistress?" Then she would dive back to work—lick, lick, lick, suck, suck, suck—pulling the pearl of her mistress's clit with a sucking of her mouth while flicking her tongue tip over and over it, all the while her face engulfed, mashed between the vulval lips of the royal pussy.

At the third cubicle, the soldier watched a demonstration of fisting. This prince had curled her hand, wearing a latex glove, into a strange kind of fist with the thumb tucked under the four fingers, and was thrusting it like a piston inside the vagina of the princess, bringing her to orgasms again and again.

The fourth couple had prearranged a scene. The prince had pasted a fake mustache of thick black hair upon her upper lip and stood up in the center of the bed. Her legs were spread, and she was bracing herself with one hand against the cubicle's wall. She barked orders to her princess to strip naked, which she did. The prince stood above her kneeling princess and produced a whip made of many leather straps radiating out of a thick handle—a toy called the cat-o'-nine-tails. She snapped it with a loud crack. She trailed the tips of the leather whip so that they ran along the fleshy backside of her kneeling penitent princess with stings of prickly pleasure. Then she began the whipping. "Crack! Crack! Crack!" went the whip.

When this chastisement was complete, and the princess had confessed her sins and was trembling in submission, the prince, standing magnificently above her slave princess, unzipped her trouser fly so that the garment dropped down the length of her legs and fell into a pile around her boots. The prince then thrust her clit into the mouth of her sweet slave princess and began pumping it into her in triumph, accompanied by shouts of "Hurrah! Hurrah!"

The soldier moved on, passing several deserted cubicles whose occupants had gone off to frolic. Then, much to her surprise, she came upon them all. As the soldier stood watching from a vantage point at the door, she saw the fifth, sixth, and seventh couples engaged in an orgy. They appeared to be just a mass of arms and legs, all of them petting, licking, sucking, humping, penetrating. Moving as one, they were like a gigantic animal, creating a life-form all their own whose cheeks, hands, thighs, and asses were wet with juices. Occasionally a face might turn up out of the crowd, its mouth dripping come and saliva, to look about, find a new stretch of flesh to explore, and then turn to feast again on this new body part. The soldier noticed that the gallant princes and their princesses engaged in safer sex, for every so often a hand would emerge from the mass to reach for a little table covered in red velvet, upon which was a bottle labeled ALCOHOL/TOY CLEANER, a box of dams, and another of condoms, all for use on their pussies and dildos to prevent the spread of disease.

Leaving the doorway, the soldier moved on, coming next upon a scene in which a princess was bent over on all fours while her butch prince humped her ass, fucking her like a dog. A small orange-covered dick strapped to the butch appeared, upon closer examination, to be a carrot stolen from the salad bar. As it had once dripped blue cheese, it now dripped lube as the prince entered the princess's pussy from the rear. The butch prince's thighs slammed against the two round royal buttocks—BAM, BAM, BAM—while one hand reached around the princess's waist and poked between her thighs to jack off the royal clit vigorously for heightened stimulus. Their cries of female passion joined in the chorus of the orgying royalty up and down the red-velvet-carpeted corridors.

In yet another room, a butch had chained her nude princess down to the sumptuous bed spread-eagled, each ankle and wrist tied to one of the four corner bedposts. As the princess tugged at her restraints, the prince tickled her with an ostrich feather and fed her strawberries and cream. The butch prince spread the cream so that it covered her thighs and tits and then licked it off, while the rosy-cheeked princess screamed in girlish glee.

The eleventh prince took off her princess's golden slippers and knelt humbly to massage her feet. Then she began to lick her toes, pink tongue flicking between each and finally drawing all five toes into her mouth to suck them all. At that moment, per the prince's instructions, the castle's servants filed in to serenade the couple with violins. While a few gay songs were played, a complete turnabout of personas occurred. The prince reached to her waist and drew out a wicked dagger with a blade of sharp, curved steel, which she flicked teasingly over her princess's flesh. She cut loose the princess's silk negligee and, with a final jerk, cut the laces of her corset. The princess's rosy flesh spilled out, and the butch prince fell upon her and ravished her by pumping the handle of the wicked curved dagger up and down in her butthole as three fingers stuffed into her cunt shot bolts of lust and power through her being.

The twelfth coupling proved to be the most dramatic. It was held in a specially prepared room draped all in black and lit by burning black candles whose ebony wax dripped into cut-glass bowls sparkling like diamond tears. Here the eldest princess was laid out like a corpse, her death pose belied only by the smirk on her face which showed that she could barely contain her excitement. Her eyelids, caked with black mascara, fluttered against her face as she tried to appear dead, while above her the kinky prince stood masturbating her clit with one end of a long black-rubber two-headed phallus. She thrust it into the open fly of her trousers, farther into the rim of soggy pubic hairs, then deeper still into her cunt at an angle which stimulated her clit so that she soon grew so horny that her hips began to hump forward and her cunt lustily devoured the phallus.

She was humping, humping so that her entire body was bucking like a bronco in midair. When she felt herself ready, she fell as though a necrophiliac upon her prey. Raising up the elegant skirts of the "corpse" of the eldest princess, she thrust the bulbous head of the long black two-headed phallus into the mouth of her pussy-hole, working it in smoothly with some lube and sinking the shaft deep inside the princess's pussy. At this point, the "dead" princess could no longer restrain herself. With unbridled passion, she grabbed the prince in a fierce embrace and began to buck her hips upward—WHAM! WHAM! WHAM!—into the prince, who had the other end still in her own cunt, so that they began to fuck themselves silly.

When they were through fucking, they rested awhile, the princesses' heads on the chests of their beloved butch princes. Then they went to rejoin the party across the water in the main room amid all the swirl of gaiety and action. Again the princes rowed them there, and soon all the couples were dancing, partying, finger-popping, flouncing their hair, firing off their little guns, and having a wild time. Each butch prince danced with the princess she loved, and the lesbian soldier danced among them unseen. When one of the princes had a cup of wine in her hand, the soldier spilled it, so that the cup was empty when she brought it to her mouth. The soldier was especially attentive to the youngest, so that she would not grow lighthearted and commit a foolish act with her butch, like run off with her, for the soldier did not like this prince at all. The youngest was alarmed at the unseen attentions, but the eldest always silenced her.

The princesses and princes danced until three o'clock in the morning, when all of their shoes were danced into holes and they were forced to stop. Then the butch princes rowed them back and forth across the lake for some time, and this time the soldier seated herself with the eldest. On the shore, they took leave of their butches and promised to return the following night.

When they reached the stairs, the soldier ran on in front and lay down in her bed. When the twelve had come up slowly and wearily and disgusted at having to return to the imprisoning confines of the castle, she was already snoring so loudly that they could all hear her from far off and the eldest said, "So far as she is concerned, we are safe." They took off their beautiful, but stained, dresses, laid them away, put their worn-out shoes under the bed, and went to sleep.

The next morning, the soldier was resolved not to speak, but to watch the wondrous goings-on and comings for a second time. She went with the princesses again that night to their secret place, and again on the third night. Each night everything was just as it had been the first time, and each time they princesses and princes fucked and partied and ate and sang and danced until their shoes were worn to pieces. The soldier even took some dental dams away with her as further tokens of the princesses' nightly doings.

All went well until, on the third night, there was a horrible accident. Two of the princes, both having an abundance of top energy, crossed paths in their boats and got into a fight. They fell into the lake and promptly drowned. That left only ten butch princes for the twelve princesses. Saddened, they returned to the castle, the soldier unseen as before, and went to bed.

The next morning, when the hour arrived for the soldier to present her findings to the Queen, she gathered up the bar napkins, matchbooks, and the dental dams and went to where the Queen awaited. Following her, the twelve hid themselves behind the door and listened to hear what she would say. When the Queen asked, "Where have my twelve danced their shoes to pieces in the night?" the soldier answered, "In an underground after-hours club with twelve princely butches." She then related how it had come to pass, and brought out the evidence. "Your daughters are mature enough to have lives of their own. They are already fucking. Look at these!" She held up the dental dams in her hand, where it could be seen upon closer inspection that the dams were soiled with cuntjuices.

The Queen summoned his/her wayward daughters and asked them if the soldier had told the truth. When they saw that they were all betrayed, and that falsehood would be of no avail, they were obliged to confess all. Thereupon the Queen asked which of them the soldier would have as a wife.

"I am no longer young," she answered modestly, "so give me the eldest. However, as I am not yet too old, give me the youngest as well."

Then the wedding of this lovely ménage à trois was celebrated on the selfsame day and the Queendom was promised to the soldier after the Queen's death. The princesses and their princes were bewitched to dance with joy and to party for many, many days, and to sing and orgasm and have fun each night. And, of course, they lived happily ever after.

Taking Flight:
The Secret of the Swan Maiden
MAM'SELLE VICTOIRE

Watching ballet is a jaggedly emotional experience for me; I find the classic ballets to be serenely, deliciously, beautiful, and also exquisitely violent and suspenseful and passionate. They are Isak Dinesen and Angela Carter come-to-life for me in gossamer and terrifying detail. As anyone who has ever escorted me to one knows, I am swept up in a turmoil of emotion at the ballet, cathartically empathizing, longing desperately to assist in the creation of perfection, and often amusing myself with the detective work the story poses.

Hence, much like other literary solutions which I have admired: to explain why the boy in Equus *might be driven to blind the horses, or why the geisha in* In the Realm of the Senses *was found resplendently carrying aloft the mutilated genitals of her lover, or how the strictly cloistered novice,* Agnes of God, *could be found to be pregnant.* Swan Lake *has always fascinated me. I ask myself, how could an impressionable young woman, imbued with intelligence and burgeoning desire, have gotten to the place where, upon meeting the Prince and being courted by him, she nevertheless protects the dark Baron who entrapped her in enchantment, and in fact spreads her wings to shield the Baron from the Prince's arrow when he draws his bow to protect her. Why is she compelled so irresistibly to return to the Baron at the end of the scenes? How could this happen? The ballet itself is told from the Prince's point of view, and the beautiful, love-struck swan-maiden flying and preening under the Baron's curse is a mystery. What on earth was the maiden thinking? This little prequel is one suggestion....*

From the minute I started bleeding, I was aware of the Baron. Lush flashes of him watching me, sharp and embarrassing as memories, flew into my head at the oddest times, coloring all my thoughts, and yet I'd never even seen him, except in paintings at school. His rich fragrance was under my nose, casting its spell, and I soon realized we were all feeling the predatory eye of the Baron in some mysterious way, captivating all of us who started our time-of-the-month.

It was easy to tell us apart, because all the rest of the girls laughed together in little circles and talked about the Prince; but it seemed as if, one by one, a growing group of us were whispering and wondering about the Baron in his unseen castle, and the mystery of his swans.

When I undressed to wash, I could feel him in the water I poured on myself; when I stretched to balance the basket on my head in the sun, I could feel him in the heat of the blinding light; when my father commented on my breasts growing, I could feel the Baron, in his long furred robes, spying me naked, and all of it made me faint and anxious, and excited and restless.

The Baron lived on the windward side of the mountain, we were told, hidden from view, in a grotto no one had ever seen. Our mothers told us it was carved into the stormy cliffs on that side, and surrounded by a glassy lake, fed by mysterious streams of heartbroken women's tears. The Baron's swans were enchanted; the flock was his prized possession, everyone said. He bred them and pampered them, and adored them to distraction. And it was said he trained them to return into his presence each night. No matter how far they ventured into the night skies, the swans were so bewitched by the Baron that they always came back to his side by moonlight.

Everyone knew the story of the Baron and his castle, even though when we looked up the mountain, all we ever saw was the Prince's palace here on the sunny side. We could see the palace from every place in the village.

The white turrets, rose-lit before the dawn light could reach us, the swans circling the buttressed arches in full moonlight, all of it grounded us. We always told our directions from our Prince's palace, and we watched the changes of the hours and the seasons from it, instead of from the fields and houses of our own village below. If fog separated us from the Prince's palace, accidents befell our grandmamas until the view was restored. When lightning hit the guard tower, babies were born suddenly.

Excitement glistened in the air, though, surely because the prince was to be married. At least we called this the Year of the Prince's Wedding, however the year was quite well nigh on, the grapes and the figs were ripening, and as yet no nuptial ball was planned.

Grand ladies had been brought from far and wide for his inspection—exotic foreign princesses, we girls presumed—but since no ball was scheduled, we all wondered among ourselves just what had happened in those sequestered royal meetings. And in the midst of all this, in the damp unending heat and fragrance of that late summer, as my neck grew hollows and my skin softened, I could feel the Baron pulling me toward him.

I stopped undressing when I washed at night. I knew he could see me, and I could feel his eyes blink as I reached the sponge under the wet muslin. My nipples were so tender sometimes, but if I touched them, he was watching. I could see him fingering the jeweled swan-head of his long cane as he stared at me, so I stopped myself, even when my nipples throbbed. Often I tried to think of what he looked like, but all I could retrieve was his smell; when my mind wandered, his face was there again, his penetrating eyes. He frightened me…and yet…

And yet I felt drawn to him; irresistibly, uncontrollably drawn to him, as I sweated, as I stretched. As I buttoned my chemise, and especially as I tied my bodice each morning, I could feel him inspecting me, expecting me to lace myself up properly.

Without realizing it, I would find myself writing poetry to the Baron, agonizing for hours over the scan of a couplet to him, only to tear it up, astonished and blushing at what I was doing. In bed one night, when the moonlight was angling in, keeping me on edge wondering with desire, I was nodding awake, nodding asleep, wrestling with the magnetic image of the Baron watching me. He was peering down from the vantage point of an immense throne with carved arms which stretched out to fill his hands, and under each swelled a polished jeweled head, just like the one on the staff he carried.

My hand was pinned under my thigh as I lay curled on the sheets, and I could feel the swansdown skin of a stranger—such a curious unfathomable smoothness, warm against the coolness of my numb fingers—before I startled at the eerie reversal of eaves-dropping on my own flesh, and shrank away from the moonlight, sure that now the Baron could see all my secrets.

I was so sleepy, yet each time I relaxed, I could hear the Baron, unmistakably coming to take me, his heavy swan-cane drumming ominously ahead of his boots. The rhythmic sound of him approaching was frightening, and jolted me awake; and yet at the same time, knowing that he was coming for me, the terrible inevitability of it lulled me like soporific ambrosia.

Then—suddenly—when I surrendered to sleep, there was nothing separating us anymore. I was standing in front of him, being inspected by him. It wasn't in my thoughts, it was really happening.

Wings were rustling very near; I could hear them. I knew we were high above the village, on the dark side of the mountain, where the swans fly at night. There was a buzzing intensity swarming all around me—I was his in my sleep—and something monumental and mysterious, something strange and cataclysmic was about to happen, I knew it.

Terrified and intrigued, I could feel myself sliding irrevocably into some kind of alluring annihilation I tried desperately to comprehend, but could not; closer and closer every time I fell asleep, and was his again. I was standing in front of him, being inspected by him, as he sat up the steps on his swan-gilded perch looking down at me. My skirts were parted on my thighs, just at the place I had touched in the moonlight, and the spicy air was molesting the very naked spot.

My arms were heavy, paralyzed in the ferocity of the moment, and I was standing in front of him, trying to pull myself away from his penetrating eye. My bodice was tighter, much tighter now, velvet and sparkling with embroidery; and everything was so beautiful.

Pulled there inexorably by his gaze, I stumbled forward onto my knees, but then lurched away from him, and woke up, wet. Was everyone going through this? Now all day I longed for sleep, but if my lids dropped, I saw the Baron, and jumped. As I braided my hair, as I unbraided it, his pungent, spicy smell was in my bed, between the sheets. If I hid myself in the covers, clutching them to protect myself from him, I could feel his breath on my throat, in my hair, no matter how I twisted in the night. When he smiled, I felt the heat in my cheeks and ears.

And yet again, sleep inebriated me, and I was standing in front of him, held there, paralyzed with wonder in all the cooing swan-song, as he stared down inspecting me, laced tightly before him.

Candlelight glinted off the curves of his beard and hair, and light seemed to emanate from the flesh stretched over his forehead and cheeks. The Baron's spicy fragrance filled the entire cavernous chamber, and I stretched to peer around me, but seemed to move not a jot.

Swans were everywhere; it was hard to tell where the lake stopped for all of the magnificent birds preening and rustling, crowded near him, restless and trembling, watching us. The golden magnificence on all sides was reflected in ranks of black-eyed swansdown, and pieces of the carved furniture assembled around us were larger than our entire house. The long table with its fire-place-island glowing in the middle, the immense credenzas weighed down by folds of tapestry from hangings too long even for this towering space; and there were curving arms of candlelight glimmering everywhere.

My arms were heavy and I rushed to run away and wake up, but wing clamor suddenly filled my ears. Something in me ruffled and flustered, and in that moment, I knew I could not escape him anymore.

I was standing before him, as the swans watched and rustled, and he was looking deeply into me, smiling into the laces of my bodice, into all my secrets. But now I was standing between his legs, up the steps of the dais, no longer looking up, but down into the icy intimidation of his eyes, as he touched me. Pressing my bound waist, stroking my hair, he was whispering into my throat; and I was leaning in the grip of his gloved paws, panting, struggling against my own arms, unable to move, as he reached toward the laces.

His spicy aura was heady and delicious, but left me dizzy and hot, and I watched, frozen, as he ungloved one hand, clasped the tiny knotted end of the laces bowed between my breasts, and pulled. The undone loops allowed the panels of punishing, rigid velvet down my belly to unthread slightly, and released a little of my bosom to his view. He stopped and regarded me coolly, like sculpture appraised for value. Then, inhaling deeply, he sighed and pressed his mouth to the exposed flesh of my breasts.

In the moment of contact, in the shocking reality of his touch, I burst out, flinging myself upward, gasping for the air above us, but realized I had not moved at all and was standing before him, unmoving, my lips trembling, as he unlaced and unlaced and unlaced me, until I was completely undone, blushing among the swans.

Next his hands rose, the gloved one and the ungloved one, climbing my torso slowly. And in the moment I realized he was going to pull the bodice and chemise entirely off my shoulders, I could feel the first tear streak my cheek.

Inside me, two sides were warring, one in outraged flight, the other leaning into my cheek, my throat, my breast, desperately craving his attention, panting for his next touch.

Even with everything that had happened, nothing prepared me for the audacity of his gloved hand reaching for my nipple and pulling me toward him. All of this was happening so much faster than I could think of it, could imagine it happening. His hands were on my back—gloved hands, ungloved hands, hot wet mouth. It was confusing and thrilling trying to remember what was leathered and what was wet as my nipples and arms and throat were covered with the overwhelming powerful sensations of his toying with me.

He was holding me up, he was pulling me more deeply into him. Some of it was irresistibly pleasurable, and even brand-new. I longed for it again, and knew I would do anything, anything to get it; and some of it burned unexpectedly, even as he stroked me gently, trying to calm me.

His touches seemed to build into a flurry of pressure, and places I had never thought of having feelings before, when I lost my balance and dropped forward, catching myself with my hand and falling onto his doeskin breeches, deep into the soft curving hardness, warmed under the spongy leather between his legs. Surely this,

this was the heart of the matter: this great rod pressing up, throbbing under my curious hand. As I stared at it mesmerized, the agitated Baron reached to unsheath it, still holding my martyred nipple imprisoned in his gloved hand. I found myself bucking under it, and yet riveted by the wonder of this new marvel. The Baron smiled inscrutably as I struggled, and then released my nipple, gripping my waist with his gauntlet. I hissed, dancing with the bee sting awakening in my breast, but soon realized I was being aimed at this great thing I was now straddling.

Begging, crying out, I squirmed, I wriggled in all directions, but every movement I made sent the great shank between his legs higher into me, jammed it up between my legs where there was no place to go. I could feel my own body betraying me and drooling gloss upon him, but there was still no room for all of him.

And just as I realized that perhaps he could not get in after all, I could feel and even hear inside me the terrible squeaky crunching as I tore open to accommodate him spearing me. In two—then three—tremendous thrusts, he was blazing inside me, one with the secrets of my belly. And even as I was sure I could never move again, I was finally reaching overhead with brilliant success, grabbing for the sky, celebrating the air with flight.

Yet another time, he was pulling me down onto him, ravaging the sore place again. I ground into him, itching for relief, spiraling madly, surrendering to this new flaming desire. But on the upward slide, I was pumping my wings into the night sky, clutching for freedom, spilling feathers.

The Baron's bewitching rod was ravaging my cloven belly, and yet in some unutterable way, also liberating my wings. In the downstroke of his rod, the savage outrage of it jamming up into my flesh, stamping me ineffably with its need, my arms were paralyzed, and I was bound in velvet and gloved fists, helpless to stop wanting it again; in the up-stroke of his release, I was surging upward, swan's neck craned for the moon…up and down, up and down again. Nauseated with pleasure, I was bristling with desire, longing for the next irresistible plundering stroke, trying frantically to escape it.

This bizarre dance was his, though, and my body plunged down on the Baron's erotic plug over and over again, enthralled by its hypnotic sliding girth stretching me open. He groaned and grappled with my waist, biting my throat, thrusting up and carving me open with his passion. He built up in waves of intensity, flinging me up and down, gripping and undulating onto him. Suddenly, with a wailing groan, he thrust himself up into me one more time and shuddered, seizing me with pleasure.

I was thrown skyward, I was blazing in the fury of sensations in his lap, eclipsing back and forth in consummation, back and forth in frazzled wonder, until without his great rod to weigh in the balance, I was free to fly, changed forever in the moonlit night.

Iron Hans
CORRINA KELLAM

I chose to rewrite this story in order to modify one of my childhood narratives to fit my own life. Fairy tales as such just didn't give me much to relate to, although there was always something charming about the old witch in "Rapunzel."

I liked "Iron Hans" because of the implications of the characters—the idea that there are good people in the world upon whom you can depend to understand you no matter what foolish things you have done. I also appreciated the fact that Jackie and Iron Hans were not related, showing me that these sorts of honest friendships could flourish regardless of how my family chose to react to me. The story gave me room to screw up: It claimed that everything would be okay in the end if your motives were kind and good. And I got to play with some intriguing power issues within caring relationships, which are always fun when they aren't overly narcissistic.

In this city you'd think you could depend on a few constants. So when the Mayor sent one of his aides out to buy some working girls for the evening, he was really surprised when his guy didn't come back. As a matter of fact, he took it fairly personally, thinking that he took his cash and disappeared. It doesn't reflect well on the boss when less than a thousand dollars is a big enough carrot for someone to jump ship. At first he was going to scream holy hell about embezzlement, but then he remembered that everyone, including his beloved and still-miraculously-chaste daughter, would realize the real reason he wore suits off the rack from Kmart with his puffed-up government salary.

So he sent two more of his associates, those of the sort who were not on the city payroll, to fetch his aide. They didn't come back either. In a panic, the Mayor called the chief of police, who called the press pool, who fabricated a tale about a terrorist who was knifing the people who were close to those in the highest political echelons. Somehow no one put three and five together, and the city had a new official war zone to warn the tourists to stay away from. So the law of averages took over, economic decay spread through-out the area, and no one wanted to hang out there anymore anyway.

One guy in the know, who waited long enough to be sure the Mayor would be itching for some action in order to secure himself a good fee for his advice on the matter, suggested that perhaps the hookers might have split because they caught wind of the aide's political connections and were leery of a police raid; and that the aide had fled in fear of dismissal over his inability to follow out his orders, and the thugs sent after him had lain low because they couldn't find their man and couldn't handle the blow their repu-tation would take if their boss found out. In short, the guy offered to go rustle up some chicks for the Mayor if he could be assured of a steady off-the-books income.

Upon being given the go-ahead, he went down deep into The Forest, the new pseudo-menacing name the press came up with for the sixteen square blocks to sell their story. It was deserted. Quick study that he was, he went into a bar that look habitable called

Deep Pockets, to see if anyone knew where he could get lucky. The front room seemed empty, but the back doorway was enticingly draped with used thigh-high stockings, kind of like 1960s hippie love beads. Intrigued, he went inside, and there they were, lounging carefree around the pool table, flocking to a big fellow with IRON HANS tattooed on the left biceps. The fellow stood up after a tricky shot, and his/her breasts bobbed up with her. The Mayor's man dropped his cash and bolted from the room. He flagged down a cop and told him that the guy who converted all the hookers was a chick. Word spread too fast that the "he" was a she, and the men rallied in front of Deep Pockets to save their women, rubbing their swollen crotches at each other in greeting as if caressing their crushed pride. It didn't take long before they broke down the bar door, splintering out the hinges for souvenirs, and lined up to take a swing at the mighty Iron Hans. Many of them risked bruising their hands under a swift kick in order to cop a bloody feel as "proof." When she finally lost consciousness and stopped resisting, they carried her around the city, dragging her head along the pavement, and finally dumped her outside of City Hall, so that anyone who wanted to could abuse her however they saw fit. In the morning, under the bright sun to avoid chants of cowardice and mass frantic lunacy, and to let the whole city come on down to watch, she would be lynched, and how. She would be the example to show other crazy-minded bitches precisely what would happen to them if they ever wanted to try out some of Iron Hans's moves for themselves.

It soon got late, and all the babies had to check in at their mothers' beds. Iron Hans was left to bleed and wait by herself. From a shaded window, a young girl watched Iron Hans writhe and quiver in the darkness. She had heard about the evil he-she from her father and the less-careful of his followers. She slipped out from his watchful eye and went out to observe the creature more closely. She moved around the prostrate body to look at the menacer's face.

"Hi."

Her breath caught in her throat. In her curiosity, she had never imagined the fallen woman to be awake, to speak to her. She imagined she would be enraged, repelled, if the lump tried to make a move toward her. It took her a moment to respond while she sorted out her emotions. Suddenly there was no way to deny what she felt—long-lost recognition. Knowing that there was only one thing left to say: "Hi."

The woman's eyes never left her face. She didn't try to move. The girl could understand fully and immediately why the hookers were willing to give up their means of economic support to be with her. "You know they're going to kill me tomorrow." Her gaze did not shift. The girl felt her face contort, tears stinging their way into vulnerable existence. "You could get me out of here." She ran to her side, tried to pull her up but couldn't. "Get a car."

"I can't." Her face dripped with tears for the impending loss. "I don't have one."

Iron Hans moved only her lips as she said, "Your father must. Take it."

"How?" She looked at her, utterly discouraged, seeing only a future filled with inevitable death.

"The keys. Get the keys. He must keep them in his bedroom. Be careful. Get them!" Iron Hans kept her position. Confidence swarmed around her almost as thickly as the mosquitoes drawn by her congealing blood. The girl turned and went back to her house. She slipped through the rooms, her breath catching with panic. She did not know what her father would do to her if he found her in his room, with his keys in hand, walking slyly back out again, sitting in his car, driving down the night-soaked streets to save his brand-new-most-hated enemy. She drove the car over the curb with the lights blackened and parked next to Iron Hans, helped her into the backseat, and whisked her away from her lynching ground, examining her bruised face in the rearview mirror while her mind whirled and her heart overbeat, and her fingers clasped themselves into grooves on the steering wheel.

"Thanks," Iron Hans said, crouching low into her seat to keep her face in the shadows.

"Uh-huh," the girl said, her rigid body showing her nervousness more clearly than any obsessive fidgeting would.

"What's your name?"

"Jackie"—her eyes never lifted from the road—"after the late great president."

"Don't you mean his wife?"

"No. My father was kind of obsessed. What about yours?"

"My father, or my name?" Iron Hans asked bemusedly.

"Your name."

"My name is Haldonna Mitchell, named after both my parents. I won't even torture you with my poor brother's variation. But everyone around here just calls me 'Iron Hans.'"

Jackie's face split into a stress-tight smile. "Iron, huh? Isn't that a little pretentious?"

Iron Hans shrugged, one maroon-splattered shoulder dipping into the light and then tucking itself back away from it again equally quickly. "I guess. But if my reputation keeps me out of trouble, I'll keep it."

"Well, Hans…"

"Please. If you're going to call me anything, call me 'Iron Hans.' I'm not some towheaded Danish guy with an impending identity crisis."

"Okay, Iron Hans, what's up? How'd you end up like this in the square?"

"I was in the wrong place in the wrong time. No, actually, I was in the right place, but I was marauded by testosterone-weakened thugs who decided to take their unhappiness with their brainlessness out on me. I thought I was safe. I let down my guard, slipped my back to the door. It only takes once, you know. I'm big enough for them to pretend I'm a threat, as if any woman I'd dig would ever give them a first glance, but not so big that there would be a real contest with four on one." Her breath rumbled through her chest as she recounted her humiliation. "Little shits even lifted my cigarettes."

"Check the glove compartment. My dad sometimes leaves a pack there," Jackie said, her eyes focused straight ahead.

"You really took this off his hands? I'll have to remember to give you more credit in the future, Jackie."

The car sped through intersections, past low-income-housing concrete roach traps, through a small park with gigantic trees tapping against the high-rise buildings across the street. Home-lessness bustled, cats and people alike. Left, right, right. Left, right, right. A steady beat of turns picked up, dictating the slow twisting spiral they made around City Hall. Jackie kept to herself most of the time, trying to get a lock on the person seated next to her as the gas gauge slowly slipped down past half a tank. Every word Iron Hans had said resonated within her. Jackie had never heard anyone speak so candidly about such antipatriarchal, antipatriotic ideas, yet every syllable felt true. She had no reason to question Iron Hans, sooth-sayer extraordinaire, only herself. Why had she never articulated these statements herself, why had she never tried to live by them as Iron Hans obviously did, why had she never even consciously thought them to herself when they fit to her so well? Curiosity was beginning to strengthen her bones, a desire to beg Iron Hans to explain exactly how she enabled herself to live this way.

She began her search with the most basic—or so it seemed—question: "Iron Hans, what was that you said about digging women?" As the words came out of her mouth, Jackie knew the answer, and knew it applied to herself as well. Iron Hans reset her butt on the seat for a moment to arrange her thoughts before addressing Jackie, but then looked at her face and saw that she didn't have to. She changed her tactic.

"What did you want to know?"

Jackie opened her mouth to speak, her eyes moving back and forth across the road as if in REM. "Would it be tacky to say 'everything'? Uhm…"

Iron Hans grabbed her shoulder and squeezed it. "I remember what you're going through right now," she said with a grin. "A couple of hours ago, I was afraid I'd never get the opportunity to watch it again."

"God—what they did—is that always going to happen?"

"Not when they kill you. Then they don't do it anymore," Iron Hans said without a touch of irony. "Speaking of which, what are you going to do now? You know what you are now. You can't forget it, and you'll never be able to pretend well enough that someone won't notice it. Your father is going to be pissed at you, at best. You'll be lucky if he doesn't have you convicted on grand theft auto for lifting his wheels and setting my repulsive ass down on his precious leather bucket seats."

Jackie's eyes welled up, not quite crying, but not quite not. "You're right. I don't know."

"Well, I'll tell you what I'd do. I'd drive this thing somewhere into The Forest and torch it so no one could trace it to you. His insurance would cover it, and then you could deal with the rest of his shit later without him waving a prison term over your head." Jackie quickly wiped a tear off her cheeks as she listened to Iron Hans. "You know, you could always come with me. I could teach you the ropes, give you a place to stay before your pop throws you out."

Jackie turned another corner, the palms of her hands abused nearly to the point of bruising by her grip. "What would I have to do?"

"Nothing." Iron Hans laughed. "Just stay away from my girl." Jackie looked incredulous and mistrustful. "I'd consider it an honor and my duty to bring another upstanding person into the community. Besides, I owe you for pulling my ass out of the square."

"You're right," Jackie said, trying to convince herself she was making the right decision. "I'll go with you. Just tell me what I have to do."

"All right! Put her there!" Iron Hans yelled as she shook Jackie's hand and directed her on how to safely get back to The Forest.

Once there, Jackie upped Iron Hans's suggestion for dumping the car by paying a couple of thugs $50 to hot wire it and drive it around some more before torching it. She warned them vigorously to avoid getting caught, because no matter what they said, they'd be charged with kidnapping. Iron Hans led her back toward the bar, sticking to nondescript alleyways to avoid any cops on the outlook. Luckily, it was still dark, so the lynching crew was still sleeping off their binge.

At one dilapidated row house, Iron Hans stopped and knocked. They went down two flights of stairs and from basement to basement down the block and across the street. They went up a full seven stories to the roof, walked two houses over, and crawled into an attic that was sealed off so there was no access to the rest of the house. A pretty woman with blonde hair slithered over to Iron Hans, her lavender gossamer wraps swirling around her thighs. She grabbed Iron Hans's face with her inch-long nails and kissed her as if she hadn't seen her in weeks, reopening sticky gashes along her eyebrows from the intense pressure. Jackie stared at them, visibly astonished at the sight of two women kissing. She pulled a long strand of her chestnut hair from its barrette and twisted it between and around her fingers, back and forth like a yo-yo slowly being spun up and down. Unconsciously, she pulled her body to the left to lean against a wall post, in order to feel the tension in her arm of her muscles fighting against the immovable wood, her fingers twisting and twisting as she watched Iron Hans's neck cords bulge and relax as she worked her mouth against this other woman's, her lips tender and tight at the same time, snapped wide open but still inoffensive from Jackie's imperfect angle.

"This is Spring," Iron Hans said when she regained her breath. "Her parents were hippies, and that's her given name, or so she claims." They traded sizzling grins.

Spring turned around, her skirt fluttering back down in place, eventually obscuring even her ankles, the soft curves of her legs easily visible even when the light wasn't shining on them. "Who is this?" she asked.

"Jackie," Iron Hans's breathy voice dropped an octave.

"Jackie," Spring repeated. She pulled a long lock down over Jackie's forehead. "Beautiful," she said, the back of her fingers brushing against Jackie's face as she stroked her hair. "Am I replaced?"

"Never." Iron Hans hugged her tight from behind and buried her face in Spring's neck. Spring pulled her hair back away from her face and smiled at Jackie. Her fingers and grin lingered, chilling Jackie. She licked her soft lips.

"I've got to go. But Jackie," Iron Hans said, linking her arm around her shoulders, "I need to make sure you understand something. This is my girl Spring. She's delightfully innocent; her conscience is as bright and clear as crystal, and I don't want you to defile her, if you know what I mean. I'll be back tonight. 'Bye, love," she said to Spring with a peck. "And don't worry about all this"—she motioned to her bruises—"I'll stay out of trouble. I promise. Keep your head about you, Jackie. I have my ways to discover cheats and traitors."

With a wave of her arm, she left them in the loft unchaperoned. Within seconds, Spring cried out, "Oh, shit!"

"What's the matter?" Jackie asked.

"Damn. I had to ask Iron Hans to do something for me, but I forgot to get her to do it while she was here."

"Don't worry," Jackie assured her. "She'll be back soon."

"Jackie," Spring cooed, "could you do me a favor?"

"Sure, I guess."

"Well, um, have you ever seen another girl's pussy?"

Jackie immediately flushed and stammered, "Well, ah, what does that have to do with anything?"

"Well," Spring continued, slowly working her way across the room toward Jackie. "I had this rather personal request I wanted to ask you, and I didn't want to shock you."

"Request?" Jackie mumbled while instinctively backing away.

"You see, I have this sort of tickle way up inside that's driving me nuts, almost to the point of pain, and my fingers aren't long enough to reach it...."

"They don't look any much smaller than mine," Jackie sputtered.

"But you'd have a better angle. Anyway, could you try to get it for me? Please?"

Jackie looked steadily away, shifting her weight from foot to foot. "Iron Hans said that I wasn't to defile you. I think that qualifies—"

"Oh, forget that sexist bullshit. And I wasn't asking you to sleep with me, just scratch a little itch." Spring lay down on a couch, pulling her dress up to her belly as she spread her legs and lifted her hips up into the air. "Oh, come on, honey. It won't kill you. Just put your middle finger right in that little hole. Come on. Come on. That's it."

Jackie slowly came closer, worry and hesitation written all over her face. "Nope, not like that. Fingernail down, toward my butt. Now be careful when you slide in, and don't go poking at me."

For the first time, Jackie felt the warm folds of another woman's cunt suck at her finger.

"Now, don't curl your knuckles up like you're scratching someone's back. Slide your finger in and out, so there's a little bit of friction but no pain. Oh, ya! There it is. Oh, ya. Now a little bit more pressure, in and out. To the left, to the left a little bit. Oh, ya, right there. Right there, Jackie. Keep it up. Oh, ya. Thanks. Thanks so much, Jackie. God, that was great. I thought that tickle was going to drive me crazy."

Jackie pulled her finger out of Spring and it glistened, coated to her palm. She stared at it, twisting it to watch the light sparkles glint like raindrops on a tree branch, until Spring distracted her by nodding toward the bathroom. She took a wad of toilet paper and wiped Spring off her hand, tossed the mess in the trash, and washed the last traces of her down the drain.

Iron Hans came home a few hours later, and with one look at Spring's big pussycat grin knew something had happened. She ransacked the bathroom immediately, looking for evidence, and spied the wad of TP in the basket. She came out and said, "Jackie, come on. We've got to discuss a few things." Jackie jumped to it, a little nervous, but feeling wholly blameless. They went back across the roof, down six floors to the sub-basement, and started off on a new subterranean trek that lead them up and out about two city blocks away from the first house they entered. They hopped a bus across town to an area bustling with tourists so they would blend in without incident. "Jackie, you're a butch, right?"

"A butch?" Jackie's face screwed up to show her lack of understanding.

"Ya, a butch. You know, like me." Iron Hans didn't look at Jackie while she spoke. She kept her voice low and kept an eye out for trouble.

"Ya, I guess." She didn't want to be disrespectful, she just had never thought about it before. Jackie's eyes had been opened to a lot of new things in the last day.

"Well, then, there's a lot of things you're going to have to understand. First of all, don't ever, ever, wear pink—not even those little cutesy triangles that are supposed to show community solidarity. Rainbows are okay if displayed sparingly and subtly, you know, with some taste; but pink is out. Second, you can't go behind somebody's back with their girl, especially if she's a pal. If you really want to be with someone who's taken, have enough self-respect to pursue her in public and take the lumps that are going to come your way. You'll have one good fight, and it'll be over. Your reputation won't be ruined forever. Now, I know Spring can be pretty persuasive...."

"I didn't do anything with Spring."

Iron Hans stopped cold and studied Jackie with a look on her face as if she were trying to convince herself not to get pissed and knock her block off. "And you have to fess up when you're caught. I saw what you left in the wastepaper basket. If you're going to try to pull one over on me, you'd better learn to cover your tracks better. I don't know what happened, and I don't *want* to know what happened, but I can't have someone staying at my place if she's going to be bopping my girl, *capisce?*"

"Okay. Sorry, Iron Hans."

"You know, the worst of it is that I really don't think you knew what you were doing. What the hell kind of teacher do I think I am if you can't even figure that one out? But your instinct must be pretty good if she gave me a grin like that," Iron Hans gave Jackie a playful punch on the arm.

"I don't know. She just said she had this tickle...."

"Ah, the tickle line," Iron Hans bobbed her head and grinned broadly. "That's how she picked me up. Just don't let it happen again."

"Sure," Jackie said with a grin.

The next morning, Iron Hans left to do her business again. Jackie puttered around, thumbing through old magazines she found in the bathroom to study up on being a butch. Just after lunch Spring came over to her, hopping from foot to foot, a pained expression on her face. "Jackie, you've got to help me out."

Fresh from her reacquaintance with the het world's lost art of butch chivalry, Jackie sprung to her feet. "What do you need?"

"I need another favor." Jackie's face fell, her gaze aimed at Spring's feet. "Not like yesterday. This will only take a second, I swear." Spring stared up at Jackie, her body moving side to side with an intense rhythm.

"Okay. What can I do for you?"

Spring grabbed her skirt, hesitating for a moment to add, "I hope this doesn't offend you." She pulled it up and spread her legs, leaning against a sofa arm for support. "There's a hair down there that doesn't belong there. Can you see it?" Jackie glanced over, then averted her eyes again. "I can't get hold of it. Can you please pick it off for me? Please?"

"Sure." Jackie reached over and snatched the long strand of blonde hair, pulling it off and out of Spring. She shuddered as it was dragged over her skin, the muscles in her thighs and cunt twitching as the invading thread was pulled free.

"Oh, thanks so much. You're a doll," Spring said with a lazy, satisfied smile.

"You're welcome." Jackie dragged her hand nervously through her hair.

"I'm going to go get dressed. Iron Hans should be home soon," Spring said with a wink as she went to her bedroom.

Iron Hans came home within minutes. Jackie shuffled around nervously, but she didn't notice her guilty pace until Spring returned in a sheer rose robe with a feline smile still plastered to her face. Iron Hans looked over at Jackie and saw a long blonde hair snaking down her face. She walked over, pulled the hair off, and stuck her nose to Jackie's forehead, taking a deep whiff in the process. She backed off, nose and eyes flaring. She pounded both fists once against the wall, looked back at Jackie, and left the apartment. Jackie only had time to look over at Spring before she returned, shaking. She grabbed Jackie by the shoulder. "Come on, kid. We have to talk." Jackie looked back and gave Spring a worried smile as Iron Hans half pushed Jackie out the door.

They didn't go far. "So what happened this time?"

Jackie looked down over the edge of the roof. "I guess she got me again, huh?" Iron Hans broke into a grin. "She said she had a hair that was bothering her. I thought a butch was supposed to be kind of like Superman, eager to help in any disaster. I didn't want to insult her by turning her down. And it seemed different—you know, like a different set of circumstances or something. I'm sorry. I guess I let you down again."

"Tell me something." Iron Hans stared at the door leading to her apartment. "What's wrong with me? What is it that I'm not doing right by her that makes her go after other women? It has to be my fault. She's a good woman. What am I missing?" Iron Hans's face was rock hard to avoid shedding tears throughout her speech.

"It's not you. I think she's caught up in the expectation that she needs to act that way. I mean, you do treat her a little sexist." Iron Hans nodded in a distracted, unfocused manner. "Maybe you need to give her a little space, let her find herself. I don't know."

"Ya, you do, Jackie. Thanks." She hugged her tight. "Now, back to your lessons. No student of mine is going to be allowed to slack off. You never get into another woman's girl. Another woman's *woman*," Iron Hans said with a grin. "Chivalry is great, but you do it to your own girl or in a group so no one can pin you with trying to make a move on her. And you don't cry in public no matter how bad it gets; and not in private, if you can help it. The only exception to that rule is if you get plowed in a bar, but I'm not recommending it. The best defense is a good offense. Remember that, Jackie. Take care of yourself, chose your friends well, and be good to your girlfriend. That's the only thing you've got going for you, no more mom and dad to run to if you get in a jam, so look out for yourself, okay?"

"Thanks, Iron Hans," Jackie hugged her. "Now let's go straighten this thing out with Spring."

"Right."

Iron Hans took care of Spring, all right. She picked her up and carried her into their bedroom with a sharp slam of the door,

Without even taking her jacket off, she kept her lady screeching and sighing for almost two full hours. They emerged holding hands and exhausted to a perfectly timed and prepared spaghetti dinner Jackie had whipped up. They spent the rest of the night playing Dirty Scrabble for pennies to match their moods.

The next morning, Iron Hans woke up late and rushed out the door, but not before telling Jackie to stay on track. "I can't put up with much more of this."

"Don't worry. I'll make you proud of me. Iron Hans grabbed a barely warm slice of bread out of the toaster and sprinted off into the morning. Jackie went into a contemplative state, musing about what it meant for her to be butch. She walked around the loft with a hand-held mirror, trying to see if she looked like a butch yet, if she had the walk down. She pulled her hair back into a low pony-tail and sat down on the couch that separated the living room from the kitchen. Tucking her hair over the back of the couch and out of sight, she held the mirror at an angle to show her lower face and body, to see if getting rid of her long hair might help. Suddenly she felt her hair being ripped back. She held the mirror up to see two fistfuls of her ponytail being pressed against Spring's cunt. She was masturbating with abandon right out in the common room. Jackie was pinned on the couch, and she didn't want to grab Spring's hands away because she promised Iron Hans that she wouldn't go there again.

"Spring! Spring, stop. What the hell are you doing? Let go of my hair! Spring, please, let go."

Iron Hans walked in to see Spring's hips and hands pumping, Jackie's head bobbing, snapped back hard on her neck. In her rush to leave she had forgotten to kiss Spring good-bye, and was return-ing for her kiss. She picked Spring up by the waist and carried her into the bedroom, barricading her in with a chair pushed up against the door. She turned around, her face slicked with sweat. Jackie looked at her, tears already dripping off her chin.

"Jackie." Iron Hans rubbed her forehead forcefully with both palms. "I told you not to cry in front of me." Jackie nodded, dejected and humiliated. "Now, kid, the way I'm looking at it is three strikes and you're out. Clean yourself off." Iron Hans tossed her a towel and looked away. Jackie started mopping Spring's pussyjuice out of her hair. "You've got to go. I can't trust you here anymore. Or I can't trust *her*. Jesus!" Iron Hans covered her eyes, then screwed the heels of her palms into them, pulling her left hand down her mouth and chin, then rested both hands on her hips. "You really were a dumb-fuck innocent, though, weren't you?" She sighed harshly, like a cough. "Listen, I don't want you to take this personally. I like you—I really do—but whether or not you meant to do it with Spring in order to fuck me up, you put a serious wrinkle in my trust for you. You know how much that means to me. Listen, kid, if you ever need anything, you come right to me. You just call out 'Iron Hans,' and I'll be there for you. I give you my word on that." Iron Hans put out her hand. Jackie took it gently, shook it, and hugged her fiercely.

With red-rimmed eyes and voice, Jackie said, "I believe you. I'm sorry, so sorry you will never know. And I know you're right. This situation was weird, no matter how helpful it was. Thanks for taking care of me, Iron Hans." Jackie hugged her again. "I'll never forget your kindness."

"Good-bye."

" 'Bye. Give my best to Spring," Jackie said while backing toward the door. "Don't take that wrong. She's your girl. I just want to look out for her, you know. For the both of you."

"I know, Jackie. Don't forget to call me if you need me."

Jackie nodded back and then reentered the world of dust and roses. She wove her way through the basements and emerged by herself, totally on her own for the first time in her life. The first thing she saw was a newspaper with a color picture of herself on the front page under the oversized headline: MISSING! She tucked her hair into her shirt and went into the first barbershop she found. She shaved her head to the skin, leaving a foot and a half of chestnut glory behind for the sweep girl. She felt liberated, as if she was leaving behind both her former het life and the disasters with Spring as she stepped back out on the street looking nothing like the made-up and coiffed picture in the newspapers. Her next destination: to find a job.

With her newly gleaming head, Jackie set off for the place she knew best: City Hall. Along the way, she discovered that she missed her hair—not for its appearance, but for its warmth. The first chance she got, she bought a baseball cap, pulled it down tightly over her ears, and vowed never to take it off again in public. Iron Hans had warned her never to wear pink; Jackie assumed that edict included avoiding blood-saturated skin trying to keep itself warm.

At City Hall, Jackie went straight to the employment office. The man behind the large faux mahogany cubicle dividing wall almost wrote her off immediately as unemployable simply because of her appearance. His argument was that a woman with no hair was unwomanly and could not use her inherent sex appeal, and therefore she was useless. When she wouldn't leave after his dismissal, he demanded that she remove her hat as a show of respect. After nearly forty-five minutes of unending abuse, he finally wearied of his game and suggested that she try the Department of Parks and Recreation, and sent her across town with deceptively vague directions.

After much articulate haranguing of anyone within speaking distance at the DPR, Jackie was offered trash detail at the courtyard section of Gardiner Park, a large grassy square popular with weekend crowds of hedonistic teenagers. Armed with her standard-issue broomstick modified with a nail poking out of one end, she began a campaign against cigarette butts. They were usually considered small enough by City Hall standards to ignore and so most often were, although most park workers would grab a scrap of paper one-quarter the size of a filter tip. The grass along the edges of the walkways and under the benches and around the wastebaskets was spread deep with a confetti of separated cigarette fibers and the occasional stub of a cigar. It was the average task demanded of any new guy, but for a new girl, and a new girl who wanted to look like a guy at that, well, they weren't going to let her rest until it was done. Nonetheless, Jackie was up to the challenge, looking for any deed with which she might prove herself, still sore and sensitive about the blow she gave Iron Hans. Jackie was a woman with a mission, her head never lifting as she stabbed with abandon into the choking grass to pull up the butts.

She looked up only when her stick hit the ground about four inches from a pair of navy flats. Jackie was about to apologize, but the words stuck in her mouth. Before her stood a sweet-looking girl who was smiling at Jackie as if she were waiting for her to say something.

"Hi. Ah…" Jackie began.

"My name is Chantelle." The girl offered her hand. Instinctively, Jackie took it and kissed it above the second knuckles of her fingers. She didn't look up again until she heard Chantelle's giggle. "Pleased to meet you."

"My name's Jackie." She gave her a proper handshake. "Um, sorry about that…"

"That's okay. I liked it," Chantelle said with an angelic smile.

Jackie's heart flipped over four times in her chest. She leaned down and picked up a sprig of tiny mayflowers. Holding them out to Chantelle, Jackie said "Wildflowers always smell more ardent. Listen, I'm working right now, but I'd love to get to know you, and to apologize properly for nearly puncturing your foot. If you wouldn't mind, could I call you sometime?"

"If you wouldn't mind, would you like to come to dinner with me tonight?" Chantelle asked.

Jackie's breath caught again. What if Chantelle didn't realize that she was a girl? How would both of them handle her inevitable revelation? Jackie stuffed those questions away as quickly as they popped up, to avoid insulting Chantelle again. "Sure, I'd love that. How should I get in touch with you?"

"How 'bout I meet you at the front gate of the park around seven?"

"Sounds great, Chantelle."

"Good, then it's a date." She winked and sauntered off down the walkway. Jackie worked at a little less than half speed the rest of the afternoon, but her wham-bam work of the morning evened it out, and no one seemed to notice.

Jackie plucked flowers from all over the park while she waited for Chantelle to reappear—daisies and dandelions and pink geraniums, which were somehow less offensively ugly than the more common red variety. By the time the hour had arrived, Jackie held a thick bouquet that crowded against itself and flopped over her fingers, concealing the entirety of her sweaty hand within the flora. Chantelle accepted her offering with a little difficulty, needing both hands to encase Jackie's fist in order to grab it. She cradled the flowers into the crook of her arm while saying, "You're supposed to tip your hat to greet a lady." She reached up to do it for her, but Jackie grabbed her hand and laced her fingers through it with a grin, her left hand wrapped loosely over their clasped hands.

"Where did you want to go to dinner?" Jackie asked instead.

They spent the next three hours together, talking and touching. Jackie never let Chantelle get far enough away for her to lose contact. She pushed Chantelle's hair out of her eyes when they giggled too jarringly and it bounced in the way, fed her from their shared ice cream cone, and wiped a spot from her lower lip. At an abandoned red light and with no whispering witnesses around, Jackie pressed her lips quickly to Chantelle's, prepared in advance only for a peck, but their lips were slow to part, Chantelle tipping her face to allow for a better contact. The streets were dead around them as the kisses came fast and slow, over and over, until a loud, long horn blasted them out of their reverie, a scream of "Fucking dykes!" sounding into the night.

Jackie pulled back slowly, her mouth slightly opened as if she were searching for inspiration, her eyes turned straight downward so she could see only the pavement between their toes. Chantelle tucked her chin down against Jackie's shoulder, her arms gripping her loosely yet protectively. Jackie returned her hug warmly and without any words, tears of gratitude and past shame trying to collect and cling to her eyelashes, rocking the two of them side to side beneath the streetlight. "I'd love to take you dancing," she said finally.

Chantelle picked up her head and looked into Jackie's eyes. "Dancing? Who said I'd ever want to do anything like that with you?" She broke into a grin, put both hands on Jackie's cheeks, and pulled her forward for another kiss, the two of them melting into each other so completely that they didn't even hear the next protesting car horn.

"God, if my father ever saw me like this," Chantelle said, leaning lazily against Jackie's chest.

"Your father?" Jackie said, stiffening slightly. She hadn't thought of her own father or his possible reaction to her new self in weeks.

"Ya, he's on the City Council. He'd probably go nuts."

"No kidding! My dad's the Mayor."

Chantelle pulled away and looked at Jackie's face again, squinting her eyes slightly in order to study her bone structure, trying to decipher it from the shadows. "God, that kid in all the news, the one they thought was murdered," Chantelle said with her mouth slack, the muscles around her eyes pulled tight.

Jackie looked worried and embarrassed. "Chantelle," she said softly in a low voice. "Please!"

"That's so horrible that he did that to you. He must have found out and wished you dead, banishing you and making up that horrible story so no one would know. God, Jackie, I'm so sorry!"

Jackie ran her hand down Chantelle's head. "Not exactly, but thanks." Her fingers smoothed her hair, comforting both of them with her slow movements. "I'll tell you all about it sometime, though. I think right now we ought to get going before someone takes notice of us personally and wants to show us the error of our ways."

"You're right," Chantelle said. "People are still itching to get somebody. Will you take me home?" Jackie's eyes widened and she sucked in an unexpected breath, half choking it out again. "Oh, I didn't mean it like that, I guess," Chantelle stammered, her face rapidly gaining the red flush of Jackie's. "I mean, walk me home, you know?"

Jackie recovered her self-composure with a quick gulp. "I'd be honored to take you home, Chantelle." She offered her arm.

"Thanks," Chantelle said, melting toward her, her cheek against Jackie's shoulder and a satisfied smile on her face as they started walking down the street.

The next morning, Jackie was awakened by a frantic phone call from Chantelle. She paraphrased a conversation she had had with her brother, describing an impending gang fight he was involved with. Her father was calling in favors all over town, but no one could guarantee her brother's safety, especially since his family ties had him on the same list as the politicians who were putting heat on the gangs, making him a high-level trophy kill. Jackie assured Chantelle that she would do what she could.

Jackie hung up and ran to the subway station, jogged through The Forest and into Deep Pockets, shouting "Iron Hans, Iron Hans!" at the top of her lungs. Iron Hans rose up out of a darkened corner, her eyes squinting and her mouth drawn with mistrust, but her angry stare was quickly replaced by worry. "Iron Hans, I need your help," Jackie said finally, huffing and puffing from her run.

Iron Hans was not interested in getting herself personally involved in a gang war, but she rounded up all her meanest-looking friends, borrowed the biggest, baddest bikes she could find, and laid in wait for the fight. When the warring groups arrived, Iron Hans and her friends roared out after them, chasing them down the side street. The bikers chased the punks all over town while Jackie led Chantelle's brother to safety before stealing off herself. Humiliated by the episode, the two gangs called a truce in order to spend their time hunting down the people responsible for their rousting instead of wasting time fighting each other. The newspapers exploded with the story, publishing exposés describing how a City Councilman's son could sink to gang membership, the lack of an effective police force to wipe out the gangs in general and, most prominently, questions and sketches about the mystery citizen who put "his" life in danger to save the boy. Chantelle gleefully related to Jackie that her father wanted to thank her personally and give her the Key to the City in a great televised ceremony, if only he could figure out who she was.

They celebrated by going to bed for the day. Jackie was nervous and uncomfortable; it was to be her first sexual experience with a woman. Chantelle thought the edginess was due to the timing; she was worried that it might feel to Jackie as if making love was a reward of some kind. She wanted to reassure her that this was not some sympathy fuck, that if the fact that Jackie had saved her brother's life had any effect on her decision, it was only to free her mind from any worries about Jackie's character, and that her heroism made Chantelle realize what a gem Jackie was so she could trust her fully now without waiting and baiting her to find her true motivations. Chantelle opened her mouth to tell this to Jackie, but then she felt fingertips on her thighs, tense at first but then suddenly warm as melted butter, and Jackie's eyes burned with true high carnal romance, telling her without words that any explanations were unnecessary. Her fingers slowly pulled the hem of her dress skyward, lingering on the skin of her thighs, her stare becoming intoxicating. Jackie's heartbeat evened out at about 175 beats per minute as she undressed Chantelle, rubbing the fabric over her body as fresh skin appeared. Chantelle stood limply and expectantly, her desire growing with each passing minute until neither woman could think of anything else in the world but the other.

They spent hours pushing their palms against each other's bodies, fitting themselves together silently in extraordinary poses and reconfigurations. When they finally started kissing and caressing each other's bodies with their tongues, they were both coated with a thin layer of musky sex sweat with all its delicious aphrodisiacal effects, and the next step came quickly. They grunted and squealed and leaked as they simultaneously drove orgasms into each other, each one subtly different, each one spiking a little farther through their bodies, each one a little sweeter and more exhausting and more time consuming until neither had the energy to seek more. Chantelle piled herself onto Jackie's chest to hear her softening heartbeat and to try to become simply herself once again. Unexpectedly, she couldn't. Her body and mind had made her commitment without consulting her first. For Chantelle, she and Jackie were as married as if they were blessed personally by the Pope—more than if they had been. Jackie had proven herself beyond a doubt, and Chantelle wanted to shout it from the rooftops. In fact, Chantelle was ready and willing to bring Jackie home to meet her parents.

But she couldn't just bring Jackie home; that would make it too easy for them to reject her. Chantelle needed to have her parents, and especially her father, meet Jackie and get to know her as a person before they found out she was her lover, or they would hate her on principle straight from the start. And Jackie needed to get to know who they were firsthand before she met them formally and inadvertently offended them with a slip of her silver-plated tongue. As luck would have it, there was yet another weekend festival on the way, complete with good-natured games and competitions to raise community spirits and quell unsanctioned intra-neighborhood rivalries. And, even more happily, Chantelle's father, as acting head of the City Council, was going to hand out the winning awards. Chantelle suggested to Jackie that she might enter a few contests to get a good look at her old man, and maybe win something, so he would have a good first impression of her.

Jackie knew that this was a job that could use the expertise of Iron Hans. After giving Chantelle an ambling kiss good-bye, she repeated her run through the city, stopping only when otherwise she would have been plowed down by cars. Finally she arrived again at Deep Pockets, baying like a banshee all the way into the back poolroom: "Iron Hans, come here, I want you." She almost screwed up a sweet shot, but Iron Hans was actually glad to see her little buddy again and to hear of all her new exploits. They pored over the festival schedule, picking out the contests that Jackie might win. The first was Friday night—precision pitching. Iron Hans insisted that Jackie look the part, digging through her closet for a well-worn baseball shirt and a broken-in but still-bright red cap. Setting them aside with a flourish, Iron Hans and Jackie went out in the street and threw balls back and forth at each other for the rest of the night, progressively throwing harder and more accurately as their pitches numbered into the hundreds.

On Friday afternoon Iron Hans came around to pitch some more to loosen Jackie up, and cheered her on as she went through her contenders one by one. They fell neatly into two categories: the lumbering oxen who could throw half a mile but couldn't hit the street dropping a ball from a moving bus, or the guys who could aim fairly accurately but didn't have enough power to ding a tin can. Jackie hit target after target. After each round, the target was dramatically pushed back a few feet farther to make it even more difficult to hit. But it was not long before she raised her mitt high in victory. Chantelle's father appeared as soon as the cameramen were in place, brandishing three golden medallions swinging on blue, white, and red ribbons. He shook Jackie's hand with a disdainful look at her scornfully cocked cap and placed the apple red ribbon securely around her neck while grumbling that there would be no media coverage when the winner refused to give "his" last name so all the relatives and former classmates could tattle and reminisce. Jackie stayed true to her anonymous state and checked out her future father-in-law from afar.

The next competition was a citywide blocks-long street game of "Simon Says." That morning Jackie went back to Deep Pockets, shouting "Iron Hans, Iron Hans!" until she was nearly hoarse. Iron Hans was actually home reading a book, but she heard Jackie squawking with abandon two blocks away and met her at the front door. The first thing they did was strip Jackie out of her jeans and find her something more photogenic. Iron Hans, always proud of her innate sense of style, outdid herself on Jackie, dressing her in a cream-colored suit and tie over a blue striped collarless shirt. To finish the look, they set her up with lambda cuff links and a dapper fedora with an excellent line.

The day was a beauty, and it looked like half of downtown had entered the game. They started in groups of about a hundred and stopped when they got down to under ten, until only seventy-five brave souls were left. This group was split into two and weeded down to four or five for the final televised game. Jackie was third from the left. Even at this close scrutiny, no one save Chantelle and Iron Hans recognized her as the winner of the day before's pitching competition or as the Mayor's missing daughter. The remaining "Simon Says" competitors were given a limbering workout by the local basketball mascot, and town kids lined up for their fifteen seconds of fame. Each child in order was to direct a command to the players, an unquestionably anonymous and random play of the game so no one could accuse anyone of cheating. With a censor at the ready to kill the sound on any kid with a vulgar mouth, the game began. These were serious contenders, but Jackie was determined to win and make both Chantelle and Iron Hans proud of her. After nearly twenty minutes of hopping and spinning and making grotesque faces, it was down to Jackie and one other woman, the crowd favorite, a popular local kindergarten teacher. With a deep breath and a quick smile at Chantelle, Jackie pressed on. A long minute later, she was declared winner. The announcer had to say it twice to be heard over the din of the disappointed voices. Jackie kept her hat on as she shook the teacher's hand and bowed to let Chantelle's father place a second red ribbon around her neck, letting the golden medallion bounce against her chest as she waved to the massive crowd and the 6:00 P.M. local news viewers.

The last contest was singing — amateur night at a popular arty nightclub. There was an eight-dollar cover and an open bar. As soon as Jackie heard this, she lost her confidence and ran back to Deep Pockets screaming: "Iron Hans! Iron Hans!" like a lunatic in heat. Her panic was fed by the nagging knowledge that she was ignoring Chantelle throughout the weekend on her quest to win over the town, and she was afraid all her work would be in vain if Chantelle got fed up with her preoccupation and broke up with her. Iron Hans saw this immediately in the look on her face and put Jackie's mind to choosing a song. After much deliberation Iron Hans and Jackie decided she should sing "Wicked Game" because she could sing it to Chantelle and romance her away from her dissatisfactions. Unfortunately, two other people had already signed up to sing that same song. After more debate and watered-down beer, they agreed that she would win over the crowd by virtue of her "sheness," providing that neither of the others would blow her away with their ability or outrageous persona. Then Spring suggested that Jackie punch up her own image and wear leather.

Iron Hans dragged a very nervous Jackie down an off-alley to a closet-sized store called Whips 'n' Clips. She paid the much-tattooed guy behind the counter discreetly, and he unlocked the back door, affording them access to a near warehouse of gleaming multicolored leathers and metals. The rows were neatly marked with handwritten gothic-lettered signs. They went past the mags, the books, the viewing booths and pre-viewed videos for sale, the lubes (including a twenty-gallon tub with a hand pump for easy hygienic access), the vibrators and other mechanical objects that took up two full rows, the butt plugs and dildos, and finally the fetish wear. Iron Hans held her chin in a Sherlockian pose, leaning back to survey what was available, and immediately started crossing things off her list. "No nipple clips, nothing holey or sheer. We don't want to turn people on and give them the wrong impression. You want to win, not show yourself off to a paying crowd. Nothing with slogans; no collars or restraints. You don't want to scare people off, just get their attention." Jackie stayed shrunken in the spot she stopped, a worried and embarrassed expression on her face as she watched Iron Hans peruse the leather underwear with the metal bones embedded over the ass. She finally returned with a stack of black leather over her arm. She popped a studded leather cap on Jackie's head and said, "You'll wear this vest and these chaps over a pair of jeans. That should give you a little area to sweat the heat off but keep you as encased in leather as possible. You can borrow my boots. What do you think?"

Jackie ran her hands over the soft leather vest, a grin splitting her face. She began nodding and said, "I think it will work." They broke out laughing and spent the next hour ruminating about who would ever actually buy such things as the dildo set at a ninety-degree angle on top of a large rubber ball like a childhood bouncing toy.

The next day Jackie sang nonstop, almost to the point of losing her voice, to everyone's unspoken horror. She had a good draw—toward the end of the contest, second of the three Wicked Gamers. Their strategy worked. Her visual presentation blew away the first singer, and by the third time around, everyone was so bored with the song that they nearly booed his uneven warbling off the stage. Jackie won by a landslide. As Chantelle's father placed the third ribbon around Jackie's neck, a twinge of recognition flitted over his face, and when he looked back at his daughter sitting in the front row of the audience, the look of love in her eyes caused the pit of his stomach to sink low into his bowels. Before he knew what was happening, ruffians in the crowd started chanting "Dyke! Dyke! Dyke! Dyke!" and pushed forward toward Jackie. One guy grabbed her leg, pulling it out from under her. She fell backward on her butt, her hat falling off as the media cameras clicked and recorded undeniable photos of the Mayor's presumed-dead daughter. She backed away in a crablike crawl and as soon as she was out of her pursuers' range she stood up and ran off the stage and out the back door. Chantelle ran up onstage, snatched her cap, and ran out after her, a crowd of would-be bashers on her heels. Jackie was not to be found. Thankfully, she was able to slink into the shadows again and avoid what might have been her death.

Chantelle strolled off, careful to avoid the menacing crowd and to keep from being followed. She wound her way through the city streets and, after about forty harrowing minutes, felt safe enough to return to Gardiner Park. She found Jackie still heaving on a bench next to a heap of still-glowing flowers. Jackie jumped up to hug Chantelle tightly, holding her to calm herself, to feel safe only in knowing that Chantelle would be there for her. Under the sharp light of the fluorescent lights, Jackie pulled the strands of hair away from Chantelle's face and said, "I love you, you know."

Chantelle waited half a beat. "I love you, too."

"I guess that's it, then." Jackie smiled at her.

"Ya," Chantelle said with a softly awed voice. A siren blew somewhere close by and a homeless man shuffled through looking for some sort of jackpot in the trash cans. "So, does this mean you'll marry me someday?"

"I'll marry you in a minute. I think I'm already married to you, actually. But I guess it's saying it that makes it real and binding, huh?" Jackie got down on her knees before Chantelle, taking her hat from her hands and putting it on the bench next to the flowers. Taking hold of both of Chantelle's hands, Jackie said, "I commit myself to you, Chantelle. I will be your lover, your friend, your guardian, your helpmate, and your life-partner forever, or as long as you want me. I promise I will be good and kind to you, that I won't hold you back from attaining your true potential, and that I will support your decisions even if on the surface they may seem to do either me or you harm. I trust that you will act in love and kindness toward yourself and me and everyone else who is worthy of your attention." Jackie swallowed hard, her eyes tearing up as she squinted to see Chantelle's face in the shadowed contrast to the light shining down over her. "Will you accept me?"

"Yes." Her gleaming smile coaxed another onto Jackie's lips.

"Chantelle." The voice was weak but unexpected; the effect upon them was the same as a booming command. Chantelle turned to see her father standing about ten feet away. Jackie got up and stood between them, preparing herself to defend her wife. The man took two steps forward and then offered her his hand. "Welcome to my family." Jackie shook his hand proudly and Chantelle half-pushed her away to hug her father. "You two should come home. The streets are no place to start a honeymoon."

The next morning, Jackie went home with Chantelle to plead her case to her parents. Her father was an ally of Chantelle's father, so he ignored the frantic calls from the media in order to call him up to discuss their daughters' situation. Neither man could tolerate the idea of losing his daughter for any reason, and both saw the possible political boon that could be gained by a family merger. The only choice they had was to accept their daughters' mutual love and commitment to each other. They held a press conference that afternoon. On the agenda was the announcement of their daughters' wedding and of the private reception that they were planning jointly to celebrate their union. The reception would be closed to the media and would take place when the women returned from their honeymoon at a secret location out of state. They also announced the creation of a new City Department to handle homosexual hate crimes, since the general hate-crimes division was notoriously lax in pursuing homosexual cases, and of a new Lesbi-Gay Antiviolence Facilitator to overlook the department. At the suggestion of their daughters, the City Council was proud to announce that the first facilitator would be Haldonna "Iron Hans" Mitchell. The first matter Iron Hans, as she chose to be called, would be attending to was to assemble a panel to study community education possibilities and to poll the lesbi-gay community to see in general how pervasive antigay violence was currently affecting the City.

Down in the Cinders
MARCY SHEINER

The story of Cinderella has been part of my life ever since I can remem-
ber. One of the reasons it resonates so strongly for me is that my relationship
with my older sister has been very intense, fraught with competitive-
ness, jealousy, and desire.

As a child I organized a group of neighborhood kids to perform
"Cinderella," in which I played the stepmother. During the 1970s I was
part of Womanrite, a feminist theater collective that performed "The
Cinderella Project," an avant-garde production emphasizing Cinderella's
sexist and patriarchal message. When I heard about this project, I knew
immediately that I would write a version of "Cinderella." In exploring
the erotic components of the story, I discovered yet another way to show
that sisters do not always have to hate one another.

Cinderella sat by the hearth gazing with pride at the excellent fire
she had just built. She brushed her blonde hair out of her face,
unmindful of the streaks of black soot left in the wake of her hands.
The flames licked at the perfect logs she had herself chopped

earlier in the day, their light and heat generating a similar feeling within Cinderella's body, which throbbed as she anticipated the return of her stepmother and stepsisters.

Dusk was her favorite time of day, the hour before Brunhilde, Grunella, and Griselda finished the important work they did out in the world and came home to be pampered by Cinderella. She gazed around at the sparkling clean house, fresh-cut flowers ornamenting every surface, pots bubbling on the stove. As always, Cinderella derived great satisfaction from her day's work; she loved creating a beautiful environment for herself and for others.

Especially for others.

She rose from the hearth, checked the soup, then headed out back with the laundry basket. It was a crisp autumn day, and the clothes she'd hung that morning were dry and sweet-smelling. Cinderella removed a pair of Griselda's panties from the line, buried her face in the crotch, and inhaled deeply. Before washing, the panties had reeked of her stepsister's hot musky juices; Cinderella had nearly fainted from the pungent aroma. But even without Griselda's juices encrusting the fine satin, the panties still gave Cinderella a thrill. Greedily she fingered the flimsy material, the little satin bow that rested just beneath her stepsister's navel, the filigreed lace that would caress Griselda's pearly thighs.

She became conscious of her own panties, their thin cotton graying from too many washings. The crotch was wet, as it usually was by evening. Though Cinderella felt ashamed of this, she simply couldn't help it. Her panties got wet when she scrubbed the floor. They got wet when she ironed her stepmother's skirts. They got wet when she made up her stepsisters' beds and fluffed their downy pillows. Serving her family made Cinderella so wet that sometimes she had to leave her chores, lie down among the cinders where she slept, and touch herself until she reached satisfaction. She had no idea what this was or why it happened, but she knew for sure it was wicked. Her stepmother had once caught her touching herself down there and had held her hands over hot coals until they blistered. Still, this punishment did not stop Cinderella, it just made her more cautious.

She continued to remove the clothes from the line, pausing to fondle a lacy bra cup, or to bury her face in a silk nightgown. Suddenly she heard the front door slam.

"I'm home!" Brunhilde shouted.

Cinderella threw the rest of the laundry into the basket and rushed to greet her stepmother in the foyer. Alas, she was too late: by the time she reached her, Brunhilde had removed her own coat and gloves. Cinderella dropped to her knees and kissed the hem of her stepmother's dress. "Forgive me, Mistress."

Brunhilde laughed wickedly, then tapped Cinderella on the shoulder with her walking stick. "Oh, nonsense, Cin, I don't know why you insist on this tedious bowing and scraping. Get up, you pathetic wretch! If you must abase yourself, at least put it to use. Fetch me a cup of mulled wine."

Cinderella scrambled to her feet, but not before bestowing a quick, stealthy kiss on her stepmother's elegant fingertips. She raced into the kitchen and poured a cup of mulled wine, then brought it to Brunhilde, who had seated herself on the couch. She knelt and removed Brunhilde's high-laced boots, polished to a gleam just that morning by Cinderella herself. Brunhilde closed her eyes and leaned her head back, cradling her mulled wine while her stepdaughter massaged her feet.

"Mmm, that's a good girl," Brunhilde murmured, wiggling her elegant toes.

Cinderella's nipples hardened instantly. Suffused with shame, she leaned against her stepmother's legs and took a deep breath, trying to calm herself.

Brunhilde kicked her away. "Stop mooning, child! Your step-sisters will be home any minute, and you know how cross they get when you're unkempt. You look as if you've been lying in the cinders all day. Go wash your face."

"Yes, Mistress." Cinderella rushed off to wash her face and comb her hair.

When she returned, Grunella and Griselda had arrived home and were tossing their outerclothes all about the room, clamoring for their wine. Cinderella scrambled about gathering up gloves and hats and coats, then served them their wine and removed their boots. Unlike their mother, the girls did not compliment Cinderella on her foot massages, but kicked and cursed as she knelt before them. This only made her panties wetter and her nipples harder. When their mother wasn't looking, Cinderella surreptitiously took her sisters' toes into her mouth and sucked them. Grunella, in particular, had a way of maneuvering her foot that drove Cinderella to distraction. Grunella would slide her smooth, delicate foot in and out of Cinderella's mouth, reaching all the way down her throat, then draw out and rub her toes along Cinderella's lips. Sometimes she'd pretend she was going to slide it in again, but just as Cinderella got ready to take it, Grunella would withdraw hastily, driving Cinderella wild with frustration. She swooned with pleasure whenever Grunella deigned to feed her an entire foot. The sensation of it against the back of her throat was exquisite, and she welcomed it as another opportunity to demonstrate her devotion.

"Cinderella!" Brunhilde shouted. "Where's supper?"

Cinderella hastened off to the kitchen. She served the family, jumping up every so often to fetch the salt, the cheese, a glass of water, eating hardly anything herself.

During supper, the sisters spoke excitedly about a ball that was to be given by the prince of their country. It was rumored that the prince was seeking a wife, and the sisters hoped that one of them would be chosen.

Cinderella had known that eventually her stepsisters must marry, but she had not realized the time might come so soon. A sense of foreboding overcame her; feeling physically ill, she begged to be excused from her duties. She ran out to the field behind the house and, collapsing behind a large haystack, heaved great heart-heavy sobs. To think that her stepsisters might leave her! Never again to sniff Griselda's panties! Never again to suck Grunella's toes! Oh, she could not bear it. True, Brunhilde would still require her services—but Brunhilde was not as consciously cruel toward Cinderella as were her daughters.

Suddenly, out of nowhere, their next-door neighbor Fanny appeared.

"Child," she asked kindly, "why are you crying?'

"Be—Because"—Cinderella gasped between sobs—"my sisters are going to the ball to try to marry the prince."

Now, Fanny had been living next door to Cinderella and her family for years, and was constantly outraged by the way in which Cinderella was treated. Once or twice she had even said something to Brunhilde, who had told her in no uncertain terms to mind her own business. Now Fanny saw an opportunity to help Cinderella at last.

"Oh, my dear, you are so right to be upset. It's very unfair. But I'll tell you what—I will help you go to the ball."

Cinderella abruptly stopped crying and stared at Fanny. "I? Go to the ball?"

Fanny clucked her tongue and stroked Cinderella's hair. "Oh, my poor, sweet girl. You cannot imagine anything so wonderful for yourself, can you?"

Actually, Cinderella could not imagine anything so horrifying for herself. She was terrified of strangers; she hated leaving home; she fainted in large crowds. She shook her head, struck dumb by terror.

'Oh, yes, child, you can go! I will see to it. I shall make you the finest dress, buy you the finest shoes, fix your beautiful golden hair with my very own hands. Now, don't breathe a word of this to your mother or sisters. You just leave it all to Aunt Fanny."

As suddenly as she had appeared, Fanny vanished. Cinderella pulled herself together, dusted the hay from her dress, and slowly walked back to the house, hoping it had all been a bad dream.

If it was a dream, then the week was a nightmare. Fanny seized numerous opportunities to ambush Cinderella in the yard and measure her waist, her breasts, even her feet. Cinderella could not bring herself to hurt the woman's feelings, so she suffered through these agonies, trying not to think about what would happen the night of the ball.

Meanwhile, the household was in a frenzy of preparations for Grunella and Griselda. Cinderella was busy sewing their gowns; many times a day she pricked her fingers, drawing blood, and would get so excited that she had to retire to the cinders to relieve herself.

The night of the ball, Cinderella was in a state of rapture as she prepared and beautified her stepsisters. When she reddened Grunella's nipples with dye she had made from berries, her sister shoved her mouth onto her full white breast, bidding her to suck. During Griselda's bath, she ordered Cinderella to rub the soap into previously forbidden crevices.

Flushed and happy, Cinderella arranged her stepsisters' hair into artful sculptures, and tenderly colored their beautiful faces. She all but forgot the purpose of these preparations—but when her sisters finally left, she remembered, and after Brunhilde retired, she crawled into the cinders to weep.

Suddenly she heard a knocking on the window.

"Psst! Cindy! Let me in!" It was that crazy Fanny—Cinderella had forgotten all about her! She quietly crept outside.

Fanny held a blue gown resplendent with frills, puffy sleeves, and scalloped hem; Cinderella thought it wasn't half as elegant as the ones she had fashioned for her stepsisters. In Fanny's other hand she held a pair of small glass slippers; again, they were no match for the white leather high-heeled boots Cinderella had lovingly selected to adorn her stepsisters' feet.

"Miss Fanny," she murmured, her head bowed respectfully, "You are very kind, but you see, I really don't want—"

"Nonsense, my child! Everything is arranged. My coachman will drive you and wait outside. If you don't show up by midnight then he'll assume you've found yourself a more interesting chauffeur." She winked lasciviously and elbowed Cinderella in the ribs.

Resigned to her fate, Cinderella allowed Fanny to dress her in the ridiculous frilly gown and the tiny glass slippers. Although fairly certain that her stepsisters wouldn't recognize her in this getup, Cinderella kept a low profile at the ball. When she spotted Griselda and Grunella dancing with handsome young men, she seethed with jealousy. Strange images invaded her head, images of her stepsisters lying beneath these handsome men, squirming, writhing, letting them take their pleasure. Half-crazed from jealousy and excitement, dazed and feverish, Cinderella suddenly found herself on the dance floor with none other than the prince himself.

He held her slim waist and steered her onto a darkened terrace.

"You," he murmured, gazing down at her upturned face, "are the most beautiful woman I have seen in my life. You are far more lovely than any other woman here."

Cinderella lowered her eyes, embarrassed. Obviously the man had not seen her stepsisters.

"And modest as well. I like that in a woman. I like you, sweetheart. In fact, I think I'm in love with you. I think I will choose you as my wife."

Cinderella was speechless.

"Ah, you're so happy you cannot speak. And well you should be. As my wife, you will have a dozen servants to fill your every need. I will pamper and spoil you. I will make love to you ever so gently."

He placed a hand on her breast and brushed her nipple with his thumb, his touch so tentative as to be almost nonexistent. Cinderella's nipple shriveled and receded. "I promise I shall never touch you any harder than that, my sweet princess." He slid his hand down her waist and rested it lightly on her hip, leaned forward and kissed her eyes, then her ears, gentle kisses that tickled like a crawling insect.

A wave of nausea engulfed Cinderella. She was struck by the memory of Grunella's foot prying her mouth open, moving relentlessly down her throat with no consideration or hesitancy. She marveled at how differently she responded to her stepsister than she did to the prince: He made her skin crawl.

Cinderella was shaken out of her musings by the sound of the clock striking midnight. "I must go!" she cried, terrified that she wouldn't reach Fanny's coachman in time and would be stuck with this simpering creature for the rest of the night. She jerked herself from his loose embrace and flew down the castle stairs. One of her slippers caught in a crack and fell off; Cinderella had no time to retrieve it. She rushed into the waiting coach, slammed the door, and said more forcefully than she'd said anything in her entire life, "Let's go!"

When she got home, Cinderella ran directly into the field, tore off her dress, and hid it behind the haystack. She went to the well and washed her face, trying to scrub off the prince's insipid touch.

"Ugh!" she said out loud, "I'm glad that's over!"

The next morning, there was a great hubbub throughout the capital. The prince ordered all houses searched for the beautiful girl who had worn the glass slipper that had been left on his stairway after the ball. Three manservants arrived at Cinderella's home and demanded to see every female in the household.

Griselda and Grunella rushed right out and tried on the glass slipper, pushing and prodding their big feet this way and that—to no avail. Cinderella sat quaking behind the stove, hoping not to be seen, but eventually one of the manservants discovered her. She kicked and shrieked and bit his arm, but he dragged her out of hiding and forced her to try on the slipper—which, of course, fit perfectly.

Grunella and Griselda gasped. "How can this be?"

In a fit of tears, Cinderella threw herself on Brunhilde. "I didn't want to go," she wailed. "Fanny made me do it. I'm so sorry. Please don't send me away." She crawled from Brunhilde to Griselda to Grunella, clutching at their hems, licking their boots in a frenzied display of groveling.

Meanwhile, the prince had arrived and saw the glass slipper sparkling on the foot of…a filthy wretch who crawled around the floor like a dog.

"How can this be?" he asked, appalled that he had promised marriage to this creature.

"Some terrible mistake," Brunhilde said, scooping Cinderella off the floor and holding her close. "She's very delicate, very excitable. I must put her to bed at once. Please go."

But the prince, accustomed to getting his way, was not to be put off.

"Madam"—he folded his arms over his chest and pointed his chin in the air—"I have proposed marriage to your wretched daughter—and you can be sure I am a man of my word. You should be grateful that I am willing to take her off your hands."

"Oh, really?" Brunhilde said, drawing herself up to her full height, which made her a good four inches taller than the prince. "Well, young man, since you *are*, after all, the *prince*, and since you *are* a man of your *word*, then by all means, you *must* take Cinderella."

An ungodly wail ensued.

"Ssh, child, it will be all right," Brunhilde whispered, patting Cinderella. "Trust me." To the prince, she said, "Take her—but her

sisters must come along and prepare her for the wedding ceremony. Cinderella is not strong enough to endure such a traumatic
change without the support and guidance of her dear sisters."

"Yes," the sisters said in unison, "we must help prepare our dear
sister for marriage."

The prince conferred with his manservants, who advised him to
agree to Brunhilde's terms.

"Well, then"—he looked with barely disguised loathing at his
bride-to-be—"let's go."

At the prince's castle, Cinderella and her stepsisters were shown
to a large chamber fit for a royal lady. The closets overflowed with
colorful gowns, precious jewels, ornate headdresses, expensive
perfumes. In the center of the room sat a large canopied bed. A
chandelier hung from the ceiling, and beveled mirrors stood in
every corner.

Cinderella watched in awe as her sisters quickly swept through
the closets, pulling out dresses and crinolines. "No, no, these will
never do!" moaned Griselda. She called for a servant and demanded
scissors, rope, and riding clothes. She sent for the stable boy and
asked to see his collection of riding crops. She summoned the
kitchen maid and had her deliver all manner of cooking utensils.

By evening Griselda and Grunella had adorned themselves from
head to toe in leather. They had dressed Cinderella in a tight
corset, garters, stockings, and the infamous glass slippers. Several
times the poor girl begged to be told what was going on; the sisters
responded by feeding her a foot or pinching her exposed nipples.
By the time they sent a servant to fetch the prince, Cinderella was
so wet and hot that she'd lost all trepidation. "Trust us," whispered Griselda, and opened the door for Prince Charming.

"Wh—What?" he asked, stunned by the scene before him. The
room glowed in candlelight. An ornate chandelier had been
replaced with a large meat hook from which a rope swayed hypnot-
ically. The sisters looked as if they were on their way to hunt with

the hounds. And his fiancée was spread out on the bed in her underwear. The prince discreetly covered his eyes.

Griselda locked the heavy wooden door. "Welcome, sweet prince," she said, savagely enunciating each syllable. "You're about to get more than you ever imagined when you chose Cinderella to be your loving princess."

The prince laughed to disguise his fear. Grunella cracked her riding crop across his calf. "Shut up, you idiot! Disrobe at once."

"Madam, I am your prince! How dare you—"

Another crack of the whip, this time from Griselda. "Disrobe! Now!"

Terrified, the prince did as he was told. To his dismay, when he removed his trousers, a fully erect penis sprang forth.

The sisters cackled gaily. "Didn't I tell you, Grunny? Didn't I peg him?"

"Peg me?" asked the prince.

"A bottom," said Grunella, placing the handle of her whip beneath his penis and raising it for inspection. "Like our dear little sister."

All eyes turned to Cinderella. She was kneeling forward on her haunches, intently watching her stepsisters and the prince. Her breasts hung over the top of her corset, the nipples elongated. One had been pierced and fitted with a diamond-studded hoop. A gold chain dangled from her neck. Her hair had been plaited into dozens of tiny braids that swayed around her innocent face.

"Lovely, isn't she?" said Griselda.

When the prince made no reply, Griselda cracked her whip across his buttocks. "I said, 'Lovely, isn't she?'"

"Y-Yes," the prince replied.

"Oh, but *you* think she's beneath you! *You* think you're doing her—and us—a *favor* by 'keeping your word.' Ugh!" She flicked her whip across the prince's member. He jumped, but his prick grew half an inch.

Griselda said, "Our little sister is a precious treasure. You won't find the likes of her among your spoiled queens and princesses. Did you really think we'd give her up without a fight?"

Cinderella was amazed; never had she heard her stepsisters praise her. Hot liquid dribbled from between her legs and onto the sheets.

"Well, we won't give her up—not unless we deem you worthy."

"What must I do?" asked the prince, who had unconsciously begun rubbing his member.

"Why, it's simple. You must learn how to treat Cinderella. How to keep her purring like a kitten." Griselda approached the bed, grabbed Cinderella's braids, and yanked her head backward. "*We* know how. We know all of her secrets—don't we, Cindy?" She stuck a finger into Cinderella's mouth. Cinderella closed her eyes and sucked. "We're perfectly willing to teach you, princey-poo. But only if you cooperate fully. Only if you trust us."

Absently squeezing his scrotum, the prince murmured, "I am your humble student."

"Good. Because we're going to teach you how to treat our sister in the manner to which she is accustomed. We're going to teach you to switch—to be a top for *her*—but you must remain subservient to *us*. Do you think you can do that?"

"I'll try," said the prince.

"I'll try, *Mistress*."

"I'll try, Mistress."

A million thoughts were swirling through Cinderella's head. Had her stepsisters known all these years the pleasure she derived from worshiping and serving them? Did they know about her wet panties, her sinful self-ministrations? Had their cruelty been deliberate? Had it been an act? She looked at Grunella, who seemed to read her mind.

"Oh, yes, Cinderella, we have always known your nature and catered to it. But don't think we didn't derive as much pleasure as you. Griselda and I are natural-born tops. We love dominating. Of course," she giggled, "sometimes we had to restrain ourselves in front of Mother."

"All right, all right," Grunella said impatiently. "Enough talking. Let's get on with it."

"Fine," said Griselda. "For now, Prince, you are to observe—just watch."

"May I touch myself, Mistress?"

"Excellent. Yes, you may touch yourself. In fact, it's mandatory." She turned to Cinderella. "On your feet."

Cinderella clambered out of bed. Griselda and Grunella quickly cuffed her hands behind her back, tied her ankles together, and clipped a chain on to each nipple. "Walk!" they ordered, each one pulling a nipple chain.

Cinderella teetered after her sisters, tits-first. By the time they reached the hanging rope, her thighs were drenched with her own juices. Griselda slid a hand between her legs, extracted some of the wetness, and shoved a finger into the prince's mouth.

"See what a little slut she is? Humiliation makes her cream. Doesn't it, Cindy?"

Cinderella moaned.

"On your knees, bitch." Cinderella sank to her knees. Grunella lifted her leather skirt. "Lick."

Cinderella avidly licked her stepsister's clitoris and labia, then snaked her tongue up inside her. Grunella grabbed her head and pressed it firmly against her while she ground her hips.

"Okay, that's enough pussying around." Griselda pulled Cinderella by the hair and forced her to stand. "Let's give her what she really wants—what we could never do at home."

She lashed Cinderella to a large cross-shaped object she'd found in the stable. It was held up by the meat hook, so Cinderella was hanging slightly above her stepsisters, who stood on either side and raised their whips. Cinderella's eyes hungrily drank in their beauty as they stood before her in their leather riding clothes, their long hair flowing behind them. She reveled in the feeling of being the object of their focused attention. Slowly they brought the whips down on both her thighs.

As much as her stepsisters had humiliated her, never before had they struck Cinderella. Something deep inside her leaped out to greet the blows, and she realized she had been wanting this for a long, long time. Each crack of the whip provided Cinderella another chance to show her sisters how much she adored them. The more it hurt, the more it proved her love. Cinderella received the blows with great joy, glad there was someone to witness her surrender.

The sisters whipped her belly, her back, even her breasts and vagina. As their blows got progressively harder, their excitement mounted. Their eyes became molten; a vein throbbed in Griselda's temple; sweat dripped down Grunella's face.

"Oh, yes," they murmured, "she likes being beaten—don't you, Cindy?"

"Yes." The more excited they became, the more Cinderella wanted them to hurt her. She arched her back, her body virtually kissing the whip. She watched the prince cupping his balls and pulling on his thick cock. Saliva trickled from his mouth. The sisters followed Cinderella's gaze.

"Ah, yes, see how hard he is. See how his muscles bulge. The weaker you get, the stronger he becomes."

It was true: the prince was being transformed from the fawning creature who had danced with her into a strong, powerful man who could provide the hardness she needed so badly. If her surrender had the power to strengthen him this way, she would gladly yield.

"Shall we stop?" Griselda teased.

"No, please, no!" Cinderella sensed that if the sisters continued, she would be taken beyond her conscious thoughts and into the realm of pure sensation. That was where Cinderella wanted to go. That was what she'd been striving for all her life.

"But Cinderella, you have marks on your skin," Griselda taunted her. "Soon you may bleed."

"Don't stop," Cinderella repeated. "Please don't stop!"

"Good God, don't stop!" shouted the prince.

The sisters laughed and resumed their whipping. When Cinderella was nearly fainting, they untied the ropes and lowered her to the floor. "Go," ordered Griselda. "Go suck your husband's cock."

Cinderella crawled across the floor. The prince towered over her and, with no hesitation, thrust his member between her parted lips.

"Suck it, you whore. Worship my royal prick."

Cinderella's flesh felt as supple as well-worn leather. Her mouth, cunt, and anus ached to be filled. Her heart palpitated with love and generosity; she wanted to serve; she wanted to give pleasure.

"Lick your husband's balls," said Grunella, and Cinderella gratefully lowered her mouth to the hanging sacs, rolling each tenderly, by turn, in her mouth. With one hand, she stroked the prince's member and, with the other, prodded his anus. The prince groaned and grabbed her by the nape of her neck, his touch that of a man taking possession. In that moment, Cinderella knew she had been given over to a new master. Eager to prove herself worthy, she grasped his prick and rubbed it lovingly all over her face, in her eyes, over her cheeks. A drop of milky fluid shimmered on the head; Cinderella licked it off, savoring its salty taste.

"Drink my royal nectar," the prince whispered. "Swallow my precious fluid."

"Oh, yes!" Cinderella gasped. "Give me your precious fluid. Anoint me." She sucked and licked and stroked until the prince released his semen and flooded her open mouth. She gulped it down.

Griselda had attached some kind of penis-shaped piece of leather onto herself with a belt. She kneeled behind Cinderella and thrust the makeshift prick into the girl's sopping hole. Grunella fastened her clit onto the prince's mouth and ordered him to lick.

Cinderella's cunt closed gratefully around whatever was inside it. She continued to lick and kiss her husband's balls and prick while Griselda pounded into her. She pressed a finger to the little button she had discovered between her legs. Soon her whole body was climbing. She pressed and bucked and reached for whatever was coming, and suddenly felt it: an explosion of a magnitude that she had never experienced in her playful little games among the cinders. Rather than just a little tremor between her legs, her entire body seemed to open and contract. Her cunt sucked on Griselda's strange appendage, and a loud moan escaped her lips, muffled by the prince's semi-erect member. She raised her hips so that Griselda could thrust even deeper, creating new waves of ecstasy deep inside her. Griselda squeezed Cinderella's buttocks and slid a finger into her anus. Behind her closed eyelids, Cinderella saw an explosion of color and light. As the contractions in her body subsided, the light burst into fragments like shooting stars, and then funny little pictures of people and animals danced behind her lids. As if from a great distance, she heard her stepsisters grunting; they, too, were experiencing ecstatic release.

"You see," Griselda quietly told the prince after a few moments, "keeping Cinderella takes a lot of work." She flexed her biceps.

The prince gazed down at the blonde head resting on his thigh, the small, delicate hand cradling his balls.

"I intend to make it my life's mission," he said.

Cinderella raised her head and kissed her fiancé. Then she kissed each of her sisters.

"Don't worry," said Griselda, "we'll check in regularly in case you need a refresher course."

"Oh," said the prince. "I'm quite sure that I will."

The Changeling
LEE LYNCH

I had three Irish grandparents, two of whom grew up in Ireland. The superstitions and beliefs of Irish culture had not left them entirely. The music of their talk is like an old melody I can call back from the depths of myself.

When my freshman English teacher decided that I would be the next great Irish poet, I plunged headlong into the Irish literature he loved. I found myself particularly drawn to the changeling stories.

These fantastical folktales felt like stories communities might tell themselves to explain the phenomena of tomboys and sissies. Parents, not wanting the blame of their strange offspring, could mourn the loss of a normal child stolen by the faeries and revile the faerie child, or changeling, left in its place.

Although some of the changeling tales are ugly, with faerie children portrayed as twisted and hateful creatures, others seem illuminated, as if told by storytellers with an appreciation for enchantment. To me, being gay has always felt like an enchanted state.

Kitty Cormac of Ballywoods on the River Slaney was indeed something to behold. Long hair colored like copper flamed up around her in the wind. She walked on the world as if it were her own red carpet, not pretending to be the Queen, but as a spirit who called others to join her. She'd don a wide-brimmed hat, festoon it with a cast-off peacock feather, crook it, and give a hoot of laughter as she boldly displayed embroidered bloomers she'd made especially for her purposes. Then she'd stride through the town like the giant who carries the sun around the world every day. Into her glow Kitty drew children and old ones and mums who should be home mending the menfolks' blouses.

Off they'd go on a sunny day to the river, on a rainy day to a canopy of trees, to do it mattered not what. But there would be merriment and song and wildberry lunches, then naps for the youngest in a river cave. When the village had its nighttime celebrations, Kitty often grabbed the bow from the fiddle player and enlivened the music, or led one of her brothers in a dance that got everyone off their duffs.

Nor was she all play. Although she declared more holidays than pleased her mum, she would do the work of two daughters the rest of the week. Often the sick asked for her companionship, the bereaved sought her soothing manner, or a farmer with a sheep, a cow, a horse off its feed came after her. Something in the way she touched the creatures, or crooned to them all night long, brought healing when hope was lost.

No one had a bad word to say about Kitty Cormac. No one, that is, but Bridget MacMahon, who was known for her bitter words and poor view of every living thing. It's said that she'd lost a child to the good people, for Daniel MacMahon, a lisping, prancing thing who'd rather watch after others' children than sire his own, was her son, thought to be a faerie babe switched in the cradle with her firstborn.

One day Kitty passed by, brandishing her walking stick as she urged a pack of gamboling kids back to their nanny goats. "She's too charmed, you'll see!" Bridget MacMahon warned a visiting neighbor as she spun the wool of her sheep while her changeling babe, now a bearded man, carded the rest.

"And where might herself be heading this storming day?" Mother MacMahon asked the neighbor. "She claims to visit over toward Coolcorthy, but that's a fair walk even for the likes of herself in her bloomers. Do the faeries carry her over? I've heard the wee folk abide in an old ruined castle out that way. Men on horses have come back with tales of seeing little figures flitting to and fro inside the building to the playing of flutes and pipes."

The neighbor held her tongue for she knew Bridget's husband had taken some men and ridden out to find his mortal son, but had come back with no child and no sighting of the castle. Perhaps it was a comfort to Bridget to think her boy happy with the good people, not here in this room, cringing at her accusing looks.

"You're saying that Kitty Cormac was left in a faerie theft?" whispered the neighbor.

"Now how would I know that, Mrs. Smallhead?" replied Bridget MacMahon with a sly look.

After this exchange, one could hear the phrase "too good to be true" in the same breath with the name of Kitty Cormac, but the girl changed not a whit. If anything, she grew more dashing and irresistible. She seemed happier with every sunrise. Some thought she had a young man out of Coolcorthy with whom she strode the woods, eager to bring forth babes as magnificent as herself.

Kitty Cormac threw back her head with its cascade of glory and laughed like a woman possessed.

At her side, on the bank of a noisy stream, Glynnis MacLaig smiled. It might well be that every last body from Ballywoods adored Kitty, but only Glynnis, who lived in the forest midway between the towns, had Kitty's love.

"Who d'you think wants to steal me away?" Kitty teased.

"Yet another suitor?" Glynnis prompted with her own laugh. She had been born with skin as soft as goose down and hair as black as a raven's feathers. Her limbs looked so delicate that the boys treated her like a fragile bird.

"The best Ballywoods has to offer," Kitty boasted, taking Glynnis's hand in hers. "He's tall and learned, and his da's got the most fertile land in the river valley. He tried to dance with me one evening, but I threatened him with my fiddle. The very next afternoon, he came to my father's house with a fancy cart, but I had Mum say I was out courting Daniel MacMahon and to be off wi' him!"

"No! You didn't," said quiet Glynnis, who dared not defy her own people and spent miserable hours with the pestering young men of Coolcorthy.

"Oh, didn't I!" Kitty said. "Then you won't believe me when I tell you young Owen Anster came to call."

"But he's a third son!"

"And defied the Church and his father to woo me! I don't know what he's thinking. He would have been a powerful priest some day."

"Did you see him?"

"He waylaid me after I left you last week."

Glynnis gasped. "Did he guess where you'd been?"

"And what if he did?" Kitty challenged, as if the boy were before her still. "With his nasty eyes that would devour a woman whole and him with a priest's tonsure already. I told him I'd have nothing to do with a man pledged to the grandest calling and marking me his temptress."

The stream seemed to chortle even louder as Kitty slid a strong arm across Glynnis's shoulders and pulled her close. " 'I have heard,' he tells me, 'how you scorn every suitor. But you'll have me.' The man makes my flesh crawl. It's as if what he wants is to prove himself among men, with me the proof."

"Perhaps," suggested Glynnis in a quavering voice, " 'tis a sign we should be off to America. Oh, hurry, Kitty. I feel it's time to go!"

Kitty sought the maiden's lips. "With the help o' goodness, we'll go soon enough, sweet lady. I've an eye on the pot of gold that will get us there. Ould miser Jack, who won't gi' for the good of a soul but his own, has plenty to keep him in splendor the rest of his days." She pulled a round wooden object from her pocket. "He'll think it faerie mischief when he finds his pot filled with wooden coins. I'll soon have the seclusion to whittle enough o' these. Pack a bag and be ready for my whistle at your wall."

Within the fortnight, Kitty did the unthinkable and moved into the abandoned shed at the edge of her father's potato field.

"Are you mad?" cried her mum, watching Kitty nail a length of canvas across a window.

"Summer's coming on," her daughter explained. "I'm tired of the house with all the babes and Da' yammering at you."

" 'Tis the way of it, my child. There's talk enough of you consorting with the wee people without moving into their bailiwick."

"You'd deprive me of the whole of the out-of-doors to keep me from their dance and song?" teased Kitty.

But her mother looked stern. "By my soul, you're no Daniel MacMahon, but I've done all a mither can for you. Sure, you can't be my own with your quare ways."

Soon, as if her mother had withdrawn a protecting charm, the talk in the village swelled. Always at the center of it, the dark-haired third son of Anster, who would have been a priest, lamented his state: bewitched by the young woman with fire for hair.

"Twinkling lights and the high sound of little voices!" he reported having seen in the woods behind Cormac's potato field.

"But where does she go of a Sunday?" they all wanted to know, "when she ought to be in church?"

Everyone loved Kitty Cormac, but they didn't understand her—she couldn't possibly be their kin.

If Owen Anster was too proud to be a priest, he was also too proud to be spurned by a woman. One Sunday, after bragging of his plan, he stole out of town behind her. Sons of the church spent their days praying, not walking, and he lagged behind Kitty's swift stride, soon losing the splendid sight of her flashing hair. He thought to catch her later, for surely the faeries' dell would be sparkling like the River Slaney on a sunny day. Even the songs of birds would be overshadowed by the music. He lay on a grassy bed just off the roadside, weary from the walk, lazy from the big Sunday meal, and slowly fell asleep to the fading strains of Kitty singing a wild low song in Irish.

With a start, he awoke to twilight and Kitty Cormac running along the road. He'd missed it all! How could he face the men of the village? He leapt up to peer at her. Ah, how she glowed with her quickened blood. A sweet smile of pleasure brightened those eyes. Would that he'd given her that smile! No doubt she'd partaken of the faeries' mead and laughed with them the whole of the afternoon.

When she was out of sight, he stole back to town in a rage. At the tavern he regaled the men with the fantastic sights he'd seen. "The wee people welcomed Kitty Cormac and led her by the hands, dancing her till she dropped, serving her golden drink, plaiting her flame of hair—"

"Flame!" cried an elder. "Scalding's how we cleanse the faerie from a mortal's soul!"

Deep in the night the sodden men stole through the potato field, Cormac the father among them, humiliated that his true child had been taken over by the tiny thieves. It was he who tossed the first torch on the roof of the shed, and Owen Anster in his drunken fury who burnt through the window Kitty had fashioned with her own lovely hands. They stood there, the crowd of farmers whose animals she'd tended and the would-be priest who would love or destroy, and watched the evil place where Kitty Cormac slept burn to the ground. That there had been not a scream or a cry for help persuaded them. Sure, the imp had escaped in a burst of bright sparks that leapt to the sky.

The next morning, Owen Anster searched the ground where the old shed had stood. Kitty's mum watched him steely-eyed, waiting in vain for him to find one sign of a mortal being.

At the same time, old miser Jack could be found running from door to door in the village setting up an alarm. His fattest, fullest pot of gold had been ruined! Instead of gold, it was filled with worthless wooden coins!

Had it happened yesterday, the townsfolk asked him. It had not been like that when he'd finished counting for the night, he replied. Well, then, the men of Ballywoods concluded, there's the proof. The faeries took it in payment for their trouble when the good men of Ballywoods drove off the changeling Kitty Cormac.

The Legend of White Snake
KITTY TSUI

I spent several years doing research for my novel, Bak Sze, White Snake, *so both the opera and the folktale are intriguing and close to my heart. In addition, I thought it would be great fun to rewrite a classical tale with an erotic twist.*

Once there was a poor student named Xu Xen who lived in the city of Hangchow, in China, the land called Middle Kingdom, for the Chinese believe they live in the center of the earth.

It was mid-afternoon on a hot summer day, and Xu Xen was walking home, depressed and forlorn. He had come from the Great Hall, where he had sat for four days and nights taking the Imperial Examinations, success at which would confer on him the title of Teacher. But, alas, he had failed it again. Now he had to return home and tell his sick mother the sad news.

He walked slowly, as if his legs were filled with wet sand, his eyes downcast. In this way, Xu Xen could not help noticing a snake by the side of the path. The snake was a magnificent specimen, its body as thick as a laborer's arm, its white scales gleaming in the sunlight.

"Hoa-ah, good," Xu Xen exclaimed aloud, for he knew he could sell the skin of the snake, and perhaps even the flesh, if it had not been dead for too long.

He found a stick and bent to prod the still form.

"Aiyah, aiyah, aiyah!"

A woman's screams filled the air.

Xu Xen dropped the stick and looked around him frantically. There was no living person in sight.

"Hah!" he snorted. "I am not superstitious like Ma. Must be hearing things. Lack of sleep and sitting for the exam with only tea for nourishment. Anyway, it is broad daylight, and there are no ghosts or fox-fairies about."

"Careful what you say, Young Master, or the ghosts and fox-fairies you cannot see will show themselves and give you a mighty fright."

"What? Who...who are you? *Wai!* Who's there?"

It was then that he happened to glance down at his feet. The white snake that he had thought was dead was looking up at him with its bright eyes.

"Hwaark," he spat. "Good, good. The snake is alive. Perhaps I can sell it to the herbalist for some taels of silver. Maybe even buy medicine for Ma so she will be well."

Xu Xen picked up the stick, intending to club the snake so that he could take it to the marketplace.

"Stop, Young Master. Wait, I beg you."

This time there was no mistake, for the student was looking straight at the snake and could see its lips moving as it mouthed the words.

"It's all right," he soothed himself. "I am hallucinating. Just one blow and I'll have it. Steady now. Aim for the head, but not too hard."

"*Wai*, what's wrong with you? Stupid, hah?"

This was another voice, the voice of a woman, high and haughty.

To his astonishment, another snake slithered into view. This was also a magnificent creature, almost as large as the first, but with bright blue scales.

"Wah! So beautiful, two snakes to take to the marketplace. My fortune is made!"

"Not so fast, fool," the blue snake spoke. "We are enchanted creatures, not common snakes to be snared and sold."

"*Man-dee*, slowly," the white snake said softly. "He is merely a mortal man and slow to understand matters of the other world."

"Hah," the other replied, "let us change him into a rock or, better yet, a grain of sand. How dare he think he can take us to market!"

The student looked at the two snakes, disbelief in his eyes.

"Young Master," the white snake offered. "Leave us to go on our way in peace and continue on with yours."

The young man broke down. "I am penniless. My mother is sick and I have failed the Imperial Examinations for the third time. I have nothing left even for the pawnbroker. You are but two snakes. Let me take one of you, then. The other can go free."

"That seems fair," said the white snake.

"You, then, you!" the blue snake cackled at the other. "Take the white snake. She is worth more money than I."

"Go then, sister. I will sacrifice myself."

The blue snake dissolved into laugher and slithered away, leaving the student with the white snake.

"Please do not hit me," she said. "I will go with you willingly."

"But why?" asked the astonished student.

"In my first life, I committed a crime. I ran away from home and eloped with my childhood love rather than marry the rich old man who wished to buy me. My parents were poor. They had nothing but me, a useless girl, and I left them. So they starved to death. As my punishment, I was turned into a snake. It is my fate now to die. Take me to the marketplace."

Xu Xen's elation turned to shame. "I cannot do that, noble snake. Go on your way. Go! Farewell."

And with that he turned and continued home.

That night Tien Di, the Lord of the Heavens, was in a generous mood. He had spent the evening feasting on suckling baby pig with crispy skin, rock-salt shrimp, roast squab, and a vegetarian stew with three kinds of mushrooms. He was drunk on fiery mao-tai wine, and his jade rod was limp after many hours spent in the arms and between the legs of his two favorite consorts, Fragrant Jasmine and Lotus Blossom Honey.

Tien Di, whose eyes see everything in the Heavens and in the Middle Kingdom, decided to grant the two snakes another chance at life. But he decreed that the blue snake, for her selfishness, must serve as the white snake's maid. Though the blue snake was not happy with this decision, she was ecstatic once again to assume a human form, for fornication was her favorite game.

The very next day, Lady White Snake and her maid, Blue Snake, traveled to the city of Hangchow.

Xu Xen and his little sister, Tranquil Peach, had spent the morning in the hills gathering herbs to sell at the marketplace. They were sweaty and dusty and dead tired when an entourage of men bearing two sedan chairs passed them.

Tranquil Peach stopped and turned to stare when a beautiful face peered out from behind an embroidered screen. She gasped out loud. She could not help herself, for it was a face of incomparable beauty, with skin white as the face of the moon framed by hair black as night. Jewels like stars sparkled in the dark tresses. Then—like a flash of lightning—the image was gone.

Tranquil Peach took a deep breath and closed her eyes,

oblivious now to the heat of the day, or in fact to anything around her. She had always been a quiet, shy girl, fond of solitude and prone to daydreaming. She had worked from an early age, gathering kindling or herbs, washing clothes, hulling rice. She escaped from the drudgery by fantasizing about pleasurable things. When she was very young, she had accidentally discovered the joy of pleasuring herself, and from that day on, she pursued it avidly. But when other girls, gathered around the stream to wash clothes, giggled about boys, Tranquil Peach thought about girls.

On this occasion, she fantasized about the woman in the sedan chair.

Tranquil Peach is holding the woman in her arms. She can smell a strange fragrance, feel the warmth of her body. The folds of the woman's gown open, revealing a glimpse of milky white flesh. She touches the smooth plane of her stomach. Reaches down to...

"Wai, *Mei-mei*, Little Sister, what are you doing?"

Tranquil Peach started. She looked down and saw that her hand was opening the slit in her trousers.

"Oh, I...I got bitten. A mosquito, I think."

"Come on. We must get to the market. Stop your dawdling and hurry up now."

Meanwhile, Lady White Snake and her maid had stopped at a roadside teahouse to rest. They were having an argument.

"Why do you want to find that poor student? Waste of time I say. Though I must admit, he is a handsome one. I think we should look up Lao Bak, the rich salt merchant. His wife just died, and I hear his concubine has been unable to produce a son."

"Xu Xen saved my life, no thanks to you." She gave Blue Snake a sharp look. "He deserves a reward for his selflessness."

"What reward? Your jade flower in his mouth?" She rolled her eyes, grabbed a steamed bun, and took a large bite.

White Snake picked up a fried dumpling in her chopsticks and savored the taste in her mouth. She ignored Blue Snake.

That night was a particularly bad one for Xu Xen's mother. She coughed blood and vomited. Tranquil Peach sat up all night and tended to her. In the morning, when she went out to fetch water, she found a basket in front of the house. Inside was a sack of rice, preserved meat, and a bunch of strange-smelling herbs tied together with string. Tranquil Peach squealed with delight. She started a fire and ran to get water.

Xu Xen belched.

"That was the first meat I've eaten in months," he said with satisfaction.

"Good rice, too," his sister added. "White and fine, without sand and grit."

Their mother stirred from her bed. "I wonder who our benefactor could be. I am feeling much better after drinking the tea made from those strange herbs."

"Rest now, Ma," said Xu Xen, "Little Sister and I are going out to look for work. I have a feeling this is going to be a lucky day for us."

On the way to the marketplace, Xu Xen and Tranquil Peach encountered two sedan chairs stopped by the side of the path. Three of the men who carried them were gathered around a fourth, who was lying in the dirt.

"What is wrong?" Xu Xen asked one of the men.

"The man fainted. Must be the heat. *Diew!*" he swore. "Now we cannot go on."

"I can offer my services," Xu Xen said excitedly, thinking of how much he might earn. "How far are you journeying?"

"To the west side of the city. But don't expect a tael of silver. A few coins and a meal is all you'll get."

"Gladly," Xu Xen replied. "But a meal for my sister, too, please."

The headman snorted. "*Hao-ah*, it is agreed. Come on, you lot, put the fallen man in the shade. When he recovers he'll have to fend for himself."

Blue Snake parted the curtains in the sedan chair and peered out at the scholar. He had taken off his shirt, and though his skin was pale, his back and arms were muscular. She licked her lips as a wicked thought crossed her mind. *I wonder if his jade rod is white as his back? I would love to kiss it, feel it grow, enlarge, engorge with blood. Fill my mouth.*

White Snake was faced with a dilemma. She knew that the best way to reward the scholar for his kindness in setting the snake free was to marry him and use her magic powers to help him finally pass the Imperial Examinations. But the last thing in the world she wanted was to marry a man. In truth, she wished to marry a woman. A woman with a straight back, strong arms, and soft breasts. A woman like Xu Xen's sister, Tranquil Peach. And she knew that Blue Snake was lusting after the scholar. But she would most likely drop him like a hot coal after she got what she wanted. What was White Snake to do?

That night both the scholar and his sister retired with full stomachs. In addition to being paid in cash, his mysterious employer had sent them home with food and a bunch of the same strange-smelling herbs that Tranquil Peach had found in the basket. They had been told to return the following day.

"Ma is feeling better, and we have good prospects for work. Ah, life is good," Xu Xen announced as he went off to bed.

Tranquil Peach had caught another glimpse of the mysterious lady in the sedan chair. When she had asked one of the sedan bearers, he had laughed and said that she was the maid. How was that possible? Such a beautiful lady and she was a maid?

Tranquil Peach got into her pallet in the tiny bedroom that she shared with her brother and her mother and turned to face the wall. There was no privacy, but still her hand moved between her legs and she brought herself to orgasm quickly, thinking of the beautiful woman with skin as white as snow.

When brother and sister arrived at the grand house on the west side of the city, they were ushered into a reception room. There, sitting on a mahogany chair with embroidered cushions was the most beautiful woman the scholar had ever seen. Standing beside her was the woman Tranquil Peach had glimpsed behind the curtains of the sedan chair. Brother and sister gasped in unison.

"I know you are both wondering why I sent for you," the lady began. "In truth, I am seeking a husband for my maid."

Now it was Blue Snake's turn to gasp. She started to say something, but White Snake held up a hand to silence her.

"She is wild and imperious, and I am seeking a man who can tame her. She comes with a dowry, of course. For her part"—at this White Snake gave her maid a fixed look—"she must remain faithful for a year and a day. Then I shall release her from my service."

The scholar looked at Blue Snake, who was regarding her mistress with an angry glare. The maid was also very beautiful, though she did look arrogant, icy, and proud. Marriage? And a dowry, too? Was he dreaming? Suddenly he remembered Tranquil Peach.

"But, Lady, what about my sister?"

"Your sister is to take my maid's place," the lady replied. "But first she is to come to my chambers. Blue Snake will instruct her in the art of service. Go, take your leave now and prepare for your marriage, Xu Xen. Your sister will be in good hands."

Servants bathed and perfumed Tranquil Peach and dressed her in silk. Though her hands and feet were oiled, the calluses on them remained rough as sand. As she was led into White Snake's bedchamber, she overheard an argument.

"I will not marry!" the maid was shrieking.

"Yes, you will. And you will remain faithful for a year and a day.

At that time, you will be free. You desired him, did you not?"

"Yes, but not to be wedded," the maid said in a horrified voice.

"Silence, Blue Snake. You will obey me; you have no choice. Ah, here is Tranquil Peach. Quiet, now, and teach her well."

Blue Snake glared at her mistress, but she knew she could not disobey. A year and a day! With one man? How was that possible? But she put it out of her mind for the moment.

Blue Snake and Tranquil Peach bathed White Snake. They dried her skin and massaged her body with sweet oils. Then they led her to the bed. Tranquil Peach thought that she was surely dreaming, but it was a dream as exquisite as the feel of silk on her body.

Two pairs of hands caressed White Snake's body. Two mouths kissed her skin, licked her nipples, stroked her legs, sucked her toes. White Snake drew Tranquil Peach to her and kissed her full on the lips. A tongue snaked inside, withdrew, and thrust in again. Soft, warm, and insistent.

Tranquil Peach shivered. She felt a familiar ache inside, and she knew that she was wet. Beside her Blue Snake was rustling something. Then Blue Snake poked her unceremoniously. She reluctantly drew away from the kiss. Blue Snake handed something to her. It was an ivory object, smooth and warm to her touch. She looked at it and immediately understood. Without a word, she put it to her lips, wet it with her saliva. She gently parted White Snake's legs and slid the ivory piece inside.

It was her first time with a woman, but she knew exactly what to do. As the motion of her hand quickened, she felt an enormous power surge through her, and she rejoiced. When she felt White Snake tense and then shudder uncontrollably, a long moan broke from her lips.

"Ahhhh, I'm dreaming or I'm in paradise!"

And they lived happily ever after.

The Little Urban Maid

LAURA ANTONIOU

The twisted morality tales of Hans Christian Andersen have always fascinated me, and the obvious Christ imagery in "The Little Mermaid" called for an examination that was pretty strong stuff for a kid. Why on earth a girl with a beautiful body, voice, and perfect grace (not to mention superb pain management) would fall for an empty-headed sixteen-year-old prince who lets her sleep on a pillow by his door (!) and doesn't even know she saved his miserable little life always puzzled me. Until, of course, I fell victim to a massive crush myself. Call it a modern-day morality tale, without all that immortal-soul silliness.

Far, far from the skylines of Manhattan, where the roads stretch dark and twisted like squid-ink fettuccine; there, where no public transportation enables you to go; there, in the chain of towns all ending in *-bay*, or *-port*, live the suburban people. So far from the towers and spires of the City, that you would have to lay many Long Island Rail Road trains end to end before you could even reach their car-pooling parking lots.

Now, you must not think that the neighborhoods so far from the center of the City are desolate and barren. No, there are the sprawling green lawns of those who don't know how to start a lawn mower and will never have to learn. There are many beautiful and well-groomed plants and trees, all grown to satisfy the purest landscape technical designer. Big cars and small tour through the twists and turns of the roads, eagerly seeking out the immense, glamorous acres of pure capitalism known as malls. And here, in this suburban area, the Fish King has built his castle. Or, rather, his four-bedroom split-level ranch, with a two-car garage, finished basement, and guaranteed genuine redwood deck.

Sol Goldman, the Fish King, (for so his trucks read, on the side: *Smoked Fish to Crown Every Table!*) had been a widower for many years. His mother kept the house for him—a proud, intelligent woman whose only fault was an overfondness for pearls, for which everyone forgave her. She took excellent care of the six—count 'em, six!— daughters that the estimable Mrs. Goldman (deceased), had borne, and raised them to be good little girls and fine young women, and cast them out into the world one at a time, to seek their fortunes.

The youngest of these daughters was the most different. She was the boldest, whose journeys took her farthest away from the lovely house and gardens that were perfectly acceptable for her older sisters. She alone sulked and protested when given new and pretty clothes to wear, and was the one most often found in the middle of scrapes and messes and complex arrangements of neighbor children that had all the local parents wondering whether therapy might help. But she was still a good girl—she was neither disobedient nor willfully cruel. And she was very, very smart.

All of the little princesses loved to hear their Grandmama tell tales of the lives elsewhere—in Big Cities, and in Other Countries, where there were many other people doing jobs the princesses couldn't imagine, and having adventures which seemed dubious, at best. But alone among them, the littlest princess loved the stories from her Tante Ester, who visited rarely and cackled and laughed and made cryptic comments which made Grandmama blush and the Fish King bluster, but left the little princesses confused. Tante Ester lived alone—or so they said—and far away, in the reaches of Brooklyn, a place Grandmama was very firm about. It was Not Safe. It was Not a Place for Princesses.

But when Tante Ester came, she brought stories not of someone else's life, but of her own. Stories of late-night shopping and dancing until dawn. Stories of exotic foods and strange places, all full of new words that the littlest princess gobbled up like sweets. The little princess knew that she would be going to these places, eating these morsels, dancing until dawn. And she knew something else, too.

She wouldn't be doing those things with any damn fool boy, either.

For that was what was expected of her and her older sisters. One at a time, as they turned the magical age of eighteen, they were decked in their finest new designer garments and given the freedom to seek out the companionship of young men, princes, to be sure, who would then squire them around, providing transportation and meals and entertainment in the hopes of a cuddle and a peck on the cheek. (Not to mention a nice job working in the Fish King empire and a very fancy wedding and a brand-new split-level ranch house, should the proper princess pronounce them acceptable.)

Each princess went forth and returned bearing tales of her adventures and making her younger sisters turn positively green with envy. And of them all, the youngest most wanted to venture beyond the suburban world. Of course, she was also the one who waited the longest before she could go. She could watch it all on TV—but the lure of the night lights of the City called to her, and she knew that her older sisters, with their whispered secrets and bold lies, never came near to the places she would have to go and the things she wanted to do. They went out just a little way, and came right back to where they felt most at home, prince in tow or not.

So she bided her time, and when finally the age came upon her, she had a plan. She took her father's birthday present, a diamond tennis bracelet—a strange gift, since she loathed the game—back to Fortunoff's and got a refund. And then she used that refund to purchase a nice Honda motorcycle. She finally had wheels. She could escape. And she knew where she was going, too.

"Brooklyn!" the Fish King thundered, shaking his castle to the very aluminum siding.

"Tsk," said Grandmama, adding things up in her head. It was clear where the little princess had gotten her brains. "I think I'll ask Ester to keep an eye on her."

"Ester? That perverted hag!" Sol thundered again. "My beautiful little girl depending on that crazy old witch?"

Grandmama ignored him and dialed the phone.

She saw which way the tide was coming in, after all.

As it turned out, Tante Ester's was the first place the little princess turned up after that long, harrowing ride west on the Long Island Expressway. And in no time at all, one visit turned into a tiny studio apartment and a job in a pet shop, a subway map and two rolls of tokens, and guaranteed dinner every Friday night. The littlest princess had found and settled in a new world.

She learned how to pinch her pennies until they dripped copper. She learned how to buy cheap, funky clothing at the used clothing stores and thrift shops, and how many ways ramen noodles can be made interesting. She found her way into the company of woman who were like her, yet so unlike her, and she followed their movements and soon started to dish with the best and dance with the drunkest. She cut her hair and threw away all her makeup and all her pumps and nearly all her dresses. She went to the movies late and ate dinner early, and learned country-western dancing and Melissa Etheridge songs. She found herself a girlfriend, and then another one, and then decided to experiment with nonmonogamy. Single again, she learned to cruise the bars, the personal ads, and even borrowed a computer to cruise all the brainy girls on-line.

Then, one night, after the sun had just set, when the clouds were the color of pale roses set against the bleeding scarlet haze of the horizon, she looked up from her perch along the piers in the West Village and saw that a star had actually peeked through the clouds and the smog to sparkle against the deepening evening sky. The air was warm, and the river quiet and not nearly as smelly as it sometimes was. The streetlights were coming on in shifts. Feeling refreshed and bold, she strolled through the streets not knowing where she was going to go, and ended up outside one of the biggest, roughest, toughest bars in the neighborhood. It had two pool tables and two bouncers and a rainbow-colored flag hanging out the front window. The evening was early, but the place was filled with gaily dressed people, so she want in, thinking a beer would be nice.

Once inside, she glanced around at the happy gathering of people and realized that she had walked into a party. And the handsomest person there was the guest of honor. She looked no older than thirty, and that was, in truth, her age. That very day was her birthday. All the festivities were for her.

She was a tall woman, and broad, in a well-broken-in leather jacket. Her dark hair was cut brutally short, even shorter than the little princess's. In fact, it looked just like an old-fashioned boy's haircut, a crew cut. But on her, it looked stunning, revealing her powerful jaw and cheekbones, leaving her strong, slender neck exposed. Her body was hard, and not very womanly—she barely seemed to have breasts at all. Of course, if she did, they might have been camouflaged by the man's shirt and tie she wore. She gestured broadly and stabbed her fingers when she spoke. She had a wide stance and a wide smile and a quick anger. She smoked and drank with a blunt hunger, sucking in the smoke and gulping down the beers, and the little princess had never seen anyone so beautiful in her entire life.

She watched this fascinating person, noticed how the other women who were dressed in man-clothing seemed to defer to her and how the women in dresses and high-heeled shoes giggled and vied for her attention. Suddenly the little princess wanted very much to light this woman's cigarettes, to fetch her a drink, and to cuddle up to that soft leather jacket and nibble on those noble-looking earlobes and find out what was under that starched white shirt. It grew late, but still she couldn't take her eyes off her. As the bar shut down and people filed out, the little princess found herself quietly wheeling her bike in the direction the leather-jacketed one had walked off in. But in trying to keep back enough to not be seen, she soon lost the woman and her flouncy, lace-bedecked chosen partner.

I must be in love, the princess thought deliriously. *I've certainly never felt so dizzy before. I must see her again!*

An ominous rumble sounded below her feet—a subway car tearing through the tunnels, echoing against the walls of the buildings she was passing. In the distance, she heard what sounded like a shout of joy—and then brakes screeching. There was a feeling in the air like a storm brewing. Nervous and panicked, she hopped onto the bike, pressed her helmet onto her head, and gunned the starter, not caring about stealth any more. One, two blocks away, she saw something terrible was happening.

A large old car had pulled up onto the sidewalk, and it was clear that it had run into someone! The little princess gunned her engine, pulled up onto the sidewalk, and gasped in horror. For the car had struck her leather-jacketed idol! The woman was lying on the sidewalk, on her back, one powerful arm thrown back as if in defiance. One look at the hysterical young woman in the beaded party dress and the little princess knew that the last gesture this bold and handsome woman had made was to push her attractive little date out of the way.

Her heart swelled for such a noble, brave, and altruistic gesture. But now was not the time for emotion. Snapping the kickstand down, she parked her bike and was off it in a second. The jabbering of the drunken driver was just noise, like seabirds squawking. She knelt beside the stricken woman and touched her throat, her temple. She was still alive! And there was a hospital just four blocks away!

The little princess didn't remember snapping, "Stay!" at the two sobbing people who were at the scene. Nor did she remember riding her bike to the emergency room, or pounding her fist against the desk for attention. But when she returned to the scene, she did remember that the woman opened her eyes when she was lifted into the wheeled stretcher, and that they looked at each other. The woman's eyes were gray, like warm steel. The little princess felt as if she could lose herself in them forever.

"Thanks," the woman croaked out. And then the emergency workers wheeled her away.

The little princess was left alone on the street. Feeling somewhat in shock, she mounted her bike and slowly headed for home, where she fell into a deep sleep and was subsequently late for work the next day. But she couldn't get that handsome woman out of her mind. She wondered about her all day: Where did she live? What did she do? What was her name? Fantasies rose like bubbles—fantasies of feeling those long, powerful arms sweeping her into hugs, those sensitive, blunt-fingered hands exploring her body. Slowly she realized that this was her prince—this was the kind of woman who would make her feel the way her Grandmama insisted a good prince should make a princess feel.

She wanted to put her newfound prince on the back of her bike and take her riding off into the sunset.

But how did one even approach such perfection?

First she had to make sure that the prince was okay. She dashed back to the hospital after work and was dismayed to find that there was no way for her to find out anything about an accident victim whose name she didn't even know. So she started going back to that same bar every other night, anxious for a glimpse of one of the women who had been there celebrating the birthday party. It was a painstaking and annoying task that kept her awake at night, which led to activities personal and lustful and terribly sad, considering she didn't even know which name to cry out at the opportune moments. She began instead to cry out, "My prince, my prince!" which worked just as well as any proper name.

In time, she had a name, and an address, and a history—and by the time the prince showed up back at the bar, one arm in a sling and a chorus of well wishers fighting for the privilege of bringing her drinks, the little princess was well prepared for her campaign of seduction. In no time at all, her prince would be in her futon, and they would find nirvana together and live happily ever after.

It didn't work.

It was as though they lived in separate worlds! When the princess tried to buy the prince a drink, she got a growl of warning and a cool stare instead of that warm smile. It was clear that the prince did not recognize her biker rescuer—and no wonder, because the little princess had been wearing a full helmet at the time. Not sure whether to identify herself, she kept quiet. After all, she didn't want to be tolerated just because she saved the woman's life! Or whatever she did with her quick action that night.

But when she tried to slide up and start a conversation, topics rapidly became bikes, babes, or bitches—bikes being things that purred and carried you around, babes being things that purred and giggled, and bitches being the last things that purred and giggled but stopped doing that before the prince was ready for them to stop. Any attempt at discussing anything personal was rebuffed, redirected, or utterly ignored.

Many a night, the little princess heard the other women talking to each other about how wonderful and tough the prince was, and she was glad that the woman was no wimp. But she remembered those warm steel eyes, and that look of dignity under the pain and sighed when she remembered the fleeting touch she had placed on the prince's body to make sure she was all right.

More and more, she grew to love the distant prince, and she wished she could find a way—any way—to be with her and love her properly. It seemed to her that the prince was larger than life—exaggerated to the point of absolutes, a thrilling figure of power and danger, and yes—pure, raw sexuality.

"What am I doing wrong?" she wailed to Tante Ester one Friday night, her fork making patterns in the sweet potatoes. "Why is this woman different? She's a dyke like me, right? So why can't I get through to her?"

"Because," Ester said with all the wisdom that was the greatest quality of her branch of the family, "it looks like you've fallen for a stone butch, baby. And you are neither butch nor femme, fowl, or, you should excuse the expression, fish."

"Well, why aren't I?" the princess asked earnestly. "I'd give anything to be what she wants, if that would get me by her side!"

"So you say. But you don't know what you'd have to change," Ester sighed. "You shouldn't even think about things like that. You should thank your lucky starfish that you don't have to! In my day, you were one or the other, and that was that! Now, you can wear a nice blouse and jeans. You can put on a little makeup and walk proud in your engineer boots. You can lead the dance one night, and follow the next, if that turns you on! Oh, no, you have it much better, baby. Eat, and find a nice girl like yourself. You don't want to mess with a stone butch."

"Oh, yes, I do!" the princess insisted. (She wasn't a princess for nothing!) "And you have to help me, too! Tell me what I have to do! Tell me what I need to change. I'll take care of the rest! Do I have to be butcher, is that it? I can do that!"

"No, honey, sweetie. To catch a stone butch, you need to be a high femme. Do you know what that means? No more jeans and boots. Grow your hair. Wear makeup, and perfume, and nice shoes. And no more job at the pet store—get something nice and ladylike, so you don't smell like beagles when you see her." Ester ticked items off on her long, slender fingers and sighed. "It's silly, sweetie. Trust me."

The little princess sighed and looked down at her sensibly trimmed nails, and pulled at her shoulder-length hair.

"Be happy the way you are," Ester said firmly, ending the conversation. "You can do anything you want."

That should have ended the situation right there, but of course it didn't. The little princess realized that she would have to focus on this and take things one at a time. As days and weeks and months passed, she started growing her hair, letting it fall down her back again the way it did when she was back at the castle. And stubbornly, despite a number of accidents at work, she grew her nails, too, and started having weekly manicures. Searching the want ads, she found a new job, sitting at a desk and answering phones. She wore her three skirts over and over, and realized that there was going to be a lot more to this high femme business than she thought. She just couldn't do it alone—and the other women at work were all too alien for her to learn from. She would have to go back to her Tante and beg for help again. But this time, she was sure to get it. This time, Tante Ester would see that she was determined!

And so, on another Friday night, she sat at the table and picked at her food until her Tante sighed and leaned back and said, "You *are* going after that butch, that prince of yours."

The little princess nodded.

"You're a fool," Tante Ester said. "But you're a fool in love, and God only knows why I'm going to do this for you except that you're in love. But I'm telling you—this is not an easy task. You'll have to give up a lot of things for this woman—and that's just to get her attention!"

"I'm willing," whispered the little princess, and she thought of her prince and winning that brave, handsome soul for her very own.

"And remember—once you're a proper high femme, there's no turning back! If you slip, it's all over for you and this butch. This woman has to fall in love with you and keep you—and you have to be able to fight to keep her. She's got to give up the hanging girls—the ones who are waiting for you to fall—and join with you so that you're two sides of the same coin. Otherwise, there's nothing but tragedy and pain in store for you.

"And did I mention the pain? The clothes, the hair—the shoes? It won't be easy, baby. It won't be one bit easy!"

"I still want to try," said the little princess.

"Okay." Tante Ester sighed again. "Let's make a list of some stuff you'll need. First, some nice dresses, and shoes, and then some stockings. We'll get you some makeup and an appointment at that place on Flatbush Avenue, where they do the nice hairstyling. And you're going to have to learn how to walk, and talk, and flirt. And everything else about how to act! Girl, you're going to wonder how anyone does the things I'm going to teach you. But you're going to do them the way I say, or else you're going to fail. Do you understand?"

"But...but...if I learn new ways to walk and talk and act and look, what will be left of me?" the little princess asked.

"Your beautiful body," her Tante Ester said honestly. "You have some natural grace, and lovely, lovely eyes. And you will have the strength and wisdom of your family inside you, and these will make her love you, if nothing else. But first, you have to walk in her world—and that I can teach you."

"Let's do it," the little princess said. "I'm ready!"

Later, she often wondered why there couldn't have been a potion for her to swallow instead of the painstaking changes she had to make in her lifestyle. First of all, and hardest to begin with, when she looked over her shopping list and her bank account, she realized that she would have to sell her motorcycle in order to buy the wardrobe her Tante described. She thought of going back home and asking the Fish King to buy her some of these items, but she realized that he would love to do that only if her prince were the proper type to bring home. Besides, this was something she was going to do for herself, wasn't it?

So she lost her wheels. It was a loss like a sword piercing her body, and each time she walked out of her apartment, she looked at the space where it used to be, and she ached for it and cried just a little. But she went to her Tante's house and put on the new clothing, and then gasped as her Tante pulled a pair of beautiful shoes from out of a colorful box.

They were white leather—not pumps, but slender high-heeled shoes of an impossible arch and height, and they fastened with the most exquisite little buckles of gold. The slipped onto her feet like softened butter, and locked on with grips like crab claws. She looked down at them nervously and set her feet on the floor and stood.

Knives! Razor-sharp knives drove into her feet! She gasped and sat back down, with leftover tears from the loss of her wheels dotting the corners of her eyes.

"Holy shit, I can't walk in these!" she cried out.

"Oh, you can and you will," Tante Ester said. "They are the traditional shoes of a high femme. You'll have several pairs, in different colors, and you will learn to wear them and walk gracefully, and your butch prince will love them. And mind your language, missy! No cursing in front of your prince; she won't like it. Learn to use euphemisms, as children do, or better yet, learn to suffer silently. And here's something else for you, too." She opened another box and pulled out a strange garment that was unlike anything the little princess had ever seen before. She was amazed when her Tante pulled it around her midsection and positioned it over her hips and under her breasts. As it began to tighten, she asked, "What is this, Tante?"

"A corset," her aunt answered, pulling the strings sharply. She grunted with satisfaction when the little princess gasped, and then pulled the strings tighter still. "You really should have played more tennis, my dear! This will give you a nice, womanly shape, with a slender waist and nice, rounded hips. I also got you a Wonder-bra—those little tits of yours could use a lift."

The little princess blushed and fell silent; not because she didn't know what to say, but because she could barely breathe with the corset drawn so tightly. She stood silently, little knife-edged spasms of pain shooting up her legs, as her Tante slipped one of the expensive dresses over her head. She turned to look in the mirror and gasped.

A beautiful young woman looked back at her: svelte, shapely, elegant, and tall, with lovely legs and long, shining hair! Was this the same girl who rode her motorcycle through the streets whooping and hollering? The woman who carried cages of budgies and cleaned fish tanks? The woman who went line dancing and arm wrestling and then talked about cyberpunk at a coffee bar all night?

Well, yes, sort of. But she was also a major, major babe. No matter how much it all hurt, her Tante was right. She was turning into the kind of woman her prince paid attention to.

She turned to her Tante and beamed. "More," she tried to say. But her usual way of breathing was restricted; the corset made it hard to be firm and loud. Instead, she whispered, "More, please."

Tante Ester nodded. Well, that was love for you. "Okay, back to talking. Remember, don't be too sharp, and don't be critical. Giggle whenever she says something funny. Be patient and don't fidget—and never look bored. She's the center of your universe—got that?"

The little princess nodded and felt very calm. That was one lesson she didn't need to learn at all.

In due time, she was ready to see whether her sacrifices and training had paid off. She showed up at the bar in her new regalia, every step still sharp as knife blades, every breath an effort. Her entire body felt like a very symphony of pain and discomfort—yet she walked into the bar with a grace that turned many heads, and slid into a seat with a set of moves that had every butch's heart pumping and quite a few of the femmes', too. She could barely move her torso—and her breathing made her Wonderbraed tits rise and fall in a rhythm that hypnotized at least half a dozen women at once, and made their girlfriends slap them. She didn't even have to raise a finger before the bartender came over to take her drink order personally.

Hey, this is not bad, she thought, trying not to move too much.

But every attention paid to her was nothing, until the prince ambled in. The little princess's heart leapt—she had nearly forgotten how handsome and dashing her prince was. And the sling was gone; apparently the injury had healed. How wonderful! Elegantly, as she had been taught, she angled her throat and looked over toward the prince, and batted her long artificial eyelashes.

It was like tugging a leash.

It was that easy.

"Hey, sweet thing, where have you been all my life?" said the prince, bowing slightly over the table. Eyes watched them from all corners of the bar, some smiling, some bitter. "And more important, care to dance?"

Ohmigod, I've wanted to for weeks! the little princess thought. But instead of speaking, she smiled gently, and gave a tiny giggle, and extended one very manicured hand and rose to dance. Every step made her believe that she was leaving bloody footprints in the sawdust, but she turned and rocked and swayed exactly as her prince led her. For the rest of the night, the prince had eyes for no other. And as she sighed and smiled and nodded and giggled, she felt that the sacrifice of any deeper conversation was worth the warmth of the woman's arms, the charm of her smile, and the gentle touch of her hands.

"Come home with me," the prince murmured while nuzzling the princess's ear.

"Yes," she sighed in response. It was a word, her Tante informed her, that butches loved to hear. The prince was no exception.

In the moonlit night, she accompanied the prince home, carefully allowing herself to be led the entire way. And, once inside, she waited until she was touched to respond, and kept her responses silky, smooth, and only in reaction. In this, too, she had been well coached.

"These nails are just too inconvenient," she had snapped at her Tante one night. "What if I....I mean, when we're close—won't they, um, hurt?"

"The only place those nails are going to do damage is on your butch's back, when you scratch and claw her in passion," Tante Ester said calmly. "Don't be thinking you'll be doing a dance on her privates. You'll be lucky if you even see them."

"What??"

"Butch and femme isn't just clothes, sweetie. The butch does, the femme gets done to. The butch leads, the femme follows. You stretch yourself back, and your butch pleasures you."

"Doesn't sound very equal to me."

"If you're lucky, you ll get a butch who opens up and lets you in some," Ester said dreamily. "That's very special. But don't take me literally, sweetie. Leave that rubber thingamajig at home, and don't ever mention that you have it."

The little princess had blushed at that, but remembered every word. And now, in the arms of her prince, she was glad that the searching hands found the sweet satin and lace undergarments instead of a leather-and-chrome harness, because the prince made such a wonderful sound of appreciation when she pulled the skirt up high and touched so boldly and sweetly! It was clear that these were the right garments to wear.

"You're so hot," the prince whispered. "God, you're perfect. Every move you make, every breath…I could hold you forever!"

"Oh, yes," the little princess sighed. And when she was finally laid down onto the bed, she forgot the pain of her feet and the pain in her chest and the unforgiving bones of the corset—all she knew was the heat, the passion, and the touch of her prince. As every sensation written and spoken about reached her, she rocked on the soft bed in wave after wave of pure ecstasy, saying nothing but "yes," over and over again.

She rapidly became the prince's favorite, eclipsing all the others. Her gentleness, demure attitude, and her silent allure gave nothing to compete against. Any other girl was too bold, too direct, too mouthy. The prince loved her completely and spoke to her for hours, holding her and wanting nothing but a murmur, a sigh, a giggle, or a sweet touch for a response. And she never realized that this was the same woman who had ridden to the scene of her accident on a motorcycle, never realized that this was the same woman who had tried so often to buy her a drink.

It was true that they never had deep conversations about the future, or politics, or anything else. There was little to talk about when your chest was so constricted that deep breathing made you dizzy, and every word had to be watched anyway. *But there's more to life than talking*, the little princess scolded herself. *I've never been so happy!*

For quite some time, this went on to their mutual satisfaction. It was true that the prince never offered the princess a ring, nor took her to be registered as domestic partners. But, according to Tante Ester, commitment was a major issue with butches, and came slowly to them. But that was okay. It was clear that the prince had eyes only for the little princess.

Until *another* princess came into the bar one night.

She is smaller than I am, the little princess thought, some new feeling rising in her that she couldn't name. *Why, I'm sure she isn't wearing a corset at all! And —look, her feet are so small, and she moves so quickly. Can it be that her shoes don't feel like razor-sharp knives to her?* For in fact, the new princess moved even more gracefully than the little one did, and her hair was a long train of shimmering gold, instead of waves of glistening copper-tinted brown.

"Holy Hannah!" said the prince as she walked into the bar. Everyone turned to see the new femme, and the little princess felt another stab of that unfamiliar emotion. *That was the way they once looked at me*, she thought. She touched the prince lightly, and the prince turned back to her and grinned. "Can't blame me for looking," she said with a laugh, and then kissed the little princess on the mouth and patted her on the hip.

But a week later, it was much more than looking.

"And then—then—the prince danced with her! In front of everybody! And I was standing there—and—and these other women came over to ask me to dance, and the prince never even noticed!" The little princess had taken her troubles to her expert Tante, and was wailing them out over a nice beef stew that was getting very cold without having ever been near her mouth.

"You've got to fight for your butch," Tante Ester said, looking down. "It's the only way. If you stand by, she'll take up with the new girl and never say boo to you again. You've got to take action this time, sweetie. Ruin the new girl. You're stronger, faster, smarter. Scare her away, and while she's gone, threaten to leave the prince. She'll be cut to the quick—it isn't her fault that she doesn't see your pain, but now she needs reminding. While she's in pain, you'll have the upper hand. Demand commitment. You've waited long enough. And when the new girl comes back, as she will, you just cut her dead with a nice ring on your finger and your clothes hanging in your prince's closet. That's the way to do it, sweetie."

"It sounds so cruel," the little princess said softly.

"It's a cruel world out there," Tante Ester said wisely. "This time you have an edge. Use it. Now! Before you lose your prince and everything you've struggled for."

It was midnight when she found the two of them, still talking and dancing in the bar. Her pains were sharp, especially the one in her stomach, where she realized that the new emotion was pure jealousy, burning through her like a heated garrote cutting her to the spine. She knew that if the prince took this new woman home, that would be the end of it—all these sacrifices and struggles for nothing, all cast away like refuse at the end of a pier. She pulled open the door of the bar and felt another twinge of pain as she realized that no one saw her—they only saw the loveliness of the new princess and the charm the prince was working on her.

The prince's warm steel eyes were happy, and it was clear that no thought had been given to the missing princess she had been squiring about for so long. Bitter hate filled the little princess as she worked her way through the bar, thinking of how she would cut this interloper down, and how she would grasp the prince's arm and make her remember who brought her so much pleasure, who saved her, and yes, who had so long desired her! And then she blinked and saw the ripple of her shoulders against the man's shirt she was wearing, and the sway of her strong hips as she danced. Suddenly she knew—the prince loved this new girl as instantly and honestly as she had once loved the little princess.

Fighting back the tears, the little princess turned and left the bar.

Stumbling, she walked on those damn shoes until she felt she had nothing but open wounds for feet. As it began to rain, she cursed, and kicked the shoes off, one after the other. Not caring about the raindrops, she tore through her own fancy, lacy dress until she found the strings of the corset and pulled and twisted them until they unbound or snapped free. People passing were astonished to see this woman contort and pull a boned lace structure from under a now torn and disarrayed dress and throw it violently into the gutter.

Taking a deep breath for once, the little princess screamed out her pain and then sank down onto the curb and folded her arms around her knees and sobbed out keening cries of anguish and sorrow, until she coughed and sputtered and realized that a river was running over her feet. She lifted them one at a time, sniffling, and realized that her expensive stockings were all twisted and run up and shredded around her ankles. But at least her feet didn't hurt so much.

Someone sat down next to her. She looked over and saw a man! A young man, very close to her age, it seemed. And, amazingly, he was wearing makeup—which made her realize that sitting in the rain had probably made her own mascara run until she looked like a raccoon. He was also wearing a gauze top that was soaked through, exposing a ring through one of his nipples, and long, soft-colored gauze pants. On his feet were army boots—a strange combination.

"Are these yours?" he asked politely, as though they were not sitting on a curb in the rain, bubbles rising around their feet. He was holding her discarded shoes.

"I threw them away," she said, astonished that an entire sentence could come out.

"Can I have them? I think they might fit," he said.

She blinked away the rain and nodded, wondering why a boy would want those shoes. Her astonishment didn't let up as he pulled his boots off and tried the shoes on. Sure enough, they fit!

"Awesome!" He stood in them. "I could never afford shoes like these! Take mine, you'll catch your death of cold sitting there with wet feet!"

The thought made her giggle—army boots with a party dress!

But she did have a long journey home, so she pulled them on and found them warm and supportive, especially when she wrapped the laces around her ankles. The boy helped her up, and she sighed in pleasure as her feet no longer felt the stabbing pains of the cursed shoes.

"I'm glad you're happy with them," she said, realizing that she could speak as much as she liked now. "They brought me nothing but pain."

"I can see that. Wanna come out and forget your troubles for a while? We're going to a new club on the East Side."

She looked at his group—for he wasn't alone. And there was the oddest collection of people she had ever seen! Two girls holding hands had purple hair and matching nose rings—and another young man had a tattoo over one eye and an arrow shooting through one eyebrow. There was a woman in black leather from head to toe, and her date who was wearing what looked like a latex miniskirt and a lace top scavenged from the trash. In fact, it was the little princess's own torn corset! There was another boy, in a long sarong and a plaid shirt, holding onto a woman in a pink party dress—and army boots.

The little princess looked down at herself, at the bedraggled lace dress and the shredded stockings and knew that she belonged with these wet, wild people. She took the hand of the sweet queer-boy who was wearing her shoes and followed them all to a lit-up club with high, high ceilings and a soaring sound system, and she heard music that no one could just rock and sway to, music that made you want to scream and throw yourself around! And she let herself be wild, moving in ways that would have shocked the prince to her royal core, and feeling the beat and the melody run through her body like gusts of wind. Hands pushed and pulled at her, and she struggled and followed, pushing back and laughing and actually allowing herself to reach the stage.

There she looked into the eyes of the lead singer, a lean and hungry-looking woman with scars and rings and a smile like an angel, and she stretched her arms wide and stood at the edge of the stage. Falling forward, she felt a sea of hands rise up to meet her, to carry her aloft and rising, until her tears faded at last and only her laughter remained. She was flying, soaring—and would never have to be bound to the razor-sharp prison of who she was not meant to be.

Jackie and the Giant Lez Beanstalk
ROBIN SWEENEY

A rite of butch passage is how "Jack and the Giant Beanstalk" reads to me now, as an adult butch woman. Struggling to do right, make something of yourself, and battle a giant, all resonate as butch challenges. So, I got to write it, including a hot Giant femme and a wonderful butch mentor.

"Fee Fie Fo Footch! I smell the blood of a baby butch!"

The Giant's terrifying cry thundered down the castle stairwell, sending Jackie running. Things were going poorly on this adventure, indeed.

Jackie jumped the last three steps and ran across the main hall of the castle. She kept running full-tilt toward the only light she saw. She scooted into an enormous kitchen. There, she ran smack-dab into a very solid torso.

"Oof!" Jackie said, falling on her butt.

"Oof, indeed, intruder. As in get oof my foot, stand the hell up, and introduce yourself, lad."

Jackie scrambled to her feet and looked at the person in front of her. Easily six feet tall, with a crew cut of short fair hair. The eyes were hard to see, since they were squinting down at her. There were tattoos of lions and tigers all over the big arms that were crossed over her chest. *My God!* Jackie thought. *It's a woman! Wow!*

Putting on her best manners, Jackie stuck out her hand. "My name's Jackie, it's nice to meet you, and could you tell me where I am, please?"

The woman looked Jackie up and down. The youngster in front of her—and anyone twenty years younger than you is a young-ster, no matter how old they are—was sandy haired and in desperate need of a haircut. She wasn't very tall, but she stood straight and made eye contact with Ace. Ace noticed her bright blue eyes, and felt a dangerous lurch of attraction. This was a very cute baby butch who had wandered up this time.

"Oh, gads, it's a baby butch. It's been a long time since a little brother wandered into the castle. The Giant's gonna have a field day with you, boy! Put it there, Jackie. I'm Ace." The older woman enveloped Jackie's hand with a huge and powerful paw and shook it.

"How the hell did you get here, Jackie? We don't get a whole lot of visitors anymore, much less strangers. Here, have a cup of coffee, boyo. Tell me about it."

Jackie took the cup gratefully, and followed Ace to the table in the middle of the kitchen. She sat down and sighed. It had been a difficult day.

"Well, it all started when Matilda asked me to go to the market and get something for dinner."

"That's always where trouble starts," Ace groaned. "With a woman."

Matilda was Jackie's girlfriend, and Jackie thought she was the prettiest girl in town. She wasn't as tall as Jackie, so when they slow danced it was easy for Matilda to put her head on Jackie's shoulder, a move that always made Jackie want to swoon. Matilda had shoulder-length dark hair, sparkling green eyes, and was round and curvy in all the places that Jackie was lean and lanky. Jackie loved Matilda, but she always seemed to be doing something wrong. Matilda was a little older than Jackie and knew more about the world. She was often frustrated with Jackie, and they often fought. The argument that happened after Jackie brought home the magic beans was a good example.

"Jackie," Matilda's voice floated out into the garden where Jackie was working. "Would you go to market and get something for dinner. Please, sweetie?" Matilda was at the kitchen door, and looked so damned cute standing there that Jackie would have done almost anything for her. Including the grocery shopping, which she was pretty bad at and loathed doing.

"Why, sure, honey. I'll get something tasty, and I'll be right back." Jackie kissed Matilda good-bye, took the coin that Matilda handed her, and set off toward the market.

Jackie was halfway to market when she heard a rustling in the bushes on the side of the road. Being a good-hearted but easily distracted sort, and much preferring exploring in the woods to grocery shopping, Jackie went into the bushes to investigate.

There was a clearing in the woods beyond the bushes, but Jackie didn't see anything moving. She assumed that it was a wild animal. She turned to head back through the bushes and continue on toward the market when she heard someone speak.

"Please, adventurer, won't you buy my beans?"

Jackie whirled around, and there in the clearing where there had been no one before, stood a beautiful woman. At first glance, it was hard to tell her age; but when Jackie stepped closer, she realized the woman was easily middle-aged, and stunning in the way a woman is when she is no longer trying to prove anything to anyone. She was dark-skinned and wore her black hair up in dozens of little braids fastened with ribbon and cloth. Bells and beads hung off the end of each braid and made tinkling noises when she moved. The woman's cloak was every color of the rainbow and shimmered in the sunlight. Her dress was white and plain, but fit her so well that it made Jackie blush to look at her. The woman took a small bag off her belt and reached out toward Jackie.

"I am no adventurer, ma'am, although I would like to be," Jackie said. "I am just a gardener who lives down the road. I'm on my way to market."

"Adventurers are adventurers even before they first adventure. These are beans that are like no others. Won't you buy them?" The woman had eyes of light amber, and Jackie found them so mesmerizing that she didn't realize she had reached for the bag.

"Well, I don't know. I have only one coin, and it's for dinner. Are they really that special?"

"For your one coin, I will sell you these beans, and your life and love will be more than you have imagined. A bargain, for all they can bring you," the woman said.

"My love will be more? Really?" Jackie reached into her pocket for the coin. "I love Matilda so much, but if there is any way to make that love be more and last forever, I'll take it."

The woman handed her the bag of beans, took the coin, and leaned down to kiss Jackie. It was just a simple peck on the cheek, but it left Jackie breathless. *Women are so amazing*, she thought, *to be able to make me feel so giddy with a single kiss*. She closed her eyes, and the woman's lips left her cheek.

"Enjoy your adventures, traveler," she said.

And when she opened her eyes, no woman stood before her. There was only the sound of bells and laughter.

Jackie rushed back to Matilda. Magic beans for only one coin!

Jackie burst through the door. Jackie was so excited that Matilda could hardly understand her.

"Beans? That's fine, dear, although I was hoping for chicken. Did you get anything to go with the beans?"

"No, Matilda, we don't need anything else. These are magic beans! We're going to have an adventure!"

"Magic beans? You spent our last money for food on magic beans?" Matilda looked baffled and annoyed, which puzzled Jackie. Didn't she understand?

"No, Matilda. The beautiful woman I met in the woods said they would make everything more than we could have ever imagined."

"The beautiful woman that you met in the woods! I can't believe it. Not only were you unable to do something as simple as go to market, you were out gallivanting with other women!"

"No, Matilda! Sweetie, I don't even know her name!" Jackie protested.

"Oh, Jackie, how could you!" At that, Matilda burst into tears and ran into the bedroom, slamming the door behind her. Jackie stood there, baffled and upset, and then went out into the yard. She went into the far corner, beyond the vegetable garden, and sat on the bench she had built there.

Great, she thought. *No dinner, no money, and my girlfriend's mad at me. Just swell.*

She took the bag that held the magic beans out of her jacket pocket, opened it, and shook the beans out onto her palm. They didn't look very interesting—just seven small brown beans.

"God, I'm a sucker!" she said out loud, and tossed the beans away.

Trying not to cry, Jackie spent a long night out on the garden bench, finally falling asleep just before dawn.

Birds were singing when Jackie finally awoke, stiff and sore from sleeping outside. She rubbed her eyes, stretching as she stood up.

Then she rubbed her eyes again.

There, in the yard behind the house she lived in with Matilda, was an enormous beanstalk. It reached far into the sky, farther than the eye could see.

"Maybe those *were* magic beans," Jackie muttered as she circled the beanstalk.

Jackie's first impulse was to fetch Matilda and show her. But remembering last night's harsh words, she hesitated. Maybe she'd just go and have an adventure by herself and see what Matilda thought of that!

Jackie started to climb the enormous beanstalk. She climbed and climbed, going miles above the ground, up high in the clouds. As she was beginning to tire, Jackie came to the edge of land. Climbing up over the edge, she saw the most amazing thing.

Nearby stood an enormous castle.

Awesome, Jackie thought. *This really is an adventure. Wait until I tell Matilda.* She walked toward the castle, over the drawbridge that crossed a moat—Jackie took a moment to check for alligators or other beasts, but didn't see any—to the castle door. After trying to figure out how to work the knocker in the shape of a high heel, she simply pushed the door, and it opened.

The castle was poorly lit, but there were candles around the enormous hall, held in sconces that looked like lovely feminine hands. There was a door off to the right, and a stairwell on the left. Jackie had started climbing the stairs when the ominous voice boomed out, sending her dashing to the kitchen and into Ace.

"That's my story," Jackie said, finishing her coffee. "I've climbed up here and now I don't know what to do. Who is that who was so loud, and who was the woman who sold me the beans, and what is this place? And what did she mean by 'baby butch?'"

"Whoa, boychick, slow down. I'm Ace, which I told you already, and I serve the Giant, Beverly. I'm mostly her servant, although I've been known to go dragon slaying and softball playing in the springtime. This is the Giant's castle, and you are the latest baby butch to be sent as a plaything by the Giant's sister, Barbara. She sells the beans to a promising specimen of butchdom, the Giant Lez Beanstalk grows, and they wander here. If they have the gumption, of course, like you. Now you'll have to engage the Giant and see if you can win your release, or spend the rest of your life in her dungeon and service. Which is not a bad way to be, believe me you, but you may not have been planning on that."

Ace continued, "And you, my friend, are a study in classic baby butch. You're young, handsome, and boyish. And a lot like a puppy."

"I am *not* a puppy, and no, I don't want to stay here! I want to go home to Matilda, my one true love."

"Ah! You're in love, huh? That's different. I usually don't help out the new boys—too much like assisting the competition, in some ways—but if you truly love your Matilda, I'm willing to help you, boyo. Tell me, do you love this Matilda truly and deeply?"

"Oh, yes, with all my heart. She is the prettiest, and kindest, and sweetest girl in the world. I have been so happy with her, Ace, really I have, even though we fight sometimes."

"All lovers fight, Jackie. But you make up and it makes you glad, right? What do you fight about?"

"Well, it's weird. It's like there are things Matilda expects or wants from me that I don't know about, and I feel like I let her down."

"Jackie, I must ask you a personal question. Is Matilda the first woman you have loved?"

Jackie blushed, and then nodded her head.

"First lover, huh? Then, my young friend, I will help you. Come with me, pay attention to all that I tell you, and tomorrow you will face the Giant with the best assistance any young butch could want. Then, you may try your hardest to return to your love."

The next morning dawned clear and crisp at the castle of Beverly the Giant. Jackie and Ace awoke in each other's arms, as comfortable and happy as a younger butch and her mentor can be. Ace showed Jackie all about harnesses and packing, and when to strut and when to be humble. She talked to Jackie about how to approach a woman when you wanted to serve her and how to grab her when it was the right time to take her.

Ace told stories of meeting and loving femmes, and all the secrets that a butch and a femme can tell each other just by dancing together. She told Jackie lots of butch secrets—about being honorable, and funny, and polite. Ace spoke of how to be tough without being hard. Ace passed on the secret of always carrying a lighter on you, even if you're a nonsmoking kind of butch, and told her of the special way a butch can sound when she says, "Please, honey."

Ace answered all the questions about how a butch knows she's butch, and how being a butch is about being masculine, but not being a man. She told Jackie to get a good suit and to buy ties that picked up the color of her eyes.

Ace also told her the long story of how she came to live with the Giant and be her consort, servant, and number one butch, and how happy that made her, which is not the story to tell here, but is a story that deserves telling. Ace made it clear how to face the Giant, answer her questions, and win her affection. That was the most important thing of all.

Then Ace taught Jackie all the truths and honest pleasures a butch can have with another butch—rough and strong and tender—all at once. Ace taught Jackie about the pleasure she could expect to feel, and how to give that pleasure back to another without embarrassment or fear.

"Let me trim that scruffy hair of yours, boyo, and then hit the shower. I'll take herself breakfast, and then you can face Beverly the Giant."

Jackie dressed carefully, even though she was still in her work boots and jeans from yesterday. Ace taught her how to put a shine on her scuffed boots, and promised her that a pair of jeans would be all right, as long as she wore a nice dress shirt. Ace loaned her one, left by another boychick who lost the confrontation with the giant, and carefully tied one of her own ties onto Jackie. It was a striped one, red on blue, that made Jackie's eyes look bright blue.

Ace helped her into a harness and selected a dildo for her. It was much bigger than Jackie had seen before, but Ace told her that size counted and just to walk tall.

She handed Jackie a bunch of flowers for the Giant—yellow roses fresh from the castle's garden—and stepped back to take a look at her. She was very young, but cute. A fine kisser, and adorable in a tie, too. The Giant would like her, and if Jackie failed the confrontation, perhaps the Giant would let Ace play with her on occasion. Jackie really did love Matilda, though, and Ace was enough of a romantic old butch to hope that Jackie got home to her love.

"There you go. You look fine. Remember what I told you, and break a leg, boy." Ace grabbed her in a quick bear hug, tousled her hair, and then slapped her butt, a trine of butch blessings. "Go get her."

Jackie strode across the main hall, feeling much more confident than she had the night before. She started up the stairs, and the voice boomed out.

"Fee, Fie, Fo, Footch! I smell the blood of a baby butch!"

Jackie swallowed, and gathered her courage.

"Hi, Ho, Hey, Hem! I sense the thrill of a scary femme!"

There was a pause, and then laughter.

"My servant has taught you well. But that simply means I won't kill you. Yet. Proceed."

Jackie got to the head of the stairs, and almost dropped the flowers. Where her sister Barbara was mysterious, elusive, and laughing, Beverly was sharp and imposing. Her black hair was cut short, close against her scalp, and she wore a score of little hoops in each ear. She was built beautifully, classically even, with strong legs and an hourglass figure. The giant had giant breasts, as well. She was the color of coffee just after you put a drop of cream in it, and Jackie thought she was stunning.

Her dark eyes flashed as she towered over Jackie. She wore several different layers of dark gold-and-green fabric that draped around her body but didn't really seem to be clothes, and over this she wore a cape of beautiful dark green velvet.

Jackie held out the flowers she carried and dropped to one knee.

"I bring you beautiful flowers, Oh beautiful Giant. Please accept them as a well-intentioned offering."

Beverly the Giant leaned over and took the flowers. She looked at them, and then looked at Jackie, still on one knee. She tossed the flowers onto a table in the corner.

"Not bad, so far. But all it means is that I won't throw you into my dungeon just yet," she said, and then smiled a self-assured smirk. "What are you going to do now, little butch?"

"Please, beautiful Giant Beverly, what would you like me to do?" Jackie said, dropping her other knee down and then lowering her head until it almost touched the floor and putting her hands behind her. Ace had made her practice that position over and over last night.

"Hmm…" the Giant rumbled, grabbing Jackie's hair and pulling her head back. "What are you up to, butchling?"

"Please, beautiful Giant, I would just like to make you happy," Jackie said, just as Ace taught her.

"Then kiss my boots, little person," she said, and let go of Jackie's hair.

Jackie dropped carefully to her belly and leaned over the Giant's boots. She kissed the toes first of one, then the other, and then settled into kissing them gently all over. She had never done this before, but it felt nice to be paying attention to the Giant this way, and it was awfully sexy, she had to admit. The boots were knee-high dark tan leather, and were so thin Jackie could feel the muscles of the Giant's legs as she flexed them. Jackie kissed and licked her way up to the top of the first boot, and then fell to the floor to work her way up the other one. The bulge in her pants seemed a part of her, and she pressed against the floor in her excitement.

She kept kissing when she got to the top of the second boot, her hands still behind her back. She kissed the Giant's knee, and then carefully licked the inside of one thigh, and then the other. She moved her head between the Giant's knees, and the Giant just barely spread her legs. Slowly and precisely, Jackie worked her mouth on every inch of the Giant's legs, until the young butch was almost standing. The Giant's mound, covered with fleecy soft dark hairs was just beyond Jackie's mouth. She blew gently on the Giant's most sensitive area.

Jackie had done this before, and she felt confident about it. She blew hot little breaths on the Giant, and then leaned forward lightly and started licking where the hairs parted. With soft moves alternating with gentle bites, she slowly parted the Giant's labia and worked her mouth over the Giant's hot cunt. It was like putting her mouth on Matilda, but much, much bigger. The Giant was built big everywhere, and her cunt was no exception. As the Giant started rocking against Jackie's mouth, working her huge clit to exactly where she wanted it against Jackie's talented tongue, Jackie worked hard to handle her size. It felt as if the Giant would be able to put all of Jackie inside her.

Then the Giant grabbed Jackie's head and moved faster, and a sudden rush of wetness covered Jackie's face.

"Yes. Yes, like that. Do it like that," the Giant cried, coming again and again.

Then she pushed Jackie away.

"All right, boy, you passed the first test, and damned well. What else are you good for?"

That made Jackie angry. She had done a good thing, going down on the Giant, and now she was being snotty. Well, she'd show that big girl a thing or two. Jackie leapt to her feet and got the Giant in a flying tackle. Now, one human, even if she's angry and turned-on and moving fast, can only make so much of a giant move. But Beverly the Giant had just come—hard—and wasn't expecting an attack from the baby butch. Usually, at this point they choked and groveled and ended up in the dungeon. *This one has spunk*, she thought as she fell backward.

"What am I good for? Are you kidding? I'm good for a lot, including fucking your brains out, scary Giant. Yeah, big Beverly the Giant. I'm gonna fuck you."

Jackie lay on top of the giant and pushed aside some of the wraps she wore. She grabbed a handful of giant tit in each hand, and pulled and twisted as the giant moaned underneath her. Jackie pushed the giant's knees apart and then reached down to unbutton her own jeans.

This was the tricky part, Ace warned her. Using your dick in a way that was respectful of the woman you were fucking—even if she was a giant who pissed you off—while still making sure you both knew who was doing the fucking was a challenge. It was especially tricky with a giant.

Jackie pulled the enormous dildo out of her jeans, struggling with it a bit. It hung almost to her knees, and she felt silly when Ace handed it to her. But now, teasing the giant's nipple that was almost as big as her hand, and watching her blush and squirm as Jackie touched her between the legs and spread her open to take her dick, Jackie realized that Ace was right. Size *did* count.

And it seemed to count in a very good way for the Giant. Jackie eased the head of her dick against the opening of the Giant's cunt, and leaned, hard, onto her tits. The giant moaned, tossed her arms over her head, and murmured something like "yes." Jackie felt the length of the dildo slide into her and started moving.

The giant liked it! She moved back against Jackie's fucking, and groaned.

"Oh, yeah, little butch, yeah. Work your dick in me!" she moaned.

"Yeah, I'm gonna. I'm fucking you, Giant. I know what you want," Jackie said, part of her brain trying to figure out where she had learned to talk like that. The rest of her brain was enjoying the feel of rocking against the Giant, fucking her slowly and fully. She fucked long, pulling her dick all the way out and plunging back into her, deep. She changed angles and slammed into the Giant.

"Oh, please, fuck me hard, fuck me hard, please, Jackie," the Giant finally said, wrapping her enormous legs around the young butch.

Jackie closed her eyes, and fucked the Giant as hard as she could. She felt the Giant start to move and buck, and start to make sounds high in her throat. Then the most amazing thing happened. Jackie felt herself start to reach the inevitable point where, no matter what, she was going to come. It was all too much, having this beautiful giant woman under her while she used her first-ever dildo. The night with Ace, the tension of the castle, and the separation from Matilda all whirled together in her and came out in one amazed howl of release. The Giant came around her then, both of them sweating and shouting with pleasure.

Jackie collapsed on top of the Giant, and they caught their breath slowly.

"Hey, you. Baby butch with the big hard-on. Where'd you learn to fuck like that?" Beverly the Giant asked.

Jackie felt herself blushing.

"Ace taught me, actually."

The Giant laughed, pushed Jackie off her, and sat up.

"Well, I'll have to talk to her about giving lessons to the victims. But you won, little one, fair and square. You not only gave me pleasure and showed me respect, you got me to trust you with precious parts of myself. I called you by name, which I'm certain Ace told you was the way to know you were free."

"I thought that was what you were saying," Jackie grinned at the Giant. "This has been most interesting and exciting, dear Giant, but I would like to ask a boon of you, and to return to my one true love, Matilda."

The Giant leaned back on one elbow and played with Jackie's hair.

"All right, if you're sure you don't want to stay. I'll give you one of my treasures, ask away."

"I would like the Wondrous Harness, please, good Giant."

"Ace told you about that, too, huh? Yes, I think that would do you well," the Giant said. "Go over to that dresser and open the bottom drawer."

Jackie got up, tucked herself back into her jeans, and buttoned up. She went to the dresser and opened the drawer. There, on a pillow of black satin, lay the Wondrous Harness. The harness always fit, never pinched, and didn't show under clothes. Most marvelous of all, when the wearer took it off, there was always a gold coin to be found somewhere on or near the wearer.

"There, now, you have your boon. Be off with you, before I decide to keep you, after all. Good-bye, Jackie, and long life," the Giant said, still lounging on the floor.

"Good-bye, and thank you, Beverly the Giant," Jackie said, leaning down to kiss her cheek.

Then she bolted down the stairs, calling a farewell to Ace, and out the castle door. She leapt upon the beanstalk, and down, down she went past the clouds and into the yard of the house she shared with Matilda.

Jackie awoke on the ground near the bench. The giant beanstalk was gone, and Jackie was quite confused. It hadn't been a dream, had it? No, it couldn't have. Her boots still shone like mirrors, and she was still wearing Ace's tie. She sat up, looked around for the Wondrous Harness, and didn't see it.

Then she put her hands on the front of her jeans and felt a bulge there. Except for her basket, Jackie didn't feel as if she was wearing anything under her pants. Then she knew that the boon bestowed upon her by the Giant was still hers.

Jackie got up and hurried into the house. She went into the bedroom, waking Matilda up with a kiss, and much more.

And they lived in the house, with always enough money and more than enough love, for a long, long time.

The Twelve Dancing Princesses
ROBIN PODOLSKY

When I was a little kid, "The Twelve Dancing Princesses" was one of those stories that would always make me cry inside. What happened to the princesses after they were found out? Did the oldest sister betray them on purpose? How could they forgive her if she did? What if the princesses didn't want to get married? And so on. I'm interested, too, in the interplay between whatever folk heritage remains in fairy tales with all the ambiguity and buried desire they contain and the "canonical" versions that are meant to serve as regulatory scripts for children. I didn't want to demonize the soldier. I identify with his sense of wonder and loss in the face of magic, his conflict over whether to surrender or try to control. Through discovering my power femme self, I've learned to identify with the princesses as well. Enough (too much?) said. Enjoy.

The soldier was no longer young, and he was tired. He arrived at the palace, his tattered uniform soiled with the blood of old wounds and dusty from the road, with a knife and a pistol at his belt and a small pack slung over his shoulders. In the pack were a tin cup, spoon, and plate, a flint, powder, bullets, and a cloak of invisibility. The cloak had been given to him by an old woman he had met in a wood into which he had run, bleeding and sick, in order to escape a battle.

The old woman had healed his wounds and nursed him until he was strong. She had given him the cloak when he told her that he was sick of war and afraid that, if the king's guard seized him, they would make him fight again.

Once on the road, the soldier kept his back to the king's palace, hoping to see it no more. Then one night, at a clamorous and sooty inn, over a deck of cards and a pitcher of ale, he heard talk that made him change his mind. One of the cardsharps, a man who more than once had tried to introduce his own deck into the play in place of the landlord's, moved and spoke with the unmistakable airs of a courtier, although his manners, like his once-fine clothes, had grown shabby from neglect. It was he who told the soldier that the king had promised one of his twelve daughters and the inheritance of all his kingdom to the man who could steal a certain secret from the princesses. That very next morning, the soldier set off for the palace. Upon arriving, he presented himself to the king at once.

When the king took the soldier's measure, he thought that here, finally, was a man ruthless, selfish, and dispassionate enough to do what must be done without falling under the sway of the princesses' charms. Pleased, he told the soldier how things were.

The king had twelve daughters, and the princesses were the most beautiful and charming women in all the land. Yet none of them had ever married. Each of them, even the youngest, had suitors from far and wide: kings and princes, poets and pirates, the richest of merchants, the boldest of rakes. But none of the princesses, not even the oldest, would give any of her admirers the time of day.

That was only half of the mystery. What most puzzled and

angered the king was this: Every night his daughters would go to bed early, disdaining the social life of the court. And every morning they would sleep so deeply that they could not be aroused, exhausted as if they had reveled until dawn. And every afternoon, each of them would require new shoes because yesterday's were so worn that the bottoms were full of holes.

When the king made his offer to the soldier, it was everything the fellow he'd met at the inn had told him it would be. The man who discovered and could prove what the princesses did at night would be rewarded with marriage to the princess of his choice and would inherit the kingdom upon the death of the king. However, there was another part to the king's proposition—something that the man who had told the soldier of the reward had neglected to mention.

Any man who attempted the task of exposing the princesses and failed would be put to death. A special graveyard outside the castle moat had been cleared out of the woods, just to contain the failed suitors of the twelve princesses.

The soldier agreed to the king's terms. That night he was conducted to a small room directly outside of the princesses' sleeping chamber where their twelve beds stood side by side. The only door through which the princesses could leave the palace was locked behind him, but the door between his room and the princesses' was left open.

The soldier made himself as comfortable as he could in the little room's only chair, an uncomfortable contraption of wooden slats. After he had settled himself, the king's oldest daughter, clad in a simple nightdress and woolen robe, her long red hair in a single braid down her back, let herself into the soldier's chamber. Without a word, she bowed and offered the soldier a glass of wine. He returned her bow and drank while she watched and smiled upon him with a kind of contemptuous affection and, perhaps, a bit of pity. When the oldest princess had left, the soldier quickly unstrapped the sponge he had tied beneath his beard to absorb any drink that he was offered.

Guessing that the wine had been drugged, the soldier feigned sleep. Sure enough, the king's youngest daughter peered into the little room to check on him.

"Well," the soldier heard the oldest daughter say, "isn't he unconscious just like the others?"

"It appears as though he is," replied the youngest princess, "but still, I feel that something is wrong. Something bad could happen to us tonight, some great misfortune from which we may never recover."

"You're always predicting things," said the oldest princess, "but if any of your prophecies have ever come true, it must be in some very subtle way that the rest of us don't understand."

The youngest princess said nothing more. From his chair outside the princesses' room, the soldier heard drawers open and shut and a great deal of movement and giggling. He heard footsteps moving away from him, toward the far end of their room.

The soldier threw on his cloak of invisibility and stepped into the princesses' chamber. There he saw all twelve princesses dressed gorgeously and ornamented with sparkling jewels, brilliant feathers, and flowers that spoke to the soldier with their insinuating perfumes.

The oldest princess, in a gown that clung to her like a thousand golden spiderwebs, her ruddy hair arrayed about her like a cape, stood by her bed and struck it with a staff. Instantly it sank into the ground, leaving a staircase as it went. Oldest to youngest, the twelve princesses descended the stairs, the soldier, wrapped in his cloak, following closely behind.

The youngest princess was sheathed in a dress that flowed over her body and fell about her feet like a mountain spring dancing with new rain. The sparkling stuff got under the soldier's boots and, by mistake, he stepped hard on the youngest princess's gown as he followed her down the stairs. "Someone is behind me!" she shrieked.

All the princesses turned to look, but saw no one. "There's nobody there," said the oldest princess, "You're always imagining things."

The youngest princess said nothing more. The princesses and the invisible soldier reached the bottom of the stairs where the oldest princess's bed stood like a sentinel with its brass posts. The steps had taken them down to a quay at the edge of a broad, fast-flowing underground river.

All around were trees that looked as though they were made of silver. Their leaves sparkled with diamonds. So that, later, he could prove to the king that what he told him was the truth, the soldier wrapped his hand in the cloak of invisibility and snapped off a silver twig with one shining diamond leaf at the end. It cracked with a resonant clang, like the peal of a silver bell.

The youngest princess started. "What was that?" she cried.

All the other princesses turned to look. In their giddy excitement and all their talk among themselves, they had heard nothing. "Will you calm down?" the oldest princess said. "You're a bundle of nerves tonight."

Down the river floated twelve slender boats with beautifully curved prows, and in each boat was a princess as lovely as any of the king's twelve daughters. As the boats pulled up to the dock, a princess got into each and began to help row the boat downstream.

Trailing the youngest princess closely, the soldier managed to follow her into a boat. In that boat was a princess arrayed in a doublet of velvet and lace fine enough for the king himself. She and the youngest princess embraced joyfully before they began to row.

"How heavy the boat is tonight!" said the youngest princess.

"It's only because we're impatient to get to where we're going," said the princess she loved. "I thought today would never be over." And they rowed hard to keep up with the others.

As the boats made their way downstream under the magical trees that glittered in the mysterious light, they were joined by others. Some of the boats carried princess couples, as happy as the twelve princesses and their companions. Others carried pairs of princes who were equally pleased with each other's company.

The landscape changed. After they left the silver forest, they came to a forest of gold in which the leaves of the trees glowed with pearls. Again, the soldier managed to break off a twig. Again, the youngest princess started at the noise that no one else seemed to hear.

They next entered a forest of bronze, whose leaves were bright with rubies. Once again the soldier seized a twig, and the youngest princess jumped at the noise. "What was that?" she cried.

Everyone looked at her. "Will you stop it?" said her oldest sister, "You're getting on everybody's nerves."

After that the youngest sister was silent. Her beloved princess stroked her hair and comforted her until, like the others, their boat docked at a pier next to a fine palace with banners and pennants flying, all lit up from within. The couples arose from their boats and went inside, the invisible soldier following close behind. Once more the youngest sister felt someone step on her dress, but she said nothing.

The princesses and princes entered the palace, which was resplendent beyond compare. The great ballroom was ablaze with the light of a thousand torches. The food was plentiful and delicious and all found it satisfying though it felt in the stomach like nothing at all. The wines and punches made everyone cheerful but affected their grace and lucidity not a whit and the musicians conjured the most irresistible tunes that got into the company's feet and commanded them to dance. The princesses in each other's arms, the princes in each other's arms, and the occasional princess and prince in each other's arms whirled and skipped until their sweat ran freely and the laughter that came from their bellies, without a trace of decorum, was loud and free.

There were hallways and rooms furnished in velvets and silks, in crystal and brocade, in leather and chains where the couples could retire to enjoy each other's company alone, or not. There were gardens and atriums where night-blooming flowers panted their heavy fragrances into the night air and made visitors happy that the grounds were strewn with hammocks, slings, and chaises longues, and with pools that invited a midnight swim.

The soldier had never seen anything like it. He tried to feel happy because he had found out the princesses' secret and he had proof and was unlikely to be caught before his work was done. But helplessly, he felt rising inside him a great, heavy grief. He watched the youngest princess, her fears forgotten, laughing with joy, undulating on the dance floor with her winsome love, their eyes locked, their pelvises not touching, but moving in unison nonetheless. He watched the oldest princess as she sat on a couch, fascinated by the words of another princess whose many braids fell over her full breasts and shone with mirrors and bright beads from within the folds of her deep purple gown. The oldest princess's face was smooth and alive, her hand locked in that of the lovely storyteller and pressed to the speaker's heart. The soldier imagined what it would be to have a wife whom he had robbed of her life's greatest joy. He tried not to watch the princes. They irritated him like scraps of memory that, refusing to harden into pictures or words, attach themselves to certain situations and flutter, agitating the air. The soldier watched the ball and thought and wasn't pleased.

There were two more unseen guests at the great dance. From deep in a wood far away, by means that are best not talked about, two watchers observed all that proceeded. They were the old woman who had given the soldier his cloak of invisibility and the princesses' half-sister, born on the wrong side of the blanket, the Inevitable Thirteenth.

"Interesting," said the old woman, "most especially the subterranean dialogue between younger and older."

"Perhaps the younger sister's power makes the old one nervous," said the Inevitable Thirteenth.

"Perhaps the youngest will never be reconciled to the older one's power until she challenges it," replied the Old Woman dryly. "You know," she went on, with the smallest of chuckles that conjured, for an instant, the kind of witch that some people might expect her to be, "sooner or later, some rebellion against the Mother is, well…inevitable."

Her companion said nothing. The old woman went on, "For instance, this story we're linked to shunts us into the broadest and most conventional channels of patriarchal power by the invocation of tropes that signify entry into and then rejection of the chthonic domain—in this case, the queer underground standing for the unchanging underworld, home of the devouring mother. Through the oldest sister's sabotage, unconscious or deliberate, of the adolescent paradise, that eternal glittering romance her sisters still cling to, the reader is pulled from the seductive allure of the underworld, is taught in fact that a condition of naming such fantasies is an eventual surrender to the normative, the everyday. Look at all that sparkle and reflection, the jewels like mirrors and the paired princesses and princes—none of our precious children may be commoners or stuck with the responsibility to rule—it shrieks with the narcissism of the *puella* and *puer*, the eternal child. To be followed of course, by expulsion into adulthood and the heterosexual union—the inescapable triumph of the Father's Law."

"Compulsory heterosexuality. And death," said the Inevitable Thirteenth.

"And taxes," said the Old Woman. "The oldest sister wants to take her place as queen. She wants to be a mother herself. She wants change. And, like it or not, if she wants those things, it means some kind of accommodation with the phallocentric matrix of power that represents what we call daily life. It also means an embrace of the kind of ruthless power that the soldier represents, the killer within us all. She has to kill her childhood and betray her sisters—the maidens—to become the mother she's ready to be."

"Nice blend of Jung and Lacan you wound up with," said the Inevitable Thirteenth. "Quite a serenity cocktail. Let's see how it all turns out after the happy ending, shall we?"

By means that are best not talked about, the watchers peered into the skein of stories that was the princesses and their lovers, all the other princesses and princes at the ball, the soldier and the king, and all the people of the land. Backward and forward through what we call time, the watchers traced the shining filaments of all their possible choices and consequent lives, unraveling the various strands. One thread, the one picked out long ago by the Brothers Grimm as that which they most wanted to display, had been decorated so brightly that it outshone all the rest. In that story, the soldier returns in safety, exposes the princesses, is believed, and marries, of course, the oldest, the one who shushed her younger sister's fears. The Grim Brothers never went on to say what happened to the youngest, to the other sisters, or even to the happy couple after they were wed.

Entering the web of story, the watchers found that thread which was the youngest sister, the slimmest strand, that shone with a pulsing, fevered glow. They saw that she never recovered from her sister's betrayal, from the loss of her own handsome princess, her one true love.

They watched the youngest sister surrender to madness—the only truth she could cling to—screaming out her visions and dreams to a world that dared not believe her. They saw three forced marriages fail after each of the grooms, youngest sons of kings with whom her father wanted very much to be allied, sickened suddenly and died inexplicable, painless deaths. They saw the youngest sister walled up, finally, by her father's order in a tower that had no entrance, watched her long golden hair trail down the tower's walls as she hauled up on ropes the water and bread that was her only sustenance, crying for a witch to climb that dazzling rope of hair and release her from her loneliness and rage. None came. They watched as she died, burned alive in her tower by villagers after an especially bad winter when their crops failed, watched while her father's guards stood by, having no orders to save her.

They watched the ten middle sisters who, married to the middle sons of kings with whom their father wished to be allied, went on to live longish, comfortable, and moderately pleasant lives and were never again quite so quick as they'd been when they danced and sweated under torchlight with the princesses they'd loved and the princes who were the only brothers they'd ever known. Toward their own daughters there would be mistrust, sometimes hatred, mixed with love. There would an affair of a soothing mirror that encouraged vanity and spite, a poisoned apple. There would be a spinning wheel, a long sleep, mutilated feet, and glass slippers. Oh, it would go on and on.

Finally, they found the strand of story that was the oldest princess, a tough, flexible, lustrous wire. They watched as the oldest sister welcomed, for a time, the sun on her face and the company of people she had never met. They watched the grace and power with which she conducted the court as her father aged and they watched her joy when she had a child, a beautiful girl. They watched as, after the death of the old king and the ascendance of the soldier to the throne, the oldest sister's power waned and she saw little of the sun, only endless rites of courtly courtesy under the torches of her husband's palace. They watched her boredom turn to bitterness and then impotent horror when she saw that her husband, the king, was still the drunken, ruthless soldier he had, with some interesting lapses, been before. She spent many nights alone in her sleeping chamber in which her husband had the bed bolted to the wall. The king began to spend altogether too much time in his daughter's room, watchful and jealous lest she find some means to escape to the underworld and find sisters and brothers there.

"The teller is the tale and the tale, the teller," said the Old Woman. "Don't you think you're taking a one-dimensional view of all this?"

"And your view of the queer underground?" asked the Inevitable Thirteenth. "An edifice of adolescent romance that must be abandoned in order to grow up? Whose story is that, anyway?"

"Are you not bitter," the old woman asked, "thrust out of the palace and into the wild?"

"And you," the Inevitable Thirteenth replied, "are you not bitter? Abandoned as well, given the most meager respect laced with not a little fear because, finally, they don't desire you and you're still alive? Having to show the merest shadow of your power, known as an eccentric, a crank, a harmless old bat who just happens to have on occasion the most marvelous gifts lying around, like a cloak of invisibility that they accept as their due with the most perfunctory of thanks? Are you not bitter? But at whom? Maybe more than a little sour toward those of us who might not be so quick to fade into rustic obscurity and who might not keep doing nice things for people who just don't appreciate it?"

"The word 'strident' is overused these days," mused the Old Woman. "However..."

"All right." The Inevitable Thirteenth settled down. "Let's watch some more. They might surprise us, all of them."

The torch flames snapped, the couples danced, the room breathed perfume and sweat and lust. Music and laughter grew wild, the drums spoke louder, and it seemed as though the moans and yells that filled the far-off rooms and gardens could be heard in the ballroom's great din. When he could stand no more, the soldier made a choice.

"Let her decide," he decided.

The soldier threw off his cloak and walked toward the oldest princess, his worn, rough form surrounded by spreading waves of silence as he moved across the floor. The oldest princess met his eyes. Facing him where she sat, she released her companion's hand, but not before pressing a kiss into the smooth palm.

When he reached her, the soldier bowed, more abruptly than he had meant to. "Will you dance, Lady?" he invited, extending his hand.

The oldest princess looked at him gravely, fearlessly. She looked at the lovely and beguiling princess at her side who was also the oldest of her own sisters, a woman whose words had begun to make the oldest sister feel that, even in the underworld, life can change wildly, unpredictably. She looked at her youngest sister, who had torn loose from her own partner's embrace and was standing before her at the soldier's side, breathing hard.

The youngest sister could not yet see what the watchers had seen, she could not know just how things might turn out. But the feelings that seized her were exactly those she would have felt if she had known, to the last detail, what the watchers knew. She stared at the oldest princess, outrage and terror erasing her prettiness, marking her face with traces of the beauty it would someday achieve.

The oldest princess realized that she was not tired of her sisters after all. She had wanted something new to happen. She did miss sunlight. She wondered about having a child, about how it would feel to reign in a court that was known to all the world. For the soldier, she felt no desire at all, only a strange fellowship. She saw that he was as tired as she. She saw, also, that she was seeing the best of him that she would ever see, if they spent all the rest of their days together.

Meeting her affectionate, distant gaze, the soldier felt more weary and sad than ever. He remembered another pair of eyes that had, for a while, looked at him as the princess had looked at the woman at her side until, one day, they turned from him in terror and disgust. Facing the princess, the soldier felt a deep regret for what he had become. He knew that, if she let him, he would still betray her secret and all would be destroyed. He hoped that she was stronger than he could be.

"Do you really think," asked the Old Woman, "that the Father's Law can be evaded by an act of willful refusal? Don't you see the futility of a phantasmic rejection of phallocentrism that depends upon that very regime for the terms of its own relevance? What do you suppose can be accomplished here?"

"I suppose," said the Inevitable Thirteenth, "that the possibilities are endless in any direction. The princess, married, might still escape the castle. Or, the princesses and princes of the underworld might find their way aboveground by another route—one that doesn't trap them in the father's palace. Or there may be more to the magic underworld than we have seen. All kinds of change may yet be possible. No, I don't think we can simply refuse the terms which, even now, construct our questions. But we can build a new thing, even if the stuff we build it with is old."

"The poor soldier," sighed the Old Woman, remembering the terrified, shivering boy he'd been when fever laid him low. "Can he build a new thing?"

"He could have once," said the Inevitable Thirteenth, "but from some acts, we don't get to come back. Remember, he's been the king's soldier for a long time."

"They made him," said the Old Woman.

"Yes," said the Inevitable Thirteenth. "But he's an example of what I mean when I say that there always is some kind of choice. It was the king, finally, who decreed the soldier's fate; but the soldier signed the decree when he bargained with a man who would sell his children and kill anyone who couldn't give him his way. Everything has consequences."

"For all of us," said the Old Woman, drawing her shawl about her in the cold, free vastness of the forest where few who were not desperate or lost ever came.

"Yes," said the Inevitable Thirteenth, drawing closer and kissing her cheek.

The soldier's heart beat quickly as the oldest princess rose to her feet.

"Of course, handsome soldier, I'll dance with you." The soldier's face and that of the youngest princess were twin masks of despair.

"But first," said the oldest princess, leading him toward the buffet, "you really must allow me to refresh you with a glass of wine. It's a very special vintage, made by ourselves, for particular occasions."

She drew, from under the table, a sealed dark bottle. When uncorked and poured, the wine was blood red. It had been given to the oldest princess, just in case of intruders, long before. Given to her by an old woman whom she had met in a wood.

They almost smiled at each other as the soldier accepted the glass from her hand. "From the looks of you, you'd better drink it all," she said. "Poor man, you're nearly dead on your feet."

ABOUT THE AUTHORS

Dorothy Allison ("The Snow Queen's Robber Girl") is the author of the poetry collection *the women who hate ME*, the Lambda Literary Award–winning short-story collection *Trash*, the National Book Award Finalist for Fiction *Bastard Out of Carolina*, the Lambda Literary Award–winning *Skin: Talking about Sex, Class, and Literature*, and *Two or Three Things I Know for Sure*.

Katya Andreevna ("Svya's Girl"), a writer and editor, has stories in *Heat Wave* and *The New Worlds of Womon*. Although a panel of Canadian judges has deemed her work obscene, she persists in turning out tales that others consider perverse. She would like to thank Tom Caffrey for the dare.

Laura Antoniou ("The Little Urban Maid") is a victim of Compulsive Publishing Syndrome, an illness which makes a person believe that she can actually make a living writing and editing in genre fiction. Therefore, she is the editor of more than a half-dozen anthologies, including *Leatherwomen I, II,* and *III, Some Women,* and *Looking for Mr. Preston.* Under the name Sara Adamson, she is also the author of the Marketplace series of erotic novels.

Red Jordan Arobateau ("The Shoes that Were Danced to Pieces") is the graffiti artist of lesbian literature. A fifty-two-year-old butch dyke of mixed-race heritage, she has been chronicling lesbian life since the late 1950s. She is the author of forty self-published, hand-typed manuscripts, two of which, *Dirty Pictures* and *Lucy and Mickey,* have been published by Masquerade Books.

Isobel Bird ("The Butch's New Clothes") is the author of the fantasy novels *The Sleeping Season* and *Dancing with the Queen of the May,* which received the Lilith Prize. Her short stories, essays, and nonfiction pieces have appeared in many different magazines, from *The Journal of Herbal Healing* to *Sidhe.* She lives, gardens, and dances beneath the moon somewhere in New England.

Francesca Lia Block ("Sleeping Beauty") is the award-winning author of a series of magic-realist-punk fairy tales for all ages. *Weetzie Bat, Witch Baby, Cherokee Bat and the Goat Guys, Missing Angel Juan,* and *Baby Be-Bop* are about a group of friends who create their own loving, if untraditional, family in the Shangri-L.A./Hell.A. of Los Angeles. She has also written *The Hanged Man,* an exploration of a young woman's descent and emergence, set in a darkly sensual, demon-haunted Los Angeles, and *Ecstasia* and *Primavera,* myth-based fantasy novels. Ms. Block's stories have been included in various books and magazines and a compilation of her stories, *Girl Goddess 9,* is forthcoming. She has written reviews and articles for *The New York Times,* the *Los Angeles Times,* and *Spin.* All of Francesca's work explores the need to confront darkness and heal pain through the forces of love and art. Currently she lives, writes, dances, and cooks vegetarian macrobiotic food in Los Angeles with her cat, Mewriel, and her springer spaniel, Vincent Van Go-Go Boots.

Kate Bornstein ("The Little Macho Girl") is a Seattle-based performance artist and the author of *Gender Outlaw: On Men, Women, and the Rest of Us* and, with co-author Caitlin Sullivan, the novel *Nearly Roadkill.* Her stage work includes the solo pieces *The Opposite Sex is Neither* and *Virtually Yours: A Game for Solo Performer with Audience.* When not writing or performing, Kate can be found cuddling with Gwydyn, following the adventures of Hothead Paisan, or prowling the Net in a never-ending search for blood, Daddy, and X-rated *Star Trek* role-playing games.

Pat Califia's ("Saint George and the Dragon") work explores boundaries: the thin lines between pleasure and pain, consent and coercion, and genders of all sorts. She has two collections of short stories in print, *Macho Sluts* and *Melting Point.* Her most recent publication is a compilation of essays and articles, *Public Sex: The Culture of Radical Sex.* She is working on two books at the moment, *Sex Changes*, a historical analysis of transgendered identities and communities, and *The Code*, a novel about a love affair between a gay leatherman and a woman, set in the 1970s.

Christa Faust ("The Girl Who Loved the Wind") is a professional Dominatrix who has recently given up life in the pro scene in order to devote herself to the entirely more masochistic pursuit of a professional writing career. Her short fiction has been featured in anthologies including *Love in Vein*, edited by her sometimes co-conspirator Poppy Z. Brite, and the forthcoming *Millenium.* She is presently working on her first novel.

Michael Ford (editor) has written lesbian, gay, bisexual, and straight erotica under many different names. Under his own name, he writes regularly about queer issues and is the author of several books, including *The World Out There: Becoming Part of the Lesbian and Gay Community*.

Dorsie Hathaway ("Goldilocks and the Three Bears") is a writer, editor, femme switch, mother-bear. She gets off on contradictions and contrast and surprises. Lover and admirer of transgressive folks everywhere who tell the truth by living their lives honestly. Fiercely protective of her clan of friends and chosen family, including a few bears and the real-life Devin. She lives in Cascadia near two rivers and a volcano, with her two baby bears and the cuddly Pooh, who makes her write.

Corrina Kellam ("Iron Hans"), poet and cunt lover, is a recent transplant to Philadelphia, although she is still a southern Maine girl at heart. Her mother suggested that she say she is a graduate student and is so overflowing with ideas that she doesn't have time to write them all down.

Jenifer Levin ("The Piper") is the author of four novels: *Water Dancer* (nominated for the PEN/Hemingway Award), *Snow*, *Shimoni's Lover*, and *The Sea of Light* (nominated for a Lambda Literary Award). Her short stories are widely anthologized, and she has written for publications including the *New York Times*, the *Washington Post*, *Rolling Stone*, *Mademoiselle*, *Ms.*, and *The Advocate*. She currently lives in New York City.

Heather Lewis ("The Story of the Youth Who Went Forth to Learn What Fear Was") is the author of the novel *House Rules*, which won the Ferro-Grumley Award, the new Voice Award, and was a Lambda Book Award finalist. Her fiction has appeared in the anthologies *Living with the Animals* and *Surface Tension*. She has completed a second novel, *Notice*, and is at work on a third novel. She lives in New York City, where she teaches at the Writer's Voice.

Lee Lynch ("The Changeling") has been writing lesbian stories since the late 1960s, when her work was published in *The Ladder*. She has published ten books, including *The Swashbuckler*, *Old Dyke Tales*, and the most recent, *Cactus Love*. Her column, "The Amazon Trail," appears in papers across the country, as do her book reviews.

Mam'selle Victoire ("Taking Flight: The Secret of the Swan Maiden") began her career as a teller of tall tales spinning fairy tales, albeit a little heavy on behavior modification, for her much-beloved little sisters, and later regaling fellow campers with perversely re-embroidered renditions of episodes of *Twilight Zone*. Would anyone remembering one of these performances kindly get in touch; we'd like to hear one of them.

Robin Podolsky ("The Twelve Dancing Princesses") is a writer who lives and works in Los Angeles, where she was born. Her essays have appeared in the *L.A. Weekly*, *Artpaper*, and *High Performance*. Among the anthologies that include her fiction and poetry are *Hers* and *Grand Passion*. Her forthcoming book, *Queer Cosmopolis*, will be published by New York University Press. After a decade as an independent artist, she has surrendered to the academy and is working toward her Bachelor of Arts degree at Pitzer College in Claremont, California.

Carol Queen ("Puss in Boots: Or, Clever Mistress Cat") is a San Francisco writer, activist, and sex educator. Her work appears frequently in sexzines and has been anthologized in *Leatherwomen*, *Dagger*, *The Erotic Impulse*, *Bi Any Other Name*, *Madonnarama*, *Best Gay Erotica 1996*, and other collections of erotic writing and sex essays.

Shar Rednour ("Rapunzel") is an erotic author and the editor of *Virgin Territory I* and *II*. She publishes *Starphkr: the best j/o 'zine to hit the planet*, and is the associate publisher and editor of *Girljock*.

Cristina Salat ("Hungry Wolf and the Three Capable Femmes") is the author of fiction and nonfiction, as well as movie novelizations and screenplays. Her work includes the award-winning children's novel *Living in Secret*. She is presently researching gray sharks in blue water.

Joan Schenkar ("Gammer Ermintrude's Revenge: A Love Letter from Snow White") is a well-known experimental playwright whose works are produced and published throughout North America and western Europe. She is the recipient of more than thirty-five grants and awards for her plays, has had more than three hundred productions, and is invited to speak about her work at college and theater festivals around the United States and Europe. Among her best-known works are *Signs of Life, Cabin Fever, The Universal Wolf, Fulfilling Koch's Postulate, Family Pride in the 50s, The Last of Hitler, Fire in the Future, The Lodger*. She is currently working on *Truly Wilde*, a biography of Oscar Wilde's outrageous niece, Dolly.

Marcy Sheiner ("Down in the Cinders") is a journalist and fiction writer who turned to writing pornography ten years ago in order to pay the rent. Discovering a natural affinity for the genre, she became highly prolific, publishing stories in *Forum, Penthouse, On Our Backs*, and *Playgirl*. Her work has been translated into Danish, Norwegian and Swedish, and has appeared in several anthologies, including *Herotica 1, 2,* and *3*. She is the editor of *Herotica 4*, as well as the forthcoming *Herotica 5*, and is working on a collection of autobiographical essays.

Linda Smukler's ("Hans and Greta") first book of poems, *Normal Sex*, was published in 1994 by Firebrand Books and was a finalist for a Lambda Literary Award in poetry. Her second book, *Home in Three Days. Don't Wash.*, with accompanying CD-ROM, was published in 1996 by Hard Press. She has received fellowships in poetry from the New York Foundation for the Arts and the Astraea Foundation. Her work has appeared in numerous journals and anthologies.

Wickie Stamps ("Go Tell Aunt Tabby") is a writer whose published works appear in *For Shelter and Beyond: Ending Violence Against Women*; *Brother and Sister*, *Looking for Mr. Preston*, *Dykescapes: Short Fiction by New Lesbian Writers*, *Doing It for Daddy*, *Leatherfolk*, *Best of Brat Attack*, *Flashpoint*, and *Queer View Mirror*. She is currently the editor of *Drummer* magazine.

Robin Sweeney ("Jackie and the Giant Lez Beanstalk") is a Bay Area writer whose work has appeared in *Dagger*, *Leatherwomen II*, *Some Women*, and *Doing it for Daddy*. With Pat Califia, she is the co-editor of *The Second Coming*.

Cecilia Tan ("The Nightingale") is a writer, editor, and sexuality activist. Her erotic fiction has appeared everywhere from *Penthouse* to *Ms.* and in many anthologies, including *Dark Angels: Lesbian Vampire Stories*, *On A Bed of Rice: An Asian-American Erotic Feast*, *No Other Tribute*, *Backstage Passes*, and *Herotica 3*. She edits anthologies of erotic science fiction for Circlet Press (1770 Massachusetts Ave. 278, Cambridge, MA 02140) and is the editor of an anthology, *S/M Visions: The Best of Circlet Press*. She is active in bisexual politics and the National Leather Association.

Kitty Tsui ("The Legend of White Snake") lives to write, eat, and have sex. Her erotic stories and poems have appeared in *Heat*

Wave, On a Bed of Rice, Asian-American Sexualities, Queer-View Mirror, The Femme Mystique, Pearls of Passion, Intricate Passions, Hear the Silence, Lesbian Love Stories, and *On Our Backs*. The author of *Words of a Woman Who Breathes Fire* and *Breathless*, she has just completed a historical novel, *Bak Sze, White Snake*. She is currently editing an anthology of erotic works by Asian-Pacific lesbian and bisexual women entitled *Who Says We Don't Talk About Sex?*

Karen X. Tulchinsky ("Avi Shmacha and the Golden Yidlock") is a Jewish dyke writer. She is the author of *In Her Nature*, a collection of short stories, and the co-editor of *Tangled Sheets: Stories and Poems of Lesbian Lust* and *Queer-View Mirror: Lesbian and Gay Short Fiction*.

MASQUERADE

N.T. MORLEY
THE PARLOR
$6.50/496-8
Lovely Kathryn gives in to the ultimate temptation. The mysterious John and Sarah ask her to be their slave—an idea that turns Kathryn on so much that she can't refuse! But who are these two mysterious strangers? Little by little, Kathryn not only learns to serve, but comes to know the inner secrets of her stunning keepers.

COME QUICKLY:
FOR COUPLES ON THE GO
$6.50/461-5
The increasing pace of daily life is no reason to forgo a little carnal pleasure whenever the mood strikes. Here are over sixty of the hottest fantasies around—all designed to get you going in less time than it takes to dial 976. A super-hot volume especially for couples on a modern schedule.

ERICA BRONTE
LUST, INC.
$6.50/467-4
Lust, Inc. explores the extremes of passion that lurk beneath even the coldest, most business-like exteriors. Join in the sexy escapades of a group of high-powered professionals whose idea of office decorum is like nothing you've ever encountered! Business attire not required....

VANESSA DURIÈS
THE TIES THAT BIND
$6.50/510-7
The incredible confessions of a thrillingly unconventional woman. From the first page, this chronicle of dominance and submission will keep you gasping with its vivid depicitons of sensual abandon. At the hand of Masters Georges, Patrick, Pierre and others, this submissive seductress experiences pleasures she never knew existed....

M. S. VALENTINE
THE CAPTIVITY OF CELIA
$6.50/453-4
Colin is mistakenly considered the prime suspect in a murder, forcing him to seek refuge with his cousin, Sir Jason Hardwicke. In exchange for Colin's safety, Jason demands Celia's unquestioning submission—knowing she will do anything to protect her lover. Sexual extortion!

AMANDA WARE
BOUND TO THE PAST
$6.50/452-6
Anne accepts a research assignment in a Tudor mansion. Upon arriving, she finds herself aroused by James, a descendant of the mansion's owners. Together they uncover the perverse desires of the mansion's long-dead master—desires that bind Anne inexorably to the past—not to mention the bedpost!

SACHI MIZUNO
PASSION IN TOKYO
$6.50/454-2
Tokyo—one of Asia's most historic and seductive cities. Come behind the closed doors of its citizens, and witness the many pleasures that await. Lusty men and women from every stratum of Japanese society free themselves of all inhibitions....

MARTINE GLOWINSKI
POINT OF VIEW
$6.50/433-X
With the assistance of her new, unexpectedly kinky lover, she discovers and explores her exhibitionist tendencies—until there is virtually nothing she won't do before the horny audiences her man arranges! Unabashed acting out for the sophisticated voyeur.

RICHARD MCGOWAN
A HARLOT OF VENUS
$6.50/425-9
A highly fanciful, epic tale of lust on Mars! Cavortia—the most famous and sought-after courtesan in the cosmopolitan city of Venus—finds love and much more during her adventures with some of the most remarkable characters in recent erotic fiction.

M. ORLANDO
THE ARCHITECTURE OF DESIRE
Introduction by Richard Manton.
$6.50/490-9
Two novels in one special volume! In *The Hotel Justine*, an elite clientele is afforded the opportunity to have any and all desires satisfied. *The Villa Sin* is inherited by a beautiful woman who soon realizes that the legacy of the ancestral estate includes bizarre erotic ceremonies.

CHET ROTHWELL
KISS ME, KATHERINE
$5.95/410-0
Beautiful Katherine can hardly believe her luck. Not only is she married to the charming and oh-so-agreeable Nelson, she's free to live out all her erotic fantasies with other men. Katherine has discovered Nelson to be far more devoted than the average spouse—and the duo soon begin exploring a relationship more demanding than marriage!

MARCO VASSI
THE STONED APOCALYPSE
$5.95/401-1/mass market
"Marco Vassi is our champion sexual energist."—VLS
During his lifetime, Marco Vassi praised by writers as diverse as Gore Vidal and Norman Mailer, and his reputation was worldwide. *The Stoned Apocalypse* is Vassi's autobiography; chronicling a cross-country trip on America's erotic byways, it offers a rare glimpse of a generation's sexual imagination.

ROBIN WILDE
TABITHA'S TEASE
$5.95/387-2
When poor Robin arrives at The Valentine Academy, he finds himself subject to the torturous teasing of Tabitha—the Academy's most notoriously domineering co-ed. But Tabitha is pledge-mistress of a secret sorority dedicated to enslaving young men. Robin finds himself the utterly helpless (and wildly excited) captive of Tabitha & Company's weird desires!

ERICA BRONTE
PIRATE'S SLAVE
$5.95/376-7
Lovely young Erica is stranded in a country where lust knows no bounds. Desperate to escape, she finds herself trading her firm, luscious body to any and all men willing and able to help her. Her adventure has its ups and downs, ins and outs—all to the undeniable pleasure of lusty Erica!

CHARLES G. WOOD
HELLFIRE
$5.95/358-9
A vicious murderer is running amok in New York's sexual underground—and Nick O'Shay, a virile detective with the NYPD, plunges deep into the case. He soon becomes embroiled in an elusive world of fleshly extremes, hunting a madman seeking to purge America with fire and blood sacrifices. Set in New York's infamous sexual underground.

OLIVIA M. RAVENSWORTH
THE MISTRESS OF CASTLE ROHMENSTADT
$5.95/372-4
Lovely Katherine inherits a secluded European castle from a mysterious relative. Upon arrival she discovers, much to her delight, that the castle is a haven of sensual pleasure. Katherine learns to shed her inhibitions and enjoy her new home's many delights. Soon, Castle Rohmenstadt is the home of every perversion known to man.

CLAIRE BAEDER, EDITOR
LA DOMME: A DOMINATRIX ANTHOLOGY
$5.95/366-X
A steamy smorgasbord of female domination! Erotic literature has long been filled with heartstopping portraits of domineering women, and now the most memorable have been brought together in one beautifully brutal volume. A must for all fans of true Woman Power.

TINY ALICE
THE GEEK
$5.95/341-4
"An accomplishment of which anybody may be proud."   —Philip José Farmer
The Geek is told from the point of view of a chicken, who reports on the various perversities he witnesses as part of a traveling carnival. When a gang of renegade lesbians kidnaps Chicken and his geek, all hell breaks loose.

CHARISSE VAN DER LYN
SEX ON THE NET
$5.95/399-6
Electrifying erotica from one of the Internet's hottest and most widely read authors. Encounters of all kinds—straight, lesbian, dominant/submissive and all sorts of extreme passions—are explored in thrilling detail.

STANLEY CARTEN
NAUGHTY MESSAGE
$5.95/333-3
Wesley Arthur discovers a lascivious message on his answering machine. Aroused beyond his wildest dreams by the acts described, Wesley becomes obsessed with tracking down the woman behind the seductive voice. His search takes him through strip clubs, sex parlors and no-tell motels—and finally to his randy reward....

MASQUERADE

AKBAR DEL PIOMBO
SKIRTS
$4.95/115-2
Randy Mr. Edward Champdick enters high society—and a whole lot more—in his quest for ultimate satisfaction. For it seems that once Mr. Champdick rises to the occasion, nothing can bring him down.
DUKE COSIMO
$4.95/3052-0
A kinky romp played out against the boudoirs, bathrooms and ballrooms of the European nobility, who seem to do nothing all day except each other. The lifestyles of the rich and licentious are revealed in all their glory.
A CRUMBLING FAÇADE
$4.95/3043-1
The return of that incorrigible rogue, Henry Pike, who continues his pursuit of sex, fair or otherwise, in the most elegant homes of the most debauched aristocrats.

CAROLE REMY
BEAUTY OF THE BEAST
$5.95/332-5
A shocking tell-all, written from the point-of-view of a prize-winning reporter. And what reporting she does! All the secrets of an uninhibited life are revealed, and each lusty tableau is painted in glowing colors.

DAVID AARON CLARK
THE MARQUIS DE SADE'S JULIETTE
$4.95/240-X
The Marquis de Sade's infamous Juliette returns—and emerges as the most perverse and destructive nightstalker modern New York will ever know.

Praise for David Aaron Clark:
"David Aaron Clark has delved into one of the most sensationalistically taboo aspects of eros, sado-masochism, and produced a novel of unmistakable literary imagination and artistic value."
—Carlo McCormick, Paper

ANONYMOUS
NADIA
$5.95/267-1
Follow the delicious but neglected Nadia as she works to wring every drop of pleasure out of life—despite an unhappy marriage. A classic title providing a peek into the secret sexual lives of another time and place.

NIGEL McPARR
THE STORY OF A VICTORIAN MAID
$5.95/241-8
What were the Victorians really like? Chances are, no one believes they were as stuffy as their Queen, but who would have imagined such unbridled libertines! Follow her from exploit to smutty exploit!

MOLLY WEATHERFIELD
CARRIE'S STORY
$5.95/444-5
"I had been Jonathan's slave for about a year when he told me he wanted to sell me at an auction. I wasn't in any condition to respond when he told me this..." Desire and depravity run rampant in this story of uncompromising mastery and irrevocable submission.

BREN FLEMMING
CHARLY'S GAME
$4.95/221-3
A rich woman's gullible daughter has run off with one of the toughest leather dykes in town—and sexy P.I. Charly is hired to lure the girl back. One by one, wise and wicked women ensnare one another in their lusty nets!

ISADORA ALMAN
ASK ISADORA
$4.95/61-0
Six years' worth of Isadora Alman's syndicated columns on sex and relationships. Today's world is more perplexing than ever—and Alman can help untangle the most personal of knots.

TITIAN BERESFORD
THE WICKED HAND
$5.95/343-0
With an Introduction by *Leg Show*'s Dian Hanson. A collection of fetishistic tales featuring the absolute subjugation of men by lovely, domineering women.
CINDERELLA
$6.50/500-X
Beresford triumphs again with this intoxicating tale, filled with castle dungeons and tightly corseted ladies-in-waiting, naughty viscounts and impossibly cruel masturbatrixes—nearly every conceivable method of erotic torture is explored and described in lush, vivid detail.

MASQUERADE

KIM'S PASSION
$4.95/162-4
The life of an insatiable seductress. Kim leaves India for London, where she quickly takes on the task of bedding every woman in sight!

CAROUSEL
$4.95/3051-2
A young American woman leaves her husband when she discovers he is having an affair with their maid. She then becomes the sexual plaything of Parisian voluptuaries.

SARAH JACKSON
SANCTUARY
$5.95/318-X
Sanctuary explores both the unspeakable debauchery of court life and the unimaginable privations of monastic solitude, leading the voracious and the virtuous on a collision course that brings history to throbbing life.

THE WILD HEART
$4.95/3007-5
A luxury hotel is the setting for this artful web of sex, desire, and love. A newlywed sees sex as a duty, while her hungry husband tries to awaken her to its tender joys. A Parisian entertains wealthy guests for the love of money. Each episode provides a new variation in this lusty Grand Hotel!

LOUISE BELHAVEL
FRAGRANT ABUSES
$4.95/88-2
The saga of Clara and Iris continues as the now-experienced girls enjoy themselves with a new circle of worldly friends whose imaginations match their own. Perversity follows the lusty ladies around the globe!

SARA H. FRENCH
MASTER OF TIMBERLAND
$5.95/327-9
A tale of sexual slavery at the ultimate paradise resort. One of our bestselling titles, this trek to Timberland has ignited passions the world over—and stands poised to become one of modern erotica's legendary tales.

RETURN TO TIMBERLAND
$5.95/257-4
Prepare for a vacation filled with delicious decadence, as each and every visitor is serviced by unimaginably talented submissives. The raunchiest camp-out ever!

CHINA BLUE
KUNG FU NUNS
$4.95/3031-8
"She lifted me out of the chair and sat me down on top of the table. She then lifted her skirt. The sight of her perfect legs clad in white stockings and a petite garter belt further mesmerized me…." China Blue returns!

ROBERT DESMOND
THE SWEETEST FRUIT
$4.95/95-5
Connie is determined to seduce and destroy the devoted Father Chadcroft. She corrupts the unsuspecting priest into forsaking all that he holds sacred, destroys his parish, and slyly manipulates him with her smoldering looks and hypnotic aura. This Magdalene drags her unsuspecting prey into a hell of unbridled lust.

LUSCIDIA WALLACE
KATY'S AWAKENING
$4.95/308-2
Katy thinks she's been rescued after a terrible car wreck. Little does she suspect that she's been ensnared by a ring of swingers, whose tastes run to domination and unimaginably depraved sex parties. With no means of escape, Katy becomes the newest initiate in this sick private club—and soon finds herself becoming more depraved than even her degenerate captors.

MARY LOVE
MASTERING MARY SUE
$5.95/351-1
Mary Sue is a rich nymphomaniac whose husband is determined to declare her mentally incompetent and gain control of her fortune. He brings her to a castle where, to Mary Sue's delight, she is unleashed for a veritable sex-fest!

THE BEST OF MARY LOVE
$4.95/3099-7
Mary Love leaves no coupling untried and no extreme unexplored in these scandalous selections from *Mastering Mary Sue, Ecstasy on Fire, Vice Park Place, Wanda*, and *Naughtier at Night*.

MASQUERADE

AMARANTHA KNIGHT
THE DARKER PASSIONS: THE PICTURE OF DORIAN GRAY
$6.50/342-2
In this latest installment in the Darker Passions series, Amarantha Knight takes on Oscar Wilde, resulting in a fabulously decadent tale of highly personal changes. One young man finds his most secret desires laid bare by a portrait far more revealing than he could have imagined....

THE DARKER PASSIONS READER
$6.50/432-1
The best moments from Knight's phenomenally popular Darker Passions series. Here are the most eerily erotic passages from her acclaimed sexual reworkings of *Dracula, Frankenstein, Dr. Jekyll & Mr. Hyde* and *The Fall of the House of Usher*. Be prepared for more than a few thrills and chills from this arousing sampler.

THE DARKER PASSIONS: FRANKENSTEIN
$5.95/248-5
What if you could create a living human? What shocking acts could it be taught to perform, to desire? Find out what pleasures await those who play God....

THE DARKER PASSIONS:
THE FALL OF THE HOUSE OF USHER
$5.95/313-9
The Master and Mistress of the house of Usher indulge in every form of decadence, and initiate their guests into the many pleasures to be found in utter submission.

THE DARKER PASSIONS:
DR. JEKYLL AND MR. HYDE
$4.95/227-2
It is a story of incredible, frightening transformations achieved through mysterious experiments. Now, Amarantha Knight explores the steamy possibilities of a tale where no one is quite who—or what—they seem. Victorian bedrooms explode with hidden demons!

THE DARKER PASSIONS: DRACULA
$5.95/326-0
The infamous erotic retelling of the Vampire legend. "Well-written and imaginative, Amarantha Knight gives fresh impetus to this myth, taking us through the sexual and sadistic scenes with details that keep us reading.... A classic in itself has been added to the shelves."
—*Divinity*

PAUL LITTLE
THE BEST OF PAUL LITTLE
$6.50/469-0
One of Masquerade's all-time best-selling authors is here represented by his most incredible moments. Known throughout the world for his fantastic portrayals of punishment and pleasure, Little never fails to push readers over the edge of sensual excitement.

ALL THE WAY
$6.95/509-3
Two excruciating novels from Paul Little in one hot volume! *Going All the Way* features an unhappy man who tries to purge himself of the memory of his lover with a series of quirky and uninhibited lovers. *Pushover* tells the story of a serial spanker and his celebrated exploits.

THE DISCIPLINE OF ODETTE
$5.95/334-1
Odette's was sure marriage would rescue her from her family's "corrections." To her horror, she discovers that her beloved has also been raised on discipline. A shocking erotic coupling!

THE PRISONER
$5.95/330-9
Judge Black has built a secret room below a penitentiary, where he sentences the prisoners to hours of exhibition and torment while his friends watch. Judge Black's House of Corrections is equipped with one purpose in mind: to administer his own brand of rough justice!

TEARS OF THE INQUISITION
$4.95/146-2
The incomparable Paul Little delivers a staggering account of pleasure and punishment. "There was a tickling inside her as her nervous system reminded her she was ready for sex. But before her was...the Inquisitor!"

DOUBLE NOVEL
$4.95/86-6
The Metamorphosis of Lisette Joyaux tells the story of a young woman initiated into a new world of lesbian lusts. *The Story of Monique* reveals the sexual rituals that beckon the ripe and willing Monique.

CHINESE JUSTICE AND OTHER STORIES
$4.95/153-5
The story of the excruciating pleasures and delicious punishments inflicted on foreigners under the leaders of the Boxer Rebellion. Each foreign woman is brought before the authorities and grilled. Scandalous deeds!

MASQUERADE

CAPTIVE MAIDENS
$5.95/440-2
Three beautiful young women find themselves powerless against the debauched landowners of 1824 England. They are banished to a sexual slave colony, and corrupted by every imaginable perversion. Soon, they come to crave the treatment of their unrelenting captors, and find themselves insatiable.

SLAVE ISLAND
$5.95/441-0
A leisure cruise is waylaid, finding itself in the domain of Lord Henry Philbrock, a sadistic genius. The ship's passengers are kidnapped and spirited to his island prison, where the women are trained to accommodate the most bizarre sexual cravings of the rich, the famous, the pampered and the perverted. An incredible bestseller, which cemented Little's reputation as a master of contemporary erotic literature.

···

ALIZARIN LAKE
SEX ON DOCTOR'S ORDERS
$5.95/402-X
A chronicle of selfless devotion to mankind! Beth, a nubile young nurse, uses her considerable skills to further medical science by offering incomparable and insatiable assistance in the gathering of important specimens. No man leaves naughty Nurse Beth's station without surrendering exactly what she needs!

THE EROTIC ADVENTURES OF HARRY TEMPLE
$4.95/127-6
Harry Temple's memoirs chronicle his amorous adventures from his initiation at the hands of insatiable sirens, through his stay at a house of hot repute, to his encounters with a chastity-belted nympho!

···

JOHN NORMAN
TARNSMAN OF GOR
$6.95/486-0
This legendary—and controversial—series returns! *Tarnsman* finds Tarl Cabot transported to Counter-Earth, better known as Gor. He must quickly accustom himself to the ways of this world, including the caste system which exalts some as Priest-Kings or Warriors, and debases others as slaves. A spectacular world unfolds in this first volume of John Norman's million-selling Gorean series.

OUTLAW OF GOR
$6.95/487-9
In this second volume, Tarl Cabot returns to Gor, where he might reclaim both his woman and his role of Warrior. But upon arriving, he discovers that his name, his city and the names of those he loves have become unspeakable. In his absence, Cabot has become an outlaw, and must discover his new purpose on this strange planet, where danger stalks the outcast, and even simple answers have their price....

PRIEST-KINGS OF GOR
$6.95/488-7
The third volume of John Norman's million-selling, controversial Gor series. Tarl Cabot, brave Tarnsman of Gor, searches for the truth about his lovely wife Talena. Does she live, or was she destroyed by the mysterious, all-powerful Priest-Kings? Cabot is determined to find out—even while knowing that no one who has approached the mountain stronghold of the Priest-Kings has ever returned alive....

···

RACHEL PEREZ
ODD WOMEN
$4.95/123-3
These women are sexy, smart, tough—some even say odd. But who cares, when their combined ass-ets are so sweet! An assortment of Sapphic sirens proves once and for all that comely ladies come best in pairs.

···

ALIZARIN LAKE
SEX ON DOCTOR'S ORDERS
$5.95/402-X
A chronicle of selfless devotion to mankind! Beth, a nubile young nurse, uses her considerable skills to further medical science by offering incomparable and insatiable assistance in the gathering of important specimens. No man leaves naughty Nurse Beth's station without surrendering exactly what she needs!

THE EROTIC ADVENTURES OF HARRY TEMPLE
$4.95/127-6
Harry Temple's memoirs chronicle his amorous adventures from his initiation at the hands of insatiable sirens, through his stay at a house of hot repute, to his encounters with a chastity-belted nympho!

MASQUERADE

AFFINITIES
$4.95/113-6
"Kelsy had a liking for cool upper-class blondes, the long-legged girls from Lake Forest and Winnetka who came into the city to cruise the lesbian bars on Halsted, looking for breathless ecstasies...." A scorching tale of lesbian libidos unleashed, from a writer more than capable of exploring every nuance of female passion in vivid detail.

SYDNEY ST. JAMES
RIVE GAUCHE
$5.95/317-1
The Latin Quarter, Paris, circa 1920. Expatriate bohemians couple with abandon—before eventually abandoning their ambitions amidst the intoxicating temptations waiting to be indulged in every bedroom.

THE HIGHWAYWOMAN
$4.95/174-8
A young filmmaker making a documentary about the life of the notorious English highwaywoman, Bess Ambrose, becomes obsessed with her mysterious subject. It seems that Bess touched more than hearts—and plundered the treasures of every man and maiden she met on the way. Incredible extremes of passion are reached by not only the voluptuous filmmaker, but her insatiable subject!

GARDEN OF DELIGHT
$4.95/3058-X
A vivid account of sexual awakening that follows an innocent but insatiably curious young woman's journey from the furtive, forbidden joys of dormitory life to the unabashed carnality of the wild world. A coming of age story unlike any other!

MARCUS VAN HELLER
TERROR
$5.95/247-7
Another shocking exploration of lust by the author of the ever-popular *Adam & Eve*. Set in Paris during the Algerian War, Terror explores the place of sexual passion in a world drunk on violence.

KIDNAP
$4.95/90-4
P. I. Harding is called in to investigate a mysterious kidnapping case involving the rich and powerful. Along the way he has the pleasure of "interrogating" an exotic dancer named Jeanne and a beautiful English reporter, as he finds himself enmeshed in the crime underworld.

ALEXANDER TROCCHI
THONGS
$4.95/217-5
"...In Spain, life is cheap, from that glittering tragedy in the bullring to the quick thrust of the stiletto in a narrow street in a Barcelona slum. No, this death would not have called for further comment had it not been for one striking fact. The naked woman had met her end in a way he had never seen before—a way that had enormous sexual significance. My God, she had been..." Trocchi's acclaimed classic returns.

HELEN AND DESIRE
$4.95/3093-8
Helen Seferis' flight from the oppressive village of her birth became a sexual tour of a harsh world. From brothels in Sydney to harems in Algiers, Helen chronicles her adventures fully in her diary. Each encounter is examined in the scorching and uncensored diary of the sensual Helen!

THE CARNAL DAYS OF HELEN SEFERIS
$4.95/3086-5
P.I. Anthony Harvest is assigned to save Helen Seferis, a beautiful Australian who has been abducted. Following clues in her explicit diary of adventures, he pursues the lovely, doomed Helen—the ultimate sexual prize.

DON WINSLOW
SECRETS OF CHEATEM MANOR
$6.50/434-8
Edward returns to his late father's estate, to find it being run by the majestic Lady Amanda. Edward can hardly believe his luck—Lady Amanda is assisted by her two beautiful, lonely daughters, Catherine and Prudence. What the randy young man soon comes to realize is the love of discipline that all three beauties share.

KATERINA IN CHARGE
$5.95/409-7
When invited to a country retreat by a mysterious couple, the two randy young ladies can hardly resist! But do they have any idea what they're in for? Whatever the case, the imperious Katerina will make her desires known very soon—and demand that they be fulfilled...

THE MANY PLEASURES OF IRONWOOD
$5.95/310-4
Seven lovely young women are employed by The Ironwood Sportsmen's Club A small and exclusive club with seven carefully selected sexual connoisseurs, Ironwood is dedicated to the relentless pursuit of sensual pleasure.

CLAIRE'S GIRLS
$5.95/442-9
You knew when she walked by that she was something special. She was one of Claire's girls, a woman carefully dressed and groomed to fill a role, to capture a look, to fit an image crafted by the sophisticated proprietress of an exclusive escort agency. High-class whores blow the roof off!

N. WHALLEN
TAU'TEVU
$6.50/426-7
In a mysterious land, the statuesque and beautiful Vivian learns to subject herself to the hand of a mysterious man. He systematically helps her prove her own strength, and brings to life in her an unimagined sensual fire. But who is this man, who goes only by the name of Orpheo?

COMPLIANCE
$5.95/356-2
Fourteen stories exploring the pleasures of release. Characters from all walks of life learn to trust in the skills of others, only to experience the thrilling liberation of submission. Here are the joys to be found in some of the most forbidden sexual practices around....

THE MASQUERADE READERS
THE VELVET TONGUE
$4.95/3029-6
An orgy of oral gratification! *The Velvet Tongue* celebrates the most mouth-watering, lip-smacking, tongue-twisting action. A feast of fellatio and *soixante-neuf* awaits readers of excellent taste at this steamy suck-fest.

A MASQUERADE READER
$4.95/84-X
A sizzling sampler. Strict lessons are learned at the hand of *The English Governess.* Scandalous confessions are found in *The Diary of an Angel,* and the story of a woman whose desires drove her to the ultimate sacrifice in *Thongs* completes the collection.

THE CLASSIC COLLECTION
PROTESTS, PLEASURES, RAPTURES
$5.95/400-3
Invited for an allegedly quiet weekend at a country vicarage, a young woman is stunned to find herself surrounded by shocking acts of sexual sadism. Soon, her curiosity is piqued, and she begins to explore her own capacities for cruelty.

THE YELLOW ROOM
$5.95/378-3
The "yellow room" holds the secrets of lust, lechery, and the lash. There, bare-bottomed, spread-eagled, and open to the world, demure Alice Darvell soon learns to love her lickings. In the second tale, hot heiress Rosa Coote and her adventures in punishment and pleasure. Two feverishly erotic descents into utter depravity.

SCHOOL DAYS IN PARIS
$5.95/325-2
The rapturous chronicles of a well-spent youth! Few Universities provide the profound and pleasurable lessons one learns in after-hours study—particularly if one is young and available, and lucky enough to have Paris as a playground. A stimulating look at the pursuits of young adulthood.

MAN WITH A MAID
$4.95/307-4
The adventures of Jack and Alice have delighted readers for eight decades! A classic of its genre, *Man with a Maid* tells an outrageous tale of desire, revenge, and submission. This tale qualifies as one of the world's most popular adult novels—with over 200,000 copies in print!

MAN WITH A MAID II
$4.95/3071-7
Jack's back! With the assistance of the perverse Alice, he embarks again on a trip through every erotic extreme. Jack leaves no one unsatisfied—least of all, himself—and Alice is always certain to outdo herself in her capacity to corrupt and control. An incendiary sequel!

MAN WITH A MAID: THE CONCLUSION
$4.95/3013-X
The conclusion to the epic saga of lust that has thrilled readers for decades.The adulterous woman who is corrected with enthusiasm and the maid who receives grueling guidance are just two who benefit from these lessons!

CONFESSIONS OF A CONCUBINE III: PLEASURE'S PRISONER
$5.95/357-0
Filled with pulse-pounding excitement—including a daring escape from the harem and an encounter with an unspeakable sadist—*Pleasure's Prisoner* adds an unforgettable chapter to this thrilling confessional.

CONFESSIONS OF A CONCUBINE II: HAREM SLAVE
$4.95/226-4
The concubinage continues, as the true pleasures and privileges of the harem are revealed. For the first time, readers are invited behind the veils that hide uninhibited, unimaginable pleasures from the world....

LADY F.
$4.95/102-0
An uncensored tale of Victorian passions. Master Kidrodstock suffers deliciously at the hands of the stunningly cruel and sensuous Lady Flayskin—the only woman capable of taming his wayward impulses. A fevered chronicle of punishing passions.

MASQUERADE

CLASSIC EROTIC BIOGRAPHIES
JENNIFER III
$5.95/292-2
The further adventures of erotica's most daring heroine. Jennifer, the quintessential beautiful blonde, has a photographer's eye for detail—particularly details of the masculine variety!
JENNIFER AGAIN
$4.95/220-5
An incendiary sequel chronicling the exploits of one of modern erotica's most famous heroines. Once again, the insatiable Jennifer seizes the day—and extracts from it every last drop of sensual pleasure! No man is immune to this vixen's charms.

JENNIFER
$4.95/107-1
From the bedroom of a notoriously insatiable dancer to an uninhibited ashram, *Jennifer* traces the exploits of one thoroughly modern woman as she lustfully explores the limits of her own sexuality.
THE ROMANCES OF BLANCHE LA MARE
$4.95/101-2
When Blanche loses her husband, it becomes clear she'll need a job. She sets her sights on the stage—and soon encounters a cast of lecherous characters intent on making her path to sucksess as hot and hard as possible!

RHINOCEROS

TRISTAN TAORMINO
& DAVID AARON CLARK, EDITORS
RITUAL SEX
$6.95/391-0
While many people believe the body and soul to occupy almost completely independent realms, the many contributors to *Ritual Sex* know—and demonstrate—that the two share more common ground than society feels comfortable acknowledging. From personal memoirs of ecstatic revelation, to fictional quests to reconcile sex and spirit, *Ritual Sex* delves into forbidden areas with gusto, providing an unprecedented look at private life. Includes work by such legendary erotic pioneers as Terence Sellers, Genesis P-Orridge, Guy Baldwin, Kate Bornstein, Annie Sprinkle, Mark Thompson, and many more.

CYBERSEX CONSORTIUM
THE PERV'S GUIDE TO THE INTERNET
$6.95/471-2
You've heard the objections: cyberspace is soaked with sex, piled high with prurience, mired in immorality. Okay—so where is it!? Tracking down the good stuff—the real good stuff—can waste an awful lot of expensive time, and frequently leave you high and dry. But now, the Cybersex Consortium presents an easy-to-use guide for those intrepid adults who know what they want. No horny hacker can afford to pass up this map to the kinkiest rest stops on the Info Superhighway.

AMELIA G, EDITOR
BACKSTAGE PASSES
$6.96/438-0
A collection of some of the most raucous writing around. Amelia G, editor of the goth-sex journal *Blue Blood*, has brought together some of today's most irreverant writers, each of whom has outdone themselves with an edgy, antic tale of modern lust. Punks, metalheads, and grunge-trash roam the pages of *Backstage Passes*, and no one knows their ways better...

PETER JASON
WAYWARD
$4.95/3004-0
A mysterious countess hires a tour bus for an unusual vacation. Traveling through Europe's most notorious cities, she picks up friends, lovers, and acquaintances from every walk of life in pursuit of pleasure.

AMARANTHA KNIGHT, EDITOR
SEDUCTIVE SPECTRES
$6.95/464-X
Breathtaking tours through the erotic supernatural via the macabre imaginations of today's best writers. Never before have ghostly encounters been so alluring, thanks to a cast of otherworldly characters well-acquainted with the pleasures of the flesh.

RHINOCEROS

DAVID MELTZER

UNDER
$6.95/290-6
The story of a sex professional living at the bottom of the social heap. After surgeries designed to increase his physical allure, corrupt government forces drive the cyber-gigolo underground—where even more bizarre cultures await him.

ORF
$6.95/110-1
He is the ultimate musician-hero—the idol of thousands, the fevered dream of many more. And like many musicians before him, he is misunderstood, misused—and totally out of control. Every last drop of feeling is squeezed from a modern-day troubadour and his lady love.

TAMMY JO ECKHART

PUNISHMENT FOR THE CRIME
$6.95/427-5
Peopled by characters of rare depth, these stories explore the true meaning of dominance and submission, and offer some surprising revelations. From an encounter between two of society's most despised individuals, to the explorations of longtime friends, these tales take you where few others have ever dared....

THOMAS S. ROCHE, EDITOR

NOIROTICA: AN ANTH. OF EROTIC CRIME STORIES
$6.95/390-2
A collection of darkly sexy tales, taking place at the crossroads of the crime and erotic genres. Thomas S. Roche has gathered together some of today's finest writers of sexual fiction, all of whom explore the murky terrain where desire runs irrevocably afoul of the law.

GERI NETTICK WITH BETH ELLIOT

MIRRORS: PORTRAIT OF A LESBIAN TRANSSEXUAL
$6.95/435-6
The alternately heartbreaking and empowering story of one woman's long road to full selfhood. Born a male, Geri Nettick knew something just didn't fit. And even after coming to terms with her own gender dysphoria—and taking steps to correct it—she still fought to be accepted by the lesbian feminist community to which she felt she belonged. A fascinating, true tale of struggle and discovery.

SEX MACABRE
$6.95/392-9
Horror tales designed for dark and sexy nights. Amarantha Knight—the woman behind the Darker Passions series, as well as the spine-tingling anthologies *Flesh Fantastic* and *Love Bites*—has gathered together erotic stories sure to make your skin crawl, and heart beat faster.

FLESH FANTASTIC
$6.95/352-X
Humans have long toyed with the idea of "playing God": creating life from nothingness, bringing life to the inanimate. Now Amarantha Knight, author of the "Darker Passions" series, collects stories exploring not only the act of Creation, but the lust that follows....

GARY BOWEN

DIARY OF A VAMPIRE
$6.95/331-7
"Gifted with a darkly sensual vision and a fresh voice, [Bowen] is a writer to watch out for."
—Cecilia Tan
The chilling, arousing, and ultimately moving memoirs of an undead—but all too human—soul. Bowen's Rafael, a red-blooded male with an insatiable hunger for the same, is the perfect antidote to the effete malcontents haunting bookstores today. *Diary of a Vampire* marks the emergence of a bold and brilliant vision, firmly rooted in past and present.

LAURA ANTONIOU, EDITOR

NO OTHER TRIBUTE
$6.95/294-9
A collection sure to challenge Political Correctness in a way few have before, with tales of women kept in bondage to their lovers by their deepest passions. Love pushes these women beyond acceptable limits, rendering them helpless to deny anything to the men and women they adore. A volume dedicated to all Slaves of Desire.

SOME WOMEN
$6.95/300-7
Over forty essays written by women actively involved in consensual dominance and submission. Professional mistresses, lifestyle leatherdykes, whipmakers, titleholders—women from every conceivable walk of life lay bare their true feelings about explosive issues.

BY HER SUBDUED
$6.95/281-X
These tales all involve women in control—of their lives, their loves, their men. So much in control that they can remorselessly break rules to become powerful goddesses of the men who sacrifice all to worship at their feet.

RENÉ MAIZEROY
FLESHLY ATTRACTIONS
$6.95/299-X
Lucien was the son of the wantonly beautiful actress, Marie-Rose Hardanges. When she decides to let a "friend" introduce her son to the pleasures of love, Marie-Rose could not have foretold the excesses that would lead to her own ruin and that of her cherished son.

JEAN STINE
THRILL CITY
$6.95/411-9
Thrill City is the seat of the world's increasing depravity, and Jean Stine's classic novel transports you there with a vivid style you'd be hard pressed to ignore. No writer is better suited to describe the unspeakable extremes of this modern Babylon.

SEASON OF THE WITCH
$6.95/268-X
"A future in which it is technically possible to transfer the total mind...of a rapist killer into the brain dead but physically living body of his female victim. Remarkable for intense psychological technique. There is eroticism but it is necessary to mark the differences between the sexes and the subtle altering of a man into a woman."
—The Science Fiction Critic

JOHN WARREN
THE TORQUEMADA KILLER
$6.95/367-8
Detective Eva Hernandez has finally gotten her first "big case": a string of vicious murders taking place within New York's SM community. Piece by piece, Eva assembles the evidence, revealing a picture of a world misunderstood and under attack—and gradually comes to understand her own place within it. A heart-stopping thriller, as well as an insider's look at the contemporary politics of "the scene"—and those threatened by it.

THE LOVING DOMINANT
$6.95/218-3
Everything you need to know about an infamous sexual variation—and an unspoken type of love. Mentor—a longtime player in scene—guides readers through this world and reveals the too-often hidden basis of the D/S relationship: care, trust and love.

GRANT ANTREWS
MY DARLING DOMINATRIX
$6.95/447-X
When a man and a woman fall in love, it's supposed to be simple, uncomplicated, easy—unless that woman happens to be a dominatrix. Curiosity gives way to unblushing desire in this story of one man's awakening to the joys of willing slavery.

LAURA ANTONIOU WRITING AS "SARA ADAMSON"
THE TRAINER
$6.95/249-3
The Marketplace—the ultimate underground sexual realm includes not only willing slaves, but the exquisite trainers who take submissives firmly in hand. And now these mentors divulge the desires that led them to become the ultimate figures of authority.

THE SLAVE
$6.95/173-X
This second volume in the "Marketplace" trilogy further elaborates the world of slaves and masters. One talented submissive longs to join the ranks of those who have proven themselves worthy of entry into the Marketplace. But the delicious price is staggeringly high....

THE MARKETPLACE
$6.95/3096-2
"Merchandise does not come easily to the Marketplace.... They haunt the clubs and the organizations.... Some are so ripe that they intimidate the poseurs, the weekend sadists and the furtive dilettantes who are so endemic to that world. And they never stop asking where we may be found...."

DAVID AARON CLARK
SISTER RADIANCE
$6.95/215-9
Rife with Clark's trademark vivisections of contemporary desires, sacred and profane. The vicissitudes of lust and romance are examined against a backdrop of urban decay in this testament to the allure of the forbidden.

RHINOCEROS

THE WET FOREVER
$6.95/117-9
The story of Janus and Madchen—a small-time hood and a beautiful sex worker on the run from one of the most dangerous men they have ever known——*The Wet Forever* examines themes of loyalty, sacrifice, redemption and obsession amidst Manhattan's sex parlors and underground S/M clubs. Its combination of sex and suspense led Terence Sellers to proclaim it "evocative and poetic."

MICHAEL PERKINS
EVIL COMPANIONS
$6.95/3067-9
Set in New York City during the tumultuous waning years of the Sixties, *Evil Companions* has been hailed as "a frightening classic." A young couple explores the nether reaches of the erotic unconscious in a shocking confrontation with the extremes of passion. With a new introduction by science fiction legend Samuel R. Delany.

THE SECRET RECORD: MODERN EROTIC LITERATURE
$6.95/3039-3
Michael Perkins surveys the field with authority and unique insight. Updated and revised to include the latest trends, tastes, and developments in this misunderstood and maligned genre.

AN ANTHOLOGY OF CLASSIC ANONYMOUS EROTIC WRITING
$6.95/140-3
Michael Perkins has collected the very best passages from the world's erotic writing. "Anonymous" is one of the most infamous bylines in publishing history —and these steamy excerpts show why! An incredible smorgasbord of forbidden delights culled from some of the most famous titles in the history of erotic literature.

LIESEL KULIG
LOVE IN WARTIME
$6.95/3044-X
Madeleine knew that the handsome SS officer was a dangerous man, but she was just a cabaret singer in Nazi-occupied Paris, trying to survive in a perilous time. When Josef fell in love with her, he discovered that a beautiful and amoral woman can sometimes be wildly dangerous.

HELEN HENLEY
ENTER WITH TRUMPETS
$6.95/197-7
Helen Henley was told that women just don't write about sex—much less the taboos she was so interested in exploring. So Henley did it alone, flying in the face of "tradition," by writing this touching tale of arousal and devotion in one couple's kinky relationship.

ALICE JOANOU
BLACK TONGUE
$6.95/258-2
"Joanou has created a series of sumptuous, brooding, dark visions of sexual obsession, and is undoubtedly a name to look out for in the future."
—*Redeemer*
Exploring lust at its most florid and unsparing, *Black Tongue* is a trove of baroque fantasies—each redolent of forbidden passions. Joanou creates some of erotica's most mesmerizing and unforgettable characters.

TOURNIQUET
$6.95/3060-1
A heady collection of stories and effusions from the pen of one our most dazzling young writers. Strange tales abound, from the story of the mysterious and cruel Cybele, to an encounter with the sadistic entertainment of a bizarre after-hours cafe. A complex and riveting series of meditations on desire.

CANNIBAL FLOWER
$4.95/72-6
The provocative debut volume from this acclaimed writer.
"She is waiting in her darkened bedroom, as she has waited throughout history, to seduce the men who are foolish enough to be blinded by her irresistible charms…. She is the goddess of sexuality, and *Cannibal Flower* is her haunting siren song."
—Michael Perkins

TUPPY OWENS
SENSATIONS
$6.95/3081-4
Tuppy Owens tells the unexpurgated story of the making of *Sensations*—the first big-budget sex flick. Originally commissioned to appear in book form after the release of the film in 1975, *Sensations* is finally released under Masquerade's stylish Rhino*ceros* imprint.

SOPHIE GALLEYMORE BIRD
MANEATER
$6.95/103-9
Through a bizarre act of creation, a man attains the "perfect" lover—by all appearances a beautiful, sensuous woman, but in reality something far darker. Once brought to life she will accept no mate, seeking instead the prey that will sate her hunger for vengeance. A biting take on the war of the sexes, this debut goes for the jugular of the "perfect woman" myth.

PHILIP JOSÉ FARMER
FLESH
$6.95/303-1
Space Commander Stagg explored the galaxies for 800 years. Upon his return, the hero Stagg, hoped to be afforded a hero's welcome. Once home, he is made the centerpiece of an incredible public ritual—one that will repeatedly take him to the heights of ecstasy, and inexorably drag him toward the depths of hell.

A FEAST UNKNOWN
$6.95/276-0
"Sprawling, brawling, shocking, suspenseful, hilarious..." —Theodore Sturgeon
Farmer's supreme anti-hero returns. "I was conceived and born in 1888." Slowly, Lord Grandrith—armed with the belief that he is the son of Jack the Ripper—tells the story of his remarkable and unbridled life. His story begins with his discovery of the secret of immortality—and progresses to encompass the furthest extremes of human behavior. A classic of speculative erotica—and proof of Farmer's long-admired genius.

THE IMAGE OF THE BEAST
$6.95/166-7
Herald Childe has seen Hell, glimpsed its horror in an act of sexual mutilation. Childe must now find and destroy an inhuman predator through the streets of a polluted and decadent Los Angeles of the future. One clue after another leads Childe to an inescapable realization about the nature of sex and evil....

DANIEL VIAN
ILLUSIONS
$6.95/3074-1
Two tales of danger and desire in Berlin on the eve of WWII. From private homes to lurid cafés, passion is exposed in stark contrast to the brutal violence of the time. Two sexy tales examining a remarkably decadent age.

PERSUASIONS
$6.95/183-7
A double novel, including the classics *Adagio* and *Gabriela and the General*, this volume traces desire around the globe. Two classics of international lust!

SAMUEL R. DELANY
THE MAD MAN
$8.99/408-9
"Reads like a pornographic reflection of Peter Ackroyd's Chatterton or A. S. Byatt's Possession.... The pornographic element... becomes more than simple shock or titillation, though, as Delany develops an insightful dichotomy between [his protagonist]'s two worlds: the one of cerebral philosophy and dry academia, the other of heedless, 'impersonal' obsessive sexual extremism. When these worlds finally collide...the novel achieves a surprisingly satisfying resolution...." —*Publishers Weekly*
For his thesis, graduate student John Marr researches the life and work of the brilliant Timothy Hasler: a philosopher whose career was cut tragically short over a decade earlier. On another front, Marr finds himself increasingly drawn toward more shocking, depraved sexual entanglements with the homeless men of his neighborhood, until it begins to seem that Hasler's death might hold some key to his own life as a gay man in the age of AIDS.

EQUINOX
$6.95/157-8
The Scorpion has sailed the seas in a quest for every possible pleasure. Her crew is a collection of the young, the twisted, the insatiable. A drifter comes into their midst and is taken on a fantastic journey to the darkest, most dangerous sexual extremes—until he is finally a victim to their boundless appetites.

ANDREI CODRESCU
THE REPENTANCE OF LORRAINE
$6.95/329-5
"One of our most prodigiously talented and magical writers." —*NYT Book Review*
By the acclaimed author of *The Hole in the Flag* and *The Blood Countess*. An aspiring writer, a professor's wife, a secretary, gold anklets, Maoists, Roman harlots—and more—swirl through this spicy tale of a harried quest for a mythic artifact. Written when the author was a young man, this lusty yarn was inspired by the heady days of the Sixties.

LEOPOLD VON SACHER-MASOCH
VENUS IN FURS
$6.95/3089-X
This classic 19th century novel is the first uncompromising exploration of the dominant/submissive relationship in literature. The alliance of Severin and Wanda epitomizes Sacher-Masoch's dark obsession with a cruel, controlling goddess and the urges that drive the man held in her thrall. This special edition includes the letters exchanged between Sacher-Masoch and Emilie Mataja, an aspiring writer he sought to cast as the avatar of the forbidden desires expressed in his most famous work.

BADBOY

CLAY CLADWELL AND AARON TRAVIS
TAG TEAM STUDS
$6.50/465-8
Thrilling tales from these two legendary eroticists. The wrestling world will never seem the same, once you've made your way through this assortment of sweaty, virile studs. But you'd better be wary—should one catch you off guard, you just might spend the rest of the night pinned to the mat....

COME QUICKLY: FOR BOYS ON THE GO
$6.50/413-5
The increasing pace of daily life is no reason a guy has to forgo a little carnal pleasure whenever the mood strikes him. Here are over sixty of the hottest fantasies around—all designed to get you going in less time than it takes to dial 976. Julian Anthony Guerra, the editor behind the phenomenally popular *Men at Work* and *Badboy Fantasies*, has put together this volume especially for you—a modern man on a modern schedule, who still appreciates a little old-fashioned action.

MATT TOWNSEND
SOLIDLY BUILT
$6.50/416-X
The tale of the tumultuous relationship between Jeff, a young photographer, and Mark, the butch electrician hired to wire Jeff's new home. For Jeff, it's love at first sight; Mark, however, has more than a few hang-ups. Soon, both are forced to reevaluate their outlooks, and are assisted by a variety of hot men....

JOHN PRESTON
MR. BENSON
$4.95/3041-5
A classic erotic novel from a time when there was no limit to what a man could dream of doing.... Jamie is an aimless young man lucky enough to encounter Mr. Benson. He is soon led down the path of erotic enlightenment, learning to accept this man as his master. From an opulent penthouse to the infamous Mineshaft, Jamie's incredible adventures never fail to excite—especially when the going gets rough! Preston's knockout novel returns to claim the territory it mapped out years ago.

TALES FROM THE DARK LORD
$5.95/323-6
A new collection of twelve stunning works from the man *Lambda Book Report* called "the Dark Lord of gay erotica." The relentless ritual of lust and surrender is explored in all its manifestations in this heart-stopping triumph of authority and vision from the Dark Lord!

TALES FROM THE DARK LORD II
$4.95/176-4
The second volume of acclaimed eroticist John Preston's masterful short stories. Also includes an interview with the author, and an explicit screenplay written for pornstar Scott O'Hara. An explosive collection from one of erotic publishing's most fertile imaginations.

THE ARENA
$4.95/3083-0
There is a place on the edge of fantasy where every desire is indulged with abandon. Men go there to unleash beasts, to let demons roam free, to abolish all limits. At the center of each tale are the men who serve there, who offer themselves for the consummation of any passion, whose own bottomless urges compel their endless subservience.

THE HEIR•THE KING
$4.95/3048-2
The ground-breaking novel *The Heir*, written in the lyric voice of the ancient myths, tells the story of a world where slaves and masters create a new sexual society. This edition also includes a completely original work, *The King*, the story of a soldier who discovers his monarch's most secret desires. Available only from Badboy.

THE MISSION OF ALEX KANE
SWEET DREAMS
$4.95/3062-8
It's the triumphant return of gay action hero Alex Kane! In *Sweet Dreams*, Alex travels to Boston where he takes on a street gang that stalks gay teenagers. Mighty Alex Kane wreaks a fierce and terrible vengeance on those who prey on gay people everywhere!

GOLDEN YEARS
$4.95/3069-5
When evil threatens the plans of a group of older gay men, Kane's got the muscle to take it head on. Along the way, he wins the support—and very specialized attentions—of a cowboy plucked right out of the Old West. But Kane and the Cowboy have a surprise waiting for them....

BADBOY

KYLE STONE

FIRE & ICE
$5.95/297-3
A collection of stories from the author of the infamous adventures of PB 500. Randy, powerful, and just plain bad, Stone's characters always promise one thing: enough hot action to burn away your desire for anyone else....

HOT BAUDS
$5.95/285-X
The author of *Fantasy Board* and *The Initiation of PB 500* combed cyberspace for the hottest fantasies of the world's horniest hackers. From bulletin boards called Studs, The Mine Shaft, Back Door and the like, Stone has assembled the first collection of the raunchy erotica so many gay men cruise the Information Superhighway for.

FANTASY BOARD
$4.95/212-4
The author of the scalding sci-fi adventures of PB 500 explores the more foreseeable future—through the intertwined lives (and private parts) of a collection of randy computer hackers. On the Lambda Gate BBS, every hot and horny male is in search of a little virtual satisfaction.

THE CITADEL
$4.95/198-5
The sequel to The Initiation of PB 500. Having proven himself worthy of his stunning master, Micah—now known only as '500'—will face new challenges and hardships after his entry into the forbidding Citadel. Only his master knows what awaits—and whether Micah will again distinguish himself as the perfect instrument of pleasure....

THE INITIATION OF PB 500
$4.95/141-1
An interstellar accident strands a young stud on an alien planet. He is a stranger on their planet, unschooled in their language, and ignorant of their customs. But this man, Micah—now known only by his number—will soon be trained in every last detail of erotic personal service. And, once nurtured and transformed into the perfect physical specimen, he must begin proving himself worthy of the master who has chosen him....

RITUALS
$4.95/168-3
Via a computer bulletin board, a young man finds himself drawn into a series of sexual rites that transform him into the willing slave of a mysterious stranger. Gradually, all vestiges of his former life are thrown off, and he learns to live for his Master's touch....

JOHN ROWBERRY

LEWD CONDUCT
$4.95/3091-1
Flesh-and-blood men vie for power, pleasure and surrender in each of these feverish stories, and no one walks away from his steamy encounter unsated. Rowberry's men are unafraid to push the limits of civilized behavior in search of the elusive and empowering conquest.

ROBERT BAHR

SEX SHOW
$4.95/225-6
Luscious dancing boys. Brazen, explicit acts. Unending stimulation. Take a seat, and get very comfortable, because the curtain's going up on a show no discriminating appetite can afford to miss.

JASON FURY

THE ROPE ABOVE, THE BED BELOW
$4.95/269-8
The irresistible Jason Fury returns—and if you thought his earlier adventures were hot, this volume will blow you away! Once again, our built, blond hero finds himself in the oddest—and most compromising—positions.

ERIC'S BODY
$4.95/151-9
Meet Jason Fury—blond, blue-eyed and up for anything. Fury's sexiest tales are collected in book form for the first time. Follow the irresistible Jason through sexual adventures unlike any you have ever read....

"BIG" BILL JACKSON

EIGHTH WONDER
$4.95/200-0
From the bright lights and back rooms of New York to the open fields and sweaty bods of a small Southern town, "Big" Bill always manages to cause a scene, and the more actors he can involve, the better! Like the man's name says, he's got more than enough for everyone, and turns nobody down....

BADBOY

LARS EIGHNER

WHISPERED IN THE DARK
$5.95/286-8
A volume demonstrating Eighner's unique combination of
strengths: poetic descriptive power, an unfailing ear for
dialogue, and a finely tuned feeling for the nuances of
male passion.

AMERICAN PRELUDE
$4.95/170-5
Eighner is widely recognized as one of our best, most exciting gay writers. He is also one of gay erotica's true
masters—and *American Prelude* shows why. Wonderfully
written, blisteringly hot tales of all-American lust.

B.M.O.C.
$4.95/3077-6
In a college town known as "the Athens of the
Southwest," studs of every stripe are up all night—studying, naturally. In *B.M.O.C.*, Lars Eighner includes the very
best of his short stories, sure to appeal to the collegian in
every man. Relive university life the way it was supposed
to be, with a cast of handsome honor students majoring in
Human Homosexuality.

EDITED BY DAVID LAURENTS

SOUTHERN COMFORT
$6.50/466-6
Editor David Laurents now unleashes another collection of
today's most provocative gay writing. The tales here focus
on the American South—and reflect not only Southern
literary tradition, but the many contributions the region has
made to the iconography of the American Male.

WANDERLUST:
HOMOEROTIC TALES OF TRAVEL
$5.95/395-3
A volume dedicated to the special pleasures of faraway
places. Gay men have always had a special interest in
travel—and not only for the scenic vistas. Wanderlust
celebrates the freedom of the open road, and the allure of
men who stray from the beaten path....

THE BADBOY BOOK OF EROTIC POETRY
$5.95/382-1
Over fifty of today's best poets. Erotic poetry has long been
the problem child of the literary world—highly creative
and provocative, but somehow too frank to be "literature."
Both learned and stimulating, *The Badboy Book of Erotic
Poetry* restores eros to its rightful place of honor in contemporary gay writing.

AARON TRAVIS

IN THE BLOOD
$5.95/283-3
Written when Travis had just begun to explore the true
power of the erotic imagination, these stories laid the
groundwork for later masterpieces. Among the many
rewarding rarities included in this volume: "In the
Blood"—a heart-pounding descent into sexual vampirism,
written with the furious erotic power that has distinguished
Travis' work from the beginning.

THE FLESH FABLES
$4.95/243-4
One of Travis' best collections, finally rereleased. *The Flesh
Fables* includes "Blue Light," his most famous story, as
well as other masterpieces that established him as the
erotic writer to watch. And watch carefully, because Travis
always buries a surprise somewhere beneath his scorching
detail....

SLAVES OF THE EMPIRE
$4.95/3054-7
The return of an undisputed classic from this master of the
erotic genre.
"*Slaves of the Empire* is a wonderful mythic tale. Set
against the backdrop of the exotic and powerful
Roman Empire, this wonderfully written novel
explores the timeless questions of light and dark in
male sexuality. Travis has shown himself expert in
manipulating the most primal themes and images.
The locale may be the ancient world, but these are the
slaves and masters of our time...." —John Preston

BOB VICKERY

SKIN DEEP
$4.95/265-5
So many varied beauties no one will go away unsatisfied.
No tantalizing morsel of manflesh is overlooked—or left
unexplored! Beauty may be only skin deep, but a handful
of beautiful skin is a tempting proposition.

BADBOY

JR
FRENCH QUARTER NIGHTS
$5.95/337-6
A randy roundup of this author's most popular tales. *French Quarter Nights* is filled with sensual snapshots of the many places where men get down and dirty—from the steamy French Quarter to the steam room at the old Everard baths. In the best tradition of gay erotica, these are nights you'll wish would go on forever....

TOM BACCHUS
RAHM
$5.95/315-5
The imagination of Tom Bacchus brings to life an extraordinary assortment of characters, from the Father of Us All to the cowpoke next door, the early gay literati to rude, queercore mosh rats. No one is better than Bacchus at staking out sexual territory with a swagger and a sly grin.
BONE
$4.95/177-2
Queer musings from the pen of one of today's hottest young talents. A fresh outlook on fleshly indulgence yields more than a few pleasant surprises. Horny Tom Bacchus maps out the tricking ground of a new generation.

KEY LINCOLN
SUBMISSION HOLDS
$4.95/266-3
A bright young talent unleashes his first collection of gay erotica. From tough to tender, the men between these covers stop at nothing to get what they want. These sweat-soaked tales show just how bad boys can really get—especially when given a little help by an equally lustful stud.

HODDY ALLEN
AL
$5.95/302-3
Al is a remarkable young man. With his long brown hair, bright green eyes and eagerness to please, many would consider him the perfect submissive. Many would like to mark him as their own—but it is at that point that Al stops. One day Al relates the entire astounding tale of his life....

CALDWELL/EIGHNER
QSFX2
$5.95/278-7
The wickedest, wildest, other-worldliest yarns from two master storytellers—Clay Caldwell and Lars Eighner. Both eroticists take a trip to the furthest reaches of the sexual imagination, sending back ten stories proving that as much as things change, one thing will always remain the same....
BIG SHOTS
$5.95/448-8
Two fierce tales in one electrifying volume. In *Beirut*, Travis tells the story of ultimate military power and erotic subjugation; *Kip*, Travis' hypersexed and sinister take on film noir, appears in unexpurgated form for the first time—including the final, overwhelming chapter. One of the rawest titles we've ever published.
EXPOSED
$4.95/126-8
A volume of shorter Travis tales, each providing a unique glimpse of the horny gay male in his natural environment! Cops, college jocks, ancient Romans—even Sherlock Holmes and his loyal Watson—cruise these pages, fresh from the throbbing pen of one of our hottest authors.
BEAST OF BURDEN
$4.95/105-5
Five ferocious tales. Innocents surrender to the brutal sexual mastery of their superiors, as taboos are shattered and replaced with the unwritten rules of masculine conquest. Intense, extreme—and totally Travis.

CLAY CALDWELL
ASK OL' BUDDY
$5.95/346-5
Set in the underground SM world, Caldwell takes you on a journey of discovery—where men initiate one another into the secrets of the rawest sexual realm of all. And when each stud's initiation is complete, he takes his places among the masters—eager to take part in the training of another hungry soul...

BADBOY

STUD SHORTS
$5.95/320-1

"If anything, Caldwell's charm is more powerful, his nostalgia more poignant, the horniness he captures more sweetly, achingly acute than ever."

—Aaron Travis

A new collection of this legend's latest sex-fiction. With his customary candor, Caldwell tells all about cops, cadets, truckers, farmboys (and many more) in these dirty jewels.

TAILPIPE TRUCKER
$5.95/296-5

With *Tailpipe Trucker*, Clay Caldwell set the cornerstone of "trucker porn"—a story revolving around the age-old fantasy of horny men on the road. In prose as free and unvarnished as a cross-country highway, Caldwell tells the truth about Trag and Curly—two men hot for the feeling of sweaty manflesh. Together, they pick up—and turn out—naive a couple of thrill-seeking punks.

SERVICE, STUD
$5.95/336-8

Another look at the gay future. The setting is the Los Angeles of a distant future. Here the all-male populace is divided between the served and the servants—guaranteeing the erotic satisfaction of all involved.

QUEERS LIKE US
$4.95/262-0

"This is Caldwell at his most charming."

—Aaron Travis

For years the name Clay Caldwell has been synonymous with the hottest, most finely crafted gay tales available. *Queers Like Us* is one of his best: the story of a randy mailman's trek through a landscape of willing, available studs.

ALL-STUD
$4.95/104-7

This classic, sex-soaked tale takes place under the watchful eye of Number Ten: an omniscient figure who has decreed unabashed promiscuity as the law of his all-male land. One stud, however, takes it upon himself to challenge the social order, daring to fall in love. Finally, he is forced to fight for not only himself, but the man to whom he has committed himself.

LARRY TOWNSEND
LEATHER AD: S
$5.95/407-0

The second half of Townsend's acclaimed tale of lust through the personals—this time told from a Top's perspective. A simple ad generates many responses, and one man finds himself in the enviable position of putting these studly applicants through their paces.....

LEATHER AD: M
$5.95/380-5

The first of this two-part classic. John's curious about what goes on between the leatherclad men he's fantasized about. He takes out a personal ad, and starts a journey of self-discovery that will leave no part of his life unchanged.

BEWARE THE GOD WHO SMILES
$5.95/321-X

Two lusty young Americans are transported to ancient Egypt—where they are embroiled in regional warfare and taken as slaves by marauding barbarians. The key to escape from this brutal bondage lies in their own rampant libidos, and urges as old as time itself.

THE CONSTRUCTION WORKER
$5.95/298-1

A young, hung construction worker is sent to a building project in Central America, where he finds that man-to-man sex is the accepted norm. The young stud quickly fits right in—until he senses that beneath the constant sexual shenanigans there moves an almost supernatural force.

2069 TRILOGY
(This one-volume collection only $6.95)244-2

For the first time, Larry Townsend's early science-fiction trilogy appears in one massive volume! Set in a future world, the *2069 Trilogy* includes the tight plotting and shameless male sexual pleasure that established him as one of gay erotica's first masters.

BADBOY

MIND MASTER
$4.95/209-4
Who better to explore the territory of erotic dominance than an author who helped define the genre—and knows that ultimate mastery always transcends the physical.

THE LONG LEATHER CORD
$4.95/201-9
Chuck's stepfather never lacks money or clandestine male visitors with whom he enacts intense sexual rituals. As Chuck comes to terms with his own desires, he begins to unravel the mystery behind his stepfather's secret life.

MAN SWORD
$4.95/188-8
The tres gai tale of France's King Henri III. Unimaginably spoiled by his mother—the infamous Catherine de Medici—Henri is groomed from a young age to assume the throne of France. Along the way, he encounters enough sexual schemers and randy politicos to alter one's picture of history forever!

THE FAUSTUS CONTRACT
$4.95/167-5
Two attractive young men desperately need $1000. Will do anything. Travel OK. Danger OK. Call anytime... Two cocky young hustlers get more than they bargained for in this story of lust and its discontents.

THE GAY ADVENTURES OF CAPTAIN GOOSE
$4.95/169-1
The hot and tender young Jerome Gander is sentenced to serve aboard the *H.M.S. Faerigold*—a ship manned by the most hardened, unrepentant criminals. In no time, Gander becomes well-versed in the ways of men at sea, and the Faerigold becomes the most notorious ship of its day.

CHAINS
$4.95/158-6
Picking up street punks has always been risky, but in Larry Townsend's classic *Chains*, it sets off a string of events that must be read to be believed. One of Townsend's most remarkable works.

KISS OF LEATHER
$4.95/161-6
A look at the acts and attitudes of an earlier generation of gay leathermen, Kiss of Leather is full to bursting with the gritty, raw action that has distinguished Townsend's work for years. Pain and pleasure mix in this tightly plotted tale.

RUN, LITTLE LEATHER BOY
$4.95/143-8
One young man's sexual awakening. A chronic underachiever, Wayne seems to be going nowhere fast. When his father puts him to work for a living, Wayne soon finds himself bored with the everyday—and increasingly drawn to the masculine intensity of a dark and mysterious sexual underground....

RUN NO MORE
$4.95/152-7
The continuation of Larry Townsend's legendary *Run, Little Leather Boy*. This volume follows the further adventures of Townsend's leatherclad narrator as he travels every sexual byway available to the S/M male.

THE SCORPIUS EQUATION
$4.95/119-5
Set in the far future, *The Scorpius Equation* is the story of a man caught between the demands of two galactic empires. Our randy hero must match wits—and more—with the incredible forces that rule his world.

THE SEXUAL ADVENTURES OF SHERLOCK HOLMES
$4.95/3097-0
Holmes' most satisfying adventures, from the unexpurgated memoirs of the faithful Mr. Watson. "A Study in Scarlet" is transformed to expose Mrs. Hudson as a man in drag, the Diogenes Club as an S/M arena, and clues only the redoubtable—and very horny—Sherlock Holmes could piece together. A baffling tale of sex and mystery.

....

DONALD VINING
CABIN FEVER AND OTHER STORIES
$5.95/338-4
Eighteen blistering stories in celebration of the most intimate of male bonding. Time after time, Donald Vining's men succumb to nature, and reaffirm both love and lust in modern gay life.

"Demonstrates the wisdom experience combined with insight and optimism can create."

—Bay Area Reporter

ORDERING IS EASY!

MC/VISA orders can be placed by calling our toll-free number

PHONE 800-375-2356 / FAX 212 986-7355

or mail this coupon to:

MASQUERADE DIRECT

DEPT. BMRK96 801 2ND AVE., NY, NY 10017

BUY ANY FOUR BOOKS AND CHOOSE ONE ADDITIONAL BOOK, OF EQUAL OR LESSER VALUE, AS YOUR FREE GIFT.

QTY.	TITLE	NO.	PRICE
			FREE
			FREE

WE NEVER SELL, GIVE OR TRADE ANY CUSTOMER'S NAME.

SUBTOTAL	
POSTAGE and HANDLING	
TOTAL	

In the U.S., please add $1.50 for the first book and 75¢ for each additional book; in Canada, add $2.00 for the first book and $1.25 for each additional book. Foreign countries: add $4.00 for the first book and $2.00 for each additional book. No C.O.D. orders. Please make all checks payable to Masquerade Books. Payable in U.S. currency only. New York state residents add 8.25% sales tax. Please allow 4-6 weeks for delivery.

NAME _____

ADDRESS _____

CITY _____ STATE _____ ZIP _____

TEL ( ) _____

PAYMENT: ☐ CHECK   ☐ MONEY ORDER   ☐ VISA   ☐ MC

CARD NO. _____ EXP. DATE _____